The
Bookkeeper

ALSO BY JAN M. WALTON

River Avenue

The Bookkeeper

A NOVEL

JAN M. WALTON

Printed in the United States of America
ISBN 978-1-7370022-2-2 (paperback)
ISBN 978-1-7370022-3-9 (ebook)
Library of Congress Control Number: 2023909046

Edited by Paula Stahel

Cover design by Roy Marshall (royboytn@gmail.com)

Author photograph by Joy Hmielewski
Photographs: J.L. Hudson building, Detroit
Historical Society, used with permission.
Ledger: iStock.com/Steve Cole Images
Bridge: iStock.com/Gary Marx

Song: "Last Night The Nightingale Woke Me"
by Halfdan K. Jerulf (public domain).

Author website: www.janmwalton.com
Windcove Publishing, Clearwater, Florida
windcovepublishing@gmail.com

For my mother, Norma Cozard Walton,
who lived her best life in Detroit.

CHAPTER 1

Detroit, June 1946

The dim bulb in the hallway lamp only dented the gloom beyond the half-open bedroom door. Calling "Ruth?" drew a muffled groan from within. Addie hesitated, judging the steps to where the bed must be. She moved around the door, and with two strides her knee bumped the mattress. Her sister's face was buried in the pillow. Addie wanted to shake Ruth awake, sit her up, but Al had said Ruth could not tolerate movement or the light. Sighing, Addie stretched back to grasp the doorknob, stepped through to the hallway, and pulled the door closed.

How long would she be like this, Addie wondered.

The last of the sun cast shadows in the living room through the windows facing the street. Children still played on the sidewalk below, the thwack of a jump-rope slapping pavement. Voices and people laughing. Under those sounds, a kind of hum, like an engine running. Addie could not decide what she wanted first—to change her clothes, use the bathroom, find a drink of something to ease her parched throat, or cry.

Crumpling into an armchair, Addie kicked off her black pumps. She had expected to celebrate her first evening in Detroit wearing the new shoes to dinner in a fancy restaurant. Her stomach grumbled. She supposed she could rustle something up in Ruth's kitchen, since she was left to fend on her own. Leaning back, she closed her eyes and rubbed at the ache in her neck, stiff from perching for hours on the edge of the train seat to keep her skirt from wrinkling.

Two years of dreaming and planning had brought her on the tedious trip from Pennsylvania, the train cars snaking through small towns from Pittsburgh to Cleveland, then hugging the shore of Lake Erie—the largest body of water Addie had ever seen—and turning north at Toledo. She felt soreness on her left side, too, from trips to the tiny ladies' washroom, where dragging a comb through her wavy hair and applying her lipstick without smearing required wedging her hips against the door frame to take the brunt of the train's lurches.

When she had boarded that train, followed the porter to her seat, and waved to Dan as the train picked up speed, Addie had bid goodbye to the girl who had lived her eighteen years among small-town country folks, confined by both the watchful eye of her older brother and the town's overbearing familiarity. Addie had browsed ladies' magazines, daydreaming about becoming the new city girl after stepping off the train in Detroit. Stylish skirts, blouses, jackets, and even trousers for the working girl jumped from the pages and mentally slipped onto her frame. Striding through the aisle to the dining car, Addie pretended the passengers admired her in a jaunty, tailored button-front dress with a gathered backpiece and pleated skirt, presenting her petite, slim figure and smallish bust to best advantage. At her table, she swept the napkin onto her lap with a confident smile. Jaunty suited her, she decided. In Detroit, she would be jaunty.

She passed time lingering in the dining car, reading the newspapers left behind by businessmen who came and went from towns along the way. Unable to make the train go faster, she spent the last few hours in her coach seat clutching her purse, snapping the brass closure open and shut, tapping her foot.

In the purse was the money Dan had given her to get started. Dan had lectured her about managing on her own. Sitting across from him at the kitchen table, she had tolerated his preaching the older-brother sermon by clutching a pencil to keep her hands calm, but her right leg jiggled below his vision. She had been managing their household accounts since the start of her high school bookkeeping classes. Each week, she reviewed the entries in the dog-eared house notebook with her brother, and he agreed with her figures. The arithmetic came easy for Addie, and she was happy to relieve him of the chore. She heard Dan's lecture as a bittersweet message that he was sad to see her go. She was the last to leave home, and he'd be alone in the house. When he pushed the bank envelope across the table, Addie counted the cash, opened a new four-column ledger book to the first page, and wrote in the starting balance. She placed the cash in a zippered pouch that went into her traveling purse.

"I will be careful with spending, and once I have a paycheck in Detroit, you won't have to give me money."

"Save for a rainy day," he advised.

She noted each expenditure she had made on the train, to be entered later in her ledger book, and recounted her cash in the pouch. Satisfied with her accounting, Addie had closed her eyes in a half-sleep, imagining herself walking along Detroit's wide avenues amidst the crowds of working men and women and arriving at a bookkeeping job each day in one of its downtown skyscrapers. She would write to her teacher, Miss Ames, once she landed a job. Addie would fill what Miss Ames called "the great need of commerce and industry."

"Most bookkeepers in business are women," Miss Ames had told the class, "and now there will be even more opportunities in the bigger companies. If I had stayed in Chicago, I would have worked my way from bookkeeper to accountant by now." Addie remembered thinking, *If I stay in this town, nothing will happen to me.*

People said Addie's class was lucky, too young to go to war, but she thought they had missed the excitement. Women had gone to the cities, lived on their own, worked and earned money in the war effort. Addie's girlfriends remained cocooned in the familiar, most having paired off with a local boy before the end of high school. Addie listened to their wedding plans with polite interest while her brain screamed, *Not for me!* One careless misstep with a boy could have trapped her. Addie knew she would be miserable living under the thumb of a man, in a house so like the one she grew up in that she could move around in it with her eyes closed.

Miss Ames had encouraged Addie's eagerness to get out into the world. Working in Chicago sounded exciting, but in Detroit Addie had the foothold of her older sister. Ruth had gone there six years earlier, to find work in the boom of wartime production. She had a steady job and her own apartment. *Lucky me, to have Ruth to get me started.* Addie would not be one of those country girls arriving with the address of an old friend or a cousin, carrying one good dress, taking a davenport or a cot in a shared room.

The train slowed and the cityscape spread in full view. Addie's heart had quickened at the sight of Michigan Central Station's tower looming ahead. A grid of tracks stretched as far as she could see. The bright sun peeked through slits in the dull, grimy clouds of smoke and haze. In the hills of a coal town, she had always lived in smog. The surprise was the flatness of Michigan's land, giving over the fullness of the horizon to the sky.

The train whistled its approach into the station yard. Addie was standing in the aisle before the bumping halt ended the train's slow glide alongside the platform. Uniformed Negro men wearing red hats waited there with luggage carts.

The porter carried her train case, led Addie onto the platform, and called out, "Red Cap." Turning to her, he said, "Miss, if you have your luggage ticket, this man will claim it for you."

Addie fished the ticket from her handbag, handed it to the Red Cap, and the man made a brisk turn of the cart toward the luggage cars at the rear of the train.

The porter pointed to the middle of the platform. "If someone is meeting you, they'll be outside the gate." Addie extended her hand with a tip, which he accepted with a smile and a doff of his cap. She had asked Ruth for advice about tipping but was unsure as she handed it over. Another thing to learn in the city.

Craning her neck and weaving around luggage carts and people greeting travelers, Addie had searched for Ruth's face among the throng outside the iron grille that separated the platform from the station lobby. The public-address announcer blared calls for departing trains. People bustled around the newsstands and shops along the far side of the station. River breezes swept through the open doors of the cavernous space, and pigeons circled each other near the vaulted ceiling.

The Red Cap wheeled his cart, loaded with her trunk, to her side. "Taxi, miss?"

"My sister should be here any minute."

He nodded and braked the cart. The clamor outside the gate lessened as people found each other and left. A clammy chill wafted over Addie. *Ruth will be here; she knows it's today.* The gate crowd had cleared, and Addie sensed the Red Cap's shifting and rearranging of the cart meant he wanted to go. Addie's parched mouth craved the water fountain but she didn't dare leave the gate until Ruth arrived. Then she heard her name, *Miss Addie Tate*, echoing over the loudspeaker; she was being called to the information desk for a message. The Red Cap pointed to the desk on the other side of the hall.

She was handed a slip of paper. Ruth was not coming. No reason, only the instruction to take a cab to her apartment. Addie crumpled the paper in her sweaty palm. She made her way back to the man with her luggage.

"Miss?"

Addie drew in a breath. "I need a taxi."

He steered the cart through the lobby with her trailing behind, her heels clicking on the marble floor in time with the faster beating of her heart. She had never been in a taxi. She knew Ruth's address, but not its direction from the station. As she stepped out of the station doors, the breadth of the sky overcame her view. The sun behind the haze pulsed a dull glare. She pulled the brim of her hat lower to focus her eyes. Her mind went to her brother Dan's face as he had hugged her on the train platform. She was on her own and the taxi was the first test.

When the taxi dispatcher asked for the address, Addie stated the street number on East Grand Boulevard. The luggage loaded, the taxi door opened for her, Addie remembered to grab money from her handbag and thanked the Red Cap. *Maybe I am doing this right*, she hoped, as he tipped his cap and closed the door when she was settled in the cab's back seat. Eying the fare card on the dashboard, she wondered how to calculate the cost of the ride so she could have the cash ready when they arrived. Sitting back, she took another deep breath, telling herself to pay attention to the streets along the way.

The driver leaned out his window to watch for an opening in the steady line of cars and taxis pulling to and from the curb along the entrance to the station. As the cab nosed into the stream, Addie heard a man shout, "Wait! Hold that cab!" The door on the curbside opened, a young man jumped onto the seat next to her, slammed the door shut and said, "Okay, driver, let's go."

Addie drew back against the door on her side. "Wait, don't go—I don't know this man."

Leaning closer, the man reached into his back pocket and took out a handkerchief. He wiped his brow, smiled, shook his head. "Sorry, didn't mean to scare you, but if I missed you, Ruth would kill me."

"You know Ruth?"

"Ruth sent me to find you. Al Kealy, happy to meet you, Addie." He extended his hand and when she didn't take it, pulled it back. He looked into her eyes with his large brown ones. Wavy dark hair framed a handsome face, his skin tinged pink as if he had gotten too much sun. "You are Ruth's sister, right?"

"Ruth's message didn't say to expect … you."

"It was last minute. She planned to come, has been talking for weeks about today, but when she couldn't, I said I'd make sure you get in."

"Ruth knows you're meeting me?"

"She expects me to, so it's a good thing I found you."

"Make up your mind, lady," the driver snapped, watching them in the rearview mirror. "You going to East Grand Boulevard or not?"

Addie looked at the driver, then at grinning Al. She was too tired to figure out what else to do. "Let's go."

The impatient driver swerved as he peeled out, throwing Addie against Al's chest. He gently righted her with one hand and, with the other, pushed her hat brim away from her face. Clammy under her armpits, with a trickle of sweat rolling down from behind an ear under her collar, an imaginary glimpse of herself as a soggy mess in his eyes, she blushed, licked her dry lips, and mumbled thanks.

Addie kept a foot of the seat between them by hanging onto the strap over the window on her side. What was Ruth thinking, expecting her to trust a strange man? Ruth had never mentioned anyone named Al. He caught her eye and grinned.

She narrowed her eyes. "How do you know Ruth?"

"We met at the store," he said. Addie nodded, satisfied for the moment he was truthful. Ruth worked at the J.L. Hudson Department Store.

The driver steered the cab at a fast clip through the traffic, blurring the mental map of right and left turns Addie tried to follow in her head. Al chattered, but Addie heard only snippets of what he was saying over the street noise. Skyscrapers loomed over the avenues, seeming to narrow the streets into tunnels where trucks, cars, buses, and streetcars competed for right-of-way with clanging bells and blaring horns. An array of people pictured in the "Arsenal of Democracy" newsreels came to life outside the cab's windows, people smoking, shouting, eating from paper bags, streaming in and out of buildings. Throngs eager to cross the wide avenues clustered at corners when red lights forced the oncoming swarm of cars and trucks to halt and block the lanes.

Al tapped the seat between them. "Look, I need to warn you. Ruth's having a migraine. She can't tolerate light when one of these takes hold. It's agony for her to turn her head. Talking hurts; she manages a few words before the pain is too much."

Addie frowned and said nothing, hiding from him she hadn't known Ruth suffered from migraines.

When the cab lurched to a stop, Addie blew the air from her tight chest in relief. The apartment house facade matched the photograph Ruth had sent her of the building where she lived. The brick structure took up the corner of the block, set back by a yard planted with maple trees and shrubs. A wrought iron door with scrollwork over the clear glass led to four floors of apartments above. From Ruth's description, Addie knew the triplet of windows on the second floor facing the street belonged to Ruth's apartment. Addie pushed open the cab door and swung her legs to the curb, hoping Al would stay in the cab. But he jumped out his side, popped open the trunk lid, got her luggage to the curb, and pulled his wallet out to pay the driver. *Whoever he is, at least he is a gentleman*, she thought.

At the door, when Addie reached out to press Ruth's bell, Al had put his hand out to stop her. Holding up a key he had taken from his pocket, he said, "No sound, remember?"

Upstairs, to Addie's relief, Al did not expect to come in with her. He put her luggage inside the apartment door, saying he would call later to check if Ruth felt better.

Now, Addie sat up in the armchair and shook off her drowsiness. Light from the streetlamps outside had replaced the setting sun. She stomped her foot at remembering she hadn't sent Dan a telegram to say she had arrived. Addie hated the thought of Dan worrying. If she hadn't been so flustered by Ruth not meeting her, she would have sent the wire. She could do it now by telephone. Addie clicked the switch on the lamp next to her chair. Then she heard a crashing sound from the bedroom.

She tripped over the heeled shoes she had tossed off and stumbled along the short hallway to the bedroom door. Flinging it open, the meager hall light exposed Ruth laying in a heap beside the bed. Addie fumbled along the wall for a light switch and found something to push. Ruth didn't react to the light coming on overhead. Sinking to her knees, Addie turned her sister's body toward her and rubbed her face. "Ruth, can you hear me? Wake up." She lay limp in Addie's arms.

Addie tried to lift Ruth, but getting one arm under her sister's weight, knew she lacked the strength to raise her. Grabbing a water glass from the bed table, Addie dunked her fingers to splash the water on Ruth's face. No reaction. *How to get help?* There was another apartment across the hall.

Pulling a pillow from the bed, she laid Ruth's head on it, then ran in stocking feet into the corridor and pounded on the other apartment door. When the neighbor lady got the gist of Addie's frantic half-sentences, she telephoned for an ambulance.

An hour later, Addie paced in a hospital waiting room.

Bumping along in the back of the speeding ambulance, Addie had blabbered about Ruth's migraine to the man taking Ruth's pulse. "How far along is your sister, miss?"

"I don't know when it started. I only arrived this evening."

"But when is the baby expected?"

The bright light inside the tight ambulance compartment shone on Ruth's prone figure buckled on the gurney. Her belly was outlined under her thin nightgown. Baffled, Addie stared at the roundness. Before she could answer, with a last wail of the siren, the ambulance screeched to a stop. The rear doors flew open, arms pulled the gurney out, and whisked Ruth away.

Addie's mind reeled with questions. *How could Ruth be having a baby? Why didn't she tell me?* Ruth was her sophisticated older sister, with ambition and prospects in the big city, not one of those girls who got into trouble. She told herself that the ambulance man must have been mistaken. Catching herself biting on her fingernail, Addie cringed, slapped her hand down to her side. She had broken that childhood habit, and now the anxiety over Ruth had pushed her finger back to her mouth. *It has to be a mistake.*

A passing nurse clucked at Addie's shoeless feet and brought her hospital slippers to wear. It was then that Addie realized she had no handbag and no key. She had jumped into the ambulance without thinking about getting back to the apartment. Her tension mixed with growing anger at Ruth for keeping her in the dark about Al, about the migraines, and possibly a baby. What else had Ruth not told her?

Nurses came calling for others who were waiting. Finally, one called out, "Who is here with Mrs. Kealy?" No one in the room answered. *Second time today I have heard that name*, Addie thought. *That Al said his name was Kealy.*

The nurse asked again, "Family for Ruth Kealy?"

Addie spoke up. "I am here for my sister, Ruth. Is there another Ruth?"

The nurse checked her clipboard. "Only a Mrs. Kealy. Come along, dear, the doctor called her husband."

Husband? Addie gawked at her until the nurse tapped the clipboard with her pen. "Are you coming, miss?"

The nurse led Addie along a hallway of curtained alcoves. She stopped at one, drew the curtains aside. Ruth lay on a hospital bed, eyes closed, damp dark curls splayed on the pillow, clutching a wad of tissues in one hand, the other lying atop her belly. At the sound of Addie saying her name close to her ear, Ruth's eyes fluttered open, and she smiled.

"Addie." Then her eyes closed. "They gave me something and I can't keep my eyes open, but I can hear you."

Addie blurted, "Why are they calling you Mrs. Kealy? Who is Al? What happened to you?"

Ruth pried her eyes open for a glimpse of Addie and raised her head some but could not sustain the effort. Letting her head fall back, Ruth sighed. "I know this is unexpected. You've just arrived, and you had to help me—"

"Help you! I had to bang on the door of a complete stranger and get in an ambulance with you! I never let Dan know I arrived because you left me stranded at the station!"

"You weren't stranded. Al was there."

As if on cue, Al Kealy pulled back the curtain and hesitated at the end of the bed, his fingers twisting his hat around and around. His face was flushed redder than it had been earlier, his pants were rumpled and his jacket stained. He smiled at Addie, then moved to Ruth's side and took her hand. "Well, we're all here. Let's get our story straight."

Addie glared at him. "What is that supposed to mean?"

Al winced, then lowered his face to Ruth's and kissed her cheek. "Can you talk, honey?"

"A little—they've given me something. We need to help Addie understand."

Addie stomped her foot. "Yes, help me understand, please, because I am losing patience."

Ruth grimaced. "You still stomp your foot? You did that when you were a little girl. For Pete's sake, Addie."

"I have a right to be mad." Addie plopped into a chair next to the bed and crossed her arms.

Ruth struggled to shift herself up on one elbow, forced her eyes open. "Al, find out if I can leave. Addie will help me get dressed." She pressed her hand to her head. "If she can do one more thing for me."

Addie stood. "Yes, I'll help you. Anything to get out of here."

Ruth flapped a hand at Al, who disappeared beyond the curtain.

Addie frowned, looking at Ruth's belly. "The ambulance man said you are expecting a baby."

Ruth winced as she sat up. "We'll talk at home."

Addie shook her head. "It's true? It's not a mistake?"

Ruth held her head between her palms. "If we can just get home." Steadying herself, Ruth made slow moves to wriggle out of the hospital gown. "Can you help me?"

Addie pulled away the hospital gown and steered Ruth's arms into the nightgown she had been wearing in the ambulance. The impulse to shake her sister flushed through Addie again. With a push, she steered Ruth's feet toward the floor. Heaving her moaning sister upright, Addie stabilized her with one arm and pulled the nightgown down her torso with the other. With their faces inches apart, Addie tugged the gown's ribbon taut around Ruth's midriff and tied a bow above the bulge. "This is some first night for me," she muttered.

Ruth clutched the bed with one hand and grabbed Addie's arm with the other. "Please, wait until we get home before you say anything more."

Addie rolled her eyes and shrugged.

Al's shoes reappeared under the curtain. Hearing Ruth say, "I'm ready," he pulled it back. A nurse was beside him with a wheelchair. When Al saw Ruth had only the nightgown to cover her, he pulled off his jacket and put it around her shoulders. They made their way along the corridor to the hospital exit, the nurse pushing Ruth in a wheelchair, Al at her side, Addie trailing behind, head down. She in her mussed skirt and blouse and hospital slippers, Ruth in a nightgown, and Al scruffy, in public, mortified her.

Outside, the nurse helped Ruth out of the chair onto Al's arm and took the wheelchair away. Al waved over a cab idling at the nearby taxi stand. After he gave the driver Ruth's address, no one spoke during the ride. Ruth, seated in the middle, leaned on Al, her eyes closed. Al caught Addie's eye and smiled. Addie ignored him. Pulling at a run in one of her stockings, Addie rehearsed in her mind the questions that demanded answers from Ruth when they got home.

When the cab pulled up to Ruth's building, Addie, who was on the curbside, jumped out and reached in to help Ruth. As Al pulled out money for the driver, Addie said, "Why don't you take this cab on home, Al? I will take care of Ruth."

Ruth, who was on her feet, locked eyes with Addie. "It's fine, Al, go home. I can manage."

Al slid over and leaned half-out of the cab. "You're sure, Ruth? I can come up."

Ruth turned to him, holding tight to Addie's arm, pinching her. "Call me," she said. He nodded, then watched her as the cab pulled away.

Ruth tugged at Addie's arm. "We can't stand here for the whole neighborhood to see." Addie, lifting an eyebrow but saying nothing, slow-walked Ruth to the door.

As they began mounting the inside steps, the woman who had called the ambulance hurried down toward them. "I saw you pull up. Let me help you, Ruth."

Ruth thanked her and said, "Mrs. Mason, once I get on my feet, we will ask you in for a proper introduction to my sister."

Mrs. Mason had a key to open Ruth's door, and Addie held it for Ruth to go inside. Mrs. Mason crossed the hall to her apartment, waited as Addie closed the door with a whispered "Good night."

Ruth made her way to the armchair. "You didn't know— Mrs. Mason is the landlady." She lowered herself onto the cushion and hunched over.

Addie shook her head. "What she must think, after this night." She spotted her black pumps shoved under the chair and bent to grab them, thinking she could model them for compliments from Ruth. As Addie raised up with a shoe in each hand, Ruth pulled the skirt of her nightgown over her mouth and vomited.

CHAPTER 2

Sunlight, streaming through the filmy window curtains along the carpet to the bed, warmed Addie awake. Blinking against the brightness, she pushed up from the pillow. The alarm clock on the bedside table read almost noon. She and Ruth had settled in the bed when it was still dark enough to hope for a night's sleep. Addie had spooned against her sister, holding a cold cloth to her forehead, hoping the nausea had run its course. Alert to Ruth's jittery movements, it had been dawn when Addie let her eyes close.

Addie rubbed at the stiffness in her neck. Beside her, Ruth breathed a soft snore. Studying her sister's face, Addie noticed Ruth's ashen pallor, the dark rings around her eyes, and what their old aunt would have called her "chicken neck." Bony wrists, puffy ankles, and the headaches. This was not the citified Ruth that Addie had last seen two years ago.

Waltzing into their family house with a stylish outfit and coiffed hair, red-red lipstick, and matching lacquered nails, that Ruth had been a movie star paper doll come to life, blurring the traces in teenage Addie's mind of the sullen sister who had left. Ruth's comments, when she peeked into the dollhouse she and her sisters had played with, and while sipping coffee at the rubbed and worn kitchen table, sounded like she was touring a place she had read about, not the home she had grown up in. Addie saw the amused glances that their other sisters and brothers exchanged, heard their gentle teasing about the changes in Ruth.

On that visit, Addie had carried Ruth's suitcase into the bedroom they used to share, watched Ruth run her hand over the chenille bedspread, dolls still propped against the pillows. Ruth laughed at the dresser strewn with hair ribbons and combs, photos of screen idols tucked into the mirror, shoes jumbled under the bed. "Looks like a sixteen-year-old girl's room." Addie decided to take that as a compliment, but she wasn't sure.

Years before, ten-year-old Ruth had protested to Dan that she belonged with her older sisters, that she should not be forced to share a room with two-year-old Addie. Losing the argument, Ruth had divided the room, arranging the single beds on opposite walls, separated by the neutral territory of the dresser in the middle. Ruth never forged the distance of their age difference.

Addie had heard the many stories about her own little girl mischief and pouting, and Ruth's resentment about the sharing, her refusing to help Addie with shoe-tying and dress-buttoning. Addie recalled Ruth yanking a hairbrush through Addie's thick waves while telling her she wished she lived somewhere else. But young Addie, not grasping Ruth's aloofness, still plopped herself on Ruth's bed, played with her dresses, tangled her hair ribbons, never paying attention to Ruth's boundaries.

Worn down by months of Ruth's complaining and Addie's tantrums, Dan had agreed to Addie living part-time at the house where their father lived with his wife and their new baby. The separation had eased the fighting between the sisters but had not changed Ruth's manner. Ruth alternated between snapping at Addie or ignoring her. When Addie was ten, Ruth graduated from high school and left home for Detroit. Addie remembered hugging Ruth goodbye, Ruth standing stiff, not hugging back.

But at the visit two years ago, Ruth had stretched out on her old bed, dolls thrown to the floor, and opened a box of her old keepsakes. She flipped through her high school class remembrance folder, sniffed at the good-luck notes written by her old girlfriends, fingered her Girl Scout badges, then threw everything back in the box and slapped the lid shut. Ruth had yielded to Addie's peppering her with questions about her apartment, her office, and the people she had met. Ruth had boasted about her important job at the J.L. Hudson Department Store. Drinking in Ruth's stories of impromptu parties after work and weekend biking on Belle Isle, Addie's wish for her own adventures ballooned. She began to picture Ruth's life as her own, imagined herself as a working girl in a circle of friends, no one treating her like the baby. She had rifled through her closet, pulling out dresses, asking for Ruth's appraisal of the styles. Addie knew that the tone of Ruth's coos about the dresses was a playful mocking of her homemade wardrobe. But Addie was sure the visit changed their relationship for the better. During the farewells as Ruth headed back to Detroit, Ruth had squeezed Addie in a tight hug.

Addie's fascination with city life only grew when she started writing to Ruth. Ruth kept the correspondence going, and Addie took that to mean Ruth enjoyed their letter conversations as much as Addie did. Schoolgirl Addie had griped to Ruth about how tired she was of being babied, that she chafed at the family's overprotection, how she wanted a different, grown-up life outside the limits of their little town. By Christmas of her senior year, Addie made up her mind to move to Detroit after graduation and live with Ruth.

She announced her plan in a letter. Ruth replied that it was too big a step, that getting a first job closer to home was the better move. It nagged at Addie that Ruth didn't quickly agree. Guessing that Ruth's hesitation was the worry she would have to take care of her baby sister, Addie had argued for her maturity in five pages written in a fast huff. Three weeks went by with no reply. Addie fretted her letter had whined like the baby sister Ruth had disliked. She regretted letting her old pouty manner annoy Ruth.

But Ruth's silence did not deter Addie's planning. At school, Addie regaled her classmates with descriptions of the city, Ruth's apartment, the clothes in the stores, the independence she would have. The vision in Addie's mind ran in bright colors, like Dorothy on the road to Oz. She would go to Detroit, even if she had to arrive on Ruth's doorstep unannounced.

Then, in early May, Dan came in from work one evening waving a letter from Ruth. She had written asking if Dan approved of their youngest sister's plan. Dan's dismay that Ruth's letter was the first he had heard of Addie's scheme stung. She realized she had hurt him by leaving him out. Addie hung her head at the look on Dan's face when she made the excuse that she had wanted to have Ruth's agreement before telling him. But she would not back down. Dan ended the conversation by saying he would send a telegram to Ruth before talking further. That he would spend the money surprised Addie, and she took it to mean he was taking her seriously.

She and Dan tiptoed around each other for several days. But Addie was not going to be deterred. She dragged the traveling trunk up from the cellar to her room upstairs. She had already bought a train ticket with the house money. On the fourth night of the tension between them, Addie sat across from Dan, picking at her dinner, fidgeting. She broke the silence. "I want a chance on my own."

Dan put his fork down. "Ruth says not to talk you out of it, if you really want to go."

Addie jumped up, trotted around the table, and threw her arms around his neck. Weeks later, after her high school graduation, they hugged again, saying goodbye on the train platform. He had whispered in her ear. "You can always come home."

Leading up to her departure, the letters she exchanged with Ruth discussed travel details and what Addie should bring with her. She never asked Ruth what had changed her mind about Addie moving to Detroit.

Now Addie reflected on Ruth's side of their correspondence, searching for something she must have missed about what was happening in Ruth's life. But she could not put her finger on any hint about Al, or a baby. Why had Ruth not told her? Annoyance about the revelations of the previous night clambered up her spine.

"Ruth, are you awake? Can you hear me?" Addie poked at Ruth's shoulder.

"Uh, stop … I hear you." Ruth's voice was hoarse. "What time is it?" She did not turn over.

"Almost noon."

"Oh. Missed church."

"Church?"

"Mass. St. Hyacinth."

"Mass? You go to a Catholic church?" *Something else Ruth hadn't mentioned in the letters.*

Ruth slowly rolled onto her back, pushed up against the pillows, and raised her head. "My head feels better, not dizzy. I think I can get up."

"Are you a papist now?"

Ruth scowled. "That's a word you heard from bigots back home who don't know any better. You don't remember when most of our neighbors were Catholics, and nobody said things like that."

Addie shrugged. "Why didn't you tell me you were a Catholic?"

"I'm not a Catholic, not yet."

"What does that mean?"

Ruth pulled up more and propped against the headboard. She took a deep breath. "Al is Catholic. For a church wedding, I should be Catholic, too."

Addie jumped off the bed. "You're getting married to Al? Because of the baby?"

Ruth steadied herself against the shake of the bed, took another breath. "I know this is a lot to take in. I planned to explain everything, but the migraine ruined things yesterday."

"I'll say." Addie crossed her arms. "You said I should come here. Without telling me the truth."

"You insisted you would move to Detroit, no matter what."

"Why didn't you tell me?"

"I didn't want to write everything."

"Such as you're having a baby? Getting married? And turning into a Catholic?"

"You wrote that you're so grown up, but I don't know."

Addie stuck her tongue out at her sister. As soon as she did it, Addie feared Ruth would remember little Addie spending afternoons in the kitchen corner after her tantrums. Addie turned away from Ruth and fingered her hair, kinky from sleeping and humidity.

The telephone rang.

Ruth swung her legs over the side of the bed, steadied herself to stand, and ran her fingertips along the walls as she walked into the living room. Addie heard Ruth say hello, then lower her voice. *It must be Al.* She grabbed a robe hanging on the back of the door and pulled it around her. She marched into the living room and plopped down on the davenport next to Ruth. Frowning, Ruth twisted away. But Addie stayed close to hear Al's voice. She made no pretense about listening.

"I hadn't gone a block when I regretted not going up with you, Ruth."

"Don't worry, I can manage."

"I should have settled you in."

"It is sweet of you to worry, but everything is okay."

"Are you sure? The way Addie talked to you … it grated on me. I don't know what ax she has to grind, but you were in no shape for that."

"I slept, I'm okay." Ruth met Addie's eyes. "She got off on the wrong foot with you, but we can fix that."

"If you're sure, I'll follow your lead. Call me at Tom's if you need me."

"Say hello to Tom for me. Bye." Hanging up, Ruth pushed at Addie's hip. "Since you listened to the whole conversation, you can move over now."

"Al has some nerve talking about me. And who is Tom?"

Ruth sighed, rubbed her forehead. "Al's cousin. And you know you were in a snit last night."

"Never mind that now. Do you have coffee? I'll make it."

"Take off my robe before you do." Addie shrugged off the robe and dumped it in Ruth's lap.

When Addie had figured out Ruth's stove, made the coffee, and carried in two cups, she found Ruth curled up on the cushions, eyes closed. She sat up when Addie said, "Here's your coffee." Addie sat in the armchair. "At the hospital, why did they call you Mrs. Kealy?"

Ruth sipped from her cup. "I married Al."

Addie's eyes widened. "Ruth! What are you saying?"

Ruth ran a hand over her belly. "We eloped."

"Why aren't you living with him, then?"

"I want to keep my job! Until we have a wedding. No one at work knows I'm married, or about the baby. They don't let pregnant women stay." She looked at Addie. "I *love* working at Hudson's. It's hard for me to picture not being there." Ruth set her cup on the lamp table. "I'm not sure Al understands, but it's different for men."

The telephone ringing again stopped their conversation. Ruth answered, then turned to Addie and mouthed "Western Union." Addie pushed closer to hear the operator read a message from their brother. Ruth disconnected that call and dialed 0 for a long-distance operator. When Dan answered, she gave Addie the handset. Hearing his voice say hello made Addie feel like crying.

"You're getting settled in?"

"I am. It's wonderful so far." In a glance at Ruth, Addie made an unspoken agreement not to say more to Dan.

Ruth moved closer to the mouthpiece. "Dan, sorry to make you worry," she called out.

"If everything is fine, don't spend money on talking to me. Write when you can, Addie, and tell me all the news."

After promising to write, and sending love to the family, Addie gave the handset to Ruth to hang up. "When are you going to tell Dan?"

"When I have managed everything. No need for him to worry."

"It hurt him when I kept my plan a secret."

"Dan will understand when I explain, in my own time. But for now, you must be careful to say nothing about this at Hudson's. I was sick at work a few times, but people there know I get migraines. I let them assume that was the reason." Ruth rubbed her neck. "And the migraines have been worse."

"I didn't know about those, either."

"The first one when I was about twelve, and ever since. You don't remember. But we pampered you, kept you from all the bad things."

"Pampered me? More like *bossed* me."

"You don't know what we protected you from."

"Like what?"

"It doesn't matter now." Ruth held her hand up as Addie started to speak. "There's no point in going over the past." Ruth looked at Addie's luggage, sitting near the door where it had been left the night before. "You have to unpack."

Ruth had hung curtains to close off an alcove at one side of the living room, making a small private space for Addie with a cot and a dresser. Unpacking the trunk, arranging shoes and hats, organizing drawers, and making room for Addie's dresses in the two cramped closets busied them for a few hours. When Addie had arranged her summer clothes, leaving her winter things in the trunk, she closed herself in the bathroom for a soak in the tub.

Pushing warm suds through handfuls of hair, rinsing, and toweling, Addie pondered over what Ruth had confided. Was becoming Catholic so complicated that a secret marriage was necessary? And everybody that Addie knew called Catholics "papists." Why did Ruth object to that when she'd said it?

Wiping steam from the mirror, Addie finger-set her curls and bobby-pinned them. Could Ruth count on Al? At her age, Ruth *would* think about a husband, Addie knew. But a guy as handsome as Al could sweet-talk someone like Ruth, lead her on. Dan had always worried over Ruth being "a soft one," quick to cry, taking the slightest hurt to heart. The ladies' magazines were full of stories about women who were not wise in the ways of men being deceived. Addie suspected that Al had taken advantage of Ruth, no matter what she said. *Watch that Al*, she told herself.

But Ruth becoming a mother? Two years of letters, no memories shared, no opening of the sealed-off place where their absent mother lay dormant. Ruth had been ten, Addie a toddler when their mother left. She had no recall of the woman in the photograph Dan kept in his room. What Addie did remember was Dan caring for them. Her father quickly married another woman. Young Addie had had a part-time role in her father's new family. He had never spoken about her mother, and her siblings told her to never ask him. Addie had come to trust her kind-hearted stepmother, who did her best to blend Addie with her two children. Addie had tested calling her "Mother." But it felt like the acting she did in the school plays, pretending to be the child of a woman standing in as her mother. What kind of mother would Ruth be?

And where does this leave me? Addie wished she could turn back time to her arrival and be greeted at the train station by the Ruth who wrote the letters. She had trusted Ruth, and Ruth had lied. That's what it amounted to, not telling Addie about her marriage. Addie finished her pin curls, put on a clean skirt and blouse. She wanted answers.

She found Ruth bustling around the rooms, finding new spots for her things displaced by the rearrangement. Folding scarves into a drawer, Ruth handed one to Addie. "Cover those pin curls."

Addie tied the scarf to hide the pins, pulled the loose strands away from her neck.

Ruth instructed her on the plan for Monday morning. "We'll leave earlier than I usually do, to have time before I clock in to take you to the Hudson's personnel office. They interview on Mondays. You'll fill out the application and take the typing test."

"I know just what to wear." Addie went to the closet and took out a dress, held it against her figure.

"Not that one." Ruth shifted the hangers, her lips pursed.

Addie stifled the impulse to argue, waiting for Ruth to choose the outfit she thought appropriate for Addie to present herself for a job at Hudson's. When Addie proposed wearing the new pumps with the dress, Ruth agreed.

Ruth showed Addie around the kitchen as she made a supper of eggs and fried potatoes with slices of fresh tomato. Addie took a chance at turning the conversation as they ate. "Al told me he met you at Hudson's."

Ruth nodded. "We did. Men from the agencies are always coming up to Advertising with product details. Sometimes the bosses send me to reception with ad copy, or to fill in for one of the other girls out front. He would stay and talk a bit when I was at the desk. The other girls said he asked about me if I wasn't up front."

"Then …?"

"He seemed to find me—we ran into each other in the hallway or had coffee at the same time in the cafeteria. It was months before he asked me out."

"What made you agree?"

Ruth smiled. "You see how handsome he is. Al has a quiet way about him and a sense of humor. He's serious but doesn't take things too seriously. Know what I mean?"

Addie nodded. "He *is* good-looking. But what happened … to lead to … married?"

"I'm not sure I can explain that."

"I know about men."

Ruth smiled. "Sure, you do."

Addie tossed her head back. "I do. I was engaged."

"What? To whom?"

"Close to the end of the war, Eddie Walsh—you probably don't remember his family; he was a year ahead of me in school—turned eighteen and enlisted. We had sort of been seeing each other, not serious, not to me anyway. But before he left, he asked me to marry him. I was so surprised! I tried to put him off as gently as I could. But he asked for some hope to carry him through. I took his ring."

"How could you promise that?"

"His sister was my best friend, and his family was so worried about him. I figured I would break it off when he got back."

Ruth looked into Addie's eyes. "He came home, didn't he?"

"Yes, he came home. But I had already written to tell him I was not waiting for him. I gave the ring to his mother. After, no one in the family would talk to me."

Ruth laughed until she saw Addie's frown. "I'm sorry. I can't imagine what you were thinking. Lucky you left that town. People there don't forget things like that."

Addie waved her off. "It doesn't matter. I got out of it. The point is, I know men take advantage."

"What do you mean?"

"They can talk you into things."

Ruth took the plates to the sink. "Al did not talk me into anything. Why do you dislike Al? You've just met, you don't know him." She ran the hot water and rubbed a soapy cloth on the dishes.

"I *don't* know him. But he is the reason for the situation you're in. What do you expect me to think?"

"I am not in 'a situation'."

Addie took the dish towel and fast-wiped plates, clattering them into a pile, satisfied with Ruth's annoyed grimace. "What about my future here? You let me think … you lied."

"I did not lie."

"It's the same thing, not telling me."

"I meant to explain things after you settled in."

"Explain now."

"When you first wrote about moving here, I thought you were too … young. After I knew about the baby, and you would not give up the idea—well, Al and I thought you could help me."

"Help you? Like a nursemaid? I am not here for that."

"No, you're here taking advantage of *my* help, being the baby, as always!"

Addie threw the dishtowel on the table and stalked out of the kitchen. She heard Ruth slam a pot into the sink.

Addie grabbed Ruth's house key from the table by the door. She glanced out the window. The sun had lowered enough to cool the evening. Addie let the apartment door slam behind her as she left. Outside, she marched to the gate, soft-kicked it with the toe of her canvas shoe. Hearing footsteps behind her, she swirled around, ready to say more to Ruth.

Mrs. Mason stood with her hands on her hips. "Kicking my gate, are you?"

"Sorry, I—" Addie shook her head.

"Is Ruth feeling better today?"

"Yes, she is. Thank you for your help last night."

"Good. I'm out for a walk. C'mon, see the neighborhood. We'll walk to the river."

Addie followed Mrs. Mason from the yard. Evening ramblers strolled along both sides of East Grand Boulevard, separated by a grassy median dotted with trees lush with the leafiness of early summer. Brick houses lined the avenue, two and three stories, with the side panels of their bay windows open to the breeze. Residents sat on their porches or in chairs in their front yards, taking advantage of the cooler air, calling out to neighbors. Addie and Mrs. Mason stepped around jump rope contests and kids racing tricycles. At the cross streets, churches, groceries, garages, and other shops clustered along the corner blocks. After they crossed Jefferson, the boulevard broadened into a promenade of trees and gardens leading onto the Belle Isle Bridge. Globes atop the iron lamp posts sparked on to light the half-mile walkway to the island in the river.

Mrs. Mason led Addie partway across the bridge. Leaning on the balustrade, Addie took in the expansive view of the skylines of Detroit, on one side of the river, and of Windsor, Canada, on the other, silhouetted in the gathering twilight.

"I love it here," Addie said.

Mrs. Mason chuckled. "You know that already, on your second day?"

"This is where my life will happen."

Mrs. Mason watched the water eddy below. "I've not felt that optimistic these last few years." She shrugged. "But life *is* happening, here, now, just as you say." The sky was darkening. "Let's go home before Ruth starts to worry about you."

Addie almost said *Ruth isn't thinking about me*, but she didn't.

CHAPTER 3

The streetcar lurched to a stop, the doors swung open, and the surge of people pushing out ejected Addie onto the curb. She shook out her skirt, tightened her arm around her purse. Masses of hats were striding toward her on the sidewalk, like a parade of ants busying in and out of their anthill. Her pumps added enough height to enable her to peek between shoulders of the rushing swarm. Amidst the jostling of passing elbows and handbags, the jitters that had kept her awake half the night notched up. Ruth, in a full-skirted day-dress and wide-brimmed hat, furrowed her brow and clenched her cheeks into a defiant warning to the oncoming throng, *Stay out of my way.* Her look reminded Addie of times when young Ruth had made demands with arms crossed and lips pursed. Addie straightened her shoulders and strode on pace to keep up with Ruth's brisk walk until Hudson's came into view.

The immensity of the J.L. Hudson building stunned Addie. She clamped her hat in place and craned her neck, gaping at the towering redbrick stories overhead. On the ground, construction was in progress, a small army of men and machines in motion, expanding the building to swallow a full square block of downtown Detroit. Old steam shovels moving earth spewed an odor so like that of coal smelting that Addie flinched. In her hometown, the smell of coal burning into coke for Pittsburgh's steel furnaces had been inseparable from the air.

Addie's abrupt stop in the middle of the sidewalk forced the crowd behind them to shift left or right, prompting glares and a few mild oaths. Ruth dragged Addie out of the stream over to the side of the building. "You can't just stop in the middle of the sidewalk."

"I couldn't help it! I can't wait to see inside. Where is the entrance?"

Ruth reached out to right Addie's hat. "Farmer Street, for the employee elevators."

Addie stuck close to Ruth as they again merged into the fast-walking crowd. At the corner of Farmer and East Grand River Avenue, the streets tunneled between the imposing buildings just like the postcard Ruth had sent her, showing an aerial view of the Detroit skyscrapers. In Addie's imagination, a tiny version of herself appeared pasted onto the rooftop of one of the tall buildings, taking in the expansive view. It had to be like flying, to perch above the bustle of the city. Addie wobbled on her heels. "Looking up made me dizzy."

Ruth took her arm. "You're sweating through your dress. Take a breath. Inside will be cooler."

A cast iron pattern of looping ribbons and flower baskets decorated the marquee over the Hudson's entry and framed the windows above. Stepping through the heavy glass doors, Addie admired the gleaming brass fixtures and sparkling crystal sconces lining the lobby walls. When the doors closed behind them, the roar of the street noise changed to that hum she had noticed when she first arrived, as if someone had struck a tuning fork and the ensemble held the note.

Showing her J. L. Hudson's employee card to the guard, Ruth explained she wished to escort Addie to Personnel, and he agreed with a tip of his cap. Addie counted ten elevators along the corridor, above each one a half-moon-shaped dial with an arrow pointing to the floor numbers moving higher or down. Waiting employees clustered in the lobby. When several elevators arrived at once, Ruth propelled Addie into a car, calling out the floor number to the operator. He levered the gated door closed, pushed a button, and the elevator car swooshed upward. There was silence in the car, and Ruth's slight shake of her head told Addie to stay quiet.

The operator announced the fourteenth floor. Ruth and Addie stepped out into a wide lobby where the double glass doors of the Personnel office loomed before them. To the right, an archway labeled Employee Cafeteria beckoned with the aroma of coffee. Addie wanted to ask if they had time for a cup, but she knew the answer.

Ruth stopped at the door to the Personnel office. "Let's look at you." She twisted a bit of Addie's hair back under her hat. "Have you got your compact?"

Addie fumbled in her bag, pulled out the compact, ran the pad over her nose, pressed her lips together to smooth out her lipstick. "How's that?"

"Better. The dress will pass but change gloves with me." Seeing the question on Addie's face, Ruth pushed her gloves at Addie and held out her other hand. "Mine are from the store. It will impress them. From now on, you will wear only Hudson's merchandise."

Pulling on Ruth's gloves, Addie nodded and licked her lips again. Before she could calm her shaky feeling, Ruth had opened the door, and Addie propelled herself forward. Overhanging milk glass globes shone light onto eight wood desks set in two rows, a woman typing at each one, the clacking of the keys competing with ringing telephones. At the entryway where they stood was a larger desk. A young woman with red hair styled into two petite buns over her ears shuffled through different colored cards in a metal file box. She gave them a big smile.

"Good morning, Ruth! I haven't seen you on this floor for a while."

"Morning, Susan. They keep me busy on nineteen. And I must hurry and get up there, but I want to introduce my sister, Addie. She'd like to apply."

Susan extended her hand to Addie. "Welcome to Hudson's, Addie. Ruth, I can do the paperwork and ask if they will see her."

"I appreciate whatever you can do."

"Addie, have a seat over there and I will call you when we're ready." She pointed to a metal-frame upholstered settee flanked by a wicker and wood armchair. A lamp table held a placard reading, "From the J. L. Hudson Co. Office Furniture Collection."

Ruth unclasped Addie's handbag and pushed a paper inside. "I hope you get the interview today—either way, call my extension when you're finished." Snapping the bag closed, Ruth whispered, "Good luck!" With that, she rushed out the door.

Addie plopped onto the settee cushion, then remembered her skirt, leaned up to smooth it, sat again holding it in place. Facing her on the opposite wall was a wood-framed poster titled, in ornate lettering, *The Firm*. Below were photographs of the senior executives of the J. L. Hudson Company. Names and titles were printed along the middle of the scroll in the same decorative lettering: Richard H. Webber, President; Oscar Webber, Vice-President and General Manager; James B. Webber, Vice-President and Merchandise Director; Joseph L. Webber, Vice-President and Merchandise Director; James B. Webber, Jr., Vice-President and Assistant General Manager; Arnold A. Petzold, Secretary and Treasurer. The Webbers all shared a squared-off jaw and set of the eyes, and the face of Petzold shadowed their features enough to believe he was a relation. Five were middle aged, in business suits and rounded wire spectacles, their portrait smiles practiced. Two were leaning in and three sitting back. The sixth man—younger, perhaps the son of one of them—wore his smile more gleeful than the others, as if he was surprised to find himself included in the array.

Their faces emitted a superiority that Addie had noticed before in prosperous upper-class men. A sensibility accustomed to refined surroundings that was matched by the atmosphere inside the building. Ruth said that Hudson's set the highest expectations for their employees. Addie saw the diligence of the typists, heads down, fingers flying over the keys. She sat up straighter, nodded her head at the Hudson's men, and decided they would find her worthy.

By the time Susan summoned her, Addie's jitters had calmed to a gentle swing of one leg crossed over the other. She gave her full attention to answering Susan's questions and filling out the personnel forms in her best penmanship. One typist moved out of her chair to seat Addie for the typing test. Susan looked over the letter of recommendation from her teacher, noted that Addie sought a bookkeeping position. After the review of the forms, Susan asked her to wait again; she would be interviewed shortly. Addie took the same seat across from the genteel gazes of the Hudson's executives and gave them a wink. This was going better than she had hoped.

Susan beckoned Addie to follow her. "Mrs. Reynolds will see you."

Opening a door at the side of the reception area, Susan led Addie into a much larger workroom running the length of one side of the building, subdivided into sections by banks of grey filing cabinets. Only the top third of the enormous windows were visible, the rest blocked by rows of metal shelving holding file boxes. Addie longed to see the view from this height, but there was no opening to look. Trailing Susan along the walking path and weaving through the maze, Addie estimated sixty women were typing, filing, speaking on telephones, and punching keys on adding machines. Signs hanging from the ceiling along the way marked areas for Payroll, Records, Safety, Pension. A trio of men talking to each other walked toward them, and when Susan stepped aside to let them pass, Addie moved behind her.

Susan stopped at a desk where a woman, wearing a dark skirt and matching jacket with a crisp white blouse, stood talking to a typist whose fingers were poised on the keys. Susan handed the suited woman a file and turned to beckon Addie closer. "This is the young lady I called about."

The woman glanced with a raised eyebrow at Addie, looked at the information in her hand. "Wait." She strode toward a door in the intersecting corridor.

Susan read the questioning look on Addie's face and patted her arm. "Don't worry about her; that's Lucille, Mrs. Reynold's gatekeeper."

Addie twisted her handbag strap for the few minutes they waited. Lucille returned, motioned with one hand for Addie to follow her, and waved Susan off with the other. Susan flashed a smile at Addie and walked away.

Addie froze. Lucille waved her fingers at Addie. "Are you coming? Mrs. Reynolds is a busy person." Addie found her feet, caught up to her as Lucille opened the door. Addie stepped over the threshold. She heard the door close behind her.

Dark wood-paneled walls framed a corner office with windows that began near the floor and stretched close to the beamed ceiling. Damask draperies opened to the sky. Hanging in Addie's direct view between two windows was a frame about six feet wide and three feet high. A black-and-white photograph depicted an aerial view of the Hudson's building, with arrows pointing to neighboring landmarks: the Skillman Branch Library, the Stott Building, Broderick Tower, Milner Hotel, Merchants Building, Grand Circus Park, Hotel Lincoln, Metropolitan Building.

The sound of a throat clearing pulled her attention to an oak desk the size of a dining table at the other end of the room. The woman sitting behind it tapped her pen on a pad. "Miss Tate?" She pointed the pen at an upholstered armchair stationed in front of the desk.

Addie stepped across the plush carpet, sat. Forcing a smile, she waited, studying the woman who was reading from the folder Lucille had given her.

Mrs. Reynolds was trim, middle-aged, and sitting erect in an executive chair upholstered to match the one where Addie sat. Black hair, cropped short like women in the factories wore it, rippled back from her forehead in waves, as though she ran a comb through when it was wet and left it to dry. She wore a striped black-and-white blouse with starched white cuffs, a loose bow of the material tied at the neck, no jewelry. On the desk was a wide blotter with dark green leather side folds embossed in gold with the logo of the J.L. Hudson Company, a matching penholder, and a telephone. After what seemed like an hour of silence, Addie's heart racing and her hands dampening Ruth's gloves with sweat, Mrs. Reynolds spoke.

"You have no experience."

Addie opened her mouth to speak, stopped by a perfectly manicured raised hand. "At Hudson's, we acquire only the best workers for every department."

Nodding, Addie clasped her hands tightly in her lap, and met the woman's eyes. "I excelled in my bookkeeping classes."

Mrs. Reynolds shook her head. "My dear, you cannot expect I would consider you for a bookkeeping position. That is out of the question." She closed the folder and held it out. "Give this to Lucille. That is all."

Addie felt the creeping flush of humiliation, like a child being sent to the corner. "Thank you, ma'am," Addie mumbled and hastened from the office.

Once she pulled the door closed behind her, tears welled in her eyes. She panicked about finding her way out of there before someone would see her cry. Lucille appeared in her blurry vision and took the folder from her hand, clucking her impatience. Addie kept her eyes on Lucille's shoes through the maze, blinking back tears, fuming at Ruth. How could Ruth not have told her about Mrs. Reynolds? Why apply if being hired was out of the question? Ruth had put her through this for nothing.

At the door to the outer office, Lucille pushed a buzzer on the wall, and Susan opened the door with a smile. "Very well, Susan, thank you." The folder and Addie handed over, Lucille closed the door.

Addie moved past Susan and made a quick wipe of her eyes. "Thank you for your help. I'll be going now."

"Are you pressed for time? We have the last details to complete."

Addie shrugged and followed Susan to her desk, where she picked up a clipboard. She held out a small white card with a green border.

"I've prepared your employee identification card. Be sure to always carry it in the store. I can take you to the department now to meet the manager; he'll go over the hours with you."

"Excuse me? I have a job here?"

"Mrs. Reynolds didn't tell you, huh? Likes to intimidate the new ones. Take the card. In this envelope is the payroll sheet with your employee number and the weekly rate. Come along, I'll take you to the Print Shop. Welcome to Hudson's!"

Later, on the street, leaning against the brick, the last ninety minutes blurring in her mind like an old silent movie played too fast, her stomach grumbling so loud she was sure those passing heard it, Addie remembered the paper with Ruth's office telephone extension. If she hadn't left the building, she could have called from one of the telephones near the employee elevators. Snapping open her purse, Addie fished out the paper and the employee identification card. Could she walk inside and go up? She pulled open one of the doors, strode to the guard, and held the card in his view. He nodded and pushed the call button for her. *Welcome to Hudson's*, Addie sang under her breath as she stepped into the elevator. The operator gave her a quizzical look, closed the gate, asked, "Floor, miss?"

"Advertising?"

"Nineteen.

"Thank you."

In the elevator lobby on the nineteenth floor, a kiosk promoted the latest issue of *The Hudsonian*, the J.L. Hudson Company employee magazine. The cover illustration was an idyllic scene of families at a lakeside swimming beach, with an array of blankets, picnic baskets, and sand toys. Headlines offered summer recipes, a dog show in the store, performances of the Hudson's Choral Club, and schedules for the employee baseball teams. Addie picked up a copy as she spotted the store telephone. When Ruth answered, Addie blurted, "I'm here, on nineteen!"

Fifteen minutes later she and Ruth sat in the cafeteria with egg salad sandwiches and coffee. Addie stuffed a huge bite from half her sandwich into her mouth.

"Slow down, Addie. Chew, then tell me what happened."

Addie swallowed, sipped coffee, sat back. "Why didn't you tell me about Mrs. Reynolds?"

Ruth shrugged. "You had to weather the interview to be hired. No need to make you more nervous."

"What a mean and nasty woman!"

"You got through it, so why fret about it? You will see her walking the floors, taking stock of how people are doing."

"But she dismissed me like I had no business applying to be a bookkeeper."

"She's right that you have no experience. You will get some."

"In the Print Shop?"

"What are you complaining about? You were hired at the best place to work in Detroit on the first try."

Addie chewed. Around the cafeteria, about a hundred women and men clustered in table groups, the hubbub of talk and laughter echoing in the high-ceilinged space. They looked happy to be there. Addie wiped her hands with a napkin. "Do you know the manager of the Print Shop, Mr. Reed?"

"I know who he is."

"He's an old-timer like Dad and Uncle Charlie, still wearing the vest and pocket watch on a chain. And the shop is full of men."

"They won't have you in the shop. You'll be at the counter, seeing to the orders going in and out." Ruth checked her watch. "You'll get used to eating on the clock. Let's go."

Outside the cafeteria, Ruth punched the elevator "up" button. "We'll talk more when I get home. You are a lucky girl!"

Leaving Addie to wait for one going down, Ruth stepped into the elevator cab. Addie made a face at Ruth as the door closed.

Addie knew Ruth had a point about getting the job, but the Print Shop was like being assigned to a dungeon. She cringed, remembering picking her way through rolls of paper and stacks of metal plates, clutching her dress from brushing against the dirty materials as Mr. Reed had led her through the thudding machinery. The system of different colored paper copies and order codes he explained muddled in her brain.

Addie rode the elevator to the ground floor. Before she would be stuck working in the Print Shop, she wanted to see the better parts of the store. She made her way to the grander customer entrance along Woodward Avenue.

Rounding the corner, Addie watched a uniformed Hudson's doorman, carrying dress boxes tied together with gold cord, escort a lady to a waiting sedan, handing the parcels off to her driver. Two more sedans pulled up, and the drivers swept the doors open for dapper men and smartly dressed women to exit. The Hudson's doorman tipped his cap, offering the "Welcome to Hudson's" greeting to each. He said it again to Addie as she sailed in behind the couples.

The ceiling soared high on the ground floor, with oversized milk glass light fixtures twinkling between immense columns lining the expanse. Polished wood floors snaked through an array of blond wood counters with glass fronts. The sales floor was active with a steady flow of customers. But the sound was hushed, a gentle discourse of lowered voices and softened tones, like inside a church.

Just ahead of Addie were the jewelry counters. One couple she had followed in looked over earrings on a velvet-covered tray. In a slow wander along the aisles, Addie admired the leather goods, handbags, scarves and belts, more merchandise than she had seen in one place before. She wished for cosmetics she saw in the Aisles of Beauty but thought better of spending her money. Each turn presented displays of enticing hats or sweaters or stockings. After seeing the ladies' part of the floor, she walked along the aisles for men. Mannequin upper bodies modeled the latest in formal shirts and ties, silk scarves, and cufflinks. Addie stood before one, imagining Al's muscular chest in the tuxedo shirt, recalling his brown eyes looking into hers. He was handsome, she would give Ruth that, but what else was he? She shook away the image.

When she came to a display of gloves, Addie remembered what Ruth said about wearing store merchandise. The saleswoman greeted her. "May I help you find your size and color, Miss?"

"Yes, please. I borrowed these gloves from my sister. They fit well and I'd like a pair."

The saleswoman raised a finger. "Let me get that style for you to try on."

The tray placed in front of Addie held a pair of gloves like Ruth's and another pair, different at the cuff, lighter in fabric. "You might like to try our newer summer style, too."

After trying a different one on each hand, Addie decided on the newer style. As the saleswoman wrote up the order, Addie said, "This is my first time in the store. I arrived in Detroit yesterday, and I have a job here, starting tomorrow."

"Oh, I'm glad you mentioned you are an employee. If you have your identification card, I can give you the discount."

Addie smiled. "I didn't know about that," she said, showing the card.

"During your first week, you will get all the details."

After she made Addie's change, the saleswoman pointed at her nametag, said, "I'm Helen. Nice to meet you, Addie, and—"

"Welcome to Hudson's!" both said together, laughing.

"Where did they put you?"

"Print Shop." Addie made a face.

"Ah, well, maybe you'll make your way to sales." Helen handed Addie the glove box wrapped in dark green paper stamped with the Hudson's logo.

That evening, Addie told Ruth about exploring the first floor and buying her gloves from Helen. Ruth found her copy of the store map to show Addie where to find the employee corridors and passageways on the sales floors. "Your starting time is half an hour earlier than mine, but I'll go with you until you learn the streetcar route."

"I can get there on my own."

Ruth shook her head. "We are *so* busy. Getting in early will help me."

"I wish I had applied for the sales floor."

Ruth threw up her hands. "Are you still complaining? How about thanking me? You don't know how many people Hudson's turns away."

Addie shrugged. "This is not the glamorous job I want to write to my friends about."

"So you aren't grateful for my help?"

Addie rolled her eyes. "Thank you, Ruth, for your help. Now, can you tell me which one of my dresses I should expose to the grime of the Print Shop on my first day?"

Ruth slapped the map on the table. "You're so smart, pick one yourself."

CHAPTER 4

At 8:35 the next morning, Mr. Reed stood behind the counter holding the order book when Addie rushed into the Print Shop. He pulled his watch from his vest pocket and made a show of clicking it open, checking the time, and snapping it shut. As Addie reached the desk, he pointed to the large clock hanging on the side wall.

"We need you at the counter at eight-thirty to begin your work."

"Good morning to you, Mr. Reed. The streetcar went slower than I expected." This was only part of the reason for Addie's lateness. Ruth had started their morning with a bout of nausea, delaying Addie's turn in the bathroom. They nixed their plan to travel to work together and Addie had gone ahead but missed the first streetcar that came along.

"Excuses do not produce the work, Miss. Let's get on with the day."

"Where can I put my things?"

Mr. Reed summoned a boy Addie had met the previous day, now shuffling boxes in heaps behind the counter. "Joe, show Miss where the lockers are." Glancing at Addie's dress, he added. "Get her a smock."

Joe nodded and started walking toward the back of the shop. Addie gave Mr. Reed a weak smile and caught up to Joe.

"Is he always grouchy?"

"Naw, he just hates getting off the schedule, even by a few minutes. You'll learn quick enough."

They walked the length of the shop, passing the men working the machines, most not looking her way, several giving her toothy grins. Addie cringed. If she must walk past them every day, she would stare ahead and ignore them. Joe led her into a wide alcove at the back where grey metal lockers lined a wall. At the side was a garment rack hung with pairs of overalls and smocks.

"The laundry delivers the clean uniforms every morning," Joe explained. He rifled through the smocks and pulled one. "This should fit over your dress." He held it out to her. "When you go to the sales floors, you leave it here."

Addie wrinkled her nose at the starched green fabric. "This is clean?"

"Clean enough to keep you from messing up your dress. You can take this empty locker."

Addie pushed her arms into the smock, billowy over her dress, and buttoned the front, dreading what she looked like, but there was no mirror. When she had stowed her handbag and forced her brimmed hat into the locker, Joe slammed the door shut, latched the lock, handed her the key. "You got your name tag? That goes on the top pocket. When you go out with orders, pin the tag on your dress."

Addie pursed her lips as she pinned the tag. On the ground floor, other girls in pristine dresses sold beautiful jewelry to refined people while she was in the dirty cave of the Print Shop in a sackcloth smock. Mrs. Reynolds had punished her with this job. It wasn't fair.

Joe glanced toward the front, where Mr. Reed waited. She shrugged herself upright, smoothed the smock, nodded to Joe. On the walk through the shop, she snubbed the ogling men with her head high and eyes straight ahead.

When they rejoined Mr. Reed, Joe finished bundling boxes onto a wheeled trolley and pushed it near the door next to piles of other boxes. He tipped an imaginary cap to Addie and disappeared into the noisy machines.

Mr. Reed pointed to a stool. The counter was two-sided, and the stool swiveled toward the door or the machines in back. Addie wobbled until she perched her heels over the bottom rung and steadied the seat to face the door.

"I will explain the current orders, Miss, and give you the morning runs to make. Then we'll see."

Addie only half-attended to Mr. Reed's review of the order book. She imagined running out into the corridor to escape the ink smell and the noise. How long would she have to endure the Print Shop before she could tell the Personnel office she wanted something else? If she learned the store while she delivered the print orders, she could ask Ruth's friend Susan to move her to a better spot.

"Miss? The telephone is ringing." Mr. Reed's eyes flicked from her to the phone. "Pick it up, please."

Addie grabbed the receiver. "Hello? This is the Print Shop ... No, I am new here. Who is this?"

Mr. Reed rubbed his forehead, grimaced.

Addie held the telephone to her chest. "Someone from the Stationery Department wants the delivery date for an order."

JAN M. WALTON

Mr. Reed held out his hand to take the telephone. "Listen to this conversation. You will handle the next one."

Addie narrowed her eyes. *All right, you mean old man, I will show you.* Grabbing a pad and pen from the counter, she scribbled notes. After the call, she got the gist of looking up a delivery date in the order book. She perused the reference list taped to the counter of departments' floors and telephone numbers.

When the telephone rang again, she answered, "Good morning, Print Shop, Addie speaking. How may I help you?" as Mr. Reed had instructed. She pushed the "hold" button when she wanted to question him without the caller hearing. After an hour's worth of calls and questions handled, and her satisfactory recall of the order color codes, Mr. Reed pointed behind her to an assortment of green stationery boxes embossed with the Hudson's logo in gold.

"The men deliver the larger orders, but you take the special print jobs to departments, particularly Bridal and Engraving. You have their orders today." Mr. Reed pressed a buzzer beneath the counter, and in a moment, Joe appeared. "Tie these for delivery and show Miss the order cart."

Joe wheeled what looked like a tearoom serving cart around the side of the counter. Engraved on the top gleaming silver tray was the name of the store, in the ornate lettering she remembered seeing on the portrait of the executives. The same dark green leather as on Mrs. Reynold's desk set covered the cart's push handle.

Joe tied gold braid around the stationery boxes, placed some on the top tray and the rest on a second tray underneath, then handed Addie the order sheet. "You take the employee elevators. Go to Bridal first," he said. "They sign for what you bring; make them verify the count of the boxes."

Mr. Reed nodded. "Follow the sheet. And hurry back."

Addie looked over the list of orders, tucked the sheet under a box on the tray, and pushed the trolley to the door. Two throats behind her cleared. She turned and saw Joe gesturing to take off the smock. She quickly pulled the buttons open, unpinned her name badge and attached it to her dress, and looped the smock over a hook by the door. Addie opened the door and pushed the cart out with a wave.

Waiting for the elevator, she checked the order sheet again. Joe had paper-clipped a map of the floors behind it. Bridal, on seven, was circled in red. When she maneuvered the cart from the employee elevator onto the thick carpet of the seventh floor, Addie smoothed her dress and wished she had combed her hair. The store offered its most elegant attire for women on the seventh floor. By the map, she was standing at the opposite end of the floor from the Bridal Salon. She realized with glee the path went through the fashion displays and decided to take her time.

Slowly rolling the cart in the aisle, Addie shifted her gaze left and right to view the mannequins outfitted in gorgeous evening gowns and wraps and heels. She had only seen such glamor in the magazines. Subtle piano music floated from hidden speakers above the different salons, one next to another. It was early in the shopping hours and few customers strolled about. Further on, the sales staff fussed over summer frocks and hats, positioning items just so on racks and counters. If they noticed her, they gave no greeting. Addie wondered if there was a rule against talking to the lowly person from the Print Shop.

She came to an archway on the left leading into a secluded room where two well-dressed women sat in plush armchairs sipping coffee. A model pirouetted in the space between them, the fabric of a halter-style evening gown swirling around her legs. The wheels of the cart caught a tuft of carpet, and the squeak when Addie pushed it free made the women look her way. The saleswoman in the salon frowned at Addie and pulled a heavy damask curtain closed. Addie sniffed and moved on.

The Bridal Salon announced itself with gold and white double doors flanked with floral arrangements set on marble pillars. A pervasive scent of lavender added to the impression that those stepping through the doors entered a special space reserved for women holding the status of being engaged. Addie hesitated outside the doors; was there a service entrance? She saw no hallways to the side or alternate door. Grabbing the glass handle, she opened one door, wedged her backside against it, pulled the cart through. The door closed behind her with a soft click. A woman with blonde curls piled on her head dressed in a form-fitting pink suit stood behind an ornate gilded desk and threw up her hands.

"Finally! We need this order right away." She pointed Addie to the left. "Through here." Addie, with the cart, followed her around a folding screen decorated with pink and gold roses that shielded the entry area from a storage alcove. The woman peered at Addie's name tag.

"We need our orders promptly each morning. We do not expect to wait. Is that clear?"

"This is my first day," Addie said.

"And you were not prompt."

Addie looked at the name on the gold pin adorning the woman's suit, an engraved piece of jewelry, not the tinplate with a typed card like Addie wore.

"Well, Miss Harris, I will try, but Mr. Reynolds is the manager of the Print Shop."

"I hold you responsible. See that I am not disappointed."

With that, Miss Harris plucked the order sheet from Addie's grasp, counted the boxes, opened one to check the accuracy of the printing, and waved a hand toward a shelf. "You may place the boxes there."

A flush of resentment crept up Addie's neck to her cheeks. Someone who knew nothing about her, who was rude, was scolding her. Addie transferred the boxes to the shelf, tilted her chin up as she turned to Miss Harris. "If you would sign the order sheet."

Miss Harris swept her ink pen across the signature line and tossed the paper onto the cart. "Good day."

Addie jerked the cart backwards and the edge bumped the middle of the standing screen, making it wobble. She kept moving as a frowning Miss Harris whipped her head around. Addie pulled open the salon door and shoved the cart through. A customer just on the other side drew back in time to avoid a collision. Praying that Miss Harris had not seen that, Addie apologized and kept going.

She aimed the cart for the elevator bank straight ahead. She intended to make the delivery to the Engraving department quick and go back to the Print Shop to complain to Mr. Reed about the ill-mannered treatment by Miss Harris. She barked to the elevator operator, "Mezzanine, please," and propelled the cart into the car.

They were alone, and the man spoke over his shoulder without closing the door. "Miss, this is the public elevator."

In her upset, she had not paid attention to which elevator she was taking when she left the Bridal Salon. She mumbled thanks, pushed the cart out of the car, made her way back to the service elevators.

On the Mezzanine, Addie shunted the cart into the sales area where more customers than on the seventh floor were milling about. The Mezzanine was smaller than the other floors, built as a balcony surrounding the main sales floor, and the departments merged from one to the next. She checked the map against the signage to get her bearings and locked eyes with Mrs. Reynolds standing in the aisle straight ahead. Addie broke the gaze and hurried to push the cart away from the main aisle, swerving left into an opening amidst a row of steamer trunks and suitcases. *Luggage department; which way from there to Engraving?* She realized it was silly to try to outfox Mrs. Reynolds, who must know Addie would be there to deliver an engraving order, those steely eyes waiting for her to make a mistake. Addie smoothed her hair and dress, calmed her walk. If she was to be fired, she would not create a scene for Mrs. Reynolds to gloat over.

When Addie reached the Stationery Department, she could see ahead to an expansive wood table with a plaque hanging above: Engraving. Arrayed across the table were bound sample books, interspersed with several of the Hudson's leather-bound blotters and a tray of fountain pens. Glancing around for Mrs. Reynolds, Addie was surprised to not see her.

A young man stood at one end of the table. He smiled at seeing the cart. "Hello. You must be the new girl from printing."

"Yes, I'm Addie. Pleased to meet you." Addie extended her hand to him.

"Addie, Mike—Michael here in the store," nodding toward his name plate, also gold like the one Miss Harris wore.

"That is the nicest greeting I've had today." Wary of Mrs. Reynolds lurking, Addie got to business. "Can you please check your order?"

Mike scooped up the boxes from the lower tray and started checking the printing. "Things haven't gone well so far?"

"No. I hate the Print Shop. The woman in Bridal scolded me. I almost took the public elevator by mistake, and down here, Mrs. Reynolds gave me her evil eye."

He grimaced. "She did, huh? She's tough on the rules."

"How long have you been working here?"

"Since my discharge." He winked. "I started in the Print Shop."

Addie laughed, then stopped at the sight of black hair waves bobbing above the display racks across the aisle. "I have to go; she's coming this way."

Mike handed her the signed order sheet. "See you, Addie, next time."

Addie turned the cart into the aisle and made a quick dash past Stationery. She skirted around Luggage and turned toward Optical. Mrs. Reynolds stepped into the aisle, holding a clipboard.

Addie faced her with a raised chin. "Good morning, Mrs. Reynolds."

"I will accompany you to the Print Shop."

They waited in silence for an elevator car to arrive. The operator stiffened at the sight of Mrs. Reynolds. The silent ascent to the twenty-first floor felt to Addie like an eternity. When the door opened, Mrs. Reynolds waved a hand for Addie to lead with the cart. Addie held the Print Shop door for Mrs. Reynolds to enter. Joe at the counter widened his eyes, called out, "Mr. Reed!"

53

Addie wheeled the cart behind the counter and left it there, kept walking to her locker. Seconds later, Joe ran into the alcove. "What the heck happened?"

Addie fumbled in her pocket for the key to the locker. "I got on the public elevator by mistake. When the operator reminded me, I got off, but she may have seen me." She opened the locker and took out her handbag. "And the woman in Bridal may have complained."

"Mrs. R is talking to Mr. Reed in the hallway."

"Think this will be my first and last day?"

Joe shrugged. "I've seen worse get off with a warning." The front desk telephone began ringing. "While you've still got a job, you should answer that."

Addie trotted to the desk and picked up the phone. The caller was pleasant and chatty, excited to meet the new girl in printing. Addie looked up an order of sales placards expected in Children's. *Too bad I won't last to deliver these to her,* she thought. She put her smock on, sat on the stool fingering her nametag, waiting for her dismissal. Addie imagined disappointing Ruth with the news that Mrs. Reynolds fired her on her first day. But surely Ruth would see that putting Addie in the Print Shop was the bigger mistake.

Mr. Reed entered the shop alone, his lips set, his thumb hooked in the vest pocket where he tucked his watch. He did not stop walking as he spoke. "Miss, please follow me to my office."

Addie trailed Mr. Reed into his cubbyhole of an office, and he closed the door. She could see only haze through the slits of the venetian blinds on the windows, grimy with ink dust like everything else in the shop. Mr. Reed cleared a pile of paper from the chair in front of the desk and nodded at Addie. She pulled the smock tight around her skirt and sat. Mr. Reed settled into his rolling desk chair, leaned back, propped his arms on the rests, and studied her.

"Miss, why do you want to work at Hudson's?"

Addie looked away, folded her hands. "This is my first job. My sister works here."

"Why do you want to work here?"

"I want to be a bookkeeper. I didn't expect to work in a print shop."

"So you are interested in working? To have employment?"

She met his eyes. "Yes, of course."

"Then please take my advice. Act like you want to be here. Follow the rules. Learn how we do things and appreciate having this position."

Addie sat up straighter. "Mrs. Reynolds is not firing me?"

Mr. Reed leaned forward and clasped his hands on the desk. "Mrs. Reynolds does not fire the staff in the Print Shop; I do. If you take my advice, you can make your way from here. However, if you decide otherwise …"

Addie stuck out her chin. "I have been here only a few hours. It's not fair to expect me to know every rule."

"I have given you the benefit of the doubt because it is your first day. What I am concerned with is not simple confusion. If you want to stay in my employ, you will need the proper attitude."

A familiar heat crawled up her neck, the feeling that had come over her in the Bridal Salon, like being scolded as a little girl. She mulled over the sassy reply that would put her out of work. She looked down, pushed her hands under her thighs. Her impulse ran under the smarter part of her that took in Mr.

Reed's implication. She had never had to prove herself outside of a schoolroom. More was required of her here. Ruth was right; Hudson's was the best place to work in Detroit. She could be a salesgirl showing jewelry to rich matrons. Or a bookkeeper. If she controlled her temper.

Mr. Reed waited for her answer.

"Mr. Reed, I will work hard and follow the rules."

"Good. After lunch, take your place at the counter, and we shall see."

Addie stepped outside the office door into the direct gaze of the six men at the nearest printing press. Faces of concern, not the sniggers she imagined they had been making while she was in the office. Joe came along the pathway, fell into step with her walking toward the front, muttered, "You fired?"

"No, just corrected."

Joe turned and gave a thumbs up to the men, who nodded and resumed their work. Seeing Addie's puzzled look, he said, "It's one for all and all for one here."

"What do you mean?"

"Don't want to see anyone get canned. The fellas worry when Mr. Reed calls someone into the office."

"But they don't even know me."

"Don't matter. We stick together."

At her lunch break, Addie left her smock on the hook and took the elevator down to the street. Outside, she bought two donuts from a street vendor. She ate them on the shady lawn outside the library on the other side of Farmer Street. What Joe had said about the men in the shop sticking together made Addie remember times in school when a teacher's reprimanding of one student rippled tension over the class. The men had worried for her despite her own rudeness. She had turned her nose up at them and if what Joe said was true, they had not held it against her. And Mr. Reed was teaching her a lesson beyond the order book. She imagined the men of "The Firm" on the poster in Personnel scowling at their new employee. She would show Mr. Reed she could do better.

When she returned to the shop, she donned her smock and sidled into the space between the two counters. She had been facing the door to the shop, keeping her back to the men. Addie moved the order book from the front to the rear counter and swiveled around on the stool to view the shop. The men were getting the machines running for the afternoon production. Joe was back there joking with them as he collected the trash. All afternoon, she took the calls and made order entries facing the machines. At the end of the day, she nodded to the men along her path to the lockers, noting the names on their coveralls. They nodded in return.

At home, recounting her first day for Ruth, she left out the Bridal Salon, Mr. Reed's admonition, and Joe's words about the men. She recreated the elevator mistake and the encounter with Mrs. Reynold's into a funny story of no-harm-done. Addie gushed with Ruth over the glamor of the seventh floor. Ruth didn't need to know Addie had stumbled on her first day. From now on, she would practice the "do it right" habits her bookkeeping teacher had drilled into her. She would live up to Hudson's standard.

The next morning, Addie arrived at the shop ten minutes early. Mr. Reed, at the counter, looked up with the hint of an upturned lip and no check of his watch, which Addie took as a positive gesture. "Good morning, Miss. No need for the smock yet. You will go to the Auditorium for the new employee training. Starts at nine, twelfth floor."

"Will I be there all day?"

"Until lunch. After lunch, come back to us."

Addie heard the "us" with new ears. "Thank you, Mr. Reed. I'll just put away my hat before I go." When Addie had stowed her hat, she made her way back through the shop, passing a cluster of the men talking together. Taking a breath, she said, "Good morning." One tipped his cap to her. She kept her stride with a smile at breaking the ice.

On the twelfth floor, men and women wearing Hudson's name tags milled around tables under a "Welcome to Hudson's" banner hung over the double-doors of the auditorium. Addie spotted Susan from Personnel and made her way through the chattering crowd. Susan caught sight of her and waved. "Addie, welcome. Come get your folder."

"Susan, good morning." Addie accepted a green folder imprinted with the Hudson's logo, a product she recalled from the order book of the Print Shop. "I'm happy to see someone I know."

"You'll meet other new people today. Take a pencil for notes. Go find a seat, look at the materials inside the folder." She giggled. "Welcome to Hudson's."

Addie tucked her folder under an arm, grabbed a pencil from the table, and passed under the banner. Columns on the left and right of the auditorium flanked a center space set with rows of metal folding chairs. On a raised platform at the front, four easels stood at attention, one holding a larger version of "The Firm" poster, another the aerial photograph of the building, and two held floor plans. Walking along the right side of the room, she scanned for a seat at the end of a row, but those were taken. The rows were filling as the bustle of people outside thronged into the room. A gong rang and a woman stepped onto the dais. "Please take your seats."

Addie excused herself through a row to get one of the few empty seats in the middle. The people she stepped past were busy talking to each other, and moved their feet left or right without looking at her. She plopped into the first vacant chair. The gong rang again, and the chatter softened. Commotion to her left came as a young woman, with bright red lipstick and a neck scarf the same color, plowed through the row without apology, aiming for the seat next to Addie. She landed as parade music came over the speakers above their heads. "Gee, just in time. They told me at the last minute to come to this."

Addie could only smile in response as the music stopped and a man stepped to the microphone.

"Good morning, new employees of the J.L. Hudson Company. I am Irving W. Wilson, head of training in our Personnel Department. Find the employee manual in your folder." He stood waiting through the rustling of papers, murmurs.

Red Lips dropped her folder, papers spilling around their feet. "Oh, crap." She scooped up the lot, plucked a booklet from the mess like a lucky card from a deck. "Got it."

The manual's green-tinted cover read *Welcome to Hudson's* in script, along with a photograph of the store's tower, viewed as if the camera had looked up from the street level. On the inside cover was a list of facts about Hudson's. Addie read that more people worked for Hudson's than lived in her hometown. Sixty operators answered telephone calls—all on the first ring. And no wonder she had gotten confused by the elevators, with over fifty of them in the store.

The headline on the first page announced "The Hudson's Creed." Now Mr. Wilson's solemn voice explained, "The Hudson's Creed is your creed. It embodies the beliefs by which the enterprise is conducted, and every employee is expected to perform. I ask each of you to read it in silence."

Addie shifted her head down, flicked her eyes left and right at others concentrating. Red Lips traced along the text with her finger. Addie read, "I believe in Hudson's because... We promise the customer that every piece of merchandise is the finest that could be produced at the price. We pledge to have faith in the store, the organization, and the ideals of this great house of industry. To be inspired by its greatness to put my best active and honest effort into the institution ..."

The stillness in the room held the weight of the Creed's expectations, as if it were a prayer. Reading it, with "The Firm" smiling upon the crowd from the dais, Mr. Reed's advice to Addie about her attitude gained significance.

Mr. Wilson called the group to attention. "Ladies and gentlemen, with your adoption of the Creed, I welcome you to Hudson's." Addie heard a whispered "Amen" from Red Lips. Addie met her eyes and nodded. They were enlisted. Addie joined in the loud applause as Mr. Wilson exited the stage.

The morning continued with presentations about the store's history, regulations, paydays, and a list of customer services to memorize. At the coffee break, Red Lips bounded out of the row before Addie could introduce herself. The woman on her other side had joined a cluster in the aisle. Alone, Addie managed to get through the crowd and grab a cup of coffee from the tables along the side. She pressed against the wall to drink without bumping into anyone. A photographer roamed around snapping candid shots of the new Hudsonians. She saw him focus on Red Lips, talking with both hands amidst a group of men.

The gong called them back to their seats. Red Lips whispered, "Sorry, I had to get to the ladies' before. I'm Rose. From Advertising."

"Addie, from the Print Shop." The speaker called for order before Addie could mention her connection to Ruth.

At the end of the training, Addie stuffed floor plans, lists, forms, and a new edition of *The Hudsonian* into her folder. Before the closing of the program, a man from Maintenance appealed for volunteers to help hang the gigantic American flag on the building for the upcoming Fourth of July celebration, drawing groans and about ten men who signed up. Mr. Wilson returned to give the new employees a send-off. The parade music played for the exiting crowd.

Red Lips stood and stretched. "Addie, I wish I could have lunch with you, but I have to run back to Advertising. Can you believe it, on my second day, they switched me to a different desk? They expect me back there now to meet my boss. Don't they know people eat lunch?"

"How did that happen?"

"The grapevine says I am filling in for someone they just fired—some girl named Ruth."

CHAPTER 5

An enormous swordfish mounted on a wooden slab hung above an aquarium where tiny iridescent fish swam among fake reeds and seashells. Spotlights anchored along the ceiling highlighted the glossy lacquered skin of the preserved giant. The live fish below pursed their lips, as if talking underwater in time with the gurgling of the tank's pump. Children wiggled their fingers along the glass, tracing the swimming fish that were following each other round and round the tank.

Across the room, not able to distract herself with a magazine, Addie gazed at the swordfish. She thought it a curious choice for a doctor's waiting room, not at all soothing. Its glassy eye watched her, the threat of its spear-like snout palpable, the taut body poised to leap from the wall and wound. It saddened Addie that the majestic creature had been wrested from the ocean to hang over a room of ailing people awaiting their turns with the doctor.

Next to Addie, Ruth clenched her fingers around her handbag, her eyes closed.

Ruth's situation simmered between them. Addie had been muddling around her sister for days like the fish caught in their tank circle.

Red Lips's news about Ruth had hurried Addie out of the auditorium to dial her sister's store extension. The Hudson's operator reported the extension as not available. Addie had telephoned the apartment every hour from the Print Shop, getting no answer. Her worry wanted her to call Al, but she didn't know how to reach him. Rushing home, she found Ruth curled up in bed, refusing to talk about what happened.

Addie brought Ruth a cup of coffee the next morning, and asked again what had happened. Ruth broke down in tears, pleaded to be left alone. After that, Addie left Ruth in her darkened room. From what Addie could tell, Ruth spent Wednesday and Thursday in her nightgown. In the evenings, Addie came home to find rumpled Ruth dozing in the armchair. Addie cooked eggs that Ruth picked at. She rebuffed Addie's attempts to talk about what happened. "Stop asking me. My head hurts." She went from the table to bed before the sun set. No calls from Al; Addie figured he telephoned Ruth while Addie was at work.

At Hudson's, Addie dreaded running into someone who knew about Ruth's firing. She had seen Susan in the cafeteria line and slipped out before Susan could notice her. When she visited the sales floors with print orders, Addie kept watch for Mrs. Reynolds, hedging against being Ruth's sister weighing on her own standing.

After work on Friday, Addie got a cheese sandwich from the corner market and walked over the Belle Isle Bridge. She sat on a bench facing the river until it was almost dark. Addie observed the ambling couples and families enjoying the warm evening breeze from the water. She wanted to stroll with friends, maybe a man friend, relaxed and carefree, not sit alone fretting over Ruth's problems.

On Saturday, Al knocked on the apartment door. "Ruth has an appointment with the baby doctor this afternoon." Addie waved him in and he went to Ruth's bedroom. After some time, Ruth, clutching her robe around her middle, hair in tangles, made her way to the bathroom. Addie rose to go to her, but Ruth said, "I'm fine. Let me be."

Al slumped into the armchair. "Would you go with Ruth? I've got to work. They don't let me into the examination room, anyway. Can you go, hear what the doctor says?"

Addie had had enough of Ruth's silence. If she went, they would have to talk. "I'll go."

Ruth came from the bathroom with her wet hair swept back and pinned, her bare face flushed. She waved off Addie's help to finish dressing, but she let Addie tie a scarf over her hair. Thinner and worn-down, Ruth took Al's arm to go down the stairs and into his car. Outside the doctor's office, after he helped Ruth to the curb, Al kissed her cheek and said, "Call me after, Ruth."

Addie said, "Where are you going to be?"

Al tilted his head at Ruth. "She knows."

Addie ushered Ruth through a door with a sign that read "Office of Dr. Edmund Tullen." Inside, Ruth gave her name to the nurse and they settled in the chairs on the opposite side of the room from the swordfish. Patients came and went. The fish in the tank swam. Addie's stomach grumbled. Then Ruth murmured close to Addie's ear, "You don't have to come with me into the room."

"Isn't that why I'm here?"

A nurse called Ruth's name. She pushed herself out of the chair, shaking off Addie's hand on her arm. They followed the stiff white cap around the wall holding the swordfish. Addie had a last glance at its eye and imagined it blinked.

Numbered doors lined both sides of the hallway. At the far end, other nurses worked around each other in an alcove lined with shelves of supplies.

"In here." The nurse opened a door for Ruth and Addie to pass through. "Let's adjust your clothing for the examination." She pointed Ruth toward the raised padded table. Ruth handed her handbag and hat to Addie, then hoisted herself onto a step-stool and backed up against the padding.

The nurse unbuttoned Ruth's skirt and shook her white cap. "You must give up the girdle, Mrs. Kealy. It is not good for the baby."

Ruth had needed to tug the girdle tight to fasten it. The nurse unhooked the girdle's side clasps and a wincing Ruth shrugged it down her hips. When she stepped out of the girdle, Addie scooped it up. The nurse waved a finger at Ruth. "Next time, no girdle and a proper maternity skirt and we won't have this trouble, will we?"

After helping Ruth lie back on the table and covering her with a sheet, the nurse left with a firm closing of the door. Ruth's hands clutched and unclutched the sheet.

"Are you nervous?" Addie whispered. Something about waiting for the door to open made her feel they should hush.

"There might be something wrong."

Could something be wrong? Was that why Al asked Addie to come? "No, it will be fine."

Ruth licked her lips. "I hope so."

A firm tap and the nurse swung the door open for the doctor to enter. Addie drew in her breath. She had expected an older man, like the doctor back home who had taken care of them all their lives. She guessed Dr. Edmund Tullen was not yet forty. He was a perfect fit for the gossipy descriptions Addie had read in the magazines of tall, dark, and handsome men. He leaned his trim frame over Ruth, not a crease in his starched white coat, and covered her small hand with his long fingers. "Hello, Ruth. How have you been feeling since your last visit?"

Ruth's drawn expression relaxed as she looked up into the doctor's chiseled face. "I've had another migraine."

"Yes, we've seen the hospital report. The injection provided relief, correct? If the migraines continue, I will prescribe pills you can take at home." He spoke to the nurse about notes for the chart, then stroked Ruth's hand and looked into her eyes. "Have your husband telephone if you have another migraine. With your history, I believe you will continue to have them." He stepped back from the examining table. "Let's see how the baby is progressing."

The nurse grasped the sheet and accordion-folded back it in four swift moves to expose Ruth's belly, from the bottom edge of her brassiere to a few inches below her navel. Ruth lay rigid, her eyes on the ceiling. Dr. Tullen placed the fingers of his right hand at the lowest point of Ruth's abdomen and walked them up over the fullness of her belly, curving his fingers against her skin. He looked at the nurse. "For the chart, 15 weeks."

The nurse handed him a funnel-shaped instrument attached to tubes with earpieces like on his stethoscope. "I am going to check for the baby's heartbeat. I'll place this at several positions on your belly, Ruth, and listen."

Ruth began to cry. Addie jumped up and grabbed Ruth's hand. "Why are you scaring her?"

Dr. Tullen shook his head. "There is nothing to be afraid of. You are …?"

"Ruth's sister."

"Hold your sister's hand, Ruth. This is nothing to worry about."

Addie squeezed Ruth's hand, who swiped at her face with her other hand. "I'm sorry. I don't know what came over me."

He placed the end of the funnel on Ruth's lower belly and adjusted the earpieces. The nurse motioned for quiet with her finger to her lips. The doctor moved the instrument an inch or two, then settled in one spot, holding it there for a long moment. He rose upright and flipped off the earpieces. "Not yet, Ruth. When I see you next time, I bet I will hear it."

Ruth cried again. Addie grabbed the end of the sheet to dry Ruth's tears, but Ruth brushed her back. Dr. Tullen put his hands in the pockets of his coat. "Now, now, Ruth, everything is going well. The nurse will talk with you about vitamins, and we will see you again next month." With that he swept out of the room.

The nurse sat Ruth up, handed over a bottle of the vitamins, and scheduled her next appointment. After the nurse left them, Addie helped Ruth off the examining table. "You like this doctor?"

"He trained at the University of Michigan."

"To make women cry?"

"Stop. Please." Ruth adjusted her skirt and blouse, pulled out her compact and ran the pad over her nose. Addie tucked the folded girdle into Ruth's handbag and held it out to her. She followed Ruth through the hallway, thinking about the doctor's hands on Ruth's belly. Fifteen weeks. What did that mean for when the baby would be born?

As they passed through the waiting room, Addie avoided eye contact with the swordfish. When they were out on the street, she tapped Ruth's elbow. "Can we talk about what the doctor said?"

"Not now." Ruth pulled away and headed for the corner. She hailed a taxi and Addie scurried to catch up as one pulled to the curb. Addie put her body between Ruth and the cab. "You have been freezing me out all week."

Ruth shifted, trying to reach around Addie for the door handle. "None of this is about you."

"I say we go see Al right now. Where is he?"

"*You* want to see Al?"

"I want some answers from both of you."

Ruth pushed around Addie and yanked the cab door open. She squirmed across the seat, giving an address to the cabbie. Addie slid in and slammed the door hard, making the cabbie scowl at her. Addie kept her gaze fixed outside the open window.

It wasn't long before the driver turned into a block of storefronts—a grocer, shoemaker, a diner. In the second stories above the street were signs for dressmaking, dentistry, fortune telling. The cabbie slowed to check the street numbers and pulled over in front of a tavern. He looked in the mirror at Ruth with raised brows.

Ruth handed him some coins. "My husband owns this place."

The driver counted the money. "Ain't none of my business."

The lighted neon sign above the entrance announced the place as Dunn's. Addie hesitated on the curb. Back home, unaccompanied women did not go into taverns. "What did you mean, your husband owns this place?"

"You'll see." Ruth grabbed the brass handle and pulled open Dunn's heavy wood door.

The door closing behind them cut off the light from the street. Diffused sun through one rectangular window high on the wall next to the door moved shadows along the ceiling. The room was narrow and deep, a long bar to their right. Eight stools sat in front of the polished oak counter, ornate carvings of acorns and leaves dressing its edge. The theme of intertwined branches and leaves continued across the breakfront built into the wall behind the bar. Glasses and bottles of various shapes and sizes lined shelves, the colors of their contents reflected in the mirror backing.

A ginger-haired man standing behind the bar toweling a glass grinned at them. "Ruth, good to see you. I didn't know you were coming in tonight."

"Hello, Tom. This is my sister, Addie. Addie, this is Al's cousin, Tom. Where is Al?"

Tom came around the bar with a hand extended to Addie. He thought to wipe it on the apron tied around his waist, then held it out again. "Addie, I've heard about you from Al. Nice to meet you." Scuffed work boots and dungarees showed below the long apron, contrasting with the starched collar and cuffs of the white shirt he wore.

Addie felt the strength in Tom's grip, noticed the muscled forearm under the rolled shirtsleeve. "Hello, Tom. What is it you've heard about me?"

Ruth looked sideways at Addie. Tom grinned. "That you have a way about you."

Ruth tapped Tom's arm. "Where is Al?"

Al came from a doorway at the back and hurried toward them. "Ruth, are you all right?"

"I need to talk with you."

Tom spoke up. "You can all sit in the back. Get Ruth off her feet."

Al nodded and took Ruth's arm. Tom bowed to Addie and moved aside for her to follow them. "See you later, Addie."

Addie smiled, but she was uneasy with his answer to her flip remark. What had Al told Tom? She didn't like the idea of Al talking about her.

Walking through the barroom, Addie noticed the sconces lighting the oak walls, polished to a sheen like the bar. Round tables sized to fit two chairs filled the center. Glass ashtrays stenciled with "Dunn's" in bright green sat on the tables. Addie laughed to herself at the memories the room brought to her mind.

When she was a girl, the family had gathered for holidays at her oldest sister Jane's roadhouse—the inn, Jane called it. Jane and her husband had turned an old watering hole into a respectable establishment. The expansive dining room, home cooking, and the tavern made the place popular with the locals. Addie remembered sneaking into the tavern through the passage connecting it to the dining room. She had first done it early one morning after spending the night in Jane's upstairs rooms. In the kitchen, young Addie was welcomed by the cooks and seated on a stool to eat bacon and eggs. Busy with their work, no one noticed when she wandered into the dining room and explored where the different doors led.

The barroom was cool and darker than the dining room. Music played from a jukebox. Sam, the dishwasher, had come in with a load of clean glasses and found her dancing. He asked if she would like to sit in a booth and have a Coke while he dried the glasses. Instead, Addie used the footrest of one barstool to climb onto another. He set a Coke, decorated with a cherry and a pink straw, in front of her. As she sipped, he asked, "Miss Addie, how do you like sitting at the bar like a grown-up lady?"

"I like it fine, Mr. Sam, I like it fine."

After that, when Addie visited, she went to the barroom in the mornings to have a Coke and talk with Mr. Sam. Addie didn't know what happened to him when Jane sold the roadhouse. But she remembered the contented feeling while sitting on the stool, sipping, talking as he dried the glasses, the music playing on the jukebox.

She wondered if Tom would be easy to talk to.

Ruth paused at an arched doorway draped with a green curtain. Al pulled it to one side and held it open for them. A dining room held square tables covered with starched white cloths, set with glassware and utensils. Ruth settled into a chair with a sigh. Al grabbed a pitcher of ice water from a side counter.

"Please, Addie, make yourself comfortable." He poured water into two glasses.

"Do you really own this place?"

"Tom and I own it, yeah."

"How did you manage that?"

Al laughed. "Long story, and I often wonder why we did."

Addie sat at the table with Ruth. "I like it."

Ruth blew the air from her cheeks. "*This* is what you like about Al?"

Al set the water glasses in front of them. He sat next to Ruth and took her hand. "Ruth, tell me what is upsetting you."

Ruth looked into Al's eyes. "The doctor tried to hear the baby's heartbeat today." She began crying. Addie fished a handkerchief from her bag, handed it to Ruth as she exchanged a glance with Al.

"Did the doctor find something wrong?"

Ruth wailed. "No, Al, but this baby will be here before we know it."

Al pushed the water glass toward Ruth. "Take a sip, honey. Try to stop crying."

Addie said to Al, "Ruth hasn't had supper. The nurse said she shouldn't skip meals."

Al looked at her. "Go tell Tom we need dinner from Ma."

Addie didn't know what he meant, but she got up and went to the front. Tom was dumping ice into a bin behind the bar. The rows of bottles shimmered under the lights in the ceiling. Tom turned from the ice bin and saw her, waved her around the bar. "Want to give me a hand?"

Addie walked the length of the bar, running her hand along the carvings. She came around to stand near Tom. Between their feet were three beer cases stacked up. He lifted the top lid and grabbed two bottles in each hand. "Into the ice." Addie grabbed a bottle in each hand, following his motion to push the bottles into the freezing mix of ice and water in the bin. Working next to Tom felt easy, like sipping Coke on a stool.

"Al sent me to tell you we need dinner for Ruth from Ma. Who is Ma?"

Tom nodded, wiped his hands on a towel, and picked up a pad laying near the cash register. "Ma runs the diner on the block. We sell meals in the evening; she's the cook." He checked the pad. "This is her menu tonight."

Addie looked over the list. "Can we get the pot roast for Ruth?"

"How about for you?"

"Oh, pot roast would be wonderful for me, too."

Tom grinned. "You ladies eating supper in our fine establishment will be good for business. We try to get the gents to bring in the wives, but most come alone." He dialed the telephone and spoke with someone on the other end. Addie, hearing his easy tone in the friendly banter, took in the curve of his back above the apron tied at his hips.

"Her girl will bring the food to the alley door. Doesn't take them long."

"How did you get this place?"

"We met old man Dunn one drunken night."

"Did you live around here?"

"I lived with Al and my aunt in Windsor after my mother died. Our fathers were American, and both married Canadian women. We raised hell on this side of the river."

He told her how he and Al rode their bikes across the bridge to have fun in the lively Detroit neighborhoods, betting that the girls they fooled around with couldn't track them down. Most taverns served whoever was tall enough to plunk down the money. Wobbling home on their bikes, they puked up the pierogies and beer, the fast-moving river making their head-spins worse.

"One night, Al crashed his bike into the door of this place. Old man Dunn came out to see Al lose his stomach on the stoop."

Dunn walked them into the back room and made them sit with black coffee until they sobered up. "Dunn told us stories of his young drinking days, said we were welcome back anytime.

After that, we would end up most nights at Dunn's. This place suckered both of us."

The old man soon had them washing glasses and running trays to the tables. He had no children, no brothers or cousins to help run the place. The two boys quenched his need for someone to appreciate what he'd made of the business. He taught them his inventory, tutored them behind the bar. Tom manned it nights when Dunn tired and took a table with the old guys.

Tom chuckled. "Dunn would eyeball how much I swigged on the sly and throw me a few bucks at the end of the night, saying I brought in more than I spilled."

Dunn had a wife in an apartment somewhere in the neighborhood, but she had never come to the place until the day he dropped dead in the back room, toppling cases of empties. The smell overwhelmed her when the cops showed her the body lying in the beer dribbles. They said she screamed curses at her dead husband; she hated the place, and she was stuck with it. She was inside crying the next morning when Al and Tom arrived. She'd heard about them from the old man and let them take over the wake. Neighborhood men paid their respects over drinks and made donations to the widow, who kept vigil in the back room with a few women. After Dunn's funeral, she shuttered the bar.

"A month later, the grocer on the corner, one of Dunn's regulars, called me saying the widow wanted to see us. We figured she thought we stole money. But, turned out, Mrs. Dunn needed an income and offered us a deal." Al and Tom would run the bar and pay her rent, plus Dunn's share as a partner.

"I had never gotten myself situated, worked here and there, nothing steady. Al was working his way in the advertising agency; he wasn't giving that up. I jumped at taking over Dunn's. I talked Al into the deal."

The bar's cash flow peaked and fell with the rhythm of the neighborhood, and they rode the waves. They paid off the widow so she could move to Cleveland. Repairs to the rickety building popped up with the regularity of the rats. Al handled inventory, kept the books, ran things a shade higher as a legit operation than Dunn had. Al came in on busy evenings to help Tom.

Tom talked with his whole body, the pleasures and challenges of the place clear in his grins and grimaces. Addie recognized the spell of a tavern, like in Jane's roadhouse. "I can tell you love this place," she said.

Tom smiled into her eyes. "Evenings, when the bar is full of men enjoying their drink, and I am the barkeep ruling over the crowd, it's great." He threw up his hands. "But I am not that happy in the wee hours when we're cleaning up the smelly mess."

Addie laughed with him. A buzzer sounded. Tom pointed toward the back. "Dinner's here."

Addie ambled back to the dining room to find Ruth holding a cloth on her forehead, her feet propped on a chair. Al came in carrying a serving tray loaded with plates. He placed one before Ruth and she inhaled the aroma from the steamy pot roast surrounded by potatoes and green beans. "It smells delicious."

Al set Addie's supper across from Ruth and pulled out her chair. She gave him a nod, let him push the chair in and hand her a large napkin to cover her skirt. When Al had set out the bread, butter, salt and pepper, he half-bowed to them. "If you ladies will excuse me, I'll go up front for a bit." Her mouth full of the tender meat, Ruth waved him away with her fork. Al pulled the curtain closed as he left.

Addie poked her fork into her meal. "Tom told me how they got this place. It reminds me of Jane's roadhouse. Remember the barroom? I used to love going there."

"You're not old enough to be in a barroom."

"Oh, Ruth, it's only reminding me of that. Are they making money? Think what Uncle George made over the years."

"George did all right with a brewery. A tavern is different. I don't know if they make money. Tom probably drinks the profits."

"What do you mean?"

"Tom works the place, sure, but he drinks as much as he likes. Al says Tom doesn't think like a businessman."

"I could help Al with the books."

Ruth dropped her fork onto the plate. "You want to help Al? What has come over you tonight? You have objected to everything about me and Al. But half an hour in the bar with Tom changes your tune?"

Addie stopped eating. "If they make a go of this place, it helps you, that's all." She lowered her voice. "Okay, if I rushed to judge Al, you can't blame me."

Ruth scoffed. "Never mind that now. Al and I are running out of time to make things right. I have to become a Catholic."

"You *have* to become a Catholic?"

"I told you. Al is Catholic, his family, his friends, all Catholic." Ruth's hands shook around her coffee cup. "I didn't think it through when we eloped."

Addie shook her head. Al came into the dining room, sat down next to Ruth. She turned to him. "I want the baby to be baptized."

"Okay, the baby will be baptized."

Ruth clenched her arms across her middle. "We've been pretending we're not married, and that I'm not expecting. What are we going to tell people?"

"That we eloped, and the baby is coming."

"Loretta says that with some classes, I can be Catholic and we can get married in church."

"Whether or not you're Catholic doesn't matter to me. Taking care of you matters to me."

"*Nothing* is settled." Ruth's face flushed, and her hand flew over her mouth as she heaved. Addie jumped up with her napkin. Too late. Ruth's dinner spurted onto the tablecloth. Addie dunked the napkin into the cold water, waited. After a moment, Ruth sat back, took the wet napkin, wiped her face. Al bundled the soiled tablecloth and took it aside.

Addie commanded, "Call a taxi." He nodded and went to the bar. Tears streamed down Ruth's cheeks. Addie sat next to her and re-wet the cloth. "You're okay, Ruth. It'll be okay."

Ruth shook her head, sniffed into the napkin. Addie got Ruth's shoes onto her feet, wiped her neck and face with more cool water.

When Al came back, Ruth let him encircle her within his arm to steady her walk. Addie followed them to the front. She thought back to her first night, Al rushing into the hospital emergency room, his clothes reeking with the odor of spilled beer and cigarette smoke. That was the smell of Dunn's. Men were now arrayed among the tables, having their drink, giving her and Ruth brazen stares. She wanted to shout at them to mind their own business.

Tom scrambled from behind the bar and yanked the street door open as the cab pulled in front. "Take care, Ruth," he said. Addie passed Tom with a half-smile.

Al settled Ruth in the cab. "Call if you need me."

Addie kept one of the wet napkins in hand, anxious to get home without Ruth being sick again. Ruth kept her eyes closed.

Long after she had helped Ruth into her bed, the sultry night air in the alcove and her distress about Ruth kept Addie restless on her cot. *She pushes me away.* Like the two sides in their old bedroom.

But Addie also thought about Tom, and the pleasant memories that Dunn's had recalled. If she offered to help Al with the bookkeeping, she'd have a reason to go back.

CHAPTER 6

Addie's second week at Hudson's began with Mr. Reed calling her into his office and handing over a binder thick with ledger pages. "The special paper stocks are drawn down more than they should be."

She set the weighty binder on the edge of Mr. Reed's desk, opened it to the first page. Department names and a list of fifty-some types of paper for flyers, banners, placards, labels, pamphlets—everything Hudson's printed in the shop. Month-by-month quantities and quarterly totals were recorded in Mr. Reed's tiny, precise script.

As she studied it, he said, "We order the amount of paper stock they plan to use. See the two columns at the right? The actual use is entered at the end of the month and totaled quarterly."

Addie saw him glance at her to make sure that she knew what quarterly meant. She scanned the columns. "It looks like the first quarter numbers lined up. We need to check the orders since then."

Mr. Reed nodded. "That's it, Miss." He pointed at Joe, clipboard in hand, perched on the ladder rolling along the metal shelving spanning the length of one shop wall. "Get the counts, make a ledger sheet with the comparison I can take upstairs."

Addie carried the binder to the counter. She paged back to April in the order book. Finding all the orders for one department meant looking line-by-line. She caught Joe's eye and motioned him over. He climbed down from the ladder, tossed the clipboard onto the counter.

"The paper counts are done," he said.

"Which departments use the special stocks most often? We'll start with those."

Addie printed the codes they were looking for on a fresh ledger sheet. The two of them spent the morning plowing through the April orders, Addie writing the ledger entries as Joe called out the quantities. They scoured the order book to find any other special paper orders. Satisfied they had accounted for all, Addie cross-checked the delivered orders against the binder numbers. After lunch, they did the same with May's orders.

When Addie lugged the binder and her completed ledger sheet to Mr. Reed's office, he waved her inside.

She handed him the ledger sheet. "In April and May, the Bridal Registry over-used the special paper. Their orders are triple what they planned."

"Misprints?" He ran his finger down the list.

"Reprints. They printed the registry booklet three times. On the second run, they added a page. Then they printed a third order for a promotion."

"Not mistakes in the shop?"

"We have the samples accepted as ordered." She stood waiting while he peered at the figures.

Mr. Reed looked up from the sheet. "You stand by this count?"

Addie swallowed. "Yes, Mr. Reed, I am sure it's correct."

"Very good, Miss, I'll take it upstairs."

Addie turned on her heel, nodded to Joe watching from the ladder. He clambered down and met her at the front counter.

"Mr. Reed's not blaming us?"

"No, he saw the figures. Registry reprinted."

Joe shrugged. "He's the one approving orders. If Registry was over their supplies, he would have known when he approved the runs."

"He asked me if I stand by the report and I said yes."

"Yeah, but he approved the orders."

"What are you saying?"

"He already knew it was Registry, but for upstairs, he made us prove it wasn't our mistakes."

On Friday, Mr. Reed called Addie and Joe into his office. "A shipment of the special paper is on the way. The cost goes against the Bridal Registry budget, not the shop." Mr. Reed nodded at them. "Finance agreed with our numbers. Good work."

Addie and Joe left the office grinning. Joe gave a thumbs up sign to the men.

Taking her time walking home from the streetcar stop, Addie wished she could tell Ruth about feeling like she had jumped a hurdle at work. But Ruth was not part of the Hudson's world anymore. Ruth had been shuffling into the kitchen to get a cup of coffee before Addie left each day, mumbling a good morning, then going back to her room. Addie would lock the door and pace her walk to meet the trolley arriving at the stop, getting off at Hudson's to be in the Print Shop at least five minutes early. The store was a refuge where her frustration with Ruth stayed tucked away. On the way home, her stomach knotted. They had had no proper dinners. Ruth said she could only eat scrambled eggs or toast. Addie stocked the kitchen with eggs, bread, and milk. Ruth ate before Addie got home and Addie dreaded another night of eating eggs alone, and the silence between them.

When Addie entered the apartment that Friday night, Ruth was sitting in the armchair basking in the waning sunlight. She wore a faded housedress, dug her bare feet into the carpet. "Hi," she said. "Are you hungry?"

Addie kicked off her shoes. "I don't want any eggs."

"Mrs. Mason brought over a casserole."

"Can we shop for groceries tomorrow?"

"I have an appointment with the priest tomorrow morning."

"Why tell me?"

"Would you go with me? In case I feel sick. I haven't been out."

"That's why you're talking to me? You haven't bothered with me all week. Isn't Al going with you?"

"I'm doing this on my own."

"Except you want me to go. Does Al agree with you about this?"

"I don't need his permission."

"Ruth, I don't understand what you are doing."

"Will you just go with me?"

It pained Addie to think Ruth pinned her hope for a wedding on the priest waving his hands, or whatever priests did. But she knew Ruth shouldn't go out alone. Addie shrugged. "I guess so." Ruth nodded and laid her head back on the chair.

In the kitchen, Addie turned on the radio, pushed the volume up. She warmed the oven and slid the casserole pan inside.

Addie washed the breakfast dishes still in the sink while she waited for the food to warm. Ruth came behind her and put her finger on the radio volume knob to turn it down. Addie's look made her pull back. Addie wiped her hands on a towel, then shoved them into the hot mitts and opened the oven door, forcing Ruth to step back. Ruth spooned food onto a plate and took it to the living room while Addie ate in the kitchen, listening to the news program. When Addie filled the sink with sudsy water for the dishes, she went to get Ruth's plate. Ruth had gone to bed.

After cleaning up the kitchen, Addie went outside. No neighbors in the yard, and after a few minutes, Addie knew why. The relentless mosquitoes nipped at her ankles, arms, and neck. Stomping upstairs, she resigned herself to the heat in her alcove.

On Saturday morning, Ruth called a taxi; her swollen ankles couldn't stand through a streetcar ride to the church. She smiled from under a wide-brimmed hat. "I feel good on this beautiful summer day."

"Then you don't need me." Addie turned away as the cab pulled up.

Ruth grabbed her arm. "Please, Addie, don't make this harder."

"I am doing you a favor, remember?" Addie said before she got into the cab.

The cab drove through neighborhoods of tidy houses, smaller than those on the Boulevard, with the same lush trees overhanging the streets, and stopped in front of a church. Ruth pushed money into the driver's palm, then pushed herself out of the back seat with a grimace. Addie climbed out of the cab into the glare of the sun bouncing off the white stone steps of St. Hyacinth Catholic Church. Her eyes watered. She pulled her sunglasses from her pocket and pushed them on.

The immense brick structure set on the corner dwarfed every house and building in the neighborhood. Used to small country churches, Addie wondered at the height of the twin bell towers. The church was, to Addie, an example of how Detroit buildings stretched themselves tall, like the biggest trees peeking above the forest.

Four sets of double wood doors spanned the width of the façade, each carved with an elaborate pattern of symbols she did not understand. Addie imagined the doors opening all at once and sucking in the light. A wooden arrow on a post planted in the lawn pointed to "Parish Rectory." Ruth wiggled a gloved hand for Addie to follow her. They turned onto a path of crushed stone, bordered by beds of lush plants and shrubs, heading to a three-story annex branching from the main building.

Embedded in a circle of flowering bushes amidst the garden trees stood a plaster statue, taller than Addie. It was of a woman dressed in blue and white robes, her hair peeking out from under a sculpted veil. Addie recognized the figure as a larger version of the Virgin Mary statues she had seen in the yards of Catholics back home. They had placed flowers around her, like in this garden. Did she grant wishes? Addie shook her head. It was a statue.

Ruth was already on the stone stoop in front of an oversized oak door. A brass plate instructed visitors to ring the bell. Ruth removed her sunglasses and straightened her full-skirted dress. Placing the glasses inside her handbag, she hooked it over her right arm and positioned the dangling bag across her middle at a covering angle. She drew in a long breath and pressed the bell. Addie tapped the toe of her shoe on the step.

"Stop, Addie."

Addie wrinkled her face at Ruth and tapped.

As Ruth reached out to ring the bell again, the door creaked opened. A petite, silver-haired woman wearing a housedress, with eyeglasses hooked on a chain dangling from her neck, looked them over, said, "Good morning."

"Good morning, I have an appointment with Father. Ruth Kealy. This is my sister."

The glasses swung sideways on the woman's chest as she pulled the door open wider. "Yes, Father is expecting you, Mrs. Kealy. Come inside."

Addie felt the temperature change from sweltering to cool as they stepped inside the entrance hall. The hum outside cut off when the door closed behind them. Polished wood paneled the walls and ceiling over a stone floor. The woman raised her hand toward a tufted bench half-way down the entrance hall. "You can wait there. Mrs. Zale is on the altar; she asked me to let her know when you arrived."

"Thank you, yes, please find Mrs. Zale." Ruth settled on the bench and the woman disappeared around a corner.

Ruth hadn't said she'd be meeting Loretta Zale at the church. Addie knew about Loretta from the letters. A year ago, she had married Leonard, Al's buddy from their war service. Ruth had become friends with Loretta since Al had been Leonard's best man. It was Loretta who got Al to bring Ruth to Mass at St. Hyacinth.

"Why is Loretta here?" Addie asked.

"She volunteers for the Altar Society." Ruth saw Addie's puzzled look. "Women of the parish clean the altar, set it up for Sunday."

Addie bit her lips to keep from making a sassy remark. She paced the hall, came to a portrait hanging in a gilt frame. A man dressed in a white robe sat with arms extended along the rests of a chair as ornate as those she had seen in photos of King George on his throne. Grey hair slicked back under a round white cap. Wide brown eyes stared from behind wire-rim glasses, and his lips pressed together as if to avoid smiling. Around his neck a gilded chain held a gold crucifix Addie judged to be a foot long, over a wide red sash around his middle. She had never seen a crucifix worn like jewelry by a man. Leaning in, she read the inscription on a brass plate at the bottom of the frame: Pope Pius XII.

Coming back to the bench and lowering herself next to Ruth, Addie faced another crucifix, about three feet from top to bottom, hanging on the wall. Its sculpted, painted body was more lifelike than on the golden necklace worn by the Pope. Addie stared at the red-rimmed eyes of Jesus, blood dribbles on his face and chest.

"Morbid, isn't it?" she whispered to Ruth.

"Be respectful."

"This gives me the creeps."

"Please, Addie, let me get through this before you tell me again how wrong I am."

Addie sat back, folded her arms, crossed one leg over the other. She wondered what Dan would say about Ruth pleading her case to a Catholic priest. Addie's foot resumed tapping on the stone floor, drawing Ruth's hand on her knee. She pushed it off as they both looked toward shoes squeaking on the tile floor.

"Loretta, hello!" Ruth jumped up to greet her friend. Addie made a face at Loretta's thick-soled leather Oxfords and white socks covering ankles more swollen than Ruth's. Her faded, checkered summer skirt reached halfway down her calves. Loretta walked with her distended middle thrust forward, one hand on her lower back, reminding Addie of science book pictures of turtles, humped and slow. Addie didn't know what number of months of pregnancy pushed out the folds of her white smock, but when Loretta hugged Ruth, the fullness of her belly filled the space between them. Letting go of Ruth, Loretta pulled her mane of black, wavy hair away from her neck.

"I should have tied my hair up for working on the altar." She let go of her hair. "This has to be Addie. C'mere, sweetie, let me hug you, too." She pulled Addie into an embrace, pushing the firmness of her pregnancy against Addie's ribs. Addie wiggled to signal enough and pulled an arm's length away from Loretta.

Loretta laughed. "Get used to it, Addie. Ruth will be huge like this soon enough!" She took Ruth's hand. "You okay?"

"Nervous. Thank you for arranging this."

"Don't worry, Ruth. Father will understand. I know he will help."

The woman who had let them in reappeared at the end of the hallway, beckoning Ruth to follow her.

"Go on, Ruth," Loretta said. "I'm going to rest here a while."

Ruth straightened her skirt, started walking down the hall. Addie came next to her, murmured, "What has she got to do with this?"

"Loretta asked the priest to meet me. Wait with her."

Addie shook her head. Ruth had asked her to come. She would not be left out in the hall. Ruth frowned and jerked her head for Addie to go back but she didn't.

The woman led them around the corner into a corridor; at an open door, she ushered Ruth and Addie into an office. Beyond a large wooden desk tall windows lined the width of the room, open to a courtyard filled with trees and flowers. Warm air flowing in mixed with the coolness of the hallway. The woman pointed at two high-back armchairs in front of the desk. Before they could sit, a man wearing the all-black version of the Pope's robes entered. Coming to Ruth's side, he extended his hand. "Good morning, I am Father Dabrowski."

Ruth shook the priest's hand. "Good morning, Father. I hope you don't mind that I brought my sister, Addie, with me."

"Not at all. Good morning." The priest wore the same rimless glasses as the Pope, but his eyes sparkled green. Addie picked up the scent of the starch in his collar, and something else, like Ivory soap.

"Good morning. Father." Addie guessed his age was close to Ruth's. She wondered what possessed a young, handsome man to wear skirts.

He swept aside the loose fabric around his legs and moved behind the desk to settle into his leather chair. The woman shuffled in again, to set a tray with a pitcher of ice water and three glasses near the edge of the desk. "Thank you, Mrs. Kowalski," the priest said.

Ruth perched on the edge of her seat, her handbag positioned in front of her middle. Addie settled next to her and eyed Father Dabrowski. He shuffled the papers in front of him. "Please help yourself to the water."

Addie jumped up and poured water into two of the glasses, handing one to Ruth. She picked up the other and held it out to the priest. "Water, Father?"

He looked up with the hint of a smile. "Thank you." When he took the glass, his fingertip brushed hers. Addie poured the third glass of water, imagined walking around the desk to run her fingers through his hair. She turned on her heel to face Ruth's glare. Addie sat, took a sip of water, composed her face.

"Now, Mrs. Kealy, as I understand things from Mrs. Zale, you are in a delicate situation."

"Yes, Father."

"Where is your husband today?"

"He works a second job on Saturdays."

"He is a baptized Catholic, is that right?"

"Yes. Not in this parish, but yes."

"And you have given serious thought to converting to Catholicism?"

"I am serious, Father, and there's not much time."

"Conversion involves study and many discussions. The process takes at least a year for someone with no ... encumbrances." He pushed his chair back from the desk and laid his arms along the chair's rests. "Tell me, what has brought you here, Mrs. Kealy?"

It may have been the softer tone, or the kindness in his eyes, that whooshed Ruth's tension away. Ruth relaxed her grip on her bag, set it on the floor, took a gulp of water, then met the priest's gaze. "I want to be married in the Church before my baby is born."

"Since you are not a Catholic, the civil ceremony is sufficient, but for your husband, the Church does not recognize a civil marriage."

"Father, he is also divorced."

Addie squirmed in her seat. *Al had a wife before?*

The priest nodded, his eyes on Ruth. "If you tell me more, I will know if I can help you."

"Before we met, Mabel—she was Al's wife—was confined in a sanitarium." Ruth's voice wavered. She gripped the icy water glass so hard that droplets ran over her fingers onto her skirt. Addie held still, let her eyes find the sky showing blue at the top of the window, biting her lips.

"Where is Mabel now?"

"We don't know."

The priest turned to Addie. Addie held still, blinking at the glare from outside creating a frame around the priest's dark hair. "I'd like to talk with Mrs. Kealy in private. Would you please wait outside?"

Ruth tapped her on the arm, nodded that Addie should leave.

"All right, I'll be in the hall." Ruth would hear the edge in her tone. Addie rose from the chair and felt the damp wrinkles of her skirt against the back of her legs. She nodded at the priest and turned away, smoothing her sweaty skirt.

Addie let the office door close behind her with a loud clack of wood-on-wood, and almost bumped into Loretta, who was standing so near the door she must have been trying to hear the conversation.

Loretta did not hide it. "I am dying to know what Father is saying," she whispered.

"He wants to speak privately with Ruth."

"Has she told him the whole story?"

Addie crossed her arms. "And what is the whole story? Hmmm? Do *you* know the whole story?"

Loretta dug her bright red nails into Addie's arm, pulling her along the hall to the bench. Addie faltered, forcing Loretta to grip harder to keep her moving. Loretta let Addie go and lowered her bulky rear until she could grasp the side of the bench and gravity plopped the front of her down. Loretta thumped the cushion with her palm. Addie straightened her damp skirt and sat.

"Your sister does not deserve sass from you," Loretta said, wagging a puffy hand in Addie's face.

She cringed at Loretta's flashy platinum engagement and wedding band embedded in her swollen flesh. Addie said, "You don't know me."

"I know you're upsetting Ruth."

"She got herself into this situation."

Loretta sat up straight and hissed into Addie's ear. "You are spoiled, just like Ruth said, and I do not see anything in you that made her believe she could count on you!"

Addie shifted away from Loretta and shook her head. "I was supposed to count on *her*! And who are you to call me spoiled?"

"That is how you are behaving. You have plenty of time to do whatever it is you think you want to do. She needs a few months from you. Is that so much to ask?"

"This is between me and Ruth. I have no choice but to help her."

"Then put your heart into it. Stop judging her."

"Is she not being judged by a priest?"

"Father will not judge her, he will advise her."

Addie huffed, folded her arms over her handbag, stared at the feet of Jesus. Loretta resettled on the seat, pushed her feet out and leaned back, her shoulder touching Addie's. Loretta twisted strands of her hair. She had removed the white smock. Addie grimaced at Loretta's maternity blouse, splattered with printed lilacs stretching over her middle. Addie was sure Loretta had not bought that at Hudson's. She had delivered print orders to Maternity. The fashionable styles offered in Hudson's were nothing like the ballooning yards of fabric Loretta wore.

Watching Loretta's deep breathing move the flowers on her blouse, Addie had a strange impulse to put her hand there to feel the baby, the way the doctor had with Ruth. Their sister Annie had been pregnant twice while Addie was growing up, and so had their stepmother. But they had never invited Addie to feel their stretching forms, to learn about the female body growing new life underneath the oversized blouses. Addie didn't recall them being this large. Did she not remember, or did they not let her see?

The sound of the door opening and Ruth thanking the priest brought them to their feet, Loretta rising with effort, Addie almost holding out a hand to her, then not. Loretta raised her brows and wagged a finger at Addie. Addie ignored her and stepped to the other side of the hall as Ruth's heels clicking on the stone floor came around the corner.

Loretta reached out to her. "Are you okay, sweetie?"

Ruth walked into Loretta's embrace. Addie did not recall as much hugging in a month at home as Loretta had done in one morning. Ruth relaxed into Loretta's hold, whispering, Loretta murmuring back. Addie tapped her foot.

As the two women separated, Addie pulled back her shoulders, stiffened to fend off Loretta's hugging her again, but Loretta faced her with both hands on her hips. "Take care of your sister."

Addie pulled on her gloves. "Nice to have met you, Mrs. Zale. Ready, Ruth?"

With a frown at the Pope, Addie strode toward the door. Without looking back, she opened it and stepped outside, letting the door click shut behind her. The aroma of the garden on the warm breeze eased her. The grass was thick and cushy looking. She slipped her heels off and enjoyed the feel of the thick turf through her stockings. She walked to the statue of the Virgin.

Mary, hands clasped in prayer, was as fixed to her pedestal as the swordfish to the wall at the doctor's office. What was she supposed to inspire? The Hudson's Creed floated through Addie's mind. There was a purpose to every action in the store. Things were counted and numbers arranged in ledgers. The dollars and cents, the merchandise, the beauty presented in every department, the pride of offering the best. Her view of her job—her attitude, as Mr. Reed said—had shifted since the employee orientation. Addie believed in the store. But this, Addie thought as she watched Ruth step out into the sun, this made no sense.

She made her way back to the gravel path, slipped her shoes on. Ruth hid her eyes behind her sunglasses. "I suppose you want to know what Father said."

"You've already told Loretta. Why tell me?"

Ruth shook her head and marched toward the street. Addie caught up to her. "Go on, tell me. What did he say?"

Ruth flagged a taxi parked down the block. "I can start my conversion, but no wedding."

"What about—"

Ruth held up a hand. "Don't. That's over and done with." She opened the cab door. "And, for your information, my conversation with Loretta? She invited you to her stork shower tomorrow, at Dunn's."

CHAPTER 7

Addie and Ruth bickered in circles during the cab ride home. Addie hurled questions about Al and Mabel; Ruth said it was none of Addie's business. Addie called Loretta a busybody; Ruth warned that if she couldn't be polite, she wouldn't be going to Loretta's stork shower. Addie said she didn't even know what a stork shower was; Ruth rolled her eyes.

Ruth had the driver stop at the market near the apartment. There, Addie grabbed a cart and pushed through the aisles, forcing Ruth to catch up. Sweat rolled down her neck as they waited in line to pay. When Ruth reached for the bagged groceries, Addie took the lighter one.

They dragged up the stairs to the apartment. Ruth threw off her hat, shut herself in the bathroom, ran the water in the tub. Addie took the fan from Ruth's bedroom into the kitchen, made half a sandwich, picked at it. Ruth, wet hair and wearing her nightgown again, came into the kitchen and pulled the fan plug from the wall. She carried it to her bedroom and closed the door.

The heat in the apartment and her frustration closed in on Addie. She ran down the stairs and took refuge in a chair under the maple trees in the side yard. She kicked off her shoes. The breeze was hot, but under the trees, the grass was cool. Addie wormed her hands up under her skirt to unhook her stockings. She couldn't afford to ruin another pair. She pushed them down to her ankles, grabbed them off, and stuffed them into her dress pocket. Addie lolled, fanning her legs with her skirt, staring up into the branches.

Mrs. Mason tramped through the gate pulling a child's wagon loaded with paper bags. She dragged it into the shady oval cast by the tree. "That sun is not giving up, is it?" She pulled a dishtowel from the wagon and mopped her face and neck.

Addie, not feeling like conversation, hoped a few polite words would do. "I am waiting it out under this tree."

"I've got a card party this evening, on the back porch. One of the gals will bring the drinks; it's my turn for the food. Nothing fancy, not in this heat." She pivoted the wagon handle to reverse away from Addie, took a few steps, then stopped. "You on your own tonight?"

Addie smirked. "I've been on my own since I got here."

"Come on, join our party." Mrs. Mason waved an arm. "You can't stay out here and get eaten by skeeters. Inside's too hot, and I'm betting you're not going roaming around by yourself. The gals will enjoy meeting you."

The calculation of her options did sound dismal, and accurate, but Addie wasn't sure of her patience for an evening with Mrs. Mason and whoever the "gals" were. "I don't play cards much."

"You'll like our game. There's plenty to eat."

Dinner. Ruth had gone to bed and the prospect of cooking for herself in the hot kitchen made Addie tired enough to skip eating at all. Mrs. Mason's kind face waited. Addie pushed out of the chair. She stepped into her shoes and reached for the wagon handle. "Lead the way, Mrs. Mason. Thank you."

"Call me Doris," she said as she led Addie along the side of the building toward the narrow yard at the back.

The back porch, a wooden platform screened all around, ran the width of the building, with four steps up to the door. Mrs. Mason motioned for Addie to pull the wagon close. "We'll take the bags and leave the wagon." She grabbed the biggest bag, mounted the steps, and held the screen door open.

Sleds hung on pegs next to snow shovels along the house wall of the porch. Mrs. Mason propped open the door with a milk crate. "People leave their boots, skates, and whatnot out here. It's perfect in summer for our games."

Two tables that looked like they came from someone's kitchen were pushed together, surrounded by six chairs. An electric fan sat on a plant stand in the corner. Mrs. Mason flicked the switch to start a breeze. "The gals will be here any minute. Help me set the table?" She pulled a flowered tablecloth, napkins, utensils, and a stack of plates from the bag. With another trip to the wagon, she retrieved baking pans covered with foil and handed them up to Addie. The last parcel in the wagon was something rolled in towels. "When it gets dark, we'll light these." Mrs. Mason unbundled two glass candelabras with triple stems for candles. She winked at Addie. "I don't save the good stuff for special occasions anymore."

Voices coming from the walkway and the scent of cigarettes announced Mrs. Mason's friends. "Hey there, you know I don't allow smoking inside. Put 'em out and come on in."

Three women in sundresses and sandals, carrying burlap bags by rope handles, called back good-natured "What a welcome" and "Nice to see you, too" greetings as they ground out cigarettes and clambered inside.

"Gals, this is Addie, new in town. She lives across the hall from me with Ruth, her sister, and she's playing with us tonight. Addie, meet Shirley, Betty, and Patsy."

Addie judged the women were somewhere around fifty. Betty was made up with bright pink cheeks and eyebrows painted on, multicolored beads around her neck. No face paint on Shirley or Patsy, only what looked like cold cream on Patsy's sunburned nose. Mrs. Mason clucked approval at their short, tight-curled hair. "Gave all of them a perm, just like mine."

Their welcomes and Addie's admiring of the curls merged with their pulling things from the burlap bags. Thermoses with lemonade and iced tea, a tin bucket leaking melting ice, and a bottle of vodka joined Mrs. Mason's glassware on the side table. Patsy declared herself the bartender. "Addie, what'll you have?"

"Make Addie's soft," said Mrs. Mason, drawing hoots from Shirley.

"You've never had a drink?"

"A sip here and there." Addie was shy to admit she had no experience with alcohol.

"Careful there, Shirl." Mrs. Mason wagged a finger. "I asked her to play cards, not drink with us. She's a kid."

"Oh, Mrs. Mason, I'm not a kid, but plain iced tea is fine for me."

"It's Doris, honey, and after a few hours with these gals, you will see how drinking turns them into sloppy card players." Laughs from the women, bustling into chairs, uncovering the serving dishes, and starting the meal.

Within minutes, Addie's nerves untied, melding into the easy rhythm of the women's flow of talk, like floating in a rowboat on a lazy river. Addie gathered that Doris Mason made regular reports of the gossip around the apartment building to her friends. They knew "that darling Ruth," and had heard about "handsome Al," but, to Addie's relief, nothing was said about the baby. Instead, the breakdown of the marriage of a woman on the top floor since the husband returned from service, the mistakes of Betty's daughter-in-law struggling with a newborn, and their judgement of the produce at the new market in the neighborhood, animated the conversation.

When they dug into the apple pie, Patsy sighed. "I waited in line for over an hour yesterday at the WMC. Won't amount to anything."

Doris clarified for Addie, "War Manpower Commission."

"That's right, nothing for *us* now. It's *man*power getting the jobs. No matter how hard we worked all the war, we're out," Shirley commiserated.

Betty wagged a finger at Shirley. "If my husband hadn't gotten back in at the plant, we'd be on the street." Shirley shrugged.

"You worked in the factories?" Addie pictured the newsreel women in headscarves and overalls, welding, riveting.

Patsy straightened up. "I was a waitress before they called for women. Learned to weld. The foreman told me I was better than any of the men he used to have. Look at my scars from before I got the hang of it." Angry red patches that ran along the inside of her left arm looked like cigarette burns. "Men started coming back, we got pink-slipped. I held on longer than most. WMC tells us to apply for the unemployment. You been there, Shirl?"

"Yep, went with the girls from the vacuum plant. White and colored, we're all out. We were making those gas masks. Don't know if they'll hire back any of us to make vacuum cleaners."

"We have all the newest vacuum cleaners at Hudson's." Four solemn faces turned to Addie. "On the tenth floor. And sewing machines, toasters, all kinds of home gadgets."

Patsy grunted and took another swig of her drink. Shirley patted Addie's arm. "Honey, some women can buy those vacuums, and some women need the jobs to make 'em."

Doris piped up. "Addie's a working woman. Hudson's is a good job."

Betty threw up her hands. "What a world now. Women should be at home, not taking jobs from men."

Patsy pushed away from the table. "I need a smoke. You, Shirl?" The two grabbed their purses and left the porch.

Doris clucked at Betty. "You see it different, but no need to rub it in. When they come back, enough of this talk. We're here for cards, so let's clear the table and get to it." Betty sighed, piled up the dessert plates.

The camaraderie returned with the start of the card game. Addie caught on to the play in two quick rounds. She offered to keep the tally of rounds, and Betty handed over the pad that held the history of points over their summer Saturdays. When the porch darkened, Doris lit the candles. Patsy kept the glasses topped up. Absorbed in play, and enough drink absorbed, the talk quieted to giggles and jibes about winners and losers as one round led to the next. Beyond the pool of candlelight, firefly sparks flitted around the dark yard.

When Patsy stretched and checked the time, the others took the cue, packed the bags with the dirty dishes and pans, and helped reload the wagon. On the walkway, Shirley and Patsy lit cigarettes, Betty and Doris linked arms. Addie pulled the wagon as they strolled to the front. The evening's cooler breeze crept up Addie's legs to balloon her skirt, damp from sitting so long. Up and down the street, candles flickered at neighboring houses where people still sat on porches taking the air. She breathed deep, tilted her head back to see the stars peeking between the treetops.

Goodbyes and hugs around, Addie promised to play with them again soon. She helped Doris ferry the contents of the wagon upstairs and into her kitchen. In the hallway between their doors, Addie thanked Doris. "Anytime, Addie. And listen, be good to your sister. She needs you." Addie nodded, thinking of Loretta's wagging finger.

The stifling heat in the dark apartment enveloped her. In the bathroom, Addie sponged cool water over her face and arms, pulled on her thinnest summer nightgown, and pinned her hair off her neck. She tied the curtain of her sleeping alcove open, hoping some breeze from the open living room windows would find her, then stretched out atop the sheets. The street quieted to a passing car, a door slammed. Addie closed her eyes, remembering summer nights at her uncle's farm when the muggy air sent them to cots on the porch.

She perspired through short drifts of sleep until she could not stand the clammy nightgown sticking to her, grabbed at the relief of pulling it off. She sat on her bed in panties, letting the sweat on her chest and back evaporate, then followed the ray of streetlight crossing the floor to the bathroom. She splashed cool water across her face, arms, breasts, letting it drip down her body, and cupped her hands to gulp from the tap. In the mirror, she saw Ruth's hot water bottle hanging in the tub and took it to the kitchen. Opening the refrigerator, Addie leaned into the coolness and pulled out an ice tray from the tiny freezer compartment. She wedged the door open with one knee, banged the ice tray into the sink and ran a trickle of water over it to release cubes. After a little melting, the cubes slid through the neck of the water bottle. Addie added some cold water, turned the stopper closed, and held the dripping rubber blob to her chest.

The glare of the overhead light bursting on startled her.

"What on earth are you doing?" Ruth, eyes wide, gripped the doorframe.

Addie shifted away from the puddle on the floor, let the refrigerator door click shut. She squeezed her arms over the rubber bottle covering her breasts. "Cooling off."

Ruth shook her head, threw a dishtowel at Addie. "You're naked, in my kitchen, making a racket in the middle of the night."

Addie swirled the dishtowel through the puddle with her foot. "I'm baking-hot. You took the fan."

Ruth flicked off the light. "Go to bed." Ruth made her way to the bedroom.

Addie kept the bottle against her chest and went to grab the pillow from her bed. She marched into Ruth's bedroom.

"Oh, no, you don't." Ruth, on the edge of her bed, shook her head. "This is my bed."

Addie climbed in on the other side, pushed her pillow under her head, and clutched the ice bottle to her middle. "Make me leave."

Ruth sighed, buried her face in her hands. She fell sideways onto her pillow, her face turned away. Her shoulders heaved with sobbing. "I can't make anybody do anything."

Addie shifted closer to Ruth, the cold rubber bottle pressing against Ruth's back. Ruth shrugged her off, pulled her legs under her nightgown, curled into herself. Addie flipped onto her back, clutched the cold bag to her front. She closed her eyes, a memory tugging at her of nights in their old room at home, Ruth's head buried under her pillow.

An old tune began playing in her head, then hummed through her closed lips. Addie sang in a low voice. "*Last night the night-in-gale woke me, last night when all was still.*" She heard Ruth sniff up tears. "*I opened my window so gently, I looked on the dreaming dew …*"

As Addie hummed the melody of the next line, Ruth rasped the lyric. "*And, oh, the bird my darling was singing, singing of you, of you.*" Addie joined Ruth in singing. "*I think of you in the daytime, I dream of you by night, I wake and would you were here, love, and tears are blinding my sight.*"

"That was Jane's favorite song," Ruth whispered, sniffing.

"Was it? I remember singing it at bedtime."

"Almost every night, after Mama left."

"It's a sad song."

"We were sad."

"I don't remember."

"You cried every night." Ruth shifted onto her back, her arm brushing Addie's.

"I've heard the stories my whole life, but I don't remember."

"We sang to calm you down."

"Did it work?"

"For a few hours, most nights."

"Maybe that's why I remember the singing."

"As far as anyone here knows, she died," Ruth said.

"What?"

"I tell people my mother died when I was young."

"I never had to talk about it. At home, people knew."

"Here, no one needs to know. She died."

Addie took that in. Their mother could be dead, for all they knew. "This is the first time we have talked about her."

"We aren't talking about her." Ruth sat up, flipped her pillow to the cool side, laid down with her back to Addie. This was one of those moments when Ruth would shut her out if she said the wrong thing.

"Why were you crying?"

"I don't know."

"You said you can't make anyone do anything." Addie tapped Ruth's thigh. "I've been a brat, I know, but I will help you."

"I'm scared."

"What are you scared of?"

Ruth choked on tears. "What if I'm like her? What if I'm a bad mother?"

Addie let the water bottle fall away, threw an arm over Ruth, hugged her tight. Ruth sobbed. Addie let go of her sister and crawled to the end of the bed, reached for the box of tissues on the dresser, but had to get up to grab it. She came around to Ruth's side, shoved tissues into her fist. Ruth blew her nose, held out her hand for more tissues, blew again. The light from the window caught the wet gleam on her face. Ruth rested her head in one hand. "Thank you." Then she looked up at Addie's bare midriff. "Get a nightgown, please."

Addie laughed, skipped to the alcove, fished a nightgown from a drawer. When she came back, Ruth patted the spot next to her on the bed. "We have to get some sleep."

Addie settled in back-to-back with Ruth and closed her eyes.

Ruth did not go to church the next morning. When Addie woke up, Ruth was in the kitchen cooking breakfast, the Sunday paper on the table with coffee and juice. With a smile, Ruth handed Addie a cup and saucer. Addie settled in a chair, sipped coffee, waited for Ruth to direct the conversation, hoping to protect their closeness from the night before. The fan's wobbly rotation on the sideboard moved the heat of another hazy day back and forth.

Ruth pointed to a page in the paper. "Hudson's has a sale on fans. We need another one." It was her first mention of the store since they had fired her.

"I can run over to that department tomorrow." Addie hesitated, then went on. "No one has said anything to me. Not many people know I am your sister, but still."

"There's nothing to talk about. Pregnant women are let go if they don't leave on their own. My mistake was thinking I could keep it a secret."

Addie recalled Patsy's upset about losing her job, Shirley's point about women needing work. Half the people in her Hudson's orientation session had been women. Certain jobs were best suited for women—the Bridal Shop came to mind. What about the Print Shop? Mr. Reed's domain was a man's world behind the front counter. Joe told Addie that a few men had started at the front counter, then trained for the printing machines. Would Mr. Reed train her for the print work if she asked? Addie presumed he would not. Still, he had given her a chance to prove that she was serious about her job. She had been on time, diligent about the order keeping, courteous in making the deliveries. The icy woman in Bridal had not complained about anything. When she made the rounds in the other departments, the salesgirls joked with her. And her report on the special paper had been taken upstairs. Addie watched

Ruth buttering toast and regretted her sister's loss. "Ruth, it doesn't seem fair."

"I miss the store." Ruth stirred her coffee. "But that's the way it is. I saved money, and now that you have a paycheck, I can pay the rent for the summer. But I worry about how Al and I will afford a baby, where we'll live. Al tells me we'll be fine. I want to believe him."

"He's supposed to take care of you." Addie took her plate to the sink. "Does the first wife get some of his money?"

"What are you talking about?"

"I read about divorce in the magazines."

"I told you—Mabel is over and done with. Don't bring her up again." Ruth clattered her plate into the sink. "Al will pick us up for the ride to Dunn's. I want to enjoy this afternoon, for Loretta's sake."

"Okay, okay," Addie said.

Addie set up the ironing board and pressed the wrinkles from her gingham dress. Loretta's scolding from the day before ran through her mind. She slipped on her dress, went into Ruth's bedroom. Ruth rifled through her summer dresses, lamented that she had not shopped for maternity outfits before she left Hudson's. After trying on three dresses with Addie working up the zippers, Ruth settled on a pleated floral sundress that buttoned in the front.

"No girdle!" Addie joked, and Ruth giggled. Then Addie said, "Loretta doesn't like me."

"Mmm."

"Called me a spoiled brat."

"Loretta speaks her mind. Her whole family does. They are kind, really. They just say what they are thinking."

105

"Sounds rude."

"Honest."

"Then you could say she and I honestly spoke our minds to each other."

"Don't worry about it. She invited you." Ruth pulled a Hudson's shopping bag from the closet. "Layette promoted stork showers for mothers-to-be. Women loved it. I bought gifts for Loretta. Add your name to the card."

They put on their hats, collected their gloves and handbags, and made their way downstairs with the gift bundles to watch for Al's car. Doris sat under the trees, Sunday shoes off, fanning herself with her church hat.

"Good morning, Doris!" Addie called. Doris waved her hat.

"You call her Doris?" Ruth asked as Al's sedan rolled up to the curb.

Addie grinned. "Yep, we're old pals now. I'll tell you later."

She had not seen Al since the night at Dunn's. He came around from the driver's side to open their doors, smiled. "Good afternoon."

Addie liked him being careful with her. With a big smile, she said, "Thank you, Al," and scooted into the back seat.

As he drove, she focused on Al's dark hair slicked back, his profile when he turned his head in Ruth's direction as they chatted in the front. Addie tried to see him from Ruth's point of view. Ruth depended on this man. To keep the peace with Ruth, she would have to get along with Al. But still watch him.

Parked cars lined both sides of the block outside Dunn's. Al pulled the sedan near the entrance, tipped his hat to the beat cop standing across the street. "A family party in a tavern on Sunday requires that we arrange an understanding with the officer," Al murmured to Ruth. "I'll unload the gifts and we'll park in the back." From the trunk, Al handed off the bundles to a trio of young girls from Loretta's family tasked with carrying them inside. Al swung the car into the alley.

When Al, Ruth, and Addie came through the back door, the clamor of voices and clanking dishes announced the party already underway in the dining room. About thirty women and girls, dressed in Sunday clothes, milled among a cluster of tables in the center. Several of the younger women bounced babies on their hips. A banquet table spanning the long wall held the serving dishes for a buffet lunch. On the opposite wall, another table was laden with beribboned gift boxes.

Loretta waddled toward them with outstretched arms, her roundness draped in a lavender dress. Loretta's form bulged at the pale purple seams of the V-neck, threatening to pop the three buttons above the voluminous skirt. Fist-size white applique daisies sprouted on the sleeves and bodice. The ends of the fabric belt around her girth were pinned together. *Not from Hudson's*, Addie thought again. Loretta embraced Ruth, then handed her off to an older woman for another hug. She faced Addie. "Nice of you to come."

"Thank you for inviting me." Addie braced for a cutting remark, but Loretta turned away to talk with someone else. Ruth's head bobbed toward the middle of the crowd of women. Addie moved to the wall near the door, looked around for water. A teenage girl came through the doorway, pushing a cart laden with pitchers of lemonade, iced tea, and water. Addie followed her to a table at the side. "Need help with those?"

"Gosh, yes, please." Grabbing two pitchers, she jerked her chin at the table where she set them down. "Just set these so people can help theirselves. Ma's waitin' on me to bring in the food." The girl skipped away. Addie unloaded the cart. Thirsty women pressed against her to fill glasses. Addie squirmed the empty cart away from the table.

Male hands grabbed an edge and dragged the cart from her grasp. Tom. "Hi, Addie. Ma needs this." He whirled it away.

A woman's hand closed around Addie's arm. "I'm Loretta's mother. Come sit." Her voice had an accent, and the dark eyes she had given to her daughter gazed at Addie from gold-framed glasses slipping down her nose. Silvery waves caught in a hair net made Addie think of her old aunt, and that Loretta's style also had been inherited. A loose, bright blue day-dress with white polka-dots and a white collar over an ample bosom covered her stout frame. At the bottom of the long skirt, her pudgy ankles and black Oxfords peeked out. She grasped Addie's hand, plodded toward a table, women moving out of her way. Addie murmured pardons for pushing through.

Pointed to a chair, Addie sat as Loretta's mother settled next to her. Greetings from the women in the other seats were a blur of names and connections to Loretta. Their conversations bubbled around Addie. A cousin said not to mind them mixing English and Polish, it was easier that way. Addie tried to catch Ruth's eye at the other end of the table, but Ruth was busy talking.

Addie leaned back and sipped from a glass of iced tea handed to her. The buzz in the room rose in pitch, competing with the clanking of plates as clusters took turns at the buffet. Addie hesitated over the steaming pans of unfamiliar foods. Loretta's mother grabbed Addie's plate from her hands, ladled portions onto it, and handed it back. Addie forked nibbles, guessing at what she was eating. Cabbage slaw, cabbage rolls filled with rice, onions and ground meat, some sort of stuffed dumplings, a creamy cucumber salad. The women around her ate with gusto.

The serving girl came around to clear the dirty plates. Tom appeared with a coffee urn on the cart, and cups were filled as women loaded clean plates with the dessert. When Addie stepped up to the table and lifted an empty plate, she felt Tom behind her before he spoke into her ear. "Take the apple." She breathed in the sweetness of an apple cake topped with a crumbly mixture of blueberries, strawberries, and cherries. He was gone before she could reply. She took a portion of the cake and sidled to the wall, looking for him. She stood there eating the cake, wondering if he would come back, or if anyone would notice if she left the party to find him.

But something about the women nesting in groups together kept Addie leaning against the wall. She looked over the huddles where the women leaned close to hear one another over the din. Squeals of joyful laughter, arms linked, a baby passed from lap to lap, the littlest girls chasing each other and tripping over handbags. Ruth sat in one circle, her neckline open, fanning herself with her hat, the lines in her face relaxed. Addie had sensed a similar feeling among women in the Hudson's lunchroom, taking over corners and niches, chairs pulled close, creating an island for their whispers. She felt it among Doris and her friends bantering over the card game, worries abandoned for a short time, a feeling like running out of school on the last day.

Addie's reverie snapped when shouts of "No men!" made a laughing Tom back out of the doorway. The green curtain was pulled closed. A trio of Loretta's cousins walked her to the center chair and held a pillow in place on it for her backside.

Loretta's mother took a chair to one side of her daughter. A cousin selected a package from the mound on the table and Loretta tore the paper open.

The little girls crawled on the floor at Loretta's feet to grab the wrappings and ribbons as she peeled them off boxes. Loretta held up tiny gowns, sweaters, booties, blankets, and bonnets to choruses of approving oohs and aahs. Addie watched Ruth's reactions, wondering if the fears of the night before bothered her now, but Ruth continued her rhythmic fanning, cooing with the others.

The serving girl crept along the wall where Addie stood, scanning for dirty glasses and coffee cups, and maneuvered around the women to gather discards on the cart. Addie held the curtain for her to pass the loaded cart through and ducked into the hall after her. She drew in a deep breath of the cooler air. Seeing the back door propped open, she stepped through to the alley. The girl stopped there with the cart. An older woman, wearing a flowered cotton housedress, a full apron tied over it, leaned against Al's car, having a smoke.

"Had enough?" The woman ground out the butt with her toe, feet in a pair of men's black leather slippers, her stockings rolled to her ankles. Bulgy varicose veins tracked up and down muscled legs; her saggy bosom lapped over a thick middle. Large hands, the skin reddened and rough, looked as though they had plunged into plenty of hot dishwater, steaming laundry tubs, and cleaning buckets. Short silver-gray hair combed straight back and held flat with what smelled like men's hair cream. Wire-frame glasses sat on a face pinched with wrinkles around her eyes and mouth. "Addie, is it? Tom tells me you're the bookkeeper."

"Are you Ma, from the diner?"

"Yeah, that's my place. I need a bookkeeper."

Addie hesitated. "I'm not …"

Ma started walking. "Come to my place for a minute."

Addie looked at the serving girl, who shrugged. Addie caught up to Ma at the door of the diner and followed her into a storage room, shelves crammed with flour sacks and boxes. Two huge refrigerators hummed on one wall.

Ma led her through into a kitchen where stainless-steel tables sat between a wall of ovens and a sink as large as a horse trough. In the front room, the cooking grill lined most of one wall, and a counter with stools spanned the length. Tables and chairs were arranged near windows dressed in red gingham curtains. The beat-up linoleum floor was scarred by years of foot traffic and chairs scraping across it, but the place was clean, smelled of lemon and bleach.

Ma rummaged under the counter, pulled out a ledger book, and thumped it in front of Addie. "I shut down in wartime. Now, it's so busy I don't have time to keep books. We're doing pie orders for grocery stores, baking on Sunday, too. Evenings, I pick up the dinners for Dunn's." She eyed Addie. "If Al has you doing their books, I figure I'll try you out."

Addie furrowed her brow. Doing books for Dunn's? "I work at Hudson's."

"A little rich for me, but folks like it."

"But I'm not a bookkeeper at Hudson's."

"So?"

Addie wiped her sweaty forehead. "Could we sit down?"

Ma waved her arm at the tables. "Sit, look over the ledger."

Addie pulled out a nearby chair and sat. The ledger landed in front of her. Ma clucked, "You look like you can use some lemonade." The slippers flopped back to the kitchen.

Opening the ledger, Addie scanned the columns and a few pages, messy with erasures and cross-outs, gaps in the dates. Receipts and bills were stuck together at the back. She looked around for a pencil. Then she stopped. Was she doing this?

Ma reappeared with a tall glass of lemonade and a bottle of beer. "Which do you want?" She laughed at Addie's expression. "I'm having the beer. Here." Addie took the glass of lemonade.

"I've looked at your ledger."

Ma swigged beer and smacked her lips. "What's your price?"

Addie blinked, took a sip of lemonade. She tested the number that came into her head. "Five dollars a week."

"Four to start; see how this works out. And pies."

"Agreed."

"Come in on Saturday before we open. Coffee's always on."

"Okay." Addie sat back. Her eyes roamed the framed photographs hung on the wall. In the largest frame, a smiling young woman wearing a two-piece bathing suit perched on the hood of a shiny sedan. Arms propped behind her, chest thrust forward, slender legs stretched over the grille, high heels poised on the fender. Around her, a crowd of men with eager faces held sketch pads and pencils. The headline atop the photo read *Miss Front End—Artists and Model Make a Dream Come True.*

"What is that about?" Addie pointed at the photo.

"Oh, Miss Front End? Some advertising guys cooked up the idea of having a chesty girl model for the car designers. Got them to draw her as a radiator ornament. Made a big splash with that."

"Why do you have it?"

"It was hanging in Dunn's. Al took it down, asked me if I wanted it. Look." She pointed. "Al's in the back, and the girl—that's Mabel."

CHAPTER 8

Hudson's frenzy of promotions in the run-up to the July Fourth holiday kept the Print Shop running overtime. Addie had not grasped the demanding scale of the work when Mr. Reed gave her the production schedule for the holiday. The blur of red, white, and blue posters, flyers, and postcards flying off the presses featured the hanging of the largest American flag in the world on the Woodward side of the building, propelling shoppers into the store for summer bargains.

The men leaned into the longer hours and smoothed their rhythm so the machines had no unexpected downtime. Addie stepped up her pace to match their momentum. Mr. Reed stationed Joe with her at the counter full-time to help log the finished orders as the men wheeled trolleys full of bundles and cartons to the front. Addie and Joe staged areas in front of the counter to hold the orders waiting for delivery or pickup. They took turns running the smaller ones around the store.

Addie had never been so tired. That week she struggled to keep her eyes open through the commute home each evening and a nibbled dinner. She was in bed before the streetlights came on. Addie dragged herself to Saturday, the start of her second job as the diner's bookkeeper.

Ruth approved Ma's hiring of Addie. "You'll get some experience."

Addie did not mention the photo of Mabel in the diner. Ruth might have seen it hanging in Dunn's. Ruth knew about Mabel. No need to rub it in. Addie wanted nothing to crack their fragile harmony since the night they had sung together.

On Saturday morning, Addie groaned at the jumble of paper Ma had strewn across two tables. Ma kept Addie's cup filled with strong coffee, but it did not keep her from yawning. She spent six hours organizing the backlog of invoices, cancelled checks, and scribbled receipts. Every time she looked up, there was Al's adoring gaze toward Mabel. Addie had seen him look that way at Ruth. What was in Al's heart?

Ma was pleased with Addie's organizing, promising to follow the instructions she gave about keeping receipts, writing out the orders. She handed Addie a pie box. "Tucked your money in there. See ya next week, girlie."

Addie slept through Sunday, and the next workdays ground together. Halfway through the morning on the next Friday, Addie rubbed her aching neck, her pencil poised over the order book, reading numbers to Joe sorting through cartons. Her pulse revved with the whirring and grinding of the presses, and she kicked one leg back and forth against the rung of the stool.

Joe missed a number, and she snapped at him. "Can you pay attention?"

"If you give it to me again, we'll be right where we're supposed to be."

She read out the order number in a louder voice.

"Addie, stop for a minute."

"What now?"

He looked at the clock. "You need a break, and after we get these orders sorted, I've got an idea for lunchtime."

She flipped her hand. "I only want to get through this day."

Joe grinned. "Let's get this done, and I promise you, you will like what I show you."

"Fine. Move on to the next order before I throw this pencil at the wall."

An hour later, Joe marked the last cartons of the morning. Half of the men grabbed their pails and hurried out for the first lunch turn. Joe wiped his hands on a rag. "Get your lunch and meet me in the hall."

Addie rolled her eyes. "This better be worth the little time we have." He waved her toward the lockers. She collected her bag, found Joe pacing in front of the elevators. He punched the "up" call button. She frowned. "Why up?"

He grinned. "You'll see."

The elevator operator greeted Joe and accepted his request for the twenty-fifth floor with a wink. When the operator pushed open the gate, Addie and Joe stepped into a cavernous space filled with huge metal tanks and grids of pipes. The machinery noise was more deafening than the Print Shop.

Addie grabbed Joe's arm. "What are we doing here?" she yelled.

He shouted, "We're going up one more." She shook her head. Around a corner, he pushed open a metal door into a stairwell. She followed, and the door closing behind them muffled the noise.

Joe started up the stairs. "Almost there."

Addie climbed behind Joe. "Wherever we're going, Mrs. Reynolds would *not* approve."

At the top, he pushed open a door, held it for Addie, watching her face. She saw the sky first, through windows as large as those in Mrs. Reynold's office. She gaped at Joe. "Are we in the tower?"

He grinned.

She skipped to see the view. Over the roof of the Farmer Street side, the Detroit skyline and the miles beyond were clear enough in the summer haze and smog. Far above her head, she could see the backsides of the red neon HUDSON'S lights, glowing the name from the four faces of the tower.

Joe came next to her. "C'mon. We've got a nice setup on the other side."

Addie trailed him through a maze of leftover window displays, signs, and special exhibitions from the war years. Between the piles, a path led to the far corner, where about fifty people sat around old cafeteria tables. Men from the Print Shop waved to her and Joe. Colored ladies from the Laundry sat together. She recognized workers from Maintenance and Equipment, who repaired the machines in the Print Shop. A cluster of cleaners, at another table. Against the wall, a table held coffee urns and plates of cookies and, next to that, a Coke machine.

"How … how did that Coke machine get here? How did any of this get here?"

"Dragged it up here when the new ones went into the cafeteria. The Maintenance guys keep it filled." He pulled two chairs to an empty table.

Addie sat, looked around, watched Joe take a huge bite of his sandwich. "How long has this been here?"

"Coupla years. Don't worry, no one comes up here except Maintenance. And us."

"Why up here?"

"These folks bring lunch, can't afford the cafeteria day to day. They don't wear the nice clothes like the salespeople. Don't feel that easy in the cafeteria. Here, it's just us."

Joe had a point about the cafeteria. With Ruth gone, Addie had felt awkward trying to find a seat where she could join a table without intruding and meet others to talk with. She had a few lunches with Helen and the salesgirls from the first floor. They were polite and chatty, but their talk focused on how to get the handsome male customers to ask them for a date. Addie appreciated Helen's kindness, but she didn't fit in with that crowd.

"Why did you bring me here?"

Joe shrugged. "Figured you would like the view. And you're in the Print Shop, too." He held his sandwich still. "Are you mad? You won't tell Mr. Reed?"

Addie smiled. "It's wonderful. I would never tell."

"Told the guys we could trust you." Joe pulled another man-sized bite off his sandwich.

Addie chewed her own sandwich. So they had talked about her. Joe had vouched for her. She caught the eye of one of the Laundry ladies, who waved an arm toward the cookies. "Help yourself, there's coffee, too." Addie left her lunch on the table and went to choose a cookie. She held up an oatmeal raisin the size of her palm, calling back, "Thanks a lot."

Joe balled his sandwich paper and aimed it at a trash barrel. "When we're not so busy, the card games up here are a hoot." Addie thought of Patsy and Shirley, their regrets about losing their jobs. They may have played in the factory lunchroom, too.

The hum of talk around the tower lunchroom sounded like different music played at each table. When she had walked in with Joe, faces had turned their way in welcome. Besides Joe, there were girls and boys her age from other departments. She might get to know the girls, have someone to see a movie with, might even get fixed up with a date.

Addie wasn't practiced at making friends. In her small town, she had grown up with the kids her age from kindergarten, knew their families, never had to explain herself to anyone. Everyone knew her family story. People didn't outright hold her mother's shame against her, but it hovered like a shadow. Here, Addie could cast that away. She had come to the city because she wanted to start fresh. Who would she be?

The anticipation she had felt on the train swelled within her. She had a respectable job in the store, and was doing book-keeping, too. Addie traveled on the streetcars and sidewalks of downtown among thousands of strangers. Before Hudson's, she had never sat in the same room with colored folks. She was learning about commerce, as Mr. Reed called it. She was making a place for herself. All of this felt ordinary. *Detroit has already changed me.*

She fished coins from her purse and went to the Coke machine for two bottles. She extended one to Joe. "Thanks for bringing me here."

Joe tapped his bottle against hers and took a swig. "Drink up. Time to get back."

Mr. Reed stayed up front with them for the afternoon. The counter phone rang with call after call from departments panicking about their orders. Addie's fingers cramped from holding the receiver. As the minutes ticked toward closing, the pile of boxes was handed off to the parade of staff coming to fetch them.

Advertising called about a last-minute print job for a Saturday promotion. Addie handed the phone over to Mr. Reed for approval. She listened to his diplomatic negotiation for time since it was so late in the day. Hanging up, he made a note in the order book. "Miss, go down to nineteen and get the copy for their run."

Addie had avoided Advertising since Ruth had been fired. She almost asked if Joe could go, but Mr. Reed called for Joe to help a man picking up large cartons.

Mr. Reed prompted her. "Go. They are waiting."

Addie unpinned her name badge from her smock, left the dusty garment on the hook, and headed out. On the elevator, she rehearsed a reply if anyone asked about Ruth. Ruth worried about her reputation in the store. Several women she worked with had telephoned, but the friendships were over with the job. Addie decided she would protect Ruth's dignity with a simple "She's fine, thanks," take the order, and get out of there.

When she stepped out of the elevator on nineteen, there was Al. "Addie, how are you?" Al was holding his hat and a large envelope.

"I have to pick up copy in Advertising, and I dread going in there."

Al shrugged. "What happened with Ruth is just business. They're too busy to bring it up."

"I hope so."

"Before you go, it's good I ran into you. I talked Ruth into going away for a week, a trip up north. A buddy of mine has a little spread on Houghton Lake, summer cabins. We're driving up in the morning. She wants to go, but she's worried about leaving you on your own for a week." Al waved his hat. "If you had the time off, you could come with us."

"I have only the holiday off."

"Right. But I want to get Ruth out of town. She's too wrapped up in the Catholic stuff."

"What do you mean?"

"Haven't you noticed? She had one class with the priest and she's been reading the catechism over and over. Keeps quoting it to me."

Addie shook her head. "I don't know. These last two weeks, when I get home, it's like I am already asleep." Addie looked Al in the eye. "This is all because of you."

Al took her elbow, walked her to the corner, lowered his voice. "Look, I never asked her to convert. Heck knows, I'm not much of a Catholic. She got this in her head after we knew about the baby. There's something about the ritual, or what she thinks Len and Loretta are part of that we're not. I don't know. I've gone along, but she is going overboard."

Addie leaned against the wall. *If Al didn't ask Ruth to convert, why was she doing it?* Ruth had a bundle of Catholic books and pamphlets in her bedroom, but Addie had not paid attention to what Ruth did while Addie was at work. "I'm not taking your side against my sister—"

"Stop right there. I am on Ruth's side. And I'm telling you, this has gotten hold of her. I'm taking her away for a week. Try to clear her head."

Ruth needed a break from the heat, and Addie could sleep in her bed while she was away. "Okay."

"She's going to fret about it to you tonight."

"I'll say I'm fine. But Al, I heard Ruth tell the priest that you had a wife." She had not planned on saying that. She watched his face change. "Miss Front End? I saw the photo in the diner."

Al leaned closer to Addie. "That's over."

Addie raised her eyebrows. "Is it? You'd *better* be on Ruth's side." She checked the clock. "I have to go." She stepped away from Al, and he pushed the elevator call button. As she opened the door to Advertising, she heard the elevator bell ding, but didn't look back.

Five minutes later, Addie was on her way back to the Print Shop. Al had been right; the girl at the desk had tossed an envelope to Addie while juggling two ringing phones. In the shop, Mr. Reed took the envelope and hurried to a man waiting at a machine in the back. She slid onto her stool.

Joe pushed the order book over to her. "All yours."

"Where are you going?"

"If we're gonna get the last jobs out, I have to be the runner in back." He trotted away.

The din of machinery maintained a steady rumble that reverberated through the counter to tingle her pencil hand. Fifteen minutes after her regular quitting time, Mr. Reed came to the counter. "Go home, Miss. Joe will bundle the last runs in the next hour. We will see you on Monday morning."

Addie smiled, shifted off the stool. "Early on Monday?"

Mr. Reed wiped his brow. "Early on Monday. With any luck, we'll close the rush by the end of the day." He nodded to her. "You kept up well this week, Miss." With a wave, he went to the machines.

Addie whispered, "Thank you, Mr. Reed."

Pushing through the door to the street, Addie lifted her face to the still bright sun. She longed to kick off her shoes at home, dreaded the tedium of the streetcar ride to get there. Addie leaned against the building for a minute to gather her energy, then walked around the corner. She stayed close to the curb on the sidewalk, keeping her eye on the line waiting for the streetcar. A car horn beeped next to her. She turned. It was Al in his sedan.

"Get in, I'll drive you home." He leaned across the front seat to open the door, and she jumped inside. Looking out his window, Al found a gap in the traffic and merged into the flow.

Addie fanned herself with her hand. "This is a lifesaver."

"Last minute business kept me around here. I thought I might catch you waiting for the streetcar."

Addie took off her hat, stretched out her legs. She glanced at Al's profile. He had confided his concern about Ruth, and Addie wanted to believe him about Mabel. She guessed he would go inside with her to talk with Ruth. She said nothing while he drove.

Al pulled in front and got out of the car. "I'll go up with you."

Addie slipped off her shoes on the stairs, stepping gingerly to protect her stockings. When she opened the apartment door, Ruth sat on the davenport, feet bare, wearing a sleeveless summer shift. Her hair was rolled and pinned. Seeing Al, Ruth covered her face with her hands. "Oh, Al, I look terrible! What are you doing here?"

With two long strides, Al took Ruth into his arms, kissed her forehead, held her close. "You are a beautiful sight." Ruth began crying into his chest.

Addie caught Al's eye and shrugged. "The crying happens a lot."

"Crying is okay, Ruth, and I want to make you laugh, too." At that, Ruth raised her face to him.

The intensity of their kiss made Addie tiptoe to the kitchen. She returned with glasses of water. Ruth settled next to Al on the davenport and tucked up her legs. "Al says you're okay with me leaving you, for us to go up north."

Addie sat down in a chair. "I'll be fine. You need the rest."

"We should get on the road early tomorrow," Al said. "The ride's about four hours." He pulled a map from his jacket pocket. "The cabins are on the far side of the lake." He laid the map on his knee, showed Ruth the route, where they could stop for a picnic lunch. As they talked, Addie's eyes fluttered closed.

When she awoke, it was almost dark. Seeing lamplight from Ruth's room, she padded through the hall. Propped up on pillows with the fan blowing, Ruth looked up from the book she was reading. "There you are. Didn't want to wake you. Are you hungry?"

"I could sleep for a week. The pace we've been running in the shop ends on Monday, thank goodness."

"I made a cold supper—chicken salad sandwiches and potato salad."

"Sounds good. What are you reading?"

Ruth waved the book. "Father gave me the catechism."

"What is that?"

"Catholic lessons. Things I must know."

"Like what?"

"The first question is, 'Who is God?'"

Addie sat on the end of the bed. Their family had gone to a Methodist church, but not every Sunday. Her stepmother played the organ for the Christmas and Easter services. She had never thought about that question.

"Ruth, why are you doing this?"

123

Ruth closed the book. "Loretta says—"

"Ruth …"

"We have nothing to fall back on." Ruth's eyes misted.

Addie looked away. She didn't want to tell Ruth that Al had said he didn't ask her to convert. He could be right about taking Ruth's mind off the catechism. She rubbed her fists into her eyes. Fatigue dragged down her thinking. She would let it go, give Al time to work on Ruth.

Ruth swung her legs off the bed. "I'll make you a plate." She went to the kitchen. Addie followed and stopped in her alcove to peel off her wrinkled dress and put on a matching pair of shorts and sleeveless blouse. When she came into the kitchen, Ruth said, "Look at you in Hudson's latest!" Addie struck a pose and Ruth laughed. She clicked on the radio. Addie ate her supper, listening to Ruth hum along.

The sun streaked its first light on the horizon when Al pulled up in his sedan. Next to her suitcase, Ruth had packed satchels with beach towels, picnic supplies, walking shoes and sandals, and a cooler of food for the road trip. Al bounded upstairs and took the suitcase and the cooler. Ruth headed down with the lightest bag. When Addie grabbed the other satchels, she saw the catechism book tucked at the side. She took the book out, carried the two bags to the car, stuffed them into the trunk.

Al had settled Ruth in the front seat. He tipped his straw hat to Addie. "Have a good week."

Addie bent to take Ruth's hand through the car window. "Enjoy the lake. Get some sun, Ruth." Al caught her eye across the roof of the car when she straightened up. Addie mouthed, "No books." Al tipped his hat again.

As she waved goodbye, a guilty twinge pulled at Addie. She brushed it aside. Al would talk Ruth out of converting, and the missing book wouldn't matter.

Addie hurried to get going to Ma's diner before the day heated. Doris had offered grateful Addie the use of her bicycle. She lugged the bike down the steps of the back porch and stowed her satchel in the basket. The breeze wafting under her skirt as she pedaled cooled her legs, but by the time she reached the diner, she had sweated through the back of her blouse. Going home would be hotter, but the bike was the fastest way to travel to the diner without spending money for a taxi. Addie parked the bike in front of the diner's window, grabbed her satchel, and breathed in the aroma of Ma's coffee as she opened the door.

Ma's two regular morning customers sat on counter stools. They were the last to leave Dunn's most nights, by Ma's account. Addie heard the squeaking of Ma's thick-soled shoes.

"Morning, Addie. Look what I got for you."

Addie gasped at seeing a Victor adding machine, like the one her bookkeeping teacher used. "Where did you get that?"

"The dentist down the block got a new model for his office girl. Sold me this one." Ma chuckled. "His wife is partial to my pies, so with those thrown in, we had a deal."

Ma set the machine on the table. Addie ran her fingers down the rows of numbers and over the Total, Sub-total, Subtract, and other keys. She pulled the lever on the right-hand side; the smooth movement of the mechanism made her smile. She punched keys to add random numbers, lifted the scroll of paper displaying the total. "This is wonderful! This will save so much time. Thank you, Ma."

"All right, then. Those fellas want pancakes, so I'll griddle you a stack, too."

Addie set her fingers on the keys, eyes on the register, and at each addition quick-pulled the lever. She flipped receipts and ran the totals. By the time Ma plated her pancakes, Addie's click-click-whirr rhythm matched her tapping foot. She pushed back her chair, grinned, stuck her tongue out at Mabel, and walked over to slide onto a stool. Ma poured her a fresh mug of coffee.

"Ma, that machine makes me happy."

"You're a silly girl, but fine by me."

Late morning, Addie stowed the adding machine on a shelf in the pantry and covered it with dishtowels to protect against the flour and dust. Ma followed her out to her bike. Addie tucked her satchel into the basket and Ma handed her a brown-paper bundle. "Supper."

"Thanks, Ma, appreciate that."

Ma folded her arms. "Tom says Ruth and Al went up north. You watch yourself on the Fourth. Folks get carried away."

"I will probably sleep through the entire day."

Ma uncrossed her arms and stuck her hands on her hips. "Another thing. Don't go to Belle Isle by yourself."

"I walk there all the time."

"Not on July Fourth. You have the bar's number?" Ma pulled the order pad from her apron pocket, scribbled, tore off the sheet and handed it to Addie. "You need anything, you call Tom."

Addie pedaled home, thinking about Tom. He knew she would be alone for the holiday. Maybe he would call her.

CHAPTER 9

A clanging noise, tinny and sharp. Addie groaned, burrowed her face in the pillow. She imagined the Print Shop dark, the machines still, the telephone quiet, the order book stowed under the counter. But the clamor pushed in.

Addie dragged herself off Ruth's bed to peer out the window. In the yard, two men hammered on a rusty oil drum. The metal gave way at the middle, and the men hoisted the halves onto a platform of bricks over a woodpile. They dragged over a tarp heaped with more wood and charcoal. Neighbors from the building were assembling tables, hauling out coolers and chairs. Addie moaned. She had promised to help Doris set up for the July Fourth cookout.

Addie slammed the window shut, bunched the curtains to close off the light. She climbed back into bed, lifted the damp fabric of her nightgown off her midriff. Hot air from the whirring fans blew across her bare legs. She pushed off the bed, unplugged one fan, and took it to the kitchen.

She flicked the radio on to hear the cheerful weatherman predicting, "Another hot one!" Perfect, she thought, for her new

Bermuda shorts outfit. The older women might cluck, but the younger crowd would admire the style and her legs.

Joe had invited Addie to go with him and his brother to the Tigers game at Briggs Stadium. Doris had given a warning like Ma's: risky for a girl alone to cross the city to Corktown and back on July Fourth. Joe's family lived on a street near the baseball field. Addie hated imposing on him to escort her to and from the game. She had asked for a rain check; he promised her a game before the season ended. She was grateful for Joe, her first friend in the city.

She wondered about Ruth as she sipped coffee. The worry worn into Ruth's face, her hard clutch of Addie's hand when the doctor listened for the baby's heartbeat. Ruth crying out her fear of being like their mother. It occurred to Addie that Ruth may have found some comfort in the catechism. She should have left the book in Ruth's satchel.

Addie was startled by a rapping on the apartment door, then Doris calling her name. She called out, "Getting dressed," and hurried to report for duty. The men had started the fire for roasting the meats. Doris sent Addie fetching things from the shed, the back porch, up and down the stairs.

The front yards of the houses along the block bustled with similar preparations for cooking and gatherings outdoors. Wood and charcoal smoke from the grills mixed with the aroma of sausages sizzling. American flags hung from porch eaves and fence posts, the fabric limp until a weak breeze unfurled the stripes. A stream of walkers and bicycles passed, going toward Belle Isle.

The men clustered with their own smokes near the grills, coolers of beer set at the side for handy grabbing. A gang of children had some kind of ball game going in the open space near the back porch. When the flurry settled and Doris took a beer, Addie claimed one of the lawn chairs set out in the shade of the maple trees.

Baby carriages were parked in a circle near the chairs. The mothers and grandmothers combined fast talking with slow bumping of a baby against a hip or shouldering one for a burp. Addie had met the neighbors in passing, but the gathering was her first opportunity to mingle with them. She didn't talk as much as listen to the banter. They had the same natural ease with each other as the sisters and aunts and cousins at Loretta's stork shower. It felt to Addie like when she first learned to read, the surprise of unlocking meaning bit by bit.

Al had said Ruth might be missing some connection she thought Loretta had with her friends and family. Addie's restless foot jiggled on the grass. She longed to feel sure of the closeness flickering between her and Ruth. Did Ruth want that, too? When Ruth had the baby, where would Addie fit into Ruth's life? She bent as if to flick a bug from her leg so the women wouldn't see tears well in her eyes.

A book landed on the grass at Addie's feet. "Oops, sorry, didn't mean to drop it." Myrtle, who lived in the apartment below Ruth and Addie, wrangled her squirming baby with one arm, and reached for the paperback. Addie grabbed it, handed it back. Myrtle shook her head. "Give that to Ruth—she's going to need Dr. Spock."

Addie turned the book up to read the title, *The Pocket Book of Baby and Child Care.*

Myrtle leaned closer. "Tell her to keep it as long as she likes." Myrtle winked. "You should read it, too. Wish I had a sister living with me." She lifted her baby off a wet spot on her skirt. Myrtle rolled her eyes. "Not again." She carried the baby at arm's length to the carriage, unpinned the diaper.

Addie looked around. Did they all know about Ruth? The chattering and baby whimpers went on. No one had shunned Ruth or been unfriendly. Ruth couldn't hide her condition much longer, anyway. Still, Addie would wait to say anything.

Addie flipped the book open, scanned the headings, started the first chapter. She appreciated Dr. Spock's plain-spoken advice. Her only experience with children was helping her stepmother with her two little ones. Addie had treated them like dolls, tying their ribbons and rocking the bassinet.

She read the first chapter and laid the book open in her lap. Addie watched the women in the yard, feeding and playing with their babies. The babies gurgling, fat cheeks dimpling in smiles. *Did my mother cuddle me?* Tears welled again, dropped onto the page. She could remember nothing of her mother. The question pulled up another agonizing one. *Did my mother love me? Did she love any of us?*

Addie blinked away the tears, kept her head down, pretending to read. When her eyes cleared, Dr. Spock's next chapter, "Equipment and Clothing," got her attention. Addie browsed the pages and realized Ruth had none of the necessary things. The pile of gifts presented to Loretta at the stork shower had seemed excessive, but her family had given her everything she needed to care for an infant. Addie closed the book. She could make a budget. The Print Shop had made the "Preparing for Baby" checklist for the Infants department. She would find time to visit the fourth floor and check prices. When Ruth and Al came home, Addie would have the checklist ready; Al would have to pay for what Ruth needed. Addie tucked the book into the pocket of her shorts.

At midday, the crowd in the yard ate heartily from the spread of potato and macaroni salads, baked beans, coleslaw, fresh garden tomatoes, pickles, sausages, grilled chicken, and hamburgers. Old laundry washtubs filled with ice kept cold jugs of lemonade and iced tea, bottles of Coke, and watermelons. Addie's worry about Ruth faded in the sociability of the neighbors who folded her into the party. There were slices of cherry and apple pies puddled in scoops of ice cream. Addie groaned with fullness but ate a slice of each.

The afternoon heat overcame the breeze. Food was stowed for later, and the grill smoldered in wait for the evening round. People spread onto blankets or went inside for naps. The kids kept cool by squirting water balloons at each other until they too flopped onto towels. Babies quieted in the carriages. The yard, and the surrounding yards, sank into a languid contentment.

Addie kicked off her sandals, settled on a blanket, and gazed up through the leaves, watching the wrens flit from branch to branch, then let her eyes close. The sound of the announcer's voice and crowd roars from radios in her yard and nearby yards tuned to the Tigers game blended and drifted over her. Addie smiled, thinking of Joe enjoying the baseball game, relieved that she was not sitting in the hot stands in a skirt and stockings. She nestled her head in her folded arms, cycling through brief naps until she heard Doris calling her name.

Addie sat up. The ball game was over, the afternoon well gone. Doris pulled Addie into a card game for the hour before they set out the dishes for the dinner round. Addie relaxed into the rhythm of the cards slapping down. For the dinner of grilled fish and pork, she joined the older folks at one of the picnic tables.

Later, on the roof watching fireworks in the dark sky over the river, the red, white, and blue explosions matched her bursting ideas about her future. Her job in the Print Shop was a good starting point, after all. But the women she had met making their own way stirred something in her. Ma had always worked for herself. Women like Patsy had proven their skills at handling factory jobs when men were short. She even admired steely Mrs. Reynolds, who had worked her way up in Hudson's. Addie had been in the city only a month. A year from now, with bookkeeping experience and references, could she have a business? Ma could introduce her to shopkeepers. Ma was gruff, but Addie felt the ice between them had broken. She would find the right moment to talk to Ma about her plan.

Addie helped with the last tasks to clean up the yard. Fireworks still crackled in the distance. Myrtle's husband doused the grill embers with water; in the early morning, he would take away the cooled drums. Doris and the others said goodnight and went upstairs.

The block quieted into a muggy night. Addie lingered on the stoop. When she tired of swatting at the mosquitos swarming her bare legs, she stood and stretched. A figure on a bicycle careened off the dark street and rode through the open gate straight up the walk toward her. Addie scrambled to get inside the door. Over her shoulder, she saw the front tire of the bike slam into the stoop. The rider tumbled onto the grass.

"Aw, are you gonna leave me like this?"

Addie recognized the voice. Tom. She spun around and hissed at him, "What are you doing, scaring me like that?"

Tom flipped onto his back and lay spreadeagled, then giggled. "Scared you? Aw, Addie, I didn't mean to scare you." He lifted his head off the ground. "Help me up?

"Get up on your own!"

He let his head fall back. "Changed my mind. I'll stay right here."

"What are you doing? Get up and go home." She waited for him to move. Tom let out a loud burp. "Have you been drinking?"

Tom rolled onto his side. "Okay, okay, I'm gonna go. Where's my bike?"

"I can't believe you crashed into my yard, drunk, in the middle of the night." She scanned the windows overhead for signs of the neighbors watching. No lights on, but she imagined their peering eyes.

Tom snored. Addie crouched at Tom's side, stage-whispered, "Wake up! Now!" No response. Addie stabbed her hand into Tom's forearm. "Get up!"

He opened his eyes. "Hi, there, Addie."

"Get up, take your bike, and go."

Tom grunted, rolled to his other side, raised up on his knees, wobbled, then pushed up to stand. Addie righted the bike next to his hip, and he grabbed the handlebar to steady himself. When he straddled the bike, she skipped back to the stoop. "Go."

She slipped inside the door, watched him put one foot on the pedal. If he fell, she didn't want to be there. Addie ran upstairs into the apartment and peered out of the front window. No Tom on the walk.

What was he thinking coming here after midnight, and drunk? On Saturday, after bookkeeping at the diner, she would march into Dunn's and tell Tom what a cad he was.

For now, she had to get up for work in the morning. Addie splashed water on her face, threw off her clothes, crawled into Ruth's bed.

The alarm clock rang at 5:30, still set for her pre-Fourth early schedule at the Print Shop. Addie pounded the knob to stop the sound, groaned at the loss of an hour's sleep. The bedroom was stifling; she had forgotten to open the window. She pulled open the curtains, raised the sash as far as it would go. The soft early light edged the yard, most of it still in the shadows.

And there was Tom, cocooned in the folds of the hammock tied between two of the maples, his bike underneath. Addie shook her head, gripped the sill. If she went down and woke him, the commotion would rouse the neighbors. It would serve Tom right for Myrtle's husband to find a vagrant in the hammock.

Addie went to the kitchen to make coffee. She downed one cup and began doing her hair. With her second cup of coffee, she peeked out of the window. Myrtle's husband was standing over the hammock, speaking to Tom. Tom rolled out of the hammock onto his feet. Tucking his shirt into his trousers, he said something that made the other man laugh. Tom righted his bike, rolled it to the curb, and pedaled away. A thunderclap broke overhead and raindrops pelted the leaves of the trees. Addie smirked at the satisfying image of Tom on the bike soaked by rain.

Addie covered her hair with a scarf and dashed to the street-car under an umbrella. Inside Hudson's entrance, she shook the wetness from her skirt. A glance at her watch showed she was on time. The elevators were less crowded than most mornings. The holiday having been on Thursday meant the lucky employees who had vacation time took Friday off.

In the Print Shop, Joe and Mr. Reed waved morning greetings at the counter. Addie strode to her locker with a smile for the men chatting around the machines. The day off had refreshed everyone. She looked forward to lunch in the tower, then remembered about going to the Infants department. Depending on where Mr. Reed sent her with orders, she might have time to stop there before lunch.

When she settled on her stool, Joe burbled on about the Tigers game and the race for the division title. Addie studied the order book to find the morning's deliveries. She tapped at a listing for Children's—it was on the fourth floor, too.

"Joe, which orders are ready to go?"

He scanned the list. "Not that one. Most departments are on half personnel today, want their orders on Monday. Big sales start next week."

"I need some time on that floor."

"Sewing Center on three takes you close. I'll check out their run."

The phone was silent. Addie propped her chin with her arm on the counter, ran the tip of the pencil up and down the list of orders. So few machines ran in the back that she could hear the wall clock ticking. Mr. Reed busied the men with cleaning and oiling of the metal gears and stampers and reorganizing the paper stocks.

Joe came back to the counter with a parcel bundled in the shop's green wrapping. "You're in luck—Sewing Center's labels for the pattern bins are ready. Mr. Reed says to take them down."

Labels delivered, Addie made her way to the fourth floor. The employee corridor snaked to a discreet archway into the customer area. Infants took up most of one side of the main aisle. A poster proclaimed "Life Begins with Storkline" and invited her to see the Pinocchio Infant Suite.

Addie stepped into a model baby nursery. Wallpaper patterned with tiny dancing sheep, white dotted curtains hanging from two windows with painted blue skies. She padded over the plush green carpet for a close look at the furniture. A chest of drawers combined with a hanging closet was a chifforobe, stated its placard, crafted from solid maple, made to order in various colors. A blue highchair was embossed, like all the furniture, with the Pinocchio character. The baby crib was pink, the toy chest white, filled with stuffed animals, tiny Pinocchios parading along its hinged top and front. A taller chest of drawers, atop it a ceramic lamp shaped like a lamb.

Addie ran her hand over the fine linens and knit blanket on the crib mattress. Tucked there was the price list, the Hudson's method of enticing the customer's desire ahead of considering their budget. Addie pursed her lips at the numbers, replaced the list as she had found it.

A walkway led out of the room to a row of the latest models of infant "coaches," quilted, padded, durable, foldable for stowing in a car trunk. Addie probed for the tags attached inside the hoods of the carriages. Her mental calculation of the cost of furniture and a carriage was producing a startling number.

The saleswoman waved to Addie from her desk in the middle of the counters and racks. Carrying the "Preparing for Baby" checklist, Addie trailed the woman as she pointed out the displays. Addie pulled her pencil from her pocket and jotted prices on the margin of the sheet. They moved through a sea of gowns, vests, bonnets, booties, dolls dressed in samples crisp and starched. Addie chuckled, remembering Myrtle's baby, fat legs kicking away at its wet gown. Then Addie checked the list to see how many gowns a baby needed. Her head swam with the numbers.

When a customer needed the saleswoman, Addie thanked her and folded the list into her pocket. Waiting at the employee elevator, she hugged her arms to her chest, tapped her foot. Outfitting a baby was expensive. Al likely had no idea how much money he would have to come up with.

After work, Addie came through the yard gate and saw Myrtle and her husband with several neighbors sitting under the trees. They waved to her. Nothing was said about Tom sleeping in the hammock. She took her time trudging up the stairs until she heard the telephone ringing, then scampered to get her key in the door, lunged for the receiver.

Ruth laughed at Addie's breathless hello. "Did you just get home?"

"Ran up the last few steps. Ruth, what's the matter?"

"Nothing's the matter. I need to tell you I am staying at the lake."

"Staying? What do you mean?"

"It's lovely here. The owners asked me to stay as their guest until Labor Day."

"That's two months!"

"I know. Dr. Tullen says the rest will do me good. I can call him anytime."

"Ruth, are you sure? What about Al?"

"Al is coming back to town tomorrow."

"He's leaving you?"

"He's going back to work."

"What do you want me to do?"

"You've got your job. Doris is there if you need anything."

"Yes, but …"

"Al's going to find us a house. I told him you must see it, make sure it's right for us, before he buys it."

"You want me to choose your house?"

Ruth chuckled. "You have a woman's eyes."

Addie's heart swelled at Ruth's trust. "I will make sure he buys a proper house, Ruth, for you and the baby."

They said goodbye with Ruth promising to call on Sundays. Addie reached into her dress pocket for the baby checklist, ran her eyes over the prices scribbled in the margins. She looked forward to shocking Al with the numbers and wielding the deciding vote for a house.

CHAPTER 10

A ddie froze in front of the window of Ma's diner, gripping the handlebars of her bike. Inside, she could see Mabel, sipping coffee at the table where Addie did the bookkeeping. She fumbled her toe over the kickstand, made two tries to lower it, and steadied the bike. Eyes down, she grabbed her satchel from the basket, turned to face the street and gulped a deep breath. *What was Mabel doing here?* Sweat trickled down her back. Addie straightened her shoulders and swiveled around to open the door. The bell chime announced her entrance.

Mabel stood up. She closed in on herself, arms hugging her chest, unpainted nails clawing her skin. Dirty-blond hair slicked back in a bun framed her pale, unmade-up face, the same ashy color Ruth took on during a migraine. The folds of her sleeveless dress bunched under a belt at her waist, like it was a size too large. Mabel made a half-smile. "I guess you know who I am."

Addie nodded toward the photograph on the wall. "Yes."

Mabel glanced over her shoulder. "That was after I met Al. My better days." She gestured to the chairs. "Will you talk with me?"

Addie looked toward the kitchen. No breakfast customers, the overhead lamps off, the only light coming from the sun streaming through the windows. "Where's Ma?"

Mabel pointed; Addie had walked past the sign on the door. "She's not opening till lunch today. We're alone for now." Mabel sat, pointed at an empty chair. "Please."

"Does Al know you're here?"

"I'm waiting for him."

Addie slammed the satchel onto the table. "To fling yourself into his arms?"

Mabel shook her head. "No chance for that to happen."

"Why should I believe you?"

Mabel gripped the edge of the table. "Just hear me out."

Addie calculated. "You have a story to match up with the one Al told Ruth?"

"Al told her the truth, I'm sure. It's not his fault things went so wrong for us."

"Why talk to me?"

"I wanted to talk to your sister, but Tom told me she's gone up north. I don't plan to stay around."

Addie tapped a foot on the linoleum. "So, what do you want?"

"Al's a good man." Mabel poured the coffee into both cups.

"Yeah, he's got Ruth believing that."

"She should believe it." Mabel sighed, twisted her hands in her lap. "Just listen, that's all I ask."

Addie sat down, crossed her legs. She picked up the coffee, raised an eyebrow at Mabel.

Mabel took a deep breath. "I met Al when we stood up together for our friends' wedding." She went on to describe Al calming his buddy George's jitters with sips from a small flask when Mabel, the maid of honor, and the bride, Peggy, climbed from a cab and ran up the church steps. The bridal couple melted into each other's arms with a passionate kiss. Al and Mabel exchanged smiles, and she had winked. "They best hurry with this wedding, don't you think?" Al had said to her as he offered his arm. "We are necessary only for the formalities." Remembering the moment, Mabel smiled. "Al made me laugh."

The bridal party and a group of friends celebrated at the Tropics Room. Mabel's telling conjured the scene as though a movie played on the wall of the diner. Addie stared at Mabel posing as Miss Front End, the beauty she had been. She imagined that other Mabel in a green satin gown, twirling with Al under colorful dance floor lights. No wonder Al was attracted to her.

"That evening is my favorite memory. All of us piled into this booth that looked like a tiki hut. George took snapshots of me on Al's lap, throwing a lei around his neck." Mabel tilted her head back, closed her eyes. "We drank and giggled our way through failed attempts at teaching Al the rumba steps. When the orchestra's final slow dance began, we were the last couple on the floor, draped around each other."

Mabel opened her eyes, leaned in. "I knew what was going to happen in his car. We went for each other. I wanted to be with him. But Al was so careful with me, kept a limit. I had never had that much to drink. He wanted to take me home. He fumbled with the car keys; his eyes were closing. He knew he was in no shape to drive." Mabel shook her head. "He covered me with a blanket in the back, and he slept in the front."

When they woke a few hours later, she climbed up front and snuggled next to Al for the drive over the bridge to Windsor. Al dropped her a block from her house with a promise to call.

"I was a sight in that gown, all wrinkled and clinging to me, scampering over lawns to my front porch. If my brothers had seen him, we'd both have gotten a beating."

Addie shot Mabel a look. "Really?"

"Really. My brothers are a whole other story, none of it good."

Mabel went on. She and Al spent time together every day for the next three weeks—lunches, dinners, afternoon and weekend drives. Whenever they were alone, one pulled the other into an eager embrace. "My lips swelled from all the kissing. Things were moving fast with us. When I wasn't with him, I thought about him touching me." Mabel hugged herself. "We eloped in the fourth week."

Their friends weren't surprised; many couples married quickly, before the men left for U.S. Army basic training or the Canadian forces. "Was it the war that pushed us? I guess we were caught up in our dreams." Mabel shook her head. "I wasn't ready for Al's mother." Mabel shook her head again and repeated, "I wasn't ready for Al's mother."

When Al brought Mabel to his family home in Windsor, his mother declared Al a fool and Mabel unwelcome. They spent two nights in a hotel before Al won his mother's begrudging agreement for Mabel to move in. The women staked out separation of the territory: downstairs, the kitchen and her bedsit were ruled by Al's mother; upstairs, their bedroom and the sewing room, Al's and Mabel's.

"Al said the dining room and front porch were the battlefields where he was captured, depending on who got the upper hand in an argument." Mabel crossed her legs, folded her arms, smirked. "Al's mother would bark instructions at me. I was a live wire then, put my stake in the ground by refusing or ignoring her. When he got his orders, Al worried about leaving us together in the house."

Mabel went to work in a factory, soldering parts repurposed to manufacture bombers. Her mother-in-law volunteered in the Canadian civilian corps. "Every day, I listened to the factory women worry about sons, brothers, and husbands overseas, and I prayed for Al. I came home to silent evenings, me at one end of the dining table, Al's mother at the other. It got to me." Mabel made the first move. "One night, I offered her Al's letter to read. She took the letter, grabbed my arm, sobbed." Mabel wiped her eyes. "She laid awake nights praying for the safety of her only child. Both of us needed Al to come home."

With their truce, Mabel asked for her mother-in-law's help to prepare for the baby Al didn't know was coming. Al's mother was thrilled about a grandchild. "She fussed over me, said it moved her fear for Al to the side, like packing away the winter clothes. For a time, you forgot how heavy they were." Mabel leaned her elbow on the table, rubbed her forehead. "We asked the neighbor to snap a photo of me and his mother waving from the front porch. We put it in an envelope with both our letters, telling Al he would be a father."

Addie breathed out. "You had a baby?"

Mabel hid her face in her hands. Her shoulders heaved. Addie held still, waited. Mabel rolled her wet face against her arm, fished a tissue from her pocket. "A little bleeding for a few days. I wanted it to be nothing. I didn't tell anyone. I hemorrhaged during my shift. The factory nurse saved my life."

When she was released from the hospital, Mabel crawled into bed at home and stayed there. Al's mother tended to her, as she had no interest in caring for herself. Weeks went by. "I couldn't write to Al. His mother had to do it." She hung her head. "But she didn't tell him how low I'd sunk."

After two months, her friend Peggy coaxed Mabel into fixing up and getting out of the house. "I let them believe I had gone back to work. But I had quit the factory. Know where I went every day?" Addie waited. Mabel pursed her lips. "Dunn's." Addie's eyes widened.

An old injury to his knee had put Tom in civilian reserve service. He opened Dunn's nights that he wasn't on duty. "He let me sit there alone until opening time." Tom kept her visits a secret, thought she'd figure herself out.

Mabel's drinking started with beer only. "My old uncles used to pack away a case, told us beer drinkers couldn't be drunks; you had to drink the hard stuff. I fooled myself with that, even when I was downing beer and shots." It wasn't long before she was fudging the stock numbers in Dunn's inventory to cover the liquor she drank.

The first time Tom found her passed out, he felt sorry for her, sobered her up with coffee, and drove her home. The second time, he couldn't keep her awake. Tom carried her through the alley to the back stairs of his apartment down the block, snuck her in to sleep it off. "I woke up on Tom's cot, no idea where I was, threw up in his sheets. Tom, bless him, cleaned me up. He told me to never come back to the bar for my own good. Said if I did, he would tell his aunt, Al's mother." Mabel blew air from her lips. "I cried on his shoulder that I'd learned my lesson, begged him not to tell anyone." She paused. "I had us both fooled."

Soon the talk reached Tom, that Mabel was drinking in the afternoons at other taverns. Tom went to see his aunt. Confronted, Mabel was contrite. For a week, she had seemed on an even keel. Had her hair done and bought clothes to look for a new job. Al's mother tried to believe her when Mabel left the house each day, saying she was looking for work. Mabel was sly about choosing places for her drinking, well away from their neighborhood. The police brought her home twice before Al's mother called the doctor.

Al got leave to visit her. "The look on his face when he saw me ... and the shock of what the doctors told him." Mabel's depression was severe. Her recovery was unpredictable. Al arranged for her to go into a hospital. When his leave was up, his mother visited twice a week. "Bless her heart, she would not give up on me. My brothers wanted no part of me, said I was Al's problem. Just as well, I would never go back to them."

Mabel hung her head. "I wish the peacefulness of the hospital could have seeped into my brain." She gazed into the stream of sun coming through the window. "I sat for hours in the gardens, staring at the lake, listening to the birds. I seesawed between numb and crying."

Al's unit returned to Detroit before the end of the war. He spent Sunday afternoons at the hospital with Mabel. "I would force my face into a smile that I didn't feel, refuse to talk, not let him touch me. The doctors said again and again: time, patience, follow the treatment regimen. I realized I wanted to live, but not with Al. I cared for him, but my problem changed me."

Mabel's voice dropped low. "I was not in love anymore. The day I told him, I remember watching his slow amble as he came toward me in the garden, the familiar way he tipped off his hat, slipped an arm around me. But the limbo of our situation was getting to him. He had stopped asking me to try living at home." Tears flowed down Mabel's cheeks. "Divorce was best for both of us. We cried together, hugged. I knew I had to let him go."

Mabel wiped her eyes, sniffed up the tears. "I left the hospital, went on a binge. My psychiatrist has all kinds of mumbo-jumbo to explain what I did, but the upshot is I ran off and stayed drunk. My looks got me a job in a bar in any town I drifted to."

Addie stared at Mabel. Never had she heard talk like this from a woman. Mabel was making no excuses for herself.

"I had sunk pretty low when Tom hunted me down, helped me get my sense back."

"Tom? Isn't Tom a drinker, too?"

"Tom has a throat on him, as my granny used to say. But he's not like me." Mabel saw Addie's quizzical look. "Tom keeps distant from the whiskeys and beers he pours, wipes his hands after each serve. If he gets a break, he downs a beer. He pours a shot for himself if men slap the money down. He says bartending changed his habits, but I don't know."

"Does Al know Tom went looking for you?"

"No."

"Are you with Tom?"

"It's not like that. He brought me to his place for last night, but I can't stay there."

"What do you want from Al?"

Mabel sighed. "I should keep seeing my doctor in Windsor. I don't have a place." She pursed her lips. "Al's mother sold her house, went to live with her cousin out west. I broke her heart when I ran off. Peggy will take me in for a short time. If I don't drink."

Addie crossed her arms. "So, you want money from Al."

Mabel rubbed her forehead. "Just to get on my feet."

146

Addie stared again at the picture of Miss Front End, the shiny hair, glossy red nails, the proud, forward thrust of her chest, the delight in the men eying her. Now worn-down Mabel was asking Addie to approve of, or at least not object to, Al giving Mabel money. What would Ruth say if Mabel had told her this story? Soft Ruth might feel sorry for Mabel.

Addie didn't. She sat back and shook her head. "You said Al was not to blame, but you want his money."

Mabel grimaced. "You make it sound like a ruse."

Addie tapped her finger on the table. "And what if Al says no to giving you money?"

"The court would say he must."

She pointed at Mabel. "How do we know that if Al gives you the money, you'll stay away?"

"I don't want to wreck his life."

Ma walked into the dining room. Mabel hung her head, gripped her coffee mug. "I've burned all my bridges here."

Addie pushed back her chair, gestured to the ledgers on the table. "I have work to do."

Mabel rose from the table. She straightened her dress, balled the tissue in her hands. "I'll be in the kitchen." Ma followed her.

Addie's hands trembled opening the ledger. Mabel's story roiled her thoughts. She pressed her fingers along her brow, checked the clock over the counter. If Al had gotten an early start, he would arrive before Dunn's opened. She began adding the receipts quickly, to get the bookkeeping out of the way before the next act of the drama occurred. The adding machine's keys took the brunt of her upset as she punched numbers.

Ma came to open the door to the first lunch customers. Addie wondered at Ma's participation in Mabel's scheme. Ma was a harsh judge of people, outspoken in her dismissal of those she deemed flawed. Yet she let Mabel sneak up on Addie and wait for Al in the diner. And she still had Miss Front End hanging on her wall.

Addie plowed through to finish the diner's records. She closed the ledger, stood for a stretch. Ma pointed to a plate set on the counter. "Got a BLT here for you."

Taking a full bite of the crunchy bacon and toasted bread, Addie studied Ma.

Ma asked, "You got something to say?"

Addie raised her brows. "You heard the story."

"I heard one side of it."

"Why are you standing up for her?"

"Depends on what happens next."

"And what will happen next?"

"Mabel and Al will work it out."

The bell chimed. Al walked in, Tom behind him. Al hesitated at the counter while Tom strode into the kitchen. Ma nodded to Al, busied herself with wiping glasses. He twisted his hat, listened to Tom greeting Mabel, her laughing.

Addie rumpled her napkin, pushed her sandwich plate away. She moved off the counter stool, glared at Al. "Mabel told me everything."

Al shook his head. "I didn't know about this."

Addie lowered her voice, tipped her head toward the kitchen. "Why did Tom help her?"

Al shrugged.

Addie went to pack up her satchel. She hiked the strap over her shoulder, planted herself in front of Al. "How was Ruth when you left her at the lake?"

"Ruth is doing well."

"Keep it that way."

Al raised his brows. "It's best if you leave."

"Ruth will call me tomorrow."

"Don't drag her into this."

Ma flung the towel over her shoulder, marched to the door, grabbed it open. "Addie, see you next week."

Addie glared at Ma, stomped out, pedaled home. Tom was partial to Mabel. Was he in love with her? Addie suspected Al would be soft on Mabel, too, and give her what she wanted. Where did that leave Ruth?

When Ruth called on Sunday, Addie could not bear to upset Ruth by telling her about Mabel. On Monday, Addie was determined to find Al and corner him into telling her about Mabel and the money. Despite manufacturing multiple reasons to visit the Advertising floor, she didn't run into Al all week.

By the next Saturday, her anger with Ma, Al, and Tom had festered. Ma opened the diner door and held up a hand before Addie could speak. "Not my place to talk about their business."

"You let her come here."

Ma shrugged. "Al will do right by Ruth."

"What makes you so sure?"

"Are ya doing my books or not?" Ma demanded, hands on hips.

Addie thumped her satchel onto the table. Ma said nothing more. When Addie finished the paperwork, Ma handed her a bundle wrapped in waxed paper. Addie accepted it with pursed lips.

Ma chuckled. "I like you don't back down easy."

Addie started on the route home. Al's sedan passed by, pulled to the curb ahead of her. She stopped her bike at his window. They looked at each other.

Al gripped the steering wheel. "I know you're mad, and you think I owe you something."

"You owe Ruth."

"Can you drive with me to Dearborn after work on Monday?"

"Dearborn?"

"To see a new house. I'll pick you up on Farmer when you get off." Al pulled into the driving lane and sped away.

Addie had collected pamphlets from Hudson's furniture and décor departments to make a budget for household goods, appliances, and furniture for different rooms in a house. With the baby list, the costs were eye-popping. But Addie shrugged off the number. She would enjoy seeing Al squirm about the money.

At closing on Monday, Addie retrieved her clipboard from her locker with her hat and bag. Al was waiting on Farmer Street when she came out of the building. They began the ten-mile drive to Dearborn by heckling each other when Addie waved the clipboard in his face. "I have a list of things Ruth needs for the house."

"I know what we need."

"Ruth wants her things from Hudson's."

"I know what Ruth cares about."

"Then why did she tell me to approve the house?"

"She didn't mean it's up to you."

"Ruth said you can't buy a house without me approving it."

"She will like this house."

Addie lifted her chin, sniffed. "Depending on what I tell her."

Al gripped the steering wheel. "What is on that list?"

"Everything for the house, and for the baby."

"The baby?"

"Furniture and clothes and things for taking care of a baby."

"And you're going to throw that at me, are you?"

Addie snickered. "There's an idea."

"Don't make this complicated."

"Speaking of complications—"

"Stop right there." His voice was sharp.

Addie crossed her arms, stared out the window. The city's density gave over to a patchwork of farms and villages. Billboards announced the coming of new housing developments. When they crossed a bridge over the River Rouge, a stench wrinkled Addie's nose. She pinched her nostrils closed. "What is that smell?"

"Progress." Al gestured upriver. "In Dearborn, it's Ford's will be done." He grabbed a newspaper from the dashboard, tossed it at her.

Addie read an advertisement for homes in Fordson, a town first developed with the sprawl of Ford's Rouge complex before the war. Newer houses built according to the original designs approved by Henry Ford now filled in the remaining open blocks.

Al turned off the main road, crawled the car along. The street was newly paved, but yellow stakes driven into the hard-packed dirt defined the sidewalk strips waiting for concrete. Two-story homes lined the block like a row of soldiers. The house paint made them identical, except for the numbers tacked above the front doors. Al pulled over in front of a house about halfway down the block. "The real estate office gave me the key for this one."

Walking from the curb to the house covered Addie's shoes with a gritty film that crept under the open toes. Up three steps, the concrete porch was only large enough for both of them if they stood sideways. Left and right, Addie had a clear view along the front porches straight down the block. "There are no trees."

Al fumbled with the key in the door lock. "Acreage around here was farmland. They'll plant a tree in front and one in back." He pushed the door open and held it for her. "If we pay extra."

Addie stepped over the threshold into hot stuffiness. Al pulled off his hat and wiped his brow with a handkerchief. "I'll find a window to open."

The inside entry was narrow. Two strides to the staircase to the second floor. A pedestal bookstand presented handbills describing the features of the house. Addie took two, handed one to Al when he rejoined her.

"Propped a kitchen window open, for the little good it will do. Let's see the nuts and bolts." Al opened a door in the hallway, saw it was a closet. He checked the handbill, pointed toward the back of the house. "Living room here, kitchen, a bedroom and bath other side. Basement door in the kitchen." Al strode through the living room and Addie heard him bounding down the stairs to the basement.

Addie took a pencil from her handbag, looped the bag's strap and her hat over a doorknob, propped her clipboard against her hip. Late-day light streamed through windows on three sides of the living room. Addie turned into the kitchen. There were gaping spots sized for a stove and a refrigerator. Modern cupboards were built into the walls, and there was space for a small table. A corner doorway opened into a passage to the bathroom and a bedroom. The bedroom windows looked out to the street in front, and on the side, a direct view into the living room of the house next door.

Addie paced from the bedroom back through the kitchen, around the living room, tapping her pencil on the clipboard. Al clomped up the basement stairs. "Enough light to see the plumbing and the furnace." He mopped his brow again. "Are those on your list?" She made a face. Al walked past her. "Have you looked upstairs?"

Sweat dribbled down the back of Addie's neck as she climbed the stairs behind Al. He opened the window on the second-floor landing. A bedroom was on both sides. Al stood in the doorway of one room, Addie entered the other. She compared the handbill's dimensions of the room against her measurements of the model baby's room.

"The nursery furniture will fit, but Ruth will run up the stairs a lot." She stood by the open window, fanned her face with the clipboard. "Carrying the baby, carrying stuff. Plus, the bathroom is downstairs."

"Let me see that list."

Addie handed over the clipboard. She watched Al's eyebrows rise as he ran a finger along the pages. He tapped through the baby list. He handed the clipboard back, leaned his hands on the windowsill, gazed into the backyard. "I don't have enough money."

Al turned and bounded down the stairs. Addie heard the kitchen window thump closed, then saw Al slam out of the front door. She rested the clipboard on the sill. The numbers were daunting, she knew. And she had more to add. Touring the rooms, Addie had noticed forgotten needs, like draperies for the many windows. Trees were extra. If Al didn't have the money, what did that mean for Ruth?

She closed the upstairs window, walked downstairs, collected her hat and bag, and opened the door. The waning sun had lowered, easing the heat. Al sat on the stoop. She smoothed her skirt and sat down next to him.

Al rested his elbows on his knees. "I'll work it out." He tapped his hat against his leg. "No need to say anything to Ruth. I'll work it out."

Addie sighed. "There isn't much time."

"Believe me, I know."

"Maybe another house …"

"The bottom line is no different. Give me the clipboard." Addie held it out to him. Al balanced it on his knees. "This isn't counting the doctor and the down payment. I've got that much. I didn't figure on all of this."

Addie shook her head. "You gave Mabel money, didn't you? You promised Ruth a house."

"Yes, I gave Mabel the money she asked for. That brings things to a close between us." He saw Addie's frown. "Before you give me your two cents, Ruth knows."

Addie raised her brows. "Ruth trusts you. I'm not Ruth."

"I give you credit, Addie, for the numbers stuff. Ma says you've straightened the diner out."

Addie shrugged. "It's easy enough."

Al stared off, then said, "I need your help."

Addie straightened up. "My help?"

Al shifted on the stoop. "I think Tom skimmed money."

"What do you mean?"

"What we order to pour and the money we take in, the numbers don't jibe. Small stuff here and there is not a worry, but this is different."

"Why would he do that?"

"I hope he's not. But I can't figure what—or who—else could short us. I'm not a hundred percent accurate with the accounts, but there was good money for us every month.

Last three months, after the bills, there's not enough for the usual draw."

"Did you talk to Tom?"

"Mentioned the draws were low, when we took our shares, but he wasn't worried about it."

"But did you ask him if he's taking the money?"

"Can't throw that in his face if I'm not sure." Al turned to Addie. "You could help."

Addie sighed, looked away. "What is it you want me to do?"

"Take over Dunn's books. Figure out where the money's going."

"But how would I? You've been keeping the accounts and *you* don't know."

"Figure out what changed." Al stood up. "Look, Addie, I don't like coming hat in hand to you, or anybody. But I've got to take care of Ruth and the baby. I was counting on the draw from Dunn's."

Addie studied Al's furrowed brow, his ruddy nose, and those brown eyes. It vexed her that he was unprepared to give Ruth the home she deserved. But his admission of being short, and his ask for help, seemed sincere.

"What could Tom be doing?"

"Selling bottles somewhere, or not putting all the drink money in the till."

"What will you tell Tom about what I'm doing?"

"He knows I get underneath the paperwork. And he knows I need cash. I'll tell him straight up."

Al stood and held out his hand to Addie. She sighed and lifted herself off the stoop. "Tomorrow, after I finish in the diner, show me the books and the inventory."

"Thank you." Al clamped his hat on his head.

"But I am not going to lie to Ruth."

"Neither am I."

They stood looking at each other. Al said, "How about some dinner? A place in the village we came through is supposed to be good."

"I am hungry."

Al went to the curb and opened the passenger car door. Before walking away, Addie took another look at the house, scribbled a note. She tucked the clipboard under her arm, picked her way along the dirt path, and climbed into the passenger seat. Al trotted around the front end to the driver's side. She settled back against the seat, stretched out her legs. Her first evening out since she arrived would be with Al.

CHAPTER 11

Addie dreamt the upstairs bedroom in the empty house had transformed into the model baby room. Pinocchio leapt from the windowsill to the chifforobe. The stuffed animals in the toy chest danced with him. He climbed into the baby crib, tapped his nose, and vanished.

Her old aunt used to say dreams were secret messages. Addie didn't believe that. She shrugged it off as she leapt out of bed. Ma would beat her to the diner, she knew, no matter how early Addie arrived; before dawn was the coolest time to bake pies. Al would meet her at Dunn's after she finished at the diner. Dressed in a cotton skirt and blouse, she pinned her hair off her face and neck, put a new ledger pad in her satchel, and tucked in pencils with fresh erasers. Addie locked the apartment door and scampered down to get her bike. Doris sat on the back porch, sipping from a mug of coffee.

"You're up early. Coffee?" She pointed at a thermos.

"Morning, Doris. I'll get some at the diner." Addie pulled the bike from the corner, stuffed her satchel in the basket.

"Have supper with me tonight." Doris had made a habit of meeting Addie in the hallway evenings on her way in from work; she was a good cook who hated to eat alone. Addie enjoyed the food and their end-of-day chatting. Addie smiled. "I impose on you too much."

Doris shook her head. "No, you don't. Supper's at six-thirty. No cards tonight, but we'll eat here on the porch."

"You're a lifesaver. I'll bring one of Ma's pies. See you later."

Addie lifted the bike down the steps and wheeled it around the building to the boulevard. The sky had brightened. The record heat the radio weatherman reported had held steady overnight. Setting a brisk pace, Addie felt the pull in her calves and sweaty dribbles down her back as she pedaled.

At the diner, the light in the kitchen meant Ma was busy with the pies. Addie rapped on the door glass to get her attention. Ma appeared in the kitchen doorway, her hands and arms flour-dusty. She scurried forward to unlock the door. "Help yourself to coffee. I've got dough to roll." Ma's slippers squeaked back to the kitchen.

Addie flicked on the overhead lights and laid her satchel on the counter. She poured a mug, doused it with cream, felt the first sips energize her thinking. Her weekly routine had transformed the haphazard clumps of papers Ma used to stuff into a breadbox into an orderly arrangement of inflows and outflows in the ledger and labeled files. Ma had learned not to skip writing orders down and to clip a day's slips together. The breadbox was her habit, though, so Addie had Ma use it to collect the week's receipts. Addie figured she'd finish before Al arrived at Dunn's. She'd come back to Ma's for lunch. Later, dinner on the porch with Doris. Addie chuckled at her luck avoiding cooking, and got to work.

She had separated the costs of the pie supplies from the regular business to see what money the pies alone brought in. Addie was tidying her files folder when Ma came behind the counter. Blueberry juice speckled the front of her apron from neck to knees. When she pulled it over her head, Addie saw her sweat-soaked cotton blouse clinging to Ma's chest.

"How do you stand the oven heat in weather like this?"

Ma's gnarled hands soaked a dishtowel in ice water, wrapped it around her neck. "Ah, girlie, a little heat bothers ya?"

Addie laughed. "Glad you can take it because your pies are bringing in good money. Want to see the numbers?"

"With pancakes?"

Addie brought the ledger book to the counter. In short order, Ma set two plates of pancakes swimming in butter and syrup at their places and eased herself onto the stool. She pulled her skirt up above her knees, hooked the slippers on the rung. "Whatcha got?"

Addie ran her finger along the ledger entries and explained the totals. "Ma, the pies are bringing in more than the diner meals. At less overall cost."

"Folks like my pies."

"My point is you could increase the pie sales. Get more help. You've only got the one girl."

"I'm making as many pies as the stores in the neighborhood ask for."

"With more stores selling the pies, you can do better."

Ma chewed and took a sip of coffee. "Stores I have, came to me. How would I get more?"

"Why not ask Al for help? He's a salesman."

"Hmm. Can I pay another girl?"

Addie began explaining the cost for a second helper, but shouts coming through the diner's open back door interrupted her. Addie and Ma exchanged a look. Ma scooted off the stool. "That's Al."

Addie trotted behind Ma through the kitchen door into the alley. Al and Tom stood nose-to-nose. There was no mistaking their angry postures. Tom took a step back, kicked at a stack of beer cases, sent the top one flying to land with the crack of broken glass. Al shouted, "That's it! Break the empties, cost us *more* money!"

Tom raised a clenched fist. "How about I break your nose?"

"You comin' at me?"

Ma got between them. "Nobody's hitting nobody, unless ya want to fight me."

Tom's fist stayed clenched. "Get outta here, Ma."

Al scowled at him over Ma's head. "Disrespectful, too? I ought to punch *you*."

Ma held firm. "Get inside. Now. Both of yas."

Tom backed off, kicked the beer case again, rattling it off the wall. Al pivoted, glowered at his cousin as Tom slammed through the door into Dunn's.

Ma grabbed Al's arm. "What's going on?"

Al caught Addie's eye and she knew: he had confronted Tom about the shortfall.

Ma saw the look, crossed her arms. "Don't tell me you've gotten her involved in somethin'."

Al shrugged. "Addie's looking at our books." He nodded to Addie.

Ma kept her gaze on Al. "Don't put her in the middle."

"Just getting answers about where our money's going. I'll wait for you here, Addie."

Ma raised her eyebrows at Al, turned and stomped to the diner. When Addie returned to the kitchen, Ma wagged her finger in Addie's face. "Do not get in the middle."

"Al asked for help with the books. Same as I do for you. Just numbers."

Ma shook her head. "Nothin' about money is just numbers."

Addie collected her things, passed by Ma pounding dough with her fists, and headed into the alley. Al was sitting in his car, his legs out the open door. "Still want to do this?"

Addie looked at the broken beer bottles. "You said you wouldn't accuse Tom."

"Tom knows where the money went."

"What? He told you?"

Al stood, shoved the car door closed. "We have ourselves quite a pickle." He grimaced. "A polite way of saying we're screwed."

Al pulled open the back door of the tavern, waved Addie through. From the front, they heard a blasting radio and the clanking of glass. Al led Addie into the dining room, where tables pushed together held a ledger. "Get settled. I'll get him."

Addie opened the thick ledger book and appreciated the neat figures written in Al's hand. But he had made the last entries a month ago. She flipped through invoices clipped together inside the cover. Payment to the beer supplier was sixty days late.

Tom marched into the room ahead of Al, who set a glass of ice water in front of Addie. Tom leaned against the wall with arms folded. Al took a chair across from Addie, nodded at the open ledger. "We're behind with the beer guy. He's been easy with us because even in slow times, we've paid in full before sixty days. I don't know what we can pay now." He looked hard at Tom.

Tom hooked a boot on a chair leg, pulled it toward him, sat. "The beat cops are shaking us down." He grunted at the puzzled look on Addie's face. "Sorry, girl, forgot you don't know how things work in the big city."

Al rapped the table with his knuckles. "Easy, there. Spell it out."

Tom scoffed. "Yeah, right, for our bookkeeper."

Addie felt the tension between the men in her hands clenching the ledger. Ma was right—she shouldn't be in the middle. Addie flipped the book closed, pushed back her chair. "I'm going home. Sorry, Al."

"No, don't go. We need your help." Al faced Tom. "We *have* to get out from under this. Stop insulting her."

Tom slapped both hands on the table. "Okay, okay. But what we need is muscle."

"Just tell Addie what happened."

Tom scowled. "The beat cop shakes us down for booze and money to keep quiet about the card room running here after hours." Addie understood Tom was talking about something different from the jar of dimes Doris and her friends played with.

Al spoke. "Neighborhood regulars playing cards here started back with old man Dunn. Penny ante. Since we've had the place, the same friendly game. Then we heard another knot of guys took over, playing for stakes. They kept it quiet. It didn't bother the front room. So we let it go."

Tom leaned forward. "But the game attracted a card sharper. Different guys started showing up at the back door Friday nights at closing. Paid their tabs, but they swiped other bottles from the back. Then the cop comes in, demands his share for not running us in for gambling."

"You should have let me in on the squeeze," Al snorted.

"I was handling it!"

"Handing it over, more like." Al slapped his hand on the table. "Maybe you can throw away your money, but I've got a family."

"Awright, awright, I get it." Tom looked at Addie. "This too much for you?"

Addie shrugged a shoulder. "My uncle bootlegged during Prohibition. My sister owned a tavern. I'm not shocked, if that's what you mean."

Tom raised his brows, sat back.

Al asked her again, "Are you willing to help?"

"What do you want me to do?"

Al tapped the ledger book. "Tell us where we stand."

"I don't want the trouble you've got."

"You just work on the books. We'll clean up the mess." Al looked at his cousin. "Right, Tom?"

Tom shrugged. "Yeah, figure out where we stand."

They got up and left Addie alone. She sorted and added and made notes on her pad. Al had done a passable job of tracking the orders and payments for beer and liquor, less so on the details of the bar's cash receipts. She saw the recent change in the weekly draws Al and Tom had taken. Addie couldn't help comparing the amount of the draw Al had been missing to the costs for the baby furniture. Before the shakedown, it would have been more than enough.

While she worked, things quieted in the front barroom. The radio played at a listening volume. She left the dining room to find Al so they could count the inventory. He was straightening bottles and cases in the storeroom. He called out the brand, counted aloud as Addie watched, and she noted the quantities.

Al stopped to wipe his hands. He pushed the storeroom door closed, lowered his voice. "Tom gave his draw to Mabel."

Addie's heel hit a box, and she stumbled back. "What the heck?"

"Yeah. Helped her move to a place." Al rubbed his brow. "He's sure she won't bother me, but he's always had a soft spot for her."

"How do you know she won't ask you for more?"

Al saw Addie's frown. "Addie, I am done with Mabel."

"For Ruth's sake, I hope you mean that."

"Yes, I do."

"What will you do about the shakedown?"

"I'd rather close Dunn's than keep paying." Al waved at the bottles and crates. "We could sell the building, pay off the debts, and walk away."

"Will Tom do that?"

"Nope. He needs this place more than I do. But we went into this together, and we'll figure it out." He tapped the clipboard. "Let's finish with the bottles behind the bar."

When they went up front, Tom moved away from the bar, busied himself cleaning tables and rearranging chairs while they counted. Addie sat on a stool. She could see Tom in the back-bar mirror. He kept his face turned away, never met her eye.

By the time Addie organized the numbers, it was past lunch. Her grumbling stomach longed for one of Ma's bacon sandwiches on fresh bread, piled with farm-ripe tomatoes. Al was thinking the same, because he asked Addie to step over to the diner with him. "Bring your pad. Tell me the bad news while we eat."

"What about Tom?"

"The numbers won't make a difference to him."

The diner was busy with Saturday lunch customers. The neighborhood knew Ma baked early on weekend mornings; the array of pies in the display case enticed a crowd. Ma, behind the counter, pointed Al and Addie toward an empty table. Ma's girl brought water, took their orders.

Addie slid her pad in front of Al. "You've got enough in the bank, plus the safe, to pay the beer guy. If you sell all the inventory, the bar can stay afloat about a month." She tapped the pad. "Will the beer guy extend credit?"

"Not sure since we got so behind. I'll talk to him."

"You have liquor inventory that doesn't sell." Addie showed Al the bottle list. "Can you return unopened bottles? Pare down your orders to only those that sell?"

Al shook his head. "No returns. But another tavern owner might barter some."

"There's no draw for you and Tom unless ..." She raised her brows for Al to take her meaning.

"Not taking a draw—neither of us can afford that." He took another look at the figures. "We've been running week-to-week, not thinking things through like this."

The busy girl half-dropped their sandwich plates at their places, smiled an apology and whirled away. Addie dug into hers, then glanced up at the wall of photos. Miss Front End was gone. She had been so intent earlier when she worked on Ma's books, she hadn't noticed the change.

Al caught her looking. "I asked Ma to take it down."

"Good." Then Addie remembered her advice to Ma about building the pie business. "You know, Al, Ma could use your help to sell pies. She wants to get more stores, increase the sales."

Al wiped his mouth on a napkin, sat back in his chair. "I'll have a talk with Ma. We might scratch each other's backs." Al pulled cash from his pants pocket, grabbed up the check.

"Here, keep this." Addie tore the sheet with the figures from her pad, handed it to Al. "Thanks for lunch."

"Thanks for your help. Don't worry, I'll manage."

"That's what Ruth always says."

"And somehow, we do it." He smiled his Al smile. "Want to drive with me to Houghton Lake for the Labor Day weekend, and we'll bring Ruth home?"

"Are you asking me to be there when you tell Ruth you didn't buy the house?"

"I've told her that wasn't the right place. You'll like the lake. It's a chance to get away."

"Thanks. I'd like to go. I miss Ruth."

"Right, then. I'll sort things out as best I can before we leave." Al stood. "I'll drive over now to see the beer guy."

Customers bustled at the counter paying their checks and buying pies. Al slapped the check and money into Ma's fist, whispered something in her ear, and she nodded. Addie caught Ma's eye, mouthed "Blueberry," and Ma took a pie box off the display, slid it over the counter. Addie took the pie to her bike, nestled it carefully in the front basket, and wheeled through the alley to Dunn's open back door.

Tom, in the back hauling ice, slammed down the block when he saw her. "I was running things fine, before." Addie said nothing, moved past him to gather her things. Tom followed her. "You understand?"

"Al's gone to see the beer guy."

"I never short us. I don't drink our stock. That night when I crashed in your yard, my buddy drowned my sorrows, as they say."

"You had some nerve. Thank goodness my neighbors didn't see me with you."

"Too good to be seen with me?"

Addie sniffed. "I'm going home." She buckled her satchel, headed for the door.

Tom said, "See you, Miss *Bookkeeper*."

Addie ignored him. Pedaling home, she mulled over the problem at Dunn's. She didn't know how Al and Tom would work their way out of it. But she knew how to get the baby furniture.

CHAPTER 12

The humidity loosened its grip for warm August days and balmy nights. The tower lunchroom buzzed with talk about fishing trips and family reunions before school started, cabins were shuttered, leaves began to fall, and the store's rush for the holiday season permitted no time off.

Ma's August routine was to close the diner on Friday until Tuesday lunch. She spent the long weekends camped in an old U.S. Army surplus tent at a lake two hours north of the city. Photos on the diner wall from previous summers pictured Ma and her fellow campers around fire pits and canoeing on the lake.

"Come out to the camp," Ma invited. "Not just old folks there. Young'uns swim out to the floats, have their parties."

"Thanks, Ma, but I'll go up north with Al to bring Ruth home." Addie stored Ma's books in the pantry, covered her adding machine. "We'll update the accounts after Labor Day."

Ma chuckled. "You've got me puppy-trained; don't think I'll mess up before then." She gave Addie a pie made with the last of the blueberries.

She pedaled away without going over to Dunn's. Addie had not heard from Al. She figured he must not have settled the bar's money problems. He would get in touch if anything changed before the drive up north to fetch Ruth.

Addie had not worked at Hudson's long enough to earn vacation time, but she shared the urgency to enjoy the still-summer days ahead of Labor Day. During the week, she explored inside the store. Hudson's eighteen customer levels offered a city within the city—everything from the tiniest buttons to the furnishings and appliances for a manor house, arranged in artful presentation, along with ten restaurants, a post office, shoemaker, dry cleaner, and salons to coif women, men, and children. She roamed the sales floors whenever she could grab time away from the Print Shop. Sometimes she indulged her fantasies in the dress and fur shops, other times she made a practical review of silver, linens, and carpets. In the Bookshop, she continued reading Dr. Spock in fifteen-minute increments, picking up where she left off the night before in her own copy. The staff in the Piano Salon were deft in the classical repertoires and Addie would slip into a nearby alcove to listen to them playing. In the Studio of Interior Decoration, on eight, she would seat herself at an oversized oak desk like the one Mrs. Reynolds had and pretend she was in charge of the store's accounts.

At lunch in the tower, Addie joined Joe and others in the card games, trading quips in their jokey competitive banter. Addie clapped with glee when Joe said, "How about that rain check for a Tigers game?"

That Saturday, he and his brother met Addie at the streetcar stop on Michigan Avenue for an afternoon game and walked her to the Briggs stadium ticket windows. Sidewalk carts sold boiled hot dogs in soft buns covered in mustard to those in the crowd milling around the stadium who couldn't wait for a grilled frankfurter inside. The sun beat down as the game began, and Addie turned her face to get as much as she could. Joe and his brother babbled their opinions of each player coming to the plate.

By the seventh inning stretch, the Tigers were ahead of the Baltimore Orioles amidst raucous cheers for the home team and booing at the visitors. When the game ended, the Tigers ran off the field, doffing their caps to the fans. Addie and the brothers shuffled down the ramps to the street on the high note of the home team's win. Addie jostled among the baseball fans on the streetcar ride home and smiled at the smear of mustard on her skirt. She wondered if Ruth and Al ever went to Tigers games. It would be fun to go to a game together next season. Could they take a baby carriage into Briggs? Joe would know.

On another Saturday, Addie roamed the downtown streets around Hudson's, stepping into the grand lobbies of the skyscrapers she viewed from the tower. She spent hours in the Detroit Public Library. She bought a sandwich and ate it sitting on the steps, watching the passing people. She marked her map with dots on the buildings and streets she had visited. She had much more of the city to see.

Addie ate her suppers with Doris, who listened to Addie's tales of the Print Shop and laughed about her encounters with characters among the store staff and customers. Their routine had become easy, close. One evening, Addie noticed a birthday greeting card propped on the lamp table in Doris's living room. "Is today your birthday?"

"Yesterday." Doris set plates on the dining table. "My fortieth."

The age surprised Addie. She had guessed Doris to be older. Her rounded figure had a matronly look, her head capped with silver hair. "Many happy returns! I wish I had known."

"About my birthday, or that I'm not as old as you figured?"

Addie blushed. "Forgive me."

"Don't fret. The women in my family are on the plump side and go grey early. My husband liked it." She had not talked about him before. "He was younger than me. I never got over my surprise that he wanted me. When the war came, he followed a romantic idea of being a Navy man." Doris sat down in a chair. "His ship went down in the Pacific." She sighed. "He wanted children; I would have liked that. But it turned out he left me this building."

Addie gasped. "You own this apartment house?"

"Yeah, and I've tried to bring good families into it. Single girls, too, like Ruth, who need a respectable place to live."

Addie hesitated, then trusted she could confide in Doris. "Al doesn't have the money for a house." She told Doris the story of meeting Mabel and the problems at Dunn's.

Doris sighed again. "I hope, for Ruth's sake, Al untangles all of his complications." She tapped her glass with a finger. "They could live here, start out in Ruth's apartment." She rose and carried the plates to the kitchen.

"What are you saying?"

From the kitchen, Doris called, "You move over here with me."

Addie straightened up at the idea.

Doris returned carrying two plates of sponge cake piled with cherries and whipped cream. She placed them on the table,

sat down. "I have the largest apartment in the building." She
took a forkful of cake. "You'll have your own bedroom. You'll
be across the hall from Ruth."

"You've thought this through, like you planned it."

"No, just came to me when you told me about their money
troubles. Seems like a plan, though, right?" Doris speared a
cherry with her fork, swirled it in the cream, and popped it in
her mouth.

Addie looked into the living room. Doris had cozy chairs
near her RCA console radio. Pillows and the afghans she had
crocheted were on the settee. The corner dining alcove where
they sat was comfortably large enough for the oak table and six
chairs. Addie imagined Thanksgiving dinner, Ruth and Al at
the table, the baby seat in the corner. What Doris offered made
sense. It would spare Ruth the trouble of moving before the
baby came, while Al figured a way out of his money problems.
Rooming with Doris was better than trying to find another
place she could afford. Would Ruth and Al go for the idea?

Addie blinked away her reverie. "Doris, you are very
kind, but why?"

Doris set her fork on her plate. "Look, I've got a building
full of people and none of my own. I'm fond of you and Ruth.
This is something I can do. Why not try? No strings attached."

"I may not be a good roommate."

"If I do the cooking, we'll be fine."

Addie laughed. It was worth the try. She raised her coffee
cup. "I'd like that." Doris clinked her cup against Addie's.

After they washed the dishes, Doris showed Addie the bedroom she would have. A table lamp glowed next to a four-poster
bed covered with a pink chenille spread. A chest of drawers,

armoire, an armchair, and a small desk by the window, framed with gauzy curtains. Doris stood in the doorway as Addie walked around the room, ran her hand along the desk. She looked at Doris and smiled. "It's perfect."

"I'll talk with Al about the lease for Ruth's apartment." Doris chuckled. "Men need to think they're in charge."

Addie went across the hall feeling a peacefulness about Doris's generous offer. The humidity had abated and the night air cooled. In bed, she drew the sheet over her bare legs, closed her eyes. She would convince Al that he must accept the plan, for Ruth's sake. With Al's help, she could rearrange Ruth's apartment for the couple. Addie had ordered the baby crib and chest of drawers as a gift for them; Hudson's could deliver the furniture to the apartment after Ruth came home. Addie turned over for sleep, satisfied that things were looking up.

The next morning, Mr. Reed waved to her as she passed by his office on the way to put away her things. She hoped he would allow her the time to arrange the furniture delivery. It was the day of the month when she went to his office to review her inventory and charge-back accounting for the Print Shop. Mr. Reed had added the monthly report to her duties after the special paper issue. She retrieved her ledgers from the counter and walked back to his office, knocked on the open door. Mr. Reed pointed to the chair in front of his desk. "Come in, Miss. Let's see the ledgers."

Addie started in on her report. Company practice was to treat the costs for departments' print jobs as debits against their budgets. Hudson's expected the shop to be efficient with paper, supplies, and equipment, to lower operating costs. For the period including the July Fourth advertising, the shop expenses met its budget.

Mr. Reed sat back and hooked a finger over the pocket watch tucked into his vest. "Well done, Miss. Take the summary sheet upstairs today."

Addie nodded and accordion-folded the extended ledger sheets back into the binder. She took a breath before making her request. "Mr. Reed, would you allow me a short time to go to the Infants Department regarding a personal order?" She saw his eyebrows shoot up and rushed to add, "A gift for my sister and her husband."

The corners of Mr. Reed's mouth turned up in what Addie had come to know as approval. "Miss, you have an appointment today. You might see to the order after the business."

"An appointment?"

Mr. Reed pushed a file folder across his desk. "I was asked to put forward a suitable candidate for an education program. I named you, and Mrs. Reynolds has accepted the nomination." He nodded at the folder. "The program information is there. Mrs. Reynolds will see you at eleven o'clock."

Addie opened the folder to read the headline on the sheet inside: Junior Accounting Program. "Mr. Reed, what does this mean?"

"The store will sponsor you to enroll in the Wayne University junior accounting program. You will work in the Print Shop on a part-time schedule."

"But ... what does this cost? I don't know how ..."

"The J. L. Hudson Company pays the tuition." Mr. Reed tapped a finger on his blotter. "Miss, this is an opportunity. Read the information, meet with Mrs. Reynolds, decide if you want to pursue it." He flicked open his pocket watch. "You have my permission to use the time before lunch as you need."

Addie looked him in the eye. "Thank you, Mr. Reed." She gathered the folder and ledgers, stood to leave. He clicked his watch closed. "Don't be late for Mrs. Reynolds."

Addie checked the wall clock as she left his office. She had an hour before the appointment with Mrs. Reynolds. She retrieved her handbag from her locker, then went to the front. Joe, perched on her stool at the counter, slid off when he saw her. "Keep the seat, Joe. I'll be away from the shop until lunch." Addie stowed the ledgers, removed her smock, transferred her name pin to her dress. Not answering Joe's puzzled look, she tucked the folder under her arm, said, "Hold the fort."

In the hall, she took a deep breath. She hadn't told Joe where she was going because she didn't know what she was getting into.

She took the elevator to the cafeteria and bought a coffee. The staggered lunch hours had not begun. She and a smattering of others had the empty-table quiet to themselves. Addie sat near a window, sipped the coffee, opened the folder.

Hudson's was one of the Detroit companies sponsoring students in the Junior Accounting Program at Wayne University to promote "workforce development." Two years of study prepared students for first-level accounting jobs. She read, "Candidates must pass a qualifying test to verify their capacities in the necessary personal traits to succeed." Addie ran her finger over the phrases "high scores in school for arithmetic," "neat work habits," "organized approach to large amounts of detail." She was good at arithmetic. Mr. Reed had recommended her, so he must be satisfied with her work habits. She had doubted he would train her for the print work, but he had thought her suitable for this program. She whispered, "Thank you, Mr. Reed."

If she passed the entry test, she would travel uptown to the college campus twice a week for classes. In the brochure were photos of girls studying side-by-side with young men. Their heads bent over ledgers, pencils in hand, or their attentive expressions fixed on professors pointing to chalkboards. Addie had never contemplated going to college. Could she be one of them?

The cafeteria clock clicked over to two minutes before eleven. Addie dreaded having to appear before Mrs. Reynolds, the Great and Powerful Oz of Hudson's. Addie scrambled the papers back into the folder, hooked her purse on her arm, and left her mug on the counter as she dashed out of the cafeteria.

She paused at the door to Personnel; no time to comb her hair or check her lipstick. She opened the door and Susan jumped up from her desk. "Addie, thank goodness. I was just about to take the group through to Mrs. Reynolds."

Three young men wearing Hudson's green blazers huddled in the center of the room, hands in pants pockets. One held his head at an angle with a bored expression; one stood stiff, wide-eyed; the third grinned at her. Susan smoothed her skirt, tapped her desk with a pen to get their attention. "Follow me to the conference room where Mrs. Reynolds will see you." She motioned for Addie to walk beside her. She spoke softly. "Congratulations, Addie. You must be excited."

"I'm confused ... and terrified."

They came to a meeting room with a long table, twelve chairs on each side, and a larger chair at the head. Addie was relieved to see placards with their names showing where they were to sit. Susan ushered them to stand behind their chairs. Lucille swished into the room, raised an eyebrow in their direction, held the door open. Mrs. Reynolds strode to the executive chair. She wore a style featured in the Woodward Shop, an all-green trouser outfit, the sleeves of her white silk blouse ballooning from the fitted vest. Addie hoped Mrs. Reynolds would notice that her dress too was from the Woodward Shop—last season's sale item, but still. Lucille closed the door.

Mrs. Reynolds sat. Lucille flipped her fingers downward to signal the four employees to take their seats. Mrs. Reynolds moved her eyes over them one by one. Addie held rigid, hands clasped in her lap, back straight. Next to her, the boy with the bored face eased his chair back, crossed his legs. Across the table, the other two leaned their arms on the table, hands folded.

Mrs. Reynolds spoke. "Hudson's has nominated you for the accounting program at Wayne University in its new School of Business Administration. Our executives are among the leaders of Detroit commerce sponsoring students, especially returning veterans."

The bored one interjected, "Then why is she here?" Addie felt her face go red. Mrs. Reynolds shifted her gaze to the interrupter. "She was nominated by her manager, as were you all."

"She's taking a spot from a man."

Mrs. Reynolds folded her hands on the table. "She is not. The list of suitable male candidates is limited to those of you here."

Bored One shrugged as though he did not believe her. Mrs. Reynolds steeled her eyes on him. "Is that all?" He shrugged again.

Mrs. Reynolds looked away from him to the group. "The company expects you to honor Hudson's reputation by achieving the degree. However, the company makes no promise of an accounting position once the degree is awarded." She let that sink in for a moment and rose. "Susan will provide the details you require. Good luck with your studies." Lucille opened the door and Mrs. Reynolds swept out of the room.

Susan handed a booklet and a bundle of forms to each of them as she gave them instructions. They would take the qualifying test the next morning in the same room. They should fill out the various forms and bring those to the test. Susan asked for any questions and answered the few the others had. The talk went on over Addie's bewilderment. She flipped through the papers. A calendar in the folder showed the classes beginning the day after Labor Day. A sheet showed her adjusted work schedule throughout the semester. All had been planned without her knowledge or consent. The Hudson's way. She heard one of the others ask, "Is our pay reduced with our hours?"

Susan shook her head. "No. You will have hours in the classroom plus the study time and your work in the store, so no pay reduction." The four students-to-be exchanged a relieved glance.

The men rose to leave. Susan reminded them of the next day's test time. When Addie and Susan were alone, Susan said, "Do you have questions?"

"Should I do this?"

Susan leaned in. "You want to be a bookkeeper? This is the way."

"Is it true she selected me because there were no men?"

"There were no other men Mrs. Reynolds considered appropriate. She wanted four candidates."

Addie walked with Susan to her office, promised to be on time for the test. She checked her watch and hurried to the elevator. She would run into the shop to get her sandwich, then to the tower. Joe would have a million questions.

When Addie returned to the Print Shop, Mr. Reed, Joe, and a cluster of the men were standing at the counter. Two of them unfurled a paper banner that read "Best of luck, Addie" and everyone burst into applause. Addie felt tears spill down her cheeks. Joe came to her rescue with his handkerchief. Addie dabbed her eyes. "Thank you, everyone. Mr. Reed, thank you for nominating me."

Mr. Reed hooked his thumb on his vest, rocked on his heels. "We expect the best from you." He turned to the men, and they took the cue. Two of them tacked the banner on the wall, and the others strode to their machines.

Addie went to the lockers to get her lunch bag. She met Joe in the hall, waiting to go up to the tower. "I hear it's you and three guys."

"How did you find out?"

Joe winked. "My sources are top secret."

"I still have to pass the test tomorrow."

"You'll pass," Joe said as they got in the elevator. "Mr. Reed is in your corner."

"Don't say anything in the tower, Joe," Addie pleaded. "It's not official yet and I need to think about this."

"Okay, but what's there to think about? This is your ticket."

When they got to the tower, her stomach roiled; she couldn't eat her lunch. Addie realized she had not gone to Infants about the furniture delivery. She told Joe she had to make a call and hurried down to the elevator. Addie made her way to Infants and arranged the delivery date for her order. Then she took an elevator to the ground floor and walked outside into the sunshine. She settled on the steps of the library across the street.

Addie thought of Miss Ames standing tall at the front of the high school class, what she had said: "Girls, you must persevere through the details to arrive at the satisfaction of the result." What would she say if Addie told her she was scared? Miss Ames would expect her to push fear aside and jump at this opportunity.

Addie rose, dusted off her skirt, and marched back to the Farmer Street entrance. She would persevere.

CHAPTER 13

Al telephoned Addie in the Print Shop on Friday morning, a week before they were to travel up north for the Labor Day weekend. Ruth had been in the grip of a migraine for five days, he said. "The pills aren't working. We can't wait until next weekend to bring her back. I'm driving up to the lake tonight. I need you to come with me." Al picked Addie up outside Hudson's at the end of her workday, then waited in the sedan while she ran inside her apartment building and threw clothes into a satchel.

Doris trailed Addie to the car, handed Al a bag of sandwiches. "I'll tidy the apartment for Ruth."

Al had not moved in yet. He had given Doris a frank outline of his finances, including the situation at Dunn's. She had offered a year's lease at the same rent Ruth paid.

Al drove with the windows open, staring ahead, jaw clenched. Addie scrunched into the passenger seat, a blanket around her shoulders, craving the clarity of the cool air as the miles took them north. She had no chatter; her mind raced with worry for Ruth. Miles of dark farm fields, interrupted by random railroad crossroads and filling stations, blurred by. Hand-painted signs near the odd general store pointed to turnoffs for this or that lake hidden from view by forests of gigantic fir trees. They had the road alone for long stretches, and Al kept a steady speed. She didn't ask him to stop. He pulled off only once, for a quick fill-up.

Addie mulled over her years with Ruth at home. Ruth said the migraines began when she was twelve. Wispy recollections tapped at Addie like branches on a windowpane during a rainstorm. After her father remarried, Addie had been sent to his house to stay for days at a time. Did the family send her away when Ruth had the headaches? Had she been too noisy, too bratty, to cope with when Dan and Jane worried over Ruth? Addie understood their keeping her away when she was little, but as she got older, shouldn't she have helped care for Ruth? Ruth said the family kept all the bad things from Addie. Over the years, they had dismissed the gaps between her memories and theirs with "You didn't need to know." But didn't that leave her out? Protecting her had kept her apart. Not only because she was a baby when their mother left, but because they decided not to let her know things that happened. She felt their exclusion, like when her old aunt sniffed at a "foreigner." Not of them.

Yet she was the one on the way to care for Ruth now.

The sedan bumped off the main road onto a gravel two-lane framed by a canopy of trees. Bugs and bats flew across the headlights and up into the overhanging branches. Another turn at a fork onto the dirt road that skirted the lake. The headlight beams caught the signs naming the camps, painted on wood planks nailed to trees where the foliage separated into a turnoff. Al slowed and turned onto a grassy path rutted by car tires. The ruts widened into a clearing and broad gravel driveway. Lights inside a log house revealed Al's friends, Norma and Guy, keeping watch from a screened porch. The couple hurried to the car.

Al jammed the gearshift into park and jumped out. "How is Ruth?"

Guy shook Al's hand. "She had a rough day. She's asleep now, worn out."

Norma came around the car to hug Addie. "You must be Addie. Ruth will be happy to see you."

The men retrieved the bags from the car's trunk and followed Addie and Norma inside. A row of tall windows set along the living room and dining area of the house faced the lakeshore. Immense fir trees dotted the lawn, sloping down to the water and docks. Pot torches blazed along the downslope path and to both sides, lighting the walkways to the cabins on the property. The lake reflected hints of the moonlight behind puffs of cloud mixed with emerging stars. Bright spots from camps around the lake sparkled along the shoreline.

An enormous chandelier of interwoven antlers hung from the vaulted ceiling of the log A-frame. Two basset hounds lazed on the stone floor before the fireplace, open to the living area and to the dining table on the other side. A cluster of cozy armchairs and ottomans, lamps, and bookcases decorated the space, with a game table tucked into a corner.

Addie looked at Al as she spoke to Norma. "Can we check on Ruth?"

Norma nodded. "She's in one of our bedrooms. You'll be in the next room."

A hallway off the entry led to four bedrooms also facing the water, with a sitting room, two bathrooms, and a laundry

room on the backside. Norma stopped at the open door of a
bedroom, reached in to flick a light switch, and set Addie's
satchel on a chair. With her finger to her lips, she led Addie
and Al to the closed door of the next room. Norma cracked it
open; a ray of the hallway lamplight leaked inside. Addie sidled
around the door, Al at her back. In the darkness, Addie heard
Ruth's deep breathing. With a sigh, Addie whispered to Al,
"Thank goodness she's asleep." They slipped into the hallway,
and Norma closed the door with a soft click.

Addie asked, "How often is she having headaches?"

Norma pursed her lips. "The last two weeks, more days
with pain than not."

Al pulled a bottle from his pocket. "Dr. Tullen prescribed
something different for her." Addie realized she hadn't thought
to call the doctor. He had known to do that.

Norma led them to the dining table where Guy met them
with a platter of hamburgers. He poured Al a glass of beer and
offered Addie iced tea. Norma sliced juicy ripe tomatoes. After
a few bites, Al sat back. "I can't thank you enough for taking
care of Ruth."

Guy wiped his mouth. "Ruth's a great gal. When she's well,
she plays games with the guests' kids in the evenings."

Norma said to Addie, "I scrounged larger blouses from
ladies around here, but she needs skirts. You'll see the change."

The talk petered out amidst yawns around the table. When
Al checked on Ruth again, she seemed deeply asleep, and he
claimed that the cot on the screened porch was fine for him.
Addie thanked Norma and Guy and went to wash up. She
climbed into the soft feather bed and snuggled into the coziness of the flannel sheets and quilts. She awoke to see the sun

creeping up, not remembering having fallen asleep. Her first thought was Ruth.

She had forgotten a robe, but a woolly wrap hung on a hook on the back of the bedroom door. Addie pulled it around her, slipped on her canvas shoes, and went into the hall. Ruth's door was ajar. Addie gave it a gentle push, saw sleeping Ruth on her back, one arm flung over her head on the pillow. Al, in the clothes he had on the night before, sat in an armchair sipping from a mug. He motioned Addie in, whispered, "She made it through the night. That's a good sign."

Addie stepped closer to the bed. Ruth's belly under the sheet looked twice as large as when Addie had watched Dr. Tullen measure her. Addie held back an impulse to place her hand there, conscious of Al watching her. Ruth's hair had grown as well, the longer locks matted from lying in bed. She had gained fullness in her arms and legs. A light tan and sunburned nose replaced her city paleness. Addie figured Norma had painted Ruth's nails bright red, as she had noticed last night hers were the same shade.

Al rose from the chair, stepped into the hallway with Addie following. He said, "If you want to wait for her to wake, I'll get you some coffee." In that moment, Al reminded Addie of her brother George, between her and Ruth in age, who had returned from the Navy a handsome, confident, capable man, someone they could depend on. Addie knew she had been harsh with Al, and while she did not regret her wariness, she felt relief in relying on him like a brother.

"Thanks, I'll get dressed, then coffee." She hesitated before going into her room. "Are you ready for this baby?"

Al half-smiled, shrugged his shoulders. "I have to be. Are you?"

"With Ruth so frail, I have to help."

"Ruth is stronger than you think."

"I hope so."

Addie stepped into her room and closed the door. She gathered her things for the bathroom, the question repeating in her mind: Are you ready? Ruth could not do this alone. Ruth needed Al. Ruth would need her, too.

In the bathroom, Addie gazed into the mirror. What if, someday, Addie needed Ruth's help with a new baby? That prospect seemed unreal, but still. They had only each other. Dan, or even Jane, would get on a train to Detroit as soon as asked, but that wasn't the same as relying on a close-by sister. The family had left her out of so much; there was no protecting her now. She was Ruth's support.

After washing and dressing, Addie strolled in bare feet to the kitchen for a mug of steaming coffee. When she passed by the living room windows, open to the air, the peacefulness of the lake, the birds singing, the trees, loosened her tense shoulders. No persistent hum of the city, no traffic noise.

In Ruth's room, window shades behind the curtains confined the bright morning sun to peeking in at the borders when a breeze moved them inward. Addie settled into the armchair and sipped. She imagined surprising Ruth with her announcement—"I'm going to college!"—and the story of her nomination to the accounting program. She rehearsed a replay of the words between Mrs. Reynolds and the bored guy who challenged her.

Susan had told Addie privately that her score on the entry test was the highest among the Hudson's group. That lowered Addie's anxiety a notch, but it rose again when she had visited the campus. She had to check the map again and again to keep her bearings. She didn't know what a "bursar" was, and panicked before a kind woman in Administration handed Addie the paper verifying Hudson's payment of the tuition, told her how to register for her classes. In the college bookstore, the clerk rang up her books with a cheery, "Welcome to Wayne."

"Coffee." Ruth's voice was husky as she slowly pushed up on the pillows. "Don't ask me how I feel."

Addie whispered, "Hello, Ruth," and took the mug to her, held it steady until she was sure of Ruth's grasp. Their eyes met as Ruth took a sip of the brew. "Hello. I must look a fright."

"We can fix that when you're feeling up to it." Addie sat on the edge of the bed. Ruth sighed, took another sip, rested the mug on her belly, and closed her eyes. A dove cooed outside; the wind rustled the trees and pushed against the window blind. Addie was about to reach for the mug when Ruth jerked forward, sending a spray of coffee onto the sheet. "I'm going to be sick!"

Addie grabbed the mug, jumped up, looked for something to place under Ruth's chin. A child's sand bucket sat on the floor next to the bed. She grabbed it, nestled it against Ruth just before she gagged.

Norma bustled in. "There, there, Ruth, it's okay, dear." She nodded at the bucket. "This happens in the mornings. Hold her hair back. I'll get a towel."

Addie gathered Ruth's curls into a bundle, swiped the hair off her forehead. Ruth heaved a few more times, then lay back. Tears squeezed from the corners of her closed eyes.

Norma came back with the towel, took the bucket from Ruth and handed it to Addie. "I'm wiping your face, Ruth. If you want to wet your lips, Addie will get water."

Ruth rasped, "No."

Norma dabbed Ruth's face and neck. "Can we do anything for you?"

Ruth's eyes fluttered. "Sleep."

Norma covered Ruth with the sheet, and she and Addie stepped into the hall. Norma sighed. "The pills make her sick. If she sleeps, her stomach might settle. Let's clean up and talk in the kitchen."

Al, in clean clothes, emerged from the bathroom. Seeing the bucket and the worry on their faces, he said, "Is Ruth …"

Addie said, "She's been sick, but she's asleep again. We'll be in the kitchen."

He ran a hand through his wet hair, strode past them to the sitting room where he had left his rucksack.

Norma was pouring pancake batter on the griddle when Al joined them in the kitchen. Addie arranged plates, poured coffee. When they sat down to eat, Norma told them about Ruth's pattern of days with pain and slow resolve. Norma had nursed her through the episodes, trying different remedies to bring her some comfort. Norma had also called Dr. Tullen. Al nodded along as Norma talked; it was clear to Addie they had been in regular touch about Ruth.

"You know, Al, it's for the best, not getting the house," Norma said. "Ruth needs to rest until the baby, not worry about moving."

"I hope she can."

Addie said, "What if the migraines don't stop?"

Al pointed to the bottle of pills on the sideboard. "That new medicine is stronger. Dr. Tullen wants to see her when we get back to town." He held out his hands. "All we can do is take care of her."

They decided on a rotation of turns in the sitting room to keep a close ear on Ruth. Al took the first turn, and a second plate of pancakes. Norma invited Addie outside to walk around the property.

The morning air was crisp. Addie thrust her hands in her jacket pockets, breathed deeply, tried to relax her shoulders. Norma's commentary about cabins and fishing and canoes was a sidetrack to her worry. How would Ruth get through the three months before the baby with the headaches? She would be alone all day while Addie and Al were working. She was too woozy to get out of bed. What if she was sick like this after the baby was born?

Addie realized Norma had stopped talking. They circled back to the beach. The lake ripples lapped at the rowboats and canoes berthed on the pebbly sand. Norma pulled Addie toward a log bench, brushed leaves off the seat. "What's on your mind?"

Addie sat, felt tears welling in her eyes. "You know what Ruth always says? 'I'll manage.' No matter what happens. But I don't know."

Norma put an arm around Addie. "Guy and me don't come down much. But if you need us, you call."

Before Addie could answer, Guy shouted Norma's name. He hobbled along the path toward them, waving his arms. Norma and Addie jumped up and trotted to him. "She's taken a turn. Al needs yous."

Addie ran. She burst into the house, heard Ruth scream. In the bedroom, Al leaned over Ruth's flailing arms and legs, trying to enfold her close to him, his voice low and steady. "I've got you, Ruth. Lean into me. I've got you." He got her legs against him with one arm, pulled her body to his chest. Ruth pushed against him, moaning, and her head rolled back. When he saw Addie, Al said, "Run a hot bath."

Addie whirled into the hallway, bumped into Norma already sprinting to the bathroom. She turned on the tap in the tub full blast. "Sometimes a bath calms her." Steam from the hot water rose and Norma closed the window. Addie slipped out and closed the bathroom door. She watched Al scoop Ruth up and lock his arms around her. Ruth lay limp against his chest. Addie pushed open the bathroom door and Al carried Ruth into the steam. Addie followed and shut the door.

Al dunked Ruth into the bath feet first, let the water creep up her legs, then her middle. He eased her bottom and her back to rest against the tub, then grabbed under her arms to hold her head above the water. "Fold a towel for under her neck."

Addie rolled a towel and held it in place as Al eased Ruth back. Ruth moaned but didn't fight. He knelt on the floor, his arm across Ruth's chest to steady her.

Norma set more towels in a pile next to the tub. "I'll make a hot water bottle for when we get her back in bed." She slipped out of the bathroom.

"How do you know what to do?" Addie asked.

With his free hand, Al pushed Ruth's wet hair back. "I don't know how to make it stop."

Addie crouched next to Al. "I'm afraid she'll never be well."

"I can't think like that."

Ruth's wet nightdress clung to her belly. Addie leaned in and rested her open palm there. She felt a flutter under her fingers. The surprise of the movement jerked her head up, and she met Al's eyes watching her. She lifted her hand away, and he put his in the same spot. After a moment, he closed his eyes and smiled.

Addie sat back on her haunches. Al shifted his hand slightly, then drew it out of the water. "You know what that is, right?"

Addie nodded. "I've read Dr. Spock's book. Twice."

They sat for a time, watching Ruth. Her body had relaxed, her eyes opened, then closed again. Al spoke to her. "You're okay, Ruth. I'm going to lift you out." Ruth squeezed his arm.

Addie held a towel ready to wrap around Ruth as Al raised her out of the water and propped her against him. Ruth, unsteady, stayed upright within the circle of Al's arms. Addie dried Ruth's legs and feet with another towel.

Ruth shivered. Al shifted her away from his chest enough to peel the towel from her shoulders. "Addie, unbutton her nightdress. We'll pull it down and re-wrap her in dry towels."

Addie's hands shook and she avoided Al's eyes. Embarrassment about undressing her sister in front of him collided with her realization that he had done this himself before. She undid the buttons and worked one and then the other of Ruth's shoulders and arms out of the sopping fabric. Al got another towel over Ruth's breasts as Addie pulled the nightdress down her hips. Al lifted Ruth for Addie to grab the gown away from her ankles.

Addie, on her knees, faced Ruth's belly. The stark reality of the baby brought tears to Addie's eyes. She kept her head down as she wrapped a towel around Ruth's middle. When Addie stood, Ruth, encircled in Al's arms, opened her eyes. "Thank you, Addie," Ruth whispered.

Al carried Ruth to the bedroom, seated her on the edge of the bed. Addie pinned up her hair, eased Ruth's arms into a clean gown. Al laid Ruth onto sheets Norma had changed. Addie left him with Ruth and collapsed into a chair on the porch overlooking the lake. Norma and Guy were on the lawn moving the picnic tables together to serve lunch for their cabin guests. They began unpacking bundles of food brought from the kitchen. Norma saw Addie and motioned for her to join them.

Al came onto the porch. "We're driving home tonight." Addie stood and looked at him. Al ran his hand through his hair. "She's got to see the doctor. The ride will be rough on her, but doing it in the dark is easier than daylight."

Addie nodded. "I'll telephone Doris."

Al gazed at the lake, hands gripping the back of a chair. "When I was a kid, we camped all summer on this lake." He blew the air from his lungs. "Wish I could make life that simple now." He went to the porch door, pushed it open and let it slam shut as he strode toward the water. He waved away Norma's offer of food, went to sit on the dock.

Addie met Guy at the grill to get a hot dog. Norma introduced her to the guests having lunch. Addie let Norma pile potato salad on her plate, poured herself a glass of iced tea from the jug, took a place on the picnic bench. Norma nestled next to her.

"Al says we'll drive home tonight."

Norma folded her arms on the table. "Hate to see you go, but she does need to see the doctor."

"Can I use your telephone to call our landlady?"

Doris reacted with her usual steadiness when she heard. She would stay up, she insisted, waiting for their arrival.

Addie kept watch over Ruth for the afternoon, packed Ruth's things and the few of her own. Ruth slept on and off, sipped water, took a few spoons of Norma's broth. Addie didn't see Al until he came to the table for the supper that Norma insisted they eat before leaving. Addie, glad for it, dug into her plate, but Al had little appetite.

After coffee, Al and Guy packed the trunk of the car with the bags and a hamper of fruit and tomatoes Norma was sending home with them. She brought out pillows and blankets to cushion Ruth's ride. Al instructed Addie before going inside to get Ruth. "Prop her against you, have the bucket ready." Norma had placed the sand bucket on the floor in the back seat. Addie waited with Guy by the car while Norma and Al fetched Ruth.

Addie said, "I don't know how to thank you."

"Just bring that baby here, soon as yous can. Norma don't have none of her own."

Ruth cried through her goodbyes to Norma and Guy. Norma cried after Addie and Ruth were settled in the back seat of the sedan. Addie circled her arm around Ruth, blankets tucked over their legs. Al shook hands with Guy, bent for Norma's kisses, got into the driver's seat, and pulled away with a light tap on the horn.

CHAPTER 14

Addie and Al hovered nearby as Dr. Tullen examined Ruth on Sunday afternoon at the apartment. Ruth was listless as a rag doll under his hands. She could not keep her eyes open in the light, moaned when he lifted her eyelids. Finished, the doctor pulled the sheet over Ruth's middle and picked up his bag. Al led the way to the living room.

"Keep her calm, resting," the doctor directed. "This migraine is waning. Get her to eat, start with plain foods, as much as she can. If her pain worsens again, call me."

Al wiped his brow. "Is there something wrong?"

"The baby measures small, but the heartbeat is steady." Dr. Tullen put on his hat. "Pregnancy has made her headaches more frequent and more painful. But she's far enough along now that she should stabilize."

Al walked Dr. Tullen to his car. From the window, Addie watched the two men shake hands, and the doctor drive off. Al bounded up the steps and Doris opened her door when he reached the landing. He waved her to follow him and held the door to the apartment open for her. When she entered, Doris exchanged a look with Addie.

Al closed the door and ran his hands through his hair. "Until she's steady on her feet, Ruth needs one of us here all the time."

Addie spoke up. "I'll come straight home from work. Be here evenings, while you're at Dunn's."

"What about your classes?"

It surprised Addie that Al remembered she had told him about starting college. "Classes start *next* week. My schedule changes then."

Doris nodded. "I'll be here while the two of you work."

Al sank into the armchair. "Thank you. If you get Ruth to eat, maybe—"

"One day at a time," Doris interrupted. "Addie, come with me into the kitchen to make a grocery list. You can shop tomorrow on the way home."

Their routine fell into place. By Thursday, when Addie came in after work, Ruth was sitting in the armchair and smiled. A breeze wafting through the windows hinted at a cool evening. Doris came out of the kitchen, drying her hands with her apron. "There you are, Addie girl. See how well Ruth is doing today?"

Addie sat on the davenport next to Ruth's chair, unbuckled her sandals. Grinning, she said, "Hello, Ruth, remember me?"

"Don't tease, Addie. I'm starting to feel like myself again. Doris is an angel."

Kicking away her shoes, Addie laughed. "Angel Doris, what is Ruth's supper tonight?"

"It's ready on the stove, table's set." Doris waved and left the apartment.

Ruth took Addie's arm to walk to the kitchen and settle in her chair. Addie chattered about the end-of-summer sales at Hudson's while she dished up the chicken with rice, peas, and corn. Doris had sliced the chicken thin and bite-sized, and simmered it in broth, so that a mouthful of the casserole needed almost no chewing. The aroma enticed Ruth to dig into her plate.

Addie had missed her sister over their weeks apart. She longed to tell Ruth about the many events that had happened at the store, anticipating Ruth's glee at hearing the gossipy stories. The tower lunchroom and the new friends she had made would surprise Ruth. And Ruth didn't yet know Mrs. Reynolds had chosen Addie for the college program. Addie was bursting to speak, but she held back while Ruth finished her food. *Was this patience*, she wondered. Ruth used to scold her as spoiled and willful. She had come to think being willful had its benefits. She did what she wanted. But spoiled was distasteful, like rotten food. Now, here she was, waiting, not tapping her foot. Addie set her fork on her plate, sat back with a smile.

The telephone rang.

Addie stood. "I'll get that." Ruth nodded, took another bite. Addie strode to the telephone table in the living room and grabbed the receiver. "Hello?"

"Addie, thank goodness you're there," Al said.

"Of course, I'm here."

"I mean, I've got bad news. It's going to be rough for Ruth to hear."

"What happened?"

"Loretta had her baby. It's not right."

"What do you mean?"

"Leonard said the doctor called in a specialist to figure out what's wrong. They didn't let Loretta see the baby."

"Oh! Oh, that's awful! What should I tell Ruth?"

"Don't tell her. I want to tell her."

"What if Loretta calls?"

"Don't let her talk to Ruth." Al's voice wavered. "Please, don't let her talk to Ruth."

"Okay, I understand." Al hung up. Addie placed the receiver in the cradle. Her gaze went to the tree outside the window where throngs of birds clustered among the branches for their evening warbling, like the instruments of an orchestra tuning all at once. She could go back to the table and make her announcement about college, pretend the call had been Al saying he'd be home early. She could give Ruth a bit more time not knowing about Loretta's baby. Ruth would know soon enough. And Addie wanted Ruth's attention. Addie flushed with a jolt of resentment toward Loretta. Soft-hearted Ruth would be entangled in her friend's despair, not look Addie's way once she heard. Addie knew she was being unfair. But still.

Ruth called to her. "Addie, who telephoned? Where are you?"

Addie stuck her hands in her pockets and strode back into the kitchen. "Al will be home early." She pushed Loretta out of her mind.

Ruth sipped her iced tea, nodded. "Tell me what's going on in the store."

"Well." Addie paused for drama, sitting back down. "Mrs. Reynolds selected me for the college program."

Ruth squealed with delight, grabbed Addie's arm across the table. As Addie told the story, Ruth's face lit with excitement. When Addie finished, Ruth's hands talked along with a rush of words about the wonderful opportunity Addie had.

Addie took in Ruth's delight, then confided her worry. "I don't know why Mrs. Reynolds chose me. Or if I can do this."

"Of *course* you can. Mrs. Reynolds does not tolerate failure. She wouldn't have chosen you unless she expected you to do well."

"She said we must be the best."

"And you *will* be."

"I hope so." Addie picked up their plates and ran water in the sink, added the dish soap. Ruth opened the evening paper to Hudson's advertisement for school clothes. "Have you been to the Hudson's High School Shop?"

Addie laughed. "Yes, indeed. The saleswomen were thrilled to fit me with skirts, blouses, sweaters, everything. When I tried on saddle shoes, the salesman told me the college girls like them scuffed up a bit." Addie shook her head. "How does he know that?"

Ruth laughed. "You'll fit right in." She brought the glasses to the sink for Addie to wash. "Al and I talked about the money, how you helped." Ruth put her arm around Addie's waist. "Thank you and thank you for moving over with Doris so we can get on our feet."

Her hands in the sudsy water, Addie bumped her hip against Ruth's. "Doris made it easy for me. We became friends while you were up north."

Ruth smiled. "You both make things easier for me. I mean it, thank you. For helping Al bring me home, and everything."

The apartment door opened and Al called out, "Ruth, I'm home."

Addie raised her brows, tilted her head toward the living room. "There's your cue, and mine." Addie didn't want to be there when he told Ruth about Loretta's baby. He had put her in the middle by asking her not to tell; she had gone along with him for her own reasons. Ruth might not understand that.

Ruth went to Al. Addie finished rinsing the dishes and wiped her hands with a towel. She heard the murmur of their voices in the other room, hoped Al would ease into the news about Loretta's baby. Addie went to pick up her sandals, purse, and hat. Al had taken Ruth into the bedroom. Addie let herself out.

Doris sat in her armchair with her knitting. Addie guessed the pastel yarns meant Doris was making another crib blanket for Ruth's baby. Addie plopped onto the davenport, watched the motion of the needles through loops of yarn.

Doris looked up, kept her hands moving. "How was dinner?"

"The casserole was delicious. But something happened." Addie filled Doris in on what Al told her about Loretta. "Al's with Ruth now."

"I am sorry to hear this." Doris held her knitting still. "Al will shoulder the burden with her."

"Ruth will fuss over Loretta."

"She will, yes."

"I came here hoping Ruth and I would be sisters, really, for the first time."

"Ruth needs a sister. Not another baby clutching at her." Doris's tone made Addie sit up. Doris softened her voice. "Look, Addie, honey, I don't mean to be harsh. Loretta's a dear friend she cares about. You're her sister. She trusts you. You stand by her, not cling to her."

Addie felt her face flush. Doris's words affected her as if Dan had spoken in her ear. He always said the six of them had a bond no one else could share. Addie fought with the old sitting-in-the-corner feeling and stood up. "I'm going to bed. Good night."

"See you in the morning." Doris rolled up her knitting.

When Addie had settled into bed, she pulled Dr. Spock's book from her nightstand. Addie had kept Myrtle's paperback and bought a new copy for Ruth. She turned to "Special Problems." She paged through twins and fatherless children and came to illnesses and birth defects. Loretta's baby might be the handicapped child, the deaf child, the blind child. One with cerebral palsy, infantile paralysis. Serious medical conditions. She slapped the book closed.

She pulled the lamp chain and settled on her side in the dark. If something like those problems had gone wrong for Loretta's baby, what might happen to Ruth's? Addie remembered the babies in the yard on the Fourth of July. Those children were fine, all of them. Not a single birth where the baby had a "special problem." Even if it had happened to Loretta's baby, she told herself, Ruth's baby would be fine.

In the morning, she woke to the aroma of brewed coffee. When she had dressed and clipped back her hair, she went to the kitchen and poured a cup, doused it with milk. Doris had gone across the hall for her talk with Al before he left for the day. He had been driving Addie to the store since he moved into the building. Neither one had named it their routine, but she hoped it was.

When she stepped into the hallway, Ruth's door was ajar. Doris stuck her head out. "Addie, 'morning. Al's gone down to the car." Doris tipped her head toward the inside of the apartment, and Addie took her meaning that Ruth was just inside.

"Okay, bye, Doris," Addie said, then called out, "Bye, Ruth, have a good day." She skipped downstairs and through the yard to the curb. Al stubbed out a cigarette and slid into the driver's seat, started the engine.

"Ruth said you quit those things." Addie slammed her car door.

"I did. Far as she knows. And I mean to. Just one for my nerves."

"How did Ruth take the news last night?"

Al pulled the car into the driving lane. "She is afraid for Loretta, but she's calm. She wants to see her, and the baby."

"Is that a good idea? What exactly is wrong with the baby?"

"Mongolism. Do you know what that is?"

Addie groaned. "Dr. Spock says that means the baby is slow in the brain."

"Leonard says the face doesn't look right, either. They don't know if it can learn to talk or do anything normal."

"Why are you saying 'it'? Did she have a boy or a girl?"

"A girl." Al glanced at Addie's face. "Sorry. The doctors advised them not to see the baby and get attached." He sighed, staring out the windshield. "Never thought I'd hear that man cry."

"I don't understand ... why?"

Al shrugged. "Because mongoloids are usually taken someplace, not home." He read the alarm on Addie's face. "Special hospitals. There's one near Kalamazoo run by nuns."

"They are going to give their baby to the nuns?" Addie's voice rose with her shock.

"They aren't sure what to do."

"What did Ruth say about that?"

"She wants to talk to Loretta." Al pulled to the curb on Farmer Street. "I'll call her later."

Addie waved as Al merged back into the traffic, then lingered on the curb, thinking. She should telephone Ruth, but she wouldn't know what to say. Loretta's baby had one of the worst problems Dr. Spock wrote about. Al had said Ruth was calm after hearing the news. Addie flashed back to the feel of Ruth's baby moving under her palm. How could Ruth be calm?

The tension in the car horns and brisk walks of those brushing by nudged her across the sidewalk to the entrance. Fridays were more hectic than other days, and the coming Labor Day holiday weekend ramped up the rush. It was the last day of her regular work schedule in the Print Shop. Addie took a breath, set her focus on organizing records and making lists for Joe as she pushed through the revolving door.

The tower crowd at lunch buzzed with talk of marching union-by-union in Monday's parade with thousands of other laborers. Addie promised to cheer them from the sidewalk. Joe scoffed. "You'll have to sleep on the curb the night before. The guys on the loading dock have a spot for us." Joe motioned to a man at another table, who saluted when Joe called to him, "Addie will see you Monday."

Before the end of their lunchtime, Joe showed Addie where to find a certain door on the street level. Metal stairs inside led to the stockrooms that ran the length of Woodward Avenue, with their second-floor windows open to the street view. Addie laughed at the cleverness of the arrangement. Hudson's was like a theater. The sales floors for the executives and the customers, and a beehive behind the scenes where the workers enjoyed the store. She promised to meet Joe on Monday to watch the parade.

The workday wound to a close. She stayed behind to update Mr. Reed on the status of the order book and pending issues for the next week. He clicked his pocket watch open and shut as she ran through her lists. "Miss, you're on an abbreviated schedule, not going around the world."

"Mr. Reed, I want to make sure nothing falls through the cracks."

"Miss, we will have no cracks. Go, have your weekend. We will see you on Wednesday."

Addie took her time going home. She got off the streetcar one stop before the usual and walked the remaining blocks to the apartment house. The mild temperature was luring people outside to visit on porches and side yards. Flags hanging from houses and storefronts fluttered in the breeze. She smelled the aromas of grilling meats and smoldering woodchips. She thought about starting on the reading for her class over the weekend. Al would be home on Saturday until Dunn's opened, and on Sunday all day. Addie would leave them alone, unless Ruth called for her.

When she opened the downstairs door, Doris's wagon sat half-loaded with baskets and bundles. Doris bustled down the steps with more in her arms. She sang out, "Addie, cards tonight! The girls are on the way."

Addie pulled off her hat and grinned. "Wonderful! How can I help?" When she had changed her clothes and washed her face, she joined Doris on the back porch. Setting out the candlesticks, Addie realized she had not checked on Ruth, and Doris had said nothing about Ruth's day. Before she could ask Doris, the gals arrived.

The group settled into the rhythm of the cards and chatter. The women were excited about Addie starting college. "You won't have to work a factory job like us," Patsy said as she shuffled the deck. "Get yourself situated better."

Addie didn't know how to answer except to say, "I hope so."

Patsy dealt the cards, saying, "I'm still looking for something. If nothing turns up, I'll be going back to waitressing." She bit her lip. "Not the same money."

Addie said, "Ma needs to hire someone at her place. She's building up the pie business. I can tell her about you." She saw Patsy narrow her eyes. "Only if you want."

Doris said, "Ma's diner is close to your house, Patsy. You wouldn't have to spend on carfare."

"You trying to talk me into something?" Patsy said to Doris. Doris flapped an arm at her. Patsy put down her cards, picked up her smokes. "Give me a minute to think about it." She went down the porch steps into the backyard.

Betty said in a low voice, "Patsy is bossy, you know. Likes to be in charge."

"Ma is bossy, too," said Addie. "Patsy says her mind. Ma likes that."

Patsy came back onto the porch. "Okay, I'll go see Ma."

Addie wrote out the address of the diner and the telephone number. "Ma will be back after Labor Day. Want me to go with you?"

Patsy waved away the suggestion. "Let her know to expect me. I'll go on my own."

Addie nodded. "I'll ask Tom to leave a note for her."

They played cards later into the night than usual. The winning hands rotated among them and all were in the mood to one-up the others. When Betty took three in a row, they called it a night.

After the friends had gone, Addie and Doris lugged the baskets and bundles up to the apartment. Addie looked over at Ruth's door. "It's too late to see Ruth. I'll knock in the morning."

Doris sighed. "I thought you knew. Ruth's gone to Loretta's house. She's staying there tonight."

"What? Does Al know?" Addie shook her head. "Of course he does. But why?"

"Loretta took her baby home. Ruth went to help her."

Addie checked her watch. "Dunn's is still open. I'm calling Al." She went to the telephone table in Doris's entryway and rummaged to find the tavern's number on a Dunn's matchbook. Doris began putting the leftovers into the refrigerator. Addie sensed Doris listening to her dialing.

Tom answered. "Evening, Dunn's."

Addie cringed at the chipper greeting, pushed back a smart remark. "Tom, put Al on." Addie could hear the voices of the tavern drinkers in the background.

"Addie!" Tom said. "Missed seeing you these last weeks."

He missed her? She heard him yell to someone, "Be right with you," then he said, "Busy here. Al's not here, went to Leonard's house."

"Do you have their telephone number?"

"Ahh, I don't."

"Never mind. Listen, leave a note for Ma. A woman is coming to see her next week about a job. Patsy's her name. Tell Ma I sent Patsy."

"Sure, I can leave the note. Patsy. Got it. When will you be over this way?"

"At the diner? Next Saturday."

"See you then." Tom hung up.

Addie pulled open the Detroit city directory and paged through the listings to find Leonard's name. Addie tapped her finger on the book. "This must be it." She wrote the number on the pad Doris kept by the telephone, picked up the receiver.

Doris flicked off the kitchen light. "Addie, it's late."

Addie said, "I need—"

Doris cut her off. "Al is with Ruth."

Addie sighed. "Oh, all right." She hung up the phone.

CHAPTER 15

Addie answered Al's early morning knock at Doris's door. He shrugged off her scrutiny of his rumpled shirt and wrinkled pants. "Do you have coffee?" Addie nodded and let him in. Al flopped into an armchair.

When Addie brought him a mug, he said, "Thanks. It was a long night. Tom said you called for me."

"You didn't tell me Ruth went to Loretta's."

"Never mind that. The big news is we cleaned out that card game at Dunn's last night. When I went back."

"What do you mean, 'cleaned out'?"

"I left Leonard's house and got back to Dunn's just at closing. The big guy in the game had gone up north for the weekend, left his cronies in charge. Tom and I took the chance to force them out. Two of our regulars stayed and backed us up. Four baseball bats coming at them broke up the game. They'll report what we did." He took a gulp of coffee. "Tom says we made it worse."

"What does he think will happen?"

"They can make us lose more than we've cost them."

"You have to protect your place."

Al scoffed. "Protection? Even if we pay, we can't win." He set down the mug. He pulled a paper from his pocket, handed it to her. "Ruth asked me to bring her clothes. Can you help me find this stuff?"

Addie read Ruth's tiny handwriting. "Is Ruth staying at Loretta's?"

"Until tomorrow. Leonard arranged for the priest to baptize their baby between the Masses. Ruth and I are the godparents." Al stood and stretched. "Give me half an hour to get cleaned up, then help me with Ruth's clothes?"

Addie nodded. "Can I call Ruth?"

Al said, "Best to wait for her to come home after the baptism. Or come with me to the church. Up to you." He let himself out.

Addie dressed and drank more coffee. She wasn't keen to go to the church, but she was curious about Loretta's baby. When she tapped on and cracked open the door across the hall, a showered and dressed Al was talking on the telephone. She walked past him to the bedroom.

She pulled open the closet and grabbed a satchel from the floor. A tumble of Al's shoes fell out. Ruth had arranged her heels on two low shelves, but there was no space for his man-sized Oxfords and boots. Addie fished out the wedges Ruth wanted. Al's suit coats and pants overloaded the hanging rod, shoving the softer fabrics of Ruth's dresses to one side. Addie needed both hands to shunt his clothes away from the dresses, then held them apart with her shoulder. She tugged and freed the green floral Ruth asked for. She rolled her eyes at the wrinkles—Ruth could not wear it like this. Addie backed out of the closet with the dress and stumbled against Al's feet behind her.

Addie found her footing and spun around. "Why are you behind me?"

"Bad timing—you didn't hear me walk in."

"I was buried in the mess in that closet." She shook out Ruth's dress. "I have to iron this."

Al nodded. "I'll get Ruth's undergarments and stockings." He opened the top drawer of the dresser.

Addie watched Al finger Ruth's lingerie. The easy intimacy of this man with her sister was both heartening and jolting. Her feeling of brotherly closeness to Al had grown since they had brought Ruth home from the lake. But she still guarded against fully trusting him. And men like Al—and Tom—stirred up confusion in her. Would she be able to love someone the way Ruth loved Al? Maybe she was too young, though plenty of her friends were already married. Or she differed from other girls.

Al's fumbling through the drawer had undone Ruth's neat folding. Addie reached in, plucked out the proper slip and the larger brassiere Ruth wore with the swelling of pregnancy, and dropped both into the satchel. Al said, "I should have let you do it." Addie sniffed and left the bedroom to set up the ironing board.

After Al drove off with the clothes, Addie found Doris in the shed at the back of the property, huddled with one of the neighbor men over the lawn mower, trying to find the cause of a stuck blade. "I want this yard trim for the Labor Day picnic." Doris wiped grease from her hands. "If we get this over to the repair shop, we might mow today." Addie helped them load the mower into the man's truck. Doris rode off with him.

Left on her own, Addie didn't want to sit home in the fine weather on her last free Saturday of the summer. She decided to pack lunch and bike to Belle Isle. Sandwiches made with leftovers from the previous night's card party, a handful of cookies, and a thermos of lemonade. Addie perused Doris's collection from the Hudson's branch of the Literary Guild Book Club. She tucked the latest Taylor Caldwell novel and her lunch into the bike basket.

The ride to the bridge reminded the muscles in her legs that she had not been on the bicycle for several weeks. On the island, Addie kept to the loop that circled around, planning to stop at a picnic table halfway. The river breezes modulated the warmth of the sun to cool her as she pedaled. She relaxed her shoulders, sat up on the bike seat, smiled at the walkers and riders she passed.

A bike horn tooted behind her. She steered to the right, kept her eyes forward. The horn tooted again. Tom pulled alongside her, grinning. He squeezed the bulb of his bike horn for another toot.

Addie shook her head. "What are you doing?"

"Saw you a mile or so back."

Addie pedaled faster. "You're following me?"

Tom matched her pace. "Catching up to you." He eyed her basket. "I bet you've got lunch."

Their bikes plowed through a puddle at a low point on the road. Tom pulled his feet up in time to avoid the spray. The muddy water splashed over Addie's canvas shoes. She groaned and braked to a stop. Water squished from her left shoe.

"I *was* having a nice Saturday before you came along."

"Aw, come on. I'm very nice."

Addie spotted a picnic table under a shade tree and slow-walked the bike to it. Tom followed. She leaned her bike against the table end and sat on the bench. She worked her fingers through the wet laces and pulled off the shoes, set them in the sun.

Tom dropped his bike on the grass, reached into her bike basket for the lunch bundle. He spotted the book and held it up with a snort. "Oh, man, what a title. *This Side of Innocence.*" He waved the book at her. "Which side of innocence are you on, hmm?"

Addie reached over and slapped his arm. He let the book fall into the basket. She stood and faced him. "You make fun of me and expect me to share my lunch with you?"

Tom held up his hands. "Truce, okay? I was teasing."

"You have to tell me what happened at Dunn's last night."

Tom raised his brows. "You talked to Al?"

Addie unwrapped the cloth bundled around the lunch, spread it over the rough table wood. "He didn't tell me much." She settled on one side of the table, pointed for Tom to sit on the other side. She placed a sandwich in front of him, poured lemonade.

"There's not much to it. We waved baseball bats and talked tough. Those guys weren't gonna draw blood when the big guy wasn't there to see their muscle. When word gets to him, though, they'll come back."

"Then what?"

"Al says we need leverage. Don't ask me—I don't know what angle he's working."

Addie munched on her sandwich, trying to keep from meeting Tom's eyes. Looking into his eyes disoriented her, like snow blindness. Yet having a picnic together seemed ordinary, as if they had done it before.

Then she remembered what Al said about Tom giving money to Mabel. She kept her eyes on her food. "Where is Mabel now?"

"Gone." Tom shook his head, said, "She got her money, she took off."

"Do you know where?"

"I don't want to know. Neither does Al." Tom crumpled his sandwich paper. He stood and stretched. "I'm meeting a fishing buddy before I head to the bar. Why don't you ride to the pier with me? You can read your book there."

She checked the dryness of her shoes. What was it about Tom? He was both aggravating and likeable. He was asking her to spend more time with him, and she wanted to. But she took her time lacing her damp shoes before she answered. "Okay—I can circle back to the bridge from there."

Tom didn't talk as they pedaled, and she relaxed into the ride. At the pier, Tom introduced her to his friend, picked up a rod, got right to the fishing. Addie settled on a nearby bench in the shade of the shoreline trees. She didn't get far into the book because she kept looking up to watch Tom. An hour passed. When he checked his watch and waved at her, she waved back. He walked his bike over to the bench. "Time for me to get to work. I'll ride you back."

"Thanks, but I'll stay a while longer." She swept her arm at the river. "Too nice to leave."

"Next time, we'll spend the day. Thanks for lunch. See you at the diner." Tom pedaled away.

Addie watched him pick up speed until she lost sight of him. Next time? Nervy to assume she wanted to spend a day with him. She opened the book to read but stared at the river flowing by. She breathed deep and turned her face to the sun. Tom had intrigued her from the first time she met him at Dunn's. The place brought back her memories of the roadhouse, but Tom gave her a giddy feeling, like having a secret Santa who left notes and trinkets leading up to Christmas. She rose, tucked her book into the bike basket, settled on the seat, and pushed off down the slope to cross in front of the pier. As she passed Tom's fishing buddy, he tipped his cap. What had Tom said to the man about her? She laughed and pedaled faster.

Doris was sweeping fresh-cut grass clippings from the walk when Addie returned to the apartment house. The two of them spent the late afternoon hours tidying the flower beds and bringing out the extra lawn chairs from the shed for the picnic. Doris watched while the men set up the barbeque drums, piling the wood and charcoal, ready for Monday. Their chores finished, Addie and Doris retreated to the shade of the back porch with cold drinks until almost dark. The neighborhood quieted to a few bird chirps and the cricket sounds.

Addie tapped a toe on the floorboard as she sipped, considered telling Doris about Tom. If she did, Doris would raise her eyebrows in that way she did, like she knew something Addie didn't. Before she could make up her mind, Doris asked, "You going to the baptism tomorrow?"

"I guess. Haven't been inside a Catholic church before."

"It's just like Ruth to stand by her friend."

Addie took that in. She remembered the closeness among the women at Loretta's stork shower, Ruth in their midst. Addie had cringed at being drawn into their fold, didn't understand what Ruth gained from the chatter and the hugging. Now, Addie saw the underlying promise. In Loretta's time of need, Ruth came to her aid, the way Doris did for Addie.

Addie said, "Doris, you're a good friend, too."

"Ah, Addie, don't get gooey on me," Doris said with a chuckle.

Just before dawn, Addie woke at the sound of a car door slam. From her window, she saw Al's car parked at the curb. He stood on the walkway, smoking a cigarette. He didn't seem at all hurt; the card sharks must have stayed away. Sundays, the bar was closed, and Al and Tom would not open on the Monday holiday. She went back to bed.

When her alarm clock jangled, Addie punched the knob down, sending the clock scuttling across the bed table and onto the floor. In the bathroom, she turned on the hot water for a sponge bath. Taking stock of her hair, Addie debated which of her hats would cover her head properly for the Catholic church. She finished in the bath, dressed, and made coffee.

Addie was downing a cup and biting into a slice of toast when she heard Al's tap on the door. She opened it, said, "I need five minutes." Already going down the stairs, he waved an arm to acknowledge he heard. Addie brushed her teeth, pushed her largest hat over her hair, and grabbed her handbag. Al paced alongside the car, then swung open the door for her to get in. Cigarettes sat on the dashboard. If he lit up, Addie knew Ruth would detect the tobacco smell. She said nothing as Al stowed them in the glove compartment. He pulled away with two hands gripped on the wheel, jaw set.

They drove without speaking through the Sunday morning streets, lively with church-going and the pre-holiday visiting among neighbors. Al's anxious mood settled on Addie. She checked her lipstick in her compact mirror, hesitated. Lipstick might not be allowed in a Catholic church. She pulled a tissue from her handbag and wiped her lips.

Al turned into the parking area for St. Hyacinth, stopping near a side entrance to the church. They went from the bright sunshine into the shadowy vestibule. Al removed his hat, led the way along the corridor to a double set of wooden doors studded with iron hardware. He strong-armed one door and held it for her.

Addie stepped into an alcove. At the far side, an archway opened to a view of the massive marble altar at the front of the church. Her gaze fixed on the brilliant blues and gold in the sunlit stained-glass windows framing the altar. Paintings in the same hues laced the ceiling and along the walls. Marble columns, more marble lining the walls. Around the altar was statuary, angels taller than she was, wings poised to the heavens. Gold embroidered linen on the altar. Behind it, on another altar, what looked like a box made of gold sat amidst tall vases of flowers. The air held the smoke of a dozen candles as fat as baseball bats set into gold pillars, and a scent that reminded Addie of burning apple wood chips.

Al touched her arm. She turned to see Ruth enter from a door in the recess. Ruth's belly mounded under the floral pattern sprayed across her dress as though they sprouted from there. Ruth's mouth turned up in a tired smile for Addie. Behind Ruth walked Father Dabrowski and a boy. A cape-like expanse of gold-and white-embroidered fabric covered the priest's black skirted robe. The boy wore a smaller version of the black robes under a too-large loose white tunic. He carried a tray holding gold vials and a gilded pitcher. Leonard escorted Loretta, holding the baby. Addie recognized the flowing christening gown and bonnet the baby wore as the outfit displayed at the stork shower, made by Loretta's grandmother. One little arm raised a fisted hand.

Father Dabrowski went to a marble basin set on a pedestal in the corner. The boy held the tray at the priest's elbow. Father nodded at Loretta. She came belly-to-belly with Ruth, staring at the baby as she settled her child in Ruth's arms. For a moment, Loretta kept her hands under the bundle of white. Tears ran down Loretta's face. Ruth pushed in closer to Loretta until their hat brims bumped. Loretta wriggled her hands away and Ruth tucked the baby at her chest. The baby protested with a wail.

Al took Ruth's elbow and together they stood before the priest, who gently laid his hand on the baby's head. Leonard put his arms around Loretta. The two of them kept their eyes on their child as Father began a chant in Latin. Addie couldn't follow the words but understood he was intoning prayers. Loretta mopped her steady tears with Leonard's handkerchief. Ruth stood tall, Al's hand at her back, the baby's gown draping over her arm. When Father paused, everyone except Addie said, "Amen."

The priest dipped a finger into a vial, smudged oil on the baby's forehead. Ruth slid the tiny white bonnet off and braced the baby's head over the edge of the basin. A fussy half-cry began when the priest raised the golden pitcher over the tiny forehead, intoned prayers, and sprinkled the water three times.

After the priest moved his hands over the child for the final blessing, Loretta reached to take her. Ruth whispered to Loretta, replaced the bonnet, tied the ribbons under the tiny chin. Leonard murmured thanks to the priest. Father and the boy left the alcove. Al clapped Leonard on the back, took him aside.

Ruth pulled Addie to Loretta. "Addie's here." Loretta raised her teary face to meet Addie's eyes. Addie looked from Loretta into the same dark eyes of the baby girl. The bonnet framed a round, flattish face. Addie sensed Loretta waiting for her to say something.

Addie smiled, whispered, "What is her name?"

"Margaret Mary."

Addie lifted one of the tiny fingers. "Hello, little Margaret Mary."

Leonard came to her side, and Loretta drew Margaret Mary up over her shoulder. Ruth and Al walked them to the door, whispering. When the door closed after them, Al shook his head, put an arm around Ruth. Ruth sniffled into her handkerchief. "Loretta's mother won't speak to them because Loretta will not send her baby to the nuns."

Al said, "Leonard's torn up."

Ruth said to Al, "I want to light a candle for them." Addie didn't follow. How would a candle help?

Leonard reappeared at the door, and called to Al. "I've got car trouble—can you believe it? Lend me a hand."

Al said to Ruth, "Sit for a few minutes while I help them." Ruth nodded, and Al followed Leonard outside.

Ruth linked her arm through Addie's and led her through the archway into the main part of the church. The boy who had assisted the priest was on the altar, lighting the candles with a long taper attached to a golden pole. Ruth stepped into one of the wooden pews that fanned out in front of the altar. She arched her back against the hard frame, patted the seat for Addie to sit. Addie nestled close, stared at the altar.

Ruth whispered, "I thought you might not come."

She matched Ruth's whisper. "I worried about you." Then she said, "Will Loretta be able to take care of Margaret Mary?"

"I hope she can."

"But her mother …"

"Her mother is wrong!" Ruth twisted on the bench to face Addie. "Any mother who gives up her child is wrong." Ruth shook her head. "You're lucky to not remember her."

Addie's lip trembled. "Don't say I was protected—or spoiled. It's worse for me than you. Dan keeps her picture. Having nothing to remember is worse." Tears spilled from Addie's eyes. She pulled the wadded handkerchief from Ruth's grip and held it to her face.

"We tried to protect you. Don't blame us for that."

"You blame me for being spoiled."

"Maybe we're all spoiled."

"What do you mean?"

"She ruined our lives."

"Are we *ruined*?"

Ruth stared at the altar. "Dr. Tullen says some mothers feel hopeless after they have a child, can't take care of the baby. Or don't want to." She saw the alarm on Addie's face. "What if that's in me, because of her?"

Addie sniffed back the tears. "You're not hopeless. *I* was the baby. Did she leave because of me?"

"Grandma used to say her daughter lost herself. Grandma got hopeless waiting for her." Ruth put her arm around Addie. "It was not because of you, or any of us."

"Wasn't I dear enough to my mother?" Addie sobbed.

Ruth took Addie's face in her hands. "You are dear to *me*. I treated you badly when we were young. I was *so* angry. I see that now." Ruth put her arms around Addie. "Help me be a good mother."

"You will be." Addie rested her head on Ruth's shoulder. Through her tears, she looked into the eyes of the Virgin Mary set in a niche in the marble wall. Mary's arms extended out to them, palms open, as if she could give them a hug. Addie nuzzled against Ruth, draped her arm across Ruth's belly.

Ruth whispered, "Don't let go."

CHAPTER 16

Addie woke, her face on a damp pillowcase, her nightgown twisted around her legs. The clock showed it was too late to join Joe at Hudson's for the Labor Day parade. She threw off the covers and got out of bed.

She had willed her tears to stop in the church, for Ruth's sake, but alone in her room that Sunday night, she had bawled until she fell asleep. Her father hated crying. He would warn her, "Stop or I'll give you something to cry about!" Addie had learned different ways to keep the tears inside. But in the church, a deep sadness had come over her. Crying on Ruth's shoulder, and crying into her pillow, had felt like popping the air from an overfilled balloon.

Addie dragged to the kitchen for coffee. Doris had made doughnuts. Addie carried her mug and plate to the window overlooking the yard. Al and Doris were setting up tables. Ruth sat in a chair under the trees. Was Tom invited? Tom didn't seem to need an invitation; he showed up when it suited him.

She dressed for the picnic in trousers and a sweater. Hanging on her closet door was a new skirt and blouse for her first day at

Wayne University. The coed uniform for marching into battle. Textbook, notebook, and pencils were ready in her bag. Addie sighed; she should try to enjoy the picnic. The last day *before*.

Rain cut the afternoon short. No Tom. They scrambled to carry the picnic dishes inside and ate around Doris's dining table. Ruth was flushed and tired, but she ate some of every dish. Al relaxed with his arm across the back of Ruth's chair. Doris entertained them with stories about the neighbors. Addie laughed with the others, but her chest fluttered and she kept checking the time on her watch. She didn't think Ruth noticed, but when they hugged good night, Ruth said, "You'll be fine tomorrow."

At half-past eight the next morning, Addie stood on the curb at the corner of Cass and Warren gazing at the Main Building, an H-shaped limestone and stucco structure, four stories high plus a clock tower in the center. Students flowed toward a pair of double doors in the stone archway at the base of the tower. She merged into the stream. Arms in the crowd grasped the doors open, propelling her inside.

Addie climbed the vestibule stairs and paused in the center atrium. Marble on the walls and columns, burnished wood, brass railings, the mosaics inlaid on the archways—she had never known a school so ornate. The hall reverberated with the talk and laughter of the students. Yet the grand space held the clamor as if wrapping them inside its opulence.

The passing rush bumped away Addie's reverie. She didn't know which of the branching hallways led to her classroom. A voice said, "Need help?" A smiling coed with blonde curls, dressed in a version of Addie's outfit, held a green umbrella overhead. "I know, the umbrella is odd, but it's eye-catching. I'm a first-day guide. What room?"

Addie looked at the registration paper crinkled in her hand. "Uh, my form says 403."

"Lecture room. Take the last staircase on the right. On the fourth floor, follow the numbers." She patted Addie's arm. "Come on, gal, you can do this. Show the men we're serious." The clock in the tower chimed. "You don't want to be late."

"Thank you," Addie said. The chime had quickened the pace in the crowded hall. She zig-zagged through to the stairs at the end. She took the first flight two steps at a time, appreciating the footing of the saddle shoes, ignoring the frowns of girls she swept by. She slowed at the landing, pressed against the wall a moment, then marched in the chain of students up the next three flights. A sign on the fourth floor pointed to her room at the far end of the hallway. When she reached the door, a young man in a white shirt and argyle sweater vest was about to kick away the doorstop. He waved Addie and the last bundle of students in, let the heavy wooden door slam shut.

Ten rows of wood desk-chairs lined the room wall-to-wall. Addie scanned over a hundred bobbing heads for an empty seat. Spotting one halfway to the front on the right, she made for the wall and sidled along it, picking her way over bags and extended legs. She gathered her skirt in one hand, held her bag close with the other, to side-step past three men seated in the row. They let her pass without looking up. She plopped into the chair by twisting her hips around the desktop. She breathed deep, felt sweat trickle down her back.

Murmuring among the students ceased when a middle-aged man in a tweedy three-piece suit, wearing the same spectacles as the Hudson's executives did, entered from a door near the front. He strode to the podium in the center and cleared his throat.

"I am Professor Harold Morse. You are beginning your study of accountancy. Detroit enterprises sponsored most of you. Our goal is to advance this school's reputation and our industries by graduating the finest accountants in the country." The professor rested his hands on the podium and scanned the rows of students.

"Accounting work is as essential to the future strength of our country as any wartime service. The arsenal of democracy has shifted from the factory floor to the management office for the growth of commerce. A lifetime of career opportunities awaits men graduating from our program." He paused. "Ladies who succeed in completing their studies will find suitable assignments."

Addie folded her arms and looked around. A handful of other girls were in the room. The professor presumed that ladies' success was less possible? Less probable? Addie found working with figures an easy process in her head, what her teacher called "natural ability." That and Mr. Reed's faith had gotten her into this program. Addie thought of when Bored One questioned Mrs. Reynolds about Addie's place in the class. She enjoyed a mental image of Mrs. Reynolds icing Professor Morse's puffed-up manner with her stare.

Professor Morse clasped his hands behind his back. "To begin, however, I see in this class an unacceptable lack of discipline. Other fields may tolerate indifferent attire among their students; Accounting does not. You will dress as does the profession. Business suits are required." Muffled groans rippled along the rows. The professor held up his hand. "If you disagree, leave the class." No one moved.

Addie pictured her one skirt suit. Wearing it with a different blouse each week would have to do. She wiggled her toes in the saddle shoes. They were comfortable and she could walk faster in them than in heels. Leaning forward, she had a view along the row of the men's shoes. They'd wear the same brogues with suits. She'd wear the saddle shoes with stockings.

The professor's teaching assistants walked the center aisle of the room, distributing stapled papers to pass down each row. Addie took one, handed off the pile to the man on her right. She sniffed at the text running crooked on the mimeographed sheaf of papers. Mr. Reed would never have allowed such copies to be used.

The man next to her ran a pencil along the top page, underlining dates. Addie took out her pencil and began reading the schedule of lectures, assignments, exams. The class met for Professor Morse's lectures on Tuesdays for three hours. On Thursdays, smaller groups led by the teaching assistants would meet in what were called accounting practicum sections. Addie had an idea that meant practice, but she would look it up to be sure. She calculated her hours working at the store, hours in class on two days, Saturdays at the diner, plus time to read and study. She'd be working seven days a week.

Professor Morse's voice intoned from the podium. No late assignments accepted. He described his grading system, forewarning the class that "An A grade is uncommon." Complete the textbook reading assignments 'one or two classes' ahead.' Related materials would be distributed as they proceeded through the topics. "Questions?" Rustling papers and sighs. "Then we shall proceed."

Like a brood of ducklings taking to the water, a hundred students opened their notebooks. The man on Addie's left slipped three point-sharp pencils into his shirt pocket, held a fourth poised over his blank page. He tilted his head and caught her eye. Addie drew her notebook from the satchel stuck between her ankles. She waved her sharp pencils with a smile. He shook his head and looked away.

Five minutes into the lecture, Addie wished for the shorthand she had not learned in high school. Professor Morse spoke without taking a breath, pacing back and forth in front of the blackboard that spanned the room. She tried to write everything he said. Her right arm bumped the left elbow of the man next to her as they both scribbled. He didn't move away. She tucked her arm closer to her body, shifted in her seat. She didn't recognize half of the words she'd scratched onto the page. Her leg jiggled under her skirt. How was she to keep up? She held the pencil to the page but stopped writing. Then she heard Mr. Reed's voice: "Pithy, Miss." He had instructed her about writing the Print Shop reports. "From the details, find the important points we must make."

Addie positioned her pencil and focused on her page as she listened to the professor's words. She pared off the fluffy and the main ideas stood out like bold print on a Hudson's poster. She noted unfamiliar terms with question marks in the margin, to look them up later. Relief flooded her when the professor said, "In summary ..." and she jotted in points she had missed.

Professor Morse poured a glass of water from the decanter on the podium, drank it down. Addie shook out her cramped fingers. He dabbed his lips with his handkerchief, continued the lecture. Forty-five minutes later he dismissed the class. As soon as he disappeared behind the recessed door, the hundred stiff bodies that had held rigid for three hours stood. Voices tumbled like a waterfall crashing from high rocks.

"Get used to it, buddy boy," said the man on Addie's right to the man on her left, towering over her head. "He's a drill sergeant, but he can get you in where you want to be."

The man on the left scoffed. "Workload doesn't bother me. What practice section are you in?" He waved a hand toward Addie like a traffic cop signaling cars to move. "Excuse me." She scrunched close to her seat and he and his briefcase bumped her in passing. She grabbed the back of the chair to steady herself. Down the row, one man from her Hudson's group was gathering his papers. He saw her at the same moment. She didn't remember his name from when they met with Mrs. Reynolds. She wanted to talk about the class with someone. If the Hudson's Creed meant anything to him, he'd be cordial. Walk her out.

Addie called to him, "What practice section are you in?"

That was the start of Addie's friendship with Louis.

Louis Carter, she learned, was related to the Webbers. "Not close enough to give me privileges in the executive dining room. They let Mrs. Reynolds give us family nobodies jobs in the store." He worked in a section of Personnel. "Mrs. Reynolds had one of the girls train me for the posting machine to record payroll. But I have worked my way into other stuff." Louis talked their way down five flights to the cafeteria in the basement of the Main Building. He insisted on buying the coffees and sandwiches—"I get an allowance"—and carried the tray to a table under a corkboard covered with notices.

Mrs. Reynolds, he said, was less scary than she appeared. He didn't worry about her watching him. "She's prancing on the sales floors most of the day, catching mistakes."

"She wouldn't fire you, would she?" Addie said. "Since you're one of the family?"

"Oh, she's fired some," Louis said. "There have been a few situations the Webbers could not overlook." He sighed. "If I don't make it through this program, she might send me to the Print Shop."

Addie sat up straight. "That's where I work. For Mr. Reed."

Louis laughed. "I know. You're *that* girl."

"What do you mean?"

"When Mr. Reed put your name forward for this program, Mrs. Reynolds scoured the store to find a man instead. She had to put me in, and the other two are grunts in Finance. There was no suitable fourth man. So, you made the list."

"From the Print Shop." Addie put her nose in the air with a smile.

"For me, Print Shop would be a demotion." He gave a thumbs-down.

"I've always been good with numbers."

"I took Latin and learned to read Greek in high school. When the army called, I took a kitbag full of books to boot camp. Lucky thing, a general plucked me from the herd to be his office aide." Louis leaned in. "The brochure for this program says ...," he pulled the pamphlet from his folder, read aloud, "'Employers want their accountants to be well read, trained with judgment and analytical ability, and able to express thoughts clearly in speech and writing.' *I* am well read."

"Okay," mused Addie, "then what's your point?"

"That a life of accounting requires no imagination." Louis wadded his napkin, set it aside. He shrugged. "I'm twenty-three. If it wasn't for the war, I'd be finished with college by now. My plan is to get through this, see what else I can get into."

"When I applied at Hudson's, I *wanted* to be a bookkeeper. Mrs. Reynolds put me in the Print Shop. I have bookkeeping work on the side."

Louis grinned. "An entrepreneur."

"Maybe someday."

"Unless the wedding comes first."

Addie shook her head. "I don't think so."

"We're all doomed by birth, one way or another." Louis shrugged and bit his sandwich.

Addie sipped her coffee. Talking with Louis was different from any conversation she'd had with a man. Her banter with Joe was of an easy-going in-this-together type. Joe caught onto her slides toward bad temper, evened things, as if he sat on the other end of her seesaw. He was jokey and plain-spoken, and a hard worker. Joe told her, "I've got my place in the world if I keep my nose to the grindstone." Not a hint of romance between them had seeped in, and that pleased her. Joe was her friend.

Louis's pedigree, as her father would say, was top line. He made a show of downplaying his family credentials but was not humble about using them. Addie could not picture Louis, reader of Greek and Latin, in the Print Shop. The folks in the tower would call him a pencil pusher, no sweat involved.

Louis had no bulk on him, not skinny but lanky, easy in the slacks and blazer he wore, a preview of the businessman he'd be one day. His dark-blonde hair curling tight reminded Addie of the perms Doris gave her friends. Louis's green eyes darted as he spoke, words flitting like dragonflies over a lake at dusk. He needed eyeglasses to read, kept a pair of circle black frames in his blazer pocket.

"You're staring at me," Louis said.

Addie blushed, checked her watch. "I don't know why we have the whole day off work when the class is in the morning. Same thing on Thursday."

Louis set his coffee mug down, looked at her. "We are off to the library."

She had thought she'd go home, see how Ruth was doing, start supper for Doris. But she wanted to go wherever Louis was going.

Louis picked up his book bag. "Let me show you how college works. Study as you go." He leapt up. "Come along, Miss Addie."

She gathered her bag and followed Louis on a journey of hallways and staircases. In the library's main room, rows of oak tables lined a central aisle between bookshelves jutting out from the walls. A placard warning "Silence" hung on the end of every bookcase.

Louis wound among the long tables until he found two empty chairs facing each other. The readers occupying the other chairs didn't look up. Louis scribbled on a page torn from his pad and flicked it across to Addie: "Read 90, break 10". She smiled and nodded. Addie unlatched her satchel, slid her textbook onto the expansive desktop, and settled across the table from Louis.

The table of contents announced "Bookkeeping" as Chapter 1 and "The Balance Sheet" as Chapter 2. Addie took her pencil in hand, blank note page ready, thinking the first chapter would be familiar. After reading five pages, she sat back. The author wrote in the dense manner that Professor Morse spoke. She reread the pages, jotted the points she could glean. When she finished the chapter, Addie tapped her pencil on her pad. The text explained bookkeeping without showing examples. She had tried to transfer the narrative to a mental ledger sheet. Why did the text explain numbers in words? She'd have to get used to college teaching.

She checked the clock and caught Louis's eye. He slapped his book closed, drawing a grimace from the student next to him. Addie took the cue from his pantomime to leave their books on the table. She tucked her wallet into her skirt pocket and followed him out to the hallway. They leaned on the sill of an open window and shared their frustrations. He argued bookkeeping was boring and pointless; she objected to the lack of practical examples. As they talked, she realized he knew bookkeeping was important, but since he would never be a bookkeeper, he brushed it off. Addie and Louis were both running toward the hurdle of making good on the sponsorship, but she suspected Hudson's would carry him over no matter what his grade was.

They returned to the library for a second stint of reading. The afternoon dragged toward five o'clock. The quiet changed to the rustle of multiple students packing up. Addie organized her papers, held her bag on her lap to stuff them in. She and Louis joined the line of students headed for the doors.

Outside, she saw a streetcar approaching the stop. "That's my trolley."

Louis shook his head. "I have my car. I'll drop you."

"It might be out of your way."

"Address?" Addie named the cross street on East Grand Boulevard.

"I'm headed to Grosse Pointe. Come on. The garage is a block over."

She admired his profile as they walked to the garage. Louis asked Addie to wait at the entrance. He disappeared inside and minutes later drove out in a Ford convertible, top down. Addie recognized it as the new "Woody" model Al had admired in a newspaper ad. Louis behind the wheel was the advertisement come to life. He popped out of the driver's seat to open the passenger door for Addie. She sensed he expected her to gush over the car. She teased him with a shrug, said, "Thank you," and slid onto the seat.

Louis put the car in gear and swung into the traffic. He grinned at her. "Hang on." He maneuvered through the downtown streets with skill and speed. Addie braced both hands on the buttery leather seat for the bump when the tires hit a rut. Louis swerved around vehicles and changed lanes, giggled at racing a trolley to beat a yellow light. He yelled, over the traffic noise, "You can buy this as a station wagon, but where's the thrill in that?"

Addie grinned. She was still grinning when they reached her block. Ahead, a green Hudson's delivery van was parked in front of her building. Louis pulled close behind it.

Addie said, "The baby furniture!" She jumped out of the convertible. "For my sister."

"You live with your sister?"

"No, across the hall, with our landlady. Where did you learn to drive like that?"

"My brothers had me driving when I was twelve. In the army, I drove a jeep."

Addie tapped her hand on the car door frame. "Thanks for the ride."

"See you in class!" He saluted and spun the wheel to pull away.

As she watched the convertible speed down the boulevard, Al's sedan approached the curb. Addie waved to him, hitched her bookbag over her shoulder, and went through the gate. Al would, no doubt, comment on Louis's convertible. The car, a

Grosse Pointe address, the family connection to the Webbers all meant Louis was not in her league. Yet he had studied all afternoon with her, driven her home. She looked forward to Thursday. He wasn't in her practicum section, but if he went to the library for the afternoon, she'd see him there.

Two Hudson's deliverymen came out of the building, tipped their hats to her. Addie reached the top of the stairs to find Ruth's door open. Inside, Ruth and Doris stood looking at the crib and dresser from the Little Lamb collection.

Addie called out, "Surprise!"

Ruth turned to her. "Addie, you ordered this furniture?"

"For you and the baby. And Al."

Ruth came to Addie and hugged her. Over Ruth's shoulder, Addie smiled at Doris's approving nod. The jumble of talk among the three women pitched high and fast as Al entered the apartment. Ruth went to meet him for an embrace, then pulled him over to admire the crib. Al's lower-key approval of the furniture satisfied Ruth.

When Doris said they should all have dinner in her apartment, Addie said, "Wait until I tell you about my first day of college!"

As they ate at Doris's table, Addie poured out the story of her class, the professor, the homework, and studying with Louis. Ruth and Doris thought he sounded charming.

"Al, did you see his car?" Addie asked.

"The Woody convertible. Not many of those around."

Addie tilted her head at Al forking his cake, surprised he was not more excited about the car.

After doing the dishes, Addie walked Ruth into the hall and hugged her good night. Al stopped before he followed Ruth into their apartment. "I'll drive you to Hudson's in the morning." Al lowered his voice. "Unless Louis Carter is picking you up."

"No, of course not. I met him just today."

Al raised his brows. "Right, you don't know him."

Al *would* try to throw cold water on her interest in Louis. Since Al had moved in with Ruth, Addie had let herself get too comfortable with him. Al was not her brother. His job was to worry about Ruth, not nose into Addie's friends.

"Sure, Al. Goodnight." Addie closed her door.

The next morning, she left before Al came down, and took the streetcar to Hudson's.

CHAPTER 17

Addie used to curl up on the davenport while her brother Dan air-conducted the orchestra during radio broadcasts by the New York Philharmonic. At full volume, the Emerson cabinet vibrated with the crescendos and bass notes, risked bursting a tube. Dan always rooted his feet in front of the speaker, arms extended, a finger pointing the imaginary baton, his upper body swaying, then twitching, with the changing rhythms in the music. When the live audience burst into applause at the finish, he rested his hands on top of the radio cabinet, eyes closed. Dan would turn and blink at Addie as though coming out of a spell.

Addie was now in a kind of fast-moving spell. September had cooled into October. Her days pulsed like a swelling of the high notes, anticipating the cymbal crash, with the effort to keep the rhythm of classes, studying, working in the Print Shop, and bookkeeping for Ma and Dunn's. Plus, going with Ruth to doctor appointments and tracking the rents for Doris. She tried not to worry further than the work in front of her, but her mind raced ahead, anxious about what she had to do next.

Addie also carried a private preoccupation with Louis. She had not spoken with him since the first day of class. The Thursday practicum sessions met in rooms scattered on different floors, and she didn't know where to find him. After her practicum on the Thursday of the week they met, Addie took the same library table and saved his chair with her bookbag, but he did not appear. Arriving early for the second Tuesday lecture, Addie positioned herself to watch for him. Louis slipped into a chair near the door at the last moment and rushed out as soon as Professor Morris left the podium. She skipped lunch, again waited in the library. Her pencil wandered from notes into doodles. After an hour, her stomach was grumbling, and she had grasped none of the details from the reading. She started again, but kept popping her head up, expecting Louis to walk in.

The third Tuesday, when Louis had not come into the library after an hour, she packed up her bookbag and left. She lectured herself during the walk to the streetcar about being silly over a boy. She *had* to shake him off.

That week on Thursday, after her practicum session, Addie wandered the length of the library looking for a different seat, not visible from the central doors. If Louis came in, let him look for her. She found a cluster of tables near the back windows, where only girls were studying. Bookshelves hid the space from the aisle. Faces looked up and smiled when she sat and opened her bag. Addie could tell from the business suit that one girl was in her program.

She glanced at her companions, heads down, pencils scratching on pads. She got to work. When her eyes needed a break, gazing out at the brilliant fall colors of the trees in the late afternoon sunlight relaxed her as though she was wrapped in one of Doris's knitted blankets. Addie worked ahead in the reading until the gong announced fifteen minutes before closing.

The business suit girl came toward her waving a pack of cigarettes. "We're in the same program. I'm Mary Clark. Got a few minutes?"

They sat together on a bench outside the Main Building. Mary had her cap set on becoming a certified public accountant. Her employer, the Michigan Bell Telephone Company, sponsored her. Mary pulled a pamphlet from her bag, "Employment Opportunities for Women in Professional Accounting." "If I get the degree, I could stay at Michigan Bell for my whole career." She pushed the booklet into Addie's hand. "Read it. You can give it back to me in class."

Addie passed the time on the trolley scanning the booklet published by the U.S. Department of Labor. Women accountants were already working in business, and more were needed. In the large companies, like Hudson's, bookkeeping could lead to higher positions. At Hudson's, Addie had heard folks call women like Mrs. Reynolds "career gals" with a tone of admiration for their devotion to the store, mixed with a sort of pity. Louis had argued that being "just a bookkeeper" was okay until Addie got married, but men like him would be the professionals Hudson's needed for the future. But both the Department of Labor and Mary said women could become professionals, the same as men. College was the ticket.

At the next lecture, Mary was waiting for Addie with a saved chair near the front. They became a pair in the lecture room and the practicum. Addie's pride kept her from turning her head to look for Louis, but at the end of class, slow moves to shake out her coat and slip it on disguised her scanning of the back rows. If Louis were to ask Addie to study, she knew she would melt. She never caught sight of him, and Addie's shaky pride held.

The Print Shop's work had escalated week by week since Labor Day, with the promotions for Halloween and the advance printing departments ordered in preparation for their Christmas displays. Mr. Reed had taken over the order book on Addie's class days, then handed it off to Joe when the shop got busier. Joe rocked on his heels in Mr. Reed fashion as Addie ran her finger down the orders he had entered. "See that neat lettering? Same as you do it."

Addie laughed. "Proving you can letter neater than the scribbles you usually make."

"That meanie in Bridal complained when my scribbles messed up an order. So, yeah."

The thirty minutes in the tower lunchroom, three days a week, were Addie's most carefree. She talked with Joe about the college mix of younger students with the returned GIs, had him laughing at her imitation of Professor Morse. But she didn't tell Joe about Louis. She could have made Louis into a story about the hoity-toity Webber family, ruminated about Louis's nervy manner, but she held back lest Joe detect her hurt feelings. Addie resolved to walk away if she encountered Louis during her rounds in the store. Not likely he would come to the sales floors, but a snub to cover her wound might prompt him to apologize. She held onto the hope that he would seek her out.

At night falling asleep, or daydreaming while she raked leaves in the yard, a movie played in Addie's imagination. Giggling in the passenger seat of Louis's convertible while he careened around Belle Isle or on the open roads outside the city.

Louis grabbing her hand, bringing it to his lips. Louis waiting for her at the bottom of the staircase in the Main Building, keeping his eyes on her as she walked down, jealous coeds sending admiring glances their way. She craved a way back to his company. Addie wondered what advice Ruth and Doris might give her, but didn't know how to explain her fascination with flighty Louis.

One evening, Addie sat in the living room fighting off thoughts of Louis, her textbook open on her lap. In the dining room, Doris's treadle sewing machine whirred. Doris had draped around Ruth maternity skirts and blouses collected from the neighbor women and was altering them to fit. "There is always someone between babies. Might as well share the clothes."

Addie gazed at Ruth sitting under the lamp beam, hemming a skirt. Ruth's belly had enlarged like a bushel basket of summer vegetables. Her skin itched and sweated under even the loosest blouses. She joked she would never wear a girdle again. If Ruth missed the stylish fashions from her Hudson's days, she did not let on. Ruth did not dress to go out. She had stopped waking Al early on Sundays to take her to Mass at St. Hyacinth. The catechism had moved from her bedside to the bookshelf in the living room. Ruth's defiance about Loretta's mother's demand had put a distance between her and whatever she had believed becoming Catholic would give her.

Addie went over and reached for the needle in Ruth's hand. "Let me do that." Ruth handed it over, stood, and rubbed her lower back. "My appointment is tomorrow evening. Help me remember to tell the doctor about my backaches."

After class the next day, Addie took two streetcars from the college to meet Ruth at Dr. Tullen's office. When Addie eyed the mighty swordfish in the reception room, she imagined its spear chasing Louis.

Dr. Tullen questioned Ruth about how often she felt the baby move. Ruth held her breath while his firm hands measured her swollen belly. The nurse marked Ruth's chart with his pronouncement of thirty-four weeks. Addie exchanged a glance with Ruth, the calendar in their heads. Six weeks to go.

No migraines since the last appointment, but Ruth complained of leg cramps and an aching back. The doctor instructed Addie where to place her hands to knead Ruth's leg muscles with a gentle motion. Addie grasped Ruth's leg and copied his long fingers moving against the bulge of her calf. Ruth sighed and closed her eyes. Dr. Tullen slid his hands away, drew the sheet over Ruth, patted her arm. She opened her eyes to meet his. "I'll see you in two weeks, Ruth, then every week. Your husband can call with any questions."

While Ruth dressed, Addie telephoned Dunn's from the doctor's reception desk to let Al know to come for them. As they waited outside in the chilly autumn wind, Ruth tucked her scarf around her neck. "You'll have to make the Thanksgiving turkey dinner this year."

Addie linked arms with her sister and smiled. "Not me— Doris has already planned the menu."

In the car, Al looked at Addie in the rearview mirror. "Ma's got her new cook making the dinner meals."

Addie said, "Ma let Patsy cook? That means she's happy with her!"

"Patsy has become her lifesaver. Ma's too busy, now that the advertising for the pies has kicked in."

Al's sales pitches to storekeepers in different neighborhoods had doubled the orders. Ma's mind worked ahead on spending the receivables. She had come back from her lake vacation declaring, "I need more ovens!" Ma also wanted to expand into the storefront between the diner and Dunn's, a two-story building owned by a tailor. He had been in the neighborhood since starting as a young man, and lived with his wife above the shop. The couple were regular campers in Ma's group at the lake. She was working on him to sell the place to her. "The wife tells me he's teetering my way."

When Addie arrived at the diner on Saturday morning, a grinning Patsy greeted her with a fresh pot of coffee. "Hey there, girl, how do you like my uniform?" Patsy wore a green-and-yellow print dress that was covered with a green, pocket apron embroidered with "Ma's Diner" on the bib. The kitchen girl, hauling dishes, wore the same, rolled her eyes as Patsy did a curtsy and said, "I told Al to put me in the ads."

Addie laughed. "Looks good on you, Patsy." In her head, Addie estimated what Ma had spent on the uniforms. Over pancakes and coffee, Addie listened to Patsy carry on about her pleasure in working in the diner. "Ma made this a great little place. I'm grateful to you, Addie."

Addie worked the figures. The payment to the tailor and taxes. Money to change the space over for pie making. Ovens. Hudson's did not sell the large baker ovens, but the man in Appliances let Addie peruse the catalogs. Ma had settled on a pricey model. There'd be wages for pie-makers. Ma couldn't make enough pies alone, would have to hire. She fussed about teaching others to replicate her technique. "My secret is in the crust," Ma said. "Nobody makes a crust like mine."

Addie updated the books, leaving the ledger sheet with the total estimated cost of the expansion for Ma. A steady drizzle tapped on the awning outside when she finished. The books at Dunn's waited. She wolfed down the grilled cheese sandwich Patsy put in front of her, put on her jacket, and covered her hair with a rain bonnet. In the warm kitchen, Ma grunted good-bye from her mixing station, Patsy blew her a kiss, and Addie quick-stepped out the back door, down the alley, and through the open back door of Dunn's.

Tom came through the hall from the barroom, wiping his hands on a towel. "Al is on the way to pick you up. Ruth's having a migraine. He wants you to stay with her so he can be here."

"Oh, no!" Addie pushed back the dripping rain bonnet. "She's been fine for a month."

Tom turned. "Come up front to watch for his car."

Addie's boots squeaked behind him to the door. He turned and came closer to her. "You're dripping on my clean floor," Tom said as he grabbed a towel from the bar. He pulled at the strings of her bonnet with one hand and lifted it away. She watched his face. Their eyes met, and she held still while he daubed the towel at the drips on her face. "That's better," he said, his breath smelling of coffee. Addie reached for her bonnet, and his fingers touched hers.

Loud honking from outside. Addie jumped. Tom threw the towel on the bar. "Cover up. I'll bring your bike inside. Al can bring it home tonight in the trunk." He unlocked the street door and went out.

Addie breathed deep, pulled the bonnet over her hair. Tom's gaze into her eyes mirrored what she had dreamed of Louis doing. Her trembling fingers tied the strings under her chin.

Al beeped the horn again. Addie stepped out into the steady rain. Tom loped to the open door, wheeling her bike. His soaked shirt clung to his chest. He grinned at Addie and ducked inside Dunn's with the bike.

Al motioned from the driver's seat for her to hurry. Addie splashed across the puddled sidewalk, jumped into the car. Al stepped on the gas, his jaw set the way it did when he worried.

"When did it start?"

"During the night, but she didn't tell me then."

"How bad?"

"As bad as at the lake." Al picked up the speed.

Addie said, "I'm scared for Ruth."

Al's hands clenched the wheel. "I called Dr. Tullen. He's at the hospital for a birth. His wife will get a message to him." Stopped at a traffic light, Al looked over at Addie. "We'll get Ruth through."

Addie nodded, understanding that he expected her to match his resolve. Al reached for the cigarettes on the dashboard, shook one from the pack, clasped it between his lips. "Don't look at me like Ruth does. I'm not lighting it."

She didn't want to judge him when her own nerves were jangled. Addie shifted the subject. "I didn't have time to work on Dunn's books."

"Nothing's changed. We're losing money, waiting for the other shoe to drop. I can't leave Tom alone there."

Addie thought of the open alley door, hoping Tom had locked it. Al and Tom had to open the barroom each night, risking the shakedown, or worse, because they needed the money. Tom wouldn't cower from a fight, but did he get a jolt from the risk? Addie glanced at Al hunkered over the wheel, squinting to see the lane between passes of the wipers. Al, the cooler head, tempered Tom's rashness. Whatever happened next, they would stand together.

Rain pounded on the roof of the sedan. In the hypnotizing swing of the windshield wipers, Addie saw Tom's face as he wiped the towel across her cheeks. The abrupt stop of the car shook her out of it.

Addie clasped the door handle, ready to make a dash for the building. Al tapped her other arm. "Let me know how she's doing, and what the doctor says." His eyes glistened. "Tell Ruth I love her." He looked away.

Addie pushed out, slammed the door shut, and ran to the stoop in one fast motion.

Doris opened Ruth's apartment door as Addie trotted up the stairs. "Ruth's quieted for now. The roof's leaking into the top floor; I've got to go up there. I'll come back when I can." Doris rushed out.

Addie peeled off her wet jacket, kicked away her boots and wet socks. She held her hands under the hot tap in the bathroom to warm them. She padded in bare feet into Ruth's bedroom. Ruth lay on her back, arms under the sheets. Tied over her face was the eyeshade Doris had made to block light. Addie sat in the armchair facing the bed. The damp edges of her trousers were cold against her ankles. She stood and slipped the trousers off, draped them over the bedstead. She dragged an extra blanket from the end of the bed to the chair, wrapped her legs in its coziness.

Rain pattered against the windowpanes. Addie looked around the bedroom, scenes flipping through her mind like pages of a photo album turning. The first night when she stumbled into this room. Spooning against Ruth during her nausea. Singing the old, sad song as they lay together.

Ruth turned onto her side, moaned. Addie tensed, ready to go to her, then heard Ruth's breathing ease back to sleep.

Addie nestled her head against the chair, hummed the song low. Her eyes closed.

Addie woke to the ring of the telephone in the living room. She stumbled out of the cocoon of blanket and heard Doris's voice answer. Addie came next to her. The doctor was on the line. Doris wrote something on the note pad, said, "Thank you, Doctor." She hung up. "He says to continue with compresses and baths, give the pills only if we must. He'll call again in the morning." She eyed Addie's bare legs.

"My trousers got soaked."

"What if Al came in here?"

"He's not leaving Dunn's tonight. Something's up."

"What do you mean?"

Addie shrugged. "I can't put a finger on it." The rain pelted the windows. "The roof?"

"Buckets and towels for tonight," Doris said.

Doris went across the hall to warm soup, and brought it back with thick brown bread and butter. Taking turns checking on Ruth, they waited out the hours, radio music low. Doris bent over her crocheting. Addie rotated between curling up on the davenport and jiggling one leg over the other. Ruth had another rough patch, and together they massaged her face and arms with hot cloths. Addie rubbed Ruth's legs the way the doctor had taught her, until Ruth flopped listlessly, slept again.

At midnight, Addie telephoned Dunn's.

One ring, Al picked up. Addie said, "Ruth's okay," heard him breathe out. She reported the doctor's orders, but left out the worst of Ruth's pain. Al's inhaling and exhaling on the line sounded like he was puffing on a cigarette. She asked, "What's going on there?"

"We locked up at ten. The rain kept the regulars home. We'll stay."

"How will the two of you—"

"Just make sure Ruth is okay." Al hung up.

Addie shooed Doris to bed, promising to wake her if Ruth worsened. She changed into one of Ruth's nightgowns, crawled in next to her sister's feverish body, pulled the blankets over them to seal in the warmth. Steady rain thrummed outside. Eyes open, Addie pictured Al and Tom pacing front to back inside Dunn's. Did they know what might come, have some warning? They had no guns in the place; Al refused to touch a gun after the war. Tom's strong arms could swing a forceful baseball bat. Would that be enough?

She closed her eyes, listened to Ruth's breathing, Jane's song running in her mind.

Addie woke at three, again at five. Ruth opened her eyes when Addie sat up. "Addie … where's Al?" Ruth asked, her voice raspy, then coughed. "Water."

Addie leaned for the water glass on the side table. Holding it for Ruth to sip, she said, "Al stayed at Dunn's with Tom."

Ruth pushed the glass away, leaned against the pillows. "My head is so heavy. I need to close my eyes." She placed her hand on Addie's arm. "Tell me about Al."

"At midnight, all was well."

"What time is it?"

"Just after five."

"If he's not here by six, call him." Ruth turned onto her side, pulled the sheet over her face.

Ruth knew the reason for Al staying all night at Dunn's, Addie realized. The precaution might be working, although Al's tone at midnight had sounded edgy.

Addie, fully awake, propped on the pillows, waiting for Al to appear, or to make the call at six. The rain had stopped. After Al came home, Addie could use her day to study. Tension in the class had risen as the calendar moved closer to the midterm exam. The teaching assistant for her practicum, a wiry graduate student with an army haircut who wore over-starched shirts that rubbed his neck red, drilled them with problems and questions. "Morse shows no mercy on his exams," the assistant warned.

She decided to make coffee, get her book from across the hall. Addie eased out of the bed. She started the percolator before scampering across the cold hallway floor and bursting through Doris's door.

Al, Tom, and Doris sat in her living room. Al jumped up, winced, grabbing his side. Tom held an ice bag against his face, grinned around it. Doris sprang from her chair and grabbed an afghan from the davenport. She threw it around Addie, pulled it together in front, covering what Addie realized the men could see through her nightgown.

Al moved toward her as he asked, "Does Ruth need me?"

Addie whispered thanks to Doris and took hold of the afghan, ignored Tom enjoying her blush. "She's better, resting. Worried about you. What happened?"

"Police raid." Al rubbed his side.

Addie gasped, gaped at him. "What?"

Doris intervened. "Addie, get dressed. I'll make coffee."

"Coffee is perking in Ruth's kitchen."

Al jerked his head at Tom. "Come on, I'll check on Ruth." Al limped past Addie, opened the door, waited for Tom to haul himself off the davenport. He held the ice bag on his cheekbone, mumbled, "Nice to see you."

Doris shooed him out, closed the door. "He's got a nasty bruise, but his cheekiness is just fine."

Addie threw off the afghan, marched to her room. Why did the police raid Dunn's? Tom was right; chasing the gamblers off had made things worse. She pulled on a pair of dungarees and a flannel blouse, rifled through a drawer for warm socks. She washed her face, pinned her hair back, stepped into her moccasins, and went back across the hall.

Doris stood over Tom, curled on the cot in the alcove, the ice bag perched on the swollen side of his face. Doris pulled the curtain across, held a finger to her lips. "Gave him aspirin," she whispered.

Addie peeked in at the bedroom door. Al sat on the edge of the bed, holding a sobbing Ruth in his arms. Al saw Addie but waved her away. She listened at the door. Al held Ruth while she cried out her fears—"What if they *killed* you?"—and her anger—"How could you let this happen?!?"

Doris tapped Addie on the shoulder. "If they need us, we'll hear." They tiptoed to the living room and let themselves out. In the hallway, Doris said, "I'm going to the top floor." The handyman was coming to assess the water damage. "He's not a churchgoer. Sunday starts his week."

Addie took coffee to her bedroom desk, opened her textbook. Next thing she knew, she woke with her head in her arms at midday and got up from her chair. She was in the kitchen fixing oatmeal when Doris bustled in. "I took a stewpot over. I've given Tom more aspirin. Hope he'll sleep longer."

"Did you see Ruth?"

"No, she's still tucked in."

"What did they tell you about the raid?"

"It was the cops that kicked in the alley door. Al and Tom flew at them with baseball bats before they knew who they were. Tom landed a blow on the first man, who smashed his nightstick in Tom's face. Al got a baton in the ribs."

"Why would they do that?"

"That's all I got from them before you walked in."

Addie started to the door. "I should go over there and talk to Al."

"You should leave them alone," Doris directed. "Ruth needs peace."

The day blurred away. Addie took her class notes to the living room, draped her legs over the armchair, tuned the radio on low. Her mind wandered from the pages to the glimpse of Tom when Doris had tended to him in the alcove. His wincing at the strain to swallow the aspirin, his groan when Doris set the ice bag on his cheek. In her little-girl days, when Addie cried with a scraped knee, one of her siblings would "kiss it and make it better," and she believed it so. She daydreamed about kissing Tom's swollen cheek.

She swung her legs to the floor. What was wrong with her? Mooning over Louis, and now Tom. Addie hauled herself from the chair, wrapped herself up against the chilly air, and bounded down the stairs. Marching toward Belle Isle, numbers swirled in her mind, and she concentrated on figures. Losses from the days Dunn's was closed, the protection money. Ma ranted about the amount every shopkeeper forked over to the beat cops for protection. If the cops roughed up your place, what was the price to get back to business?

She trudged a mile on the island, fought the wind walking home. Addie ate warmed-over stew while Doris made another trip across the hall, came back and reported, "All is quiet."

Addie cleaned up the kitchen, flicked off the lights. She would get up early in the morning, to study before work, and to get Al alone on the drive to Hudson's.

CHAPTER 18

The Monday morning edition of *The Detroit Free Press* ran a photo in the back pages of cops milling in front of Dunn's, "Raided for suspected illegal activity." Not saying the bar was closed when it was raided, and that they found nothing. Addie threw the paper across the table in Hudson's cafeteria.

She was already in the sedan when Al came down to give her a ride to work. He had eased into the driver's seat, holding his side. "That's gonna hurt for a while."

"How did Ruth make it through the night?"

"Better than me." He started the car.

"I've been waiting in this cold car for you to tell me the story."

He did. After the blows at the back door, two burly cops had shoved Al and Tom spreadeagled against the bar, rapped their knuckles when Tom cursed them. They listened to glass shattering in the back room. Al tried reasoning with the sergeant, but it did no good. "He tapped his baton against his leg with a smile on his face, like he didn't see his men smashing bottles and cracking the legs off chairs. But they didn't smash all the inventory," Al said. "They just stole it. I got a glimpse of them carting boxes out the back."

The beefy pair guarding them shunted Al and Tom out the front door and kicked them to their knees on the sidewalk. The sergeant slapped a padlock on the door hasp, jammed it secured. "See here?" he had jeered. "On the alley door, too. You'll not be gettin' in." A paddy wagon careened out of the alley, slowed for their fellows to jump in, revved away.

Bruised and soaked from the rain, Al had felt inside his pocket for the key to the sedan. "I was ready to drive away even if they had slashed my tires." He found it, dangled the key in front of Tom, steadied him on his feet. They made their way through the alley, littered with glass from smashed bottles. They laughed with relief at the sight of full tires. Heading the opposite direction from the paddy wagon—"They might have been waiting to hammer us," Al said—he zig-zagged through side streets to the apartment building.

"Smashed or stolen, the inventory is gone."

"But thank goodness, you and Tom are okay."

"Yeah. Out of our place, but okay."

"How was Tom feeling this morning?"

"He can manage. Doris kept the aspirin coming during the night, and the ice got the swelling down."

Addie raised her brows; she didn't know Doris had tended Tom during the night.

Al pulled over to let Addie out. He said, "Right now, I don't know which end it up. Tom says we keep standing our ground."

She wanted to ask him what that meant, but she got out of the car. In the Hudson's cafeteria, she had picked up the morning newspaper and found the photo.

The wall clock in the cafeteria dinged 7:45. Addie picked up her bookbag. So much for early morning studying.

When she entered the Print Shop, Mr. Reed's dour face matched her mood. Addie used to assume that something she'd done or not done caused his upsets; she had learned from his habits, and the departments' see-sawing orders, to wait for him to explain.

"Joe is out sick. His mother says it's flu."

Addie flinched. Joe had never been out sick. "That's awful."

Mr. Reed sighed. "Signs and flyers for the Sewing Center's Halloween fabric sale are due there today. And the Candy Shop doubled the poster order."

Without Joe, that meant Addie's work doubled, too. She hurried to her locker, shoved her bookbag at the bottom. If she got a lunch break, she'd come back for the textbook.

The men in the shop worked the machines nonstop, handing off by turns for shortened breaks. An open window in the locker room circulated enough crisp air to moderate the heat coming off the machinery. At noon, Mr. Reed surprised her with a box lunch delivered from the cafeteria. He got one for himself, too. "Miss, I apologize there's no time for a break today."

Addie plopped onto her stool with a smile. "Thank you, Mr. Reed. This is perfect." He nodded and took his box to his office. Addie bit into her sandwich, picked up her pencil to continue calculating prices. No time for the class reading. She would have to spend the hours after dinner catching up.

At the close of the day, Addie walked through the maze of orders boxed and piled at the front of the shop. She rechecked the quantities and taped the price sheet to each bundle. The din of the machinery tapered to a stop. Addie bid goodnight to the parade of men leaving. Mr. Reed came to the front, rolling down his shirtsleeves.

She held out the day's checklist for his approval. "The men came through today, Mr. Reed."

"That they did. So did you. But tomorrow we'll be without you *and* Joe." He set the clipboard on the counter, hooked his thumbs in his vest pockets.

Addie pursed her lips. Her class day would be a hardship in the shop. "Do you want me to work tomorrow afternoon?"

Mr. Reed leaned against the counter. "Miss, do you remember when I asked why you wanted to work here?"

Addie flushed. Her first day seemed long ago. "I had a lot to learn."

"Right, Miss. There's more to learn—at the college. You have a head for this business. *If* you want to go forward."

Addie looked away. Textbook pages shuffled in her mind like a flicker book, the numbers dancing, Professor Morse squinting behind his spectacles, Louis laughing with a finger pointed at her. Addie blinked it away, turned to Mr. Reed. His belief in her was a lighthouse, shining the way clear. She accepted his wisdom with a nod. "Thank you, Mr. Reed."

"We'll see you on Wednesday." He closed the order book.

When Addie arrived home, Al, Ruth, and Tom sat around Doris's dining room table. Doris was spooning macaroni and cheese onto plates. Tom lifted the fingers of one hand in a wave as Addie came in. His face looked like a Halloween mask. The bruising on his cheek was a blend of red, purple, and yellow.

Doris had set Addie a place next to Tom. She put her coat on the hook, went into the bathroom to wash her hands.

She combed out the curls in her hair, pinched her cheeks. Addie breathed deep, arched against the tightness in her shoulders. In the dining room, she slid into the chair, averting her eyes from Tom to focus on Ruth. "You look like you are feeling better."

Ruth shook her napkin onto her lap. "The baby has been jumping all day. Like my nerves."

Addie turned to Al. "Did you see the paper?"

Al pursed his lips. "Yep."

Tom swallowed a forkful, massaged his jaw. Addie clenched her fingers tight around her fork to stop thinking of "kiss and make it better." She managed to say, "I hope you're feeling better."

"Doris is my Florence Nightingale. She's got me feeling fine."

Addie had never seen a blush on Doris like the pink she turned at Tom's words. Addie looked at her plate and moved her fork through the food. Something seemed to be happening between Doris and Tom. *Was she smitten with him?*

Al cleared his throat. "I'm taking tomorrow off work. We'll cut those padlocks off. Clean up, figure out the damage. We reopen tomorrow night."

Addie's fork clattered on her plate. "How can you? With what inventory?"

"They didn't take the kegs." Al looked at Tom.

Tom said, "The keg beer is what we sell most."

Al said, "Ma tells me the neighborhood is churning mad about the raid. Our regulars will come in tomorrow night."

Tom said, "And she says nobody's been nosing around my flat. I can go home."

Ruth sat back, rested a hand on her belly. "You'll be in their sights again. It won't be safe."

253

Al put his arm around her shoulders. "Ruth, honey, we've talked and talked about this. We *have* to reopen."

Addie agreed with Al. They needed every cent from pouring the kegs. They might make enough that the beer guy would not cut them off. "You could serve only from kegs for a while. Make more per pour than from bottles." Addie looked at Tom. "As you said, that's what you sell most."

Ruth's furrowed brow implied she had expected Addie to be on her side.

Al said, "Ma is spreading the word that Dunn's will be open. The cops won't take on the entire neighborhood."

Doris spoke up. "We can get more people there. I'll go. I'll talk it up around the building."

Addie saw Ruth's frown. "Ruth, I'll be here with you, after the library."

Ruth shook her head. "No, I'll go with Doris." She turned to Al. "If you're doing this, we're in this mess together." Then Ruth wagged her finger at Addie. "But you stay away from Dunn's until further notice." She pointed her finger toward Al. "If you need Addie's bookkeeping help, she has to do it here."

Tom spoke up. "What about Saturday?" Addie kept her eyes on her plate. She hoped Tom meant he wanted to see her in Dunn's.

Ruth said, "Too soon."

Addie opened her mouth to protest, but Al said, "Let's take it one day at a time, okay?"

Ruth looked at Addie. "Tomorrow night, you study."

Addie sighed. "I have to."

Al looked at his watch, asked Ruth if she wanted him to walk her across the hall before he drove Tom home. Ruth said, "Addie can do that. You go ahead."

Tom came around the table to where Doris stood stacking the dishes. He put his arms around Doris, kissed her on the forehead. "You saved me. Thank you."

Addie's heart beat hard. She saw Doris lean into Tom, then pull back, her face red. Doris tapped him on the shoulder. "Let me go, you big lug. Just don't get yourself clobbered again."

Addie jumped up and collected the used glasses, went into the kitchen, started the hot water in the sink. Tom and Al called out goodnight to her as they left, and she called back. She leaned against the sink, fanned her face with the dishtowel.

Doris brought in the plates. "That man is something," she said.

Addie sank the plates into the sudsy water. Tom *was* something, something she didn't know how to figure. And if Doris had eyes for him …

Ruth called for Addie from the living room and Doris said, "I'll finish here."

Addie dried her hands, went to Ruth. She clasped Ruth's extended hand and stepped back, helping with a pull as Ruth grunted to stand. Linking arms, they walked across the hall.

"Do you think they can make enough money to keep the bar?" Ruth asked.

"With any luck, maybe."

Ruth flicked on a lamp. The cot, stripped of sheets, stood to the side, folded and strapped shut. "Al was supposed to take that to the attic. With the crib and the baby's chest in our room, the only place for our dresser is the alcove."

Addie said, "I'm sorry, I haven't been helping you much."

Ruth said, "There's still plenty to do." Then Ruth's face lit up. She grabbed Addie's hand, placed it flat on her belly. Ruth locked eyes with Addie, waited.

Addie whispered, "Ooh." Ruth kept still. The bumping against Addie's palm continued.

Ruth had tears in her eyes. "Tell me everything will be okay."

Addie pulled Ruth closer. "You will be okay. I know you will."

On Tuesday morning, Addie was first in the door as the college library opened. Reading for an hour before the lecture grounded her in the topic enough to grasp most of Professor Morse's points and scribble questions to look up later. Next to her, Mary wrote at a casual pace. Addie hoped that meant Mary had studied ahead and Addie could copy her notes. After class, they went to the cafeteria for a quick sandwich before heading to the library.

During their study break in the afternoon, Addie stepped into the cool hallway and gazed through the windows at the full-color brilliance of the foliage outside. She rubbed her neck, flexed her fingers. A year ago, she had been sewing her costume for the high school Halloween dance. She didn't recognize the girl who had fussed over recreating Dorothy's farm girl outfit from *The Wizard of Oz*. Addie shoved her hands into her jacket pockets. The twists and turns in Detroit had been like the yellow brick road. Not to Oz, but where?

Mary came up beside her on her way back from the water fountain. "Shall we?" she said, and opened the library door. Addie smiled and walked ahead.

As they took their places at the study table, Addie thought of Louis for the first time that day. She hadn't looked for him in the lecture room. Bigger fish to fry, as Dan would say; let him go. Her loud sigh raised heads around the table. Addie put her finger to her lips and opened her notebook.

When they parted outside later, Mary said, "If we keep up this concentration, we'll pass."

"You'll definitely pass," Addie said. "Me, the jury is still out."

That evening, Addie welcomed the quiet of the empty apartment. Doris left a note saying dinner was in the refrigerator. Addie carried her plate to the dining table, propped the textbook next to it, plopped into the chair Tom had sat in the night before. She thought about calling Dunn's. If she did, Tom would cloud her mind. Bigger fish, she reminded herself with a sigh.

At ten, Addie was still at the table, her plate shoved to the side, book and notes spread out. She rubbed her eyes with stiff fingers, heard Ruth and Doris on the stairs. Addie opened the door as they reached the landing. Ruth huffed from the effort, dark circles under her eyes. "I can't wait to take these shoes off. Doris will tell you about the night."

Addie got ahead of Ruth to open her door. "Are you sure?"

Ruth waved her off. "Al will be back in an hour. Goodnight." She closed her door.

Doris took off her hat. "The ladies and gents of the neighborhood filled the place. Best night they've had in a year. I gave Patsy a hand with the dinners."

"That's great news!"

Doris chuckled. "You should have seen Tom running the bar, showing off his battle scars." The crowd at Dunn's, it seemed, had provoked Tom's defiance. Addie admired his bravado; he wasn't afraid of a fight.

Addie waited up to catch Al when she heard him in the hall. She kept her voice low. "Doris gave me the lowdown. Any problems?"

"Two cops in a car eyed the crowd lined up on the block. They were gone when we locked up. I used the tailor's garage in the next alley to hide the sedan."

"Kegs?"

"Dry. Sold it all. Tomorrow, I beg the beer guy for mercy." Al leaned against the wall. "If we had more nights like tonight, we might make it. Ruth thought so, too." He slapped his hat on his thigh. "It's a crap shoot."

"Good luck with the beer guy."

"If he'll give us the kegs, we'll open again Saturday. Goodnight." After Al closed his door, Addie heard the lock turn. She did the same on her side, turned off the lamp, and glanced at the street below. The space at the curb meant cautious Al had left the sedan in the back shed instead of out front.

The next afternoon at Hudson's, Addie stepped out of the elevator on nineteen to find Al about to step into a car going down. He said, "Kegs, Saturday." Addie smiled her acknowledgement of the good news. She made a rough mental calculation. Keg sales alone, two nights out of the usual six in the week. Dunn's couldn't survive on that for more than a month even if they sold every drop.

Bigger fish, bigger fish, bigger fish, played like a radio jingle in her head. Her worry about Dunn's would have to take a back seat.

At their previous study session, Addie and Mary had combined their notes, and before their Thursday practicum, Mary typed a study guide for the midterm. "As the Bible says, two are better than one," she said, presenting the carbon copy to Addie as they entered the practicum classroom.

Tapping the copy, Addie said, "*This* is my bible."

Professor Morse's teaching assistant announced a practice test. "Correctly answering questions from the previous exams the Professor has given is a good marker of your proficiency." He distributed papers to the group, called for silence.

Addie twisted a pencil in her sweaty palm, scanned the first two questions. "Explain the matching principle for the recording of expenses," "The balance sheet compares the assets to the sum of the liabilities and equity, true or false." Mary, head down, was confident enough to write with an ink pen.

Addie took a deep breath. Her leg jiggled. The teaching assistant sat with his hands folded on the desk, watching the students, eyes flicking at the clock. The look on his face reminded her of Bored One when Mrs. Reynolds announced they would represent Hudson's in the program, questioning "Why is she here?" In the lecture room, Addie held her head high when Bored One passed or caught her eye. *I have earned my spot.* Addie planted her feet, wiped her hand dry, read the first question again. *I know this.* Mr. Reed was right. College was her yellow brick road.

Later, in the library, Addie and Mary compared what they had written against the correct answers the Professor's assistant gave out afterward. He had laughed at the gasps from the students when he pronounced their responses "Inn-co-*rect.*"

"His sing-song voice made me want to choke him," Addie said.

Mary clucked. "Was it his voice, or the ones you had wrong?"

Addie sighed. "Walk me through question eight again, will you? I was stuck there."

Mary looked over Addie's test paper. "On eight, and ten, fourteen, sixteen …"

Addie held up her hands. "I get the message, believe me." She opened the study guide, dug into the details.

At five, Mary packed up to go home. Addie walked her out, grabbed cookies in the cafeteria, and returned to the library. Mary had helped her to narrow in on the gaps in her knowledge. Addie knew bookkeeping inside out, had mastered the balance sheet concepts, but was shaky on classification of activities in profit-and-loss accounts. She had confused capital assets and working assets, but had a handle on the differences now.

The fifteen-minutes-to-closing bell sounded. Sighs mixed with books thumping shut, chairs scraping on the wood floor. Her fellow business students, wearing another day of study on their faces, pulled on coats and jackets, shuffled to the doors. Addie nodded to her tablemates, packed her satchel. She stepped into the hallway amidst the stragglers. The librarian jangled the keys to hurry them out. Addie heard feet pounding up the staircase, a familiar voice yelling, "Hold the door!"

Louis.

Taking the stairs two at a time, his curly hair shaking rain drops onto his rumpled grey suit jacket, his wadded-up necktie sticking out of a pocket. Addie backed to the side as he reached the top step. Louis yelled at the librarian, "I left my bag!" and lunged for the door.

The librarian shrugged her shoulders, pointed at the clock. "You've got one minute." He barreled into the library and the librarian closed the door.

Had he seen her? Addie's pride tangled with her impulse to wait for him. She took one slow step down, then another. The few other students moved past her at a quick pace. If she was the only one left when he came out, he'd know she waited. Addie stepped down to the next landing where the staircase turned. She fluffed her curls, straightened her blouse and jacket, rued that she had worn trousers instead of a skirt.

She heard the librarian shooing Louis out, the heavy door locking. Addie's heart thumped in her ears. She looked up at Louis bounding down the stairs, grinning at her. "Got what I came for." He patted the bag slung over his shoulder. He stopped in front of Addie, cocked his head. "Were you in the library all afternoon?"

She forced her bantering voice to answer. "Of course. Weren't you?"

Louis shook his head. "All those heads concentrating give me the jumps. I left after an hour."

"*You* preached to *me* about studying in the library."

"And you should. I found a place more suited to my style."

Addie picked up his rhythm. "I can just imagine. Someplace Mrs. Reynolds would find appalling, I bet." She gripped the stair railing with a sweaty palm, started down.

Louis laughed and loped ahead to the next landing. "Mrs. Reynolds will never find me." Logic said Louis had not been studying, wherever he was. Addie pushed logic to the side with pride and laughed, too.

They reached the atrium. Rain tapped against the windowpanes. Addie, with no umbrella, pulled the hood of her jacket over her hair and looped her book bag strap across her body. She longed for Louis to offer her a ride, tested him. "Looks like I'll have a wet run for the trolley."

Louis pulled the door and held it open. "C'mon. My car's at the curb." The convertible gleamed shiny wet in the streetlamp's glow.

Addie zig-zagged on the walkway to avoid puddles and soggy piles of yellow and red leaves. Louis reached for her and said, "Give me your hand." Addie plopped her wet hand into his warm palm. Louis pulled her into a fast trot to the side of his car. She held on until he unfurled his fingers, ran the tips across her palm. Laughing, he fumbled in different pockets for the keys, got the door open. She let her hand touch his as she grasped the door frame. He laughed again. "I'm getting wet here."

Someone shouted her name.

Addie twisted to look behind her. The headlights from a car pulled up to the rear end of the convertible shone into her eyes. Her name was shouted again. She bent away from the lights, saw a man coming toward her. Tom.

"Addie, get in the sedan," Tom yelled.

"What are you doing here?" she said. She looked at Louis. "I don't know what's going on."

Louis said, "You know this guy?"

Tom planted himself a foot away. "She knows me. Get away from her."

Louis let go of the car door, took a step toward Tom. Addie slid along the side of the convertible, grabbed Tom's sleeve. "Tom, what are you doing?"

Tom kept eyes on Louis while he spun Addie behind him. "Get in the sedan!"

Before Addie could answer, Tom punched Louis in the face, shouting, "You son of a bitch!"

Louis went down on one knee, grabbed his jaw. Then he lunged for Tom. Slick leaves underfoot toppled them, flailing at one another.

Addie screamed, "Stop, stop!" She maneuvered to grab hold of Tom's jacket. She lost her grip and fell back into the leaves when Tom lurched forward to land another blow on Louis's cheek. Louis lay sprawled with his face in the leaves. His legs moved, but he didn't get up. Tom was down too. Addie leapt forward and went to Louis.

Tom pushed up to his knees, gasping. "Get in the damn car."

She ignored him and bent over Louis.

Tom got on his feet, grabbed her wrist. "*Listen* to me. You don't know about this guy."

Addie hit Tom's hand away. He put his hands on her shoulders, turned her around, and moved her with him to the sedan. "We're getting out of here."

He yanked the car door open, tugged at her jacket, and she landed in the passenger seat. He slammed the door closed, scrambled to the driver's seat, and put the car in gear. In the headlight beam, Addie saw Louis leaning on a knee against the convertible, holding his arm against his eyes. Tom peeled away from the curb.

Addie yelled, "What is *wrong* with you? Why did you hit Louis? Why are you here?"

Tom checked the rearview mirror, swiped back his dripping hair. "You don't know what your boyfriend back there has been up to."

Addie slapped the seat with her fist. "What are you talking about?"

"Louis, as you call him, is the big fish in the card game at Dunn's."

Addie stared at Tom. "No, no, you're making this up."

"No I'm not. *He's* the troublemaker."

JAN M. WALTON

Addie shook her head. "No."

Tom scoffed. "Yeah? Don't believe me? Ask Al."

"Why did you come here?"

"To take you to the hospital—Ruth's having the baby."

CHAPTER 19

Addie shivered, her teeth chattering. Tom cranked his window closed, flicked on the dashboard heater. The tepid air blowing against her wet jacket made Addie colder. "Turn it off," she stuttered.

Tom yanked at the knob. "Grab the blanket in the back." He rolled to a stop at a traffic light. Addie stared ahead, shaking. "Addie, grab the blanket in the back."

When she still didn't move, Tom stretched an arm over the seat, felt for the blanket, tugged it forward. The blanket bunched between them, and he flipped it onto Addie's lap. The signal turned green, and he drove on. Addie clutched the edge of the blanket and pulled it to her chin. Goosebumps tingled along her arms, but the shivering eased.

"Almost there," Tom said.

"You have some nerve," she said.

Tom glanced at her. "Don't cry over *that* guy."

"I won't listen to you." Addie pulled the strap of her book bag over her head and shoved the bag between her feet. She threw back the hood of her jacket, pulled her arms out of the sleeves. Dragging the soggy garment off her back, she tossed it over the seat. She wrapped the blanket around her shoulders, stared out her window. She would not look at Tom. How dare he accuse Louis, a member of the Webber family, of causing the trouble at Dunn's? How would she explain Tom to Louis? Louis would never speak to her again after Tom's stupid punch. So what if she did want Louis to be her boyfriend? It was none of Tom's business. Did Tom think he had some call on her?

Addie ran her hands through her hair, pressed her fingers on her temples and forced herself to concentrate on Ruth having the baby. *It's too soon.* The car jerked to a stop at the hospital entrance. Addie threw off the blanket, jumped out, didn't bother closing the car door. The hell with Tom.

Her wet shoes squeaked across the linoleum to the reception desk. Addie blurted Ruth's name to a frowning nurse, then jogged up the two flights to the maternity floor. Another desk, where a nurse asked for the patient's name, clucked at Addie's demand to go to Ruth's room. "You may wait with the father." Addie signed the register under Al's scrawl.

The nurse pointed at a door marked "Fathers." As Addie opened it, a fog of cigarette smoke swamped her. She coughed, pulled her handkerchief from her pocket to cover her nose and mouth. Three smoking heads, clustered around a table radio, swiveled, then relaxed when they saw she was not a nurse. She recognized the oak-armed settee and chairs the men sat on as pieces from Hudson's Office Collection.

"Addie, back here." Al gestured from the far end of the room. She waved the handkerchief like a scythe, cutting a path through the smoke. A Coca-Cola vending machine, one with cigarettes, and another offering candy and chewing gum, stood like tin soldiers along the short wall of an alcove. In front of the machines, a dinette set from Hudson's Kitchen collection. Bright overhead lights reflected off the shiny linoleum floor. Two pay telephones hung on the wall next to a sign reading, "Please ask the nurse for change."

Al stood with hands on his hips, his shirtsleeves rolled up, slacks wrinkled. "Ruth is doing okay, last I heard." He pulled out a chair for Addie.

"I want to see her."

Al shrugged. "Me, too."

"Why aren't you with her?"

"I was until the nurse made me leave. Here, sit. Want a Coke?"

Addie bumped the chair with her knee. "How can you just wait here? Tell me what happened to Ruth."

Al held out his hands. "Take it easy. The nurse knows to find me here."

Tom walked in, carrying Addie's bag and jacket. "Smoke in here is worse than Dunn's."

"Why are you here?" Addie demanded of Tom.

Al eyed Addie, then Tom. "What's going on?"

Addie stomped her foot. "Never mind him. Tell me about Ruth. It's too soon for the baby."

Al rubbed his brow. "She had pain in her back, then low in her belly. It didn't stop, made her cry. I got the nurse on the phone. Dr. Tullen said to get her in here." He blushed red. "In the car, her water broke." Al said to Tom, "Don't ask me what that means."

Addie slumped into a chair. Tom set her bag on the table, hung her jacket on a wall hook. He slipped coins into the Coke machine, pulled out three bottles, stuck them one at a time in the bottle opener to pop the caps. He plunked the bottles onto the table, pushed one to Addie. "We might as well relax."

"You can leave," Addie said, turning away from him.

Tom scoffed. "You know why she's mad, Al? She's in love with none other than Louis Carter, known in Detroit's back rooms as young Mr. C."

Al's eyebrows shot up. "What?"

Addie shoved the chair back from the table, picked up her bag. "I am not listening to this."

She marched out, asked the desk nurse to direct her to the ladies' room. Addie whipped around a corner and dodged a collision with Dr. Tullen's nurse. The nurse wore a long-sleeved green cotton shift over her uniform, tied tight at her collar. Instead of the starched white cap, a wrap like the headscarf Ma wore for baking covered her hair. Both stopped short in mutual recognition. The nurse took a step back, wrinkled her nose. Addie realized she must reek of cigarette smoke.

"I was in the fathers' room with Ruth's husband. How is Ruth?"

"Mrs. Kealy is in the labor room. Dr. Tullen doesn't want to wait much longer."

"What does that mean?"

"She's close to delivering the baby."

"It's too soon! Take me to my sister. Please! She needs me."

The nurse pursed her lips, looked Addie up and down. "Wait here." She went back the way she came, disappeared at the other end of the hall. Addie leaned against the tiled wall, caught her reflection in the glass of a display case on the opposite side. She moved closer to inspect her hair, fished in her bag for bobby pins. She swept the front curls away from her face and pinned them. In the glass, the deep-set eyes, slim nose—she saw her mother's face, in the photograph Dan kept.

Addie jumped back at the nurse's voice. "Come along. It's not the usual procedure, but Dr. Tullen will allow you to be with Mrs. Kealy."

Addie matched the nurse's quick pace. "Is something wrong?"

"Mrs. Kealy will have an easier delivery if she is calmer." The nurse opened a door to a closet, selected a folded shift and a head covering like the ones she wore. She pushed the bundle into Addie's arms, led her through a doorway labeled "Nurses Only." Lockers along the walls, benches in between, and to the side, a room of toilet stalls.

The nurse opened a locker. "Leave the wet trousers here, roll up your sleeves before you put on the tunic. Wrap your hair completely under the scarf. Find me in the hall when you are ready." At the door she said, "Use the toilet—you won't have another chance."

Addie scooted to the first stall, peeled off the trousers, and peed. Did Ruth's water breaking feel relieving like this? No, the baby was coming early. Ruth would panic. Addie hurried to the sink, rolled the blouse sleeves above her elbow, and washed her hands. She grabbed the tunic from over the stall door where she had tossed it, pulled it over her head, tied the strings at the back of her neck. The rough cotton fabric brushed her bare thighs but fell below her knees to cover her underpants.

Guided by the mirror, Addie yanked her hair off her neck, pulled the scarf up and around twice, tucked the ends. She stuck her tongue out at her reflection. "I am not my mother, and neither is Ruth." She grabbed up her clothes and bag, stuffed them into the locker, and slammed it shut. In the hall, the nurse looked her over and gestured for Addie to follow.

They pushed through double doors into a washroom so brightly lit that Addie blinked. Gleaming white porcelain sinks lined two walls. The nurse instructed Addie to scrub her hands and arms with disinfecting soap. When they finished, the nurse backed into a push-door marked "Labor 1." She jerked her head at Addie to step through. "Touch only Ruth's hands and face. Nothing else."

"Addie, thank God," Ruth groaned. She lay on a gurney with a sheet covering her belly and legs. She clenched the sheet with both hands, grimaced, moaned like Addie had heard her do during migraines. Addie cradled Ruth's head, pushed away her damp curls from her face. Ruth arched her back, her feet moving to push up her knees.

"I'm here, Ruth, it's okay, I'm not leaving you." Addie grabbed Ruth's hand, received the pain of Ruth's nails digging into her palm. She whispered in Ruth's ear, "I will not let go."

The nurse propelled Ruth's feet into metal rests that extended from the end of the gurney. Her knees bent and her thighs parted wide under the sheet. The nurse folded back the sheet to uncover Ruth's legs. Her eyes darted wildly from side to side. Her howls of pain made Addie jump, but she kept hold of Ruth's hand.

Dr. Tullen strode in, shrouded in a white long-sleeved coat, like the butcher wore, and baggy white pants, his hair covered in what looked like a baseball cap missing the bill. "Ruth, I am going to examine you." He pulled a mask over his nose and mouth. "You'll feel my fingers." He sat on a low stool and rolled between Ruth's feet.

Ruth wailed at the doctor's touch. Sweat dribbled from her face and neck. Dr. Tullen rolled the stool back. "Ruth, it's time to push."

Addie wasn't sure Ruth heard. But Ruth answered, "I'm so tired."

"Not long now, Ruth." Dr. Tullen said to Addie. "Do you want to stay?"

Addie had never been present for a birth. When their sister Annie had her babies, Addie had been too young to help the midwife. In the movies, mothers made little fuss as labor began and looked pretty when it was over. Ruth's bulging veins, the guttural sounds coming from her, the indignity of her wide-open thighs—none of this was pretty.

Addie took a deep breath, nodded. "Yes."

"Hold your sister's hand. The nurse will tell Ruth when to push with the contractions."

The nurse wiped Ruth's face and neck with a cold cloth. "Ruth, you're doing really well. Your baby will be here soon." Her calm voice reminded Addie of her stepmother's unruffled tone about a bloody nose or gashed knee. The nurse put her arm under Ruth's shoulders, checked her watch to time the contractions. Ruth raised her head from the pillow. Her face contorted.

Addie kept hold of Ruth's hand. Her fingers flexed and dug into Addie's palm as her body shuddered with the effort to push. Two gowned and masked nurses came through the door, one wheeling a cart with a tray of instruments, the other a baby bed. Dr. Tullen's white cap bobbed between Ruth's thighs.

The contractions came one after another. In the short breaks between, Ruth mumbled, "I can't ... I can't." Addie and the nurse soothed her with cold cloths, saying "Yes, you can."

At last Dr. Tullen called for Ruth to push once more, this time with all her might. Ruth screeched through the effort. Then came a whimper and a gurgle.

"Ruth, you have a daughter."

Ruth's hand went limp in Addie's palm, her head lolled back. "Thank God."

Another squeaky cry. Addie let the tears squeeze from her eyes. But she couldn't see the baby on Dr. Tullen's lap. The doctor called for the bassinet, handed off the baby. He murmured instructions to the two assisting nurses. They bent over the bassinet making quick movements, blocking Addie's view of the baby.

"Where's my baby?" Ruth tried to sit up.

Dr. Tullen said, "Lay still, Ruth."

The nurse restrained Ruth with a hand firm against her shoulder. "There, there, Ruth, Doctor is not finished. Baby is in good care."

Ruth startled at the doctor's hand running over her belly.

Addie instinct told her something was not right. While the doctor tended to Ruth, Addie listened for the baby's cry. Wasn't the baby supposed to cry?

Ruth squirmed, tried to close her legs. Dr. Tullen said, "Okay, Ruth, the birth is complete." He murmured something to one of the nurses attending to the baby. She lifted the swaddled bundle for Ruth to see the tiny face, eyes squeezed shut. Ruth reached for her.

Dr. Tullen stood and put his hand on Ruth's knee. "Ruth, your baby's breathing is slow. She was born earlier than expected, and she weighs only five pounds. She's going to a warming crib in the nursery." He nodded to the nurse, who laid the baby in the bassinet and whisked it out of the room.

Ruth wailed, "I want my baby!"

Addie rubbed Ruth's arm, afraid of upsetting her by asking questions. Dr. Tullen squeezed Ruth's knee. "Ruth, let us take care of her. I'll talk to your husband. I'll see you when you're settled in the ward." He left.

The two remaining nurses met at Ruth's feet. One said, "Mrs. Kealy, after a wash, we'll sit you up, change your gown." Their hands began moving under the sheet along Ruth's legs. Ruth writhed and clutched at Addie. She sputtered through sobs, "Go with the baby. Get Al."

Addie trotted through the washroom to the main hallway. She spotted the nurse wheeling the baby, ran after her. The nurse turned her head at the thump of Addie's shoes behind her. "Stay back," she warned.

Addie peered into the crib; the little face wasn't moving. "Where are you taking her?" she demanded.

The nurse kept her stride, pointing to a sign overhead. "You can watch us incubate her from the observation window." She pushed the baby crib through a door labeled "Nursery–No Admittance."

Incubate her. Warnings from Dr. Spock's chapter on "The Premature Baby" rang alarm bells in Addie's head. She ran.

Grim-faced Al stared through the observation window, Dr. Tullen at his side. The doctor clapped Al on the back and strode away. Al leaned both hands on the window ledge. When Addie came next to him, he choked on his words. "She might not make it."

On the other side of the window, the nurses opened the incubator, a glass and steel crib box hooked to wires and tubes. Steady and swift, they transferred Ruth's baby girl from the bassinet. Hands unwrapped the swaddling, laid her on her back, clad only in a diaper and a beanie cap, head sideways, eyes closed. Addie judged her body was small enough to fit in Al's hand. A finger twitch and the slight rise of her chest signaled a breath. Al groaned when they closed the glass lid of the box, turned dials to start the control lights blinking.

Addie took his arm. "Ruth needs you."

Al nodded. "Tom is in the waiting room. Tell him, will you?"

"Yes." Addie looked into Al's eyes, reading his worry mirroring her own.

Al whispered, "We have to prepare Ruth for the worst."

"No, that can't happen." Tears trickled down Addie's cheeks.

Al gave her a quick hug, walked away. She gazed at the tiny form, squinting to see evidence of breathing. She leaned her forehead against the glass. *Breathe, breathe, breathe,* she urged the baby, and herself. She thought of using the pay telephone in the fathers' waiting room, calling Dan, to hear her brother reassure her the baby would live. Addie knew that was no use, but she craved hope.

She turned away from the window. When Addie entered the fathers' room, the men in the nearest chairs jumped, and she realized she still wore the nurses tunic. With no trousers underneath.

Tom rushed up to her. "What the heck happened?"

Addie fell against his chest and began to cry.

"Oh, Jesus," Tom said, circling his arms around her. The men gawked as Tom coaxed Addie to the alcove. She leaned into him, her legs moving only because his did. He sat her on a chair, brought her a cup of water. When she tried to speak, more tears flowed. He pulled his chair close next to her, laid his arm across the back of hers, waited.

When Addie could talk, she burbled about Ruth's labor, the baby's breathing, the incubator, and Dr. Spock while swiping her tears with her arm. At last, she sipped the water, breathed deep, and looked at Tom. His grimace crinkled the arcs of the still greenish-yellow bruising near his eye. He pulled her to his chest with both arms, and her hand slid around his neck. They sat like that until they heard Al say, "C'mon, we need you."

Addie jumped up. "Has Ruth seen the baby?"

Al leaned against the wall as though he needed support. He rubbed his eyes, kicked at the cigarette machine. "Not yet. Ruth can't stop crying. I've called the priest to come."

Addie and Tom exchanged a look. Tom went to Al, grasped his shoulder. "What do you want us to do?"

Al rubbed his brow, said, "Be godparents for the baptism."

Addie said, "I'm not Catholic."

"Doesn't matter. Ruth wants you. She's in such a state." Al straightened up, ran a hand through his hair. "We can only watch from the window. You'll just stand there."

Addie pulled at the tunic. "My trousers are in the nurses' locker room." Al and Tom followed her as she rushed there to change. She tugged off the tunic, pulled on her damp pants. She undid the head wrap, fluffed her hair with her fingers, and picked up her bag. Tom was waiting in the hall. He answered her questioning look. "Al went for Ruth."

Addie and Tom waited at the nursery window. Three rows of open cribs lined the room, spaced so the nurses could move among the babies, squirming, crying, fists waving. Pink or blue blanket, pink or blue bear drawn on the name card affixed to each crib.

Addie heard Ruth weeping before Al turned her wheelchair into the corridor. Addie went to Ruth and took her hand. Al positioned the chair close to the window and took Ruth's other hand. Tom came around next to Addie. When he felt for her hand, she entwined her fingers with his.

Ruth wailed, "I can't hold her."

Addie said, "I know, Ruth. Soon you will. Have you named her?"

Ruth sniffed, whispered, "Katherine Jane."

Addie smiled. Their older sister, Jane, would bask in that honor.

A nurse wheeled the warming crib close to the window. Tom breathed out at the sight of the tiny body inside. Addie felt him lean into her as she did to him.

Ruth said to Al, "Tell me she's breathing."

Al choked up. "Honey, she *is* breathing."

Father Dabrowski strode into the nursery, his black robes overlaid with a white doctor's gown. A nurse held a tray with vials like the ones he had used to baptize Loretta's baby. Another nurse opened the top of the incubator part way. The priest prayed. The nurses clasped their hands and bowed their heads. He dipped his pinky finger into a vial, made the lightest contact with baby's chest to mark the sign of the cross. Ruth, tears running, murmured "Amen" with Al. As the priest withdrew his arm, the nurse closed the crib. Father's lips continued to move in prayer. Turning, he made another sign of the cross in the air, blessing all the babies.

Addie let go of Tom's hand, stooped over, and put her arms around Ruth's shoulders. Ruth buried her face in Addie's blouse, crying harder. Al said, "I've got to take her to the ward," just as a nurse came toward them, motioning to Al.

Addie asked him, "Will they let me stay with her?"

"Go with Ruth until they kick you out. I need to talk with Tom." Al bent to whisper in Ruth's ear, kissed her cheek. Ruth folded in on herself, nails digging at her arms.

Addie took the wheelchair handles. The nurse led the way into the ward. Iron bedsteads, three and three, were arrayed on the two long walls, shades drawn on windows lining the far wall. The overhead lights were off; huddled forms lay under blankets in all but one bed. Next to the empty bed, turned down for Ruth, was a table with a telephone and a reading lamp. The nurse flicked on the lamp, helped Ruth from the chair. Ruth shifted her hip to rest against the bed. "I'm so tired."

Addie saw a bloodstain on Ruth's gown. The nurse said to Addie, "Step out while I settle her in."

Addie squeezed Ruth's arm. "I'll be close by, Ruth."

She slumped on a bench in the hall, checked her watch. After midnight, and she was due in the Print Shop at eight. If she stayed with Ruth, could she make herself presentable for Hudson's? Her suit jacket was crumpled, the legs of her trouser pants stained and wrinkled. The blouse might do, and she could pin up her hair, but she had no cosmetics with her. If she went to work with no sleep, would she make it through the day?

The nurse stuck her head out of the ward door. "Mrs. Kealy is sound asleep. You can see her tomorrow for the visiting hours." She closed the door.

Thankful that Ruth was resting, Addie waited for Al. He came around the corner with the keys to the sedan in one hand and her jacket in the other. "I'll drive you home."

"You should stay. Tom can drive me home."

Al shook his head. "He can't. I telephoned Ma to take in the keg delivery tomorrow. She got wind of trouble."

"What do you mean?"

"Louis has tough guys looking for Tom. Tom's on the run."

CHAPTER 20

Al drove along the quiet streets, the rain coming down faster than the wipers could flick it away. "Do you want to hear about Louis?"

Addie sighed. "I wish I didn't."

"He had a reputation long before he made his way to Dunn's."

Louis, Al told her, was familiar in the taverns tucked into the nooks and crannies of Detroit, neighborhood places his family would never set foot in or hear an inkling of his pursuits. He played cards evenings after work, didn't hide who he was, strolled in wearing suit and tie, carrying cash in his briefcase.

"He played with working men, bought them rounds, acted dumb about the game," Al said. Until his cocky glee over his winnings rubbed the locals he fleeced the wrong way, and their friendly mood turned. "He moved his action enough times that word got around." When Louis discovered the game at Dunn's, the cardsharper in the backroom game welcomed him. "The sharper used Louis as a bigger-money draw to raise the stakes."

Ma soon heard the low-down on Dunn's new player from a beat cop, Al told her. "The cops knew Louis and his pattern.

Louis had no problem paying the cops' tributes to claim a seat in any back room."

Ma warned Tom the sharper was bringing a tougher crowd to the game. "Tom never told me Ma gave him a heads up," Al said. "The sharper's nasty temper unnerved him. Tom hoped he could keep them happy and the game would stay quiet."

The sharper's buddies bragged to Tom about taking easy money from "Mr. C" of the Webber family. Louis's play drifted when he drank. Skirting around the table with shots for the players, Tom saw the hands around, watched Louis giggle as he bet. Tipsy Louis was outmatched by the cronies working the con on him. He lost big, but he never caught on or he believed he could play them out.

Al said, "Louis bragged about wagering with the family money. He brought in a cousin who staked him for a few games."

The night Tom and Al took up bats, Louis was out of town for a family wedding. When he heard that Al and Tom had forced the game out of Dunn's, Louis paid the cops to get Al and Tom out of the way with a raid.

Al shook his head. "He must have paid big. The cops gave Louis the keys to the padlocks."

Louis bragged to the sharper about a bankroll, talked his way into a game with double the buy in. "The sharper figured Louis was putting his roll on one big game to sweep up his losses. They didn't know where his cash was coming from, but they didn't care, as long as they rigged it so he lost."

But Al and Tom reopened Dunn's before the night of the big game, with the neighborhood in their corner. The sharper wanted to muscle Al and Tom to hold the game at Dunn's, but the cops demanded more payoff to look the other way. The sharper didn't like the squeeze, or the trouble Louis caused. "The tough guy moved the game and cut Louis out. But Mr. C had other ideas. He put out the word he would pay big to crash the game."

"How do you know?"

"Ma. She's been on the block so long, people talk to her."

Addie said, "When I ran into him after studying, Louis was in a panic about having left his briefcase in the library."

"He must have been carrying cash. It was bad timing that Tom showed up when Louis was going to drive you home."

"Tom didn't know that Louis was in my class, but you did. That day you saw his car."

"I never figured Louis would be our trouble. I worried about the sharper. I was wrong. Louis has a temper. He got steamed when we messed up his game, and he's upped the ante since Tom punched him."

Gambler Louis, who paid men to hurt Tom, was not the Louis that Addie had laughed with or dreamed about. She had heard stories in the tower about people who blew a week's pay on cards, horses, dice. Gambling got a grip some could not shake. But Louis? He was a thrill-seeker, she saw that, and unpredictable. She had fawned over college-man Louis, who read Greek and Latin. Louis, who giggled and held her hand. A different Louis had rolled in the wet leaves fighting Tom.

Tom had punched away her dreams. But she had held Tom's hand, too, last night.

"Where has Tom gone?"

Al shook his head. "Not saying. For your own sake."

Addie fumed. "This is crazy, all of it. I don't want to hear any more about either of them. I'm worried sick about Ruth and the baby. *I* am due at work in a few hours. I *have* to study. I take my exam on Tuesday."

"I am worried sick about the baby too! It's a fluke Louis and Tom ran into each other, with you in the middle."

"Tom did *not* have to punch him."

"Tom came to your rescue!"

"I didn't need to be rescued!"

In front of their building, Addie pushed the handle to open the door before Al came to a full stop. Dead quiet in the yard, a light in Doris's window. Addie dragged her exhaustion up the stairs. Doris, in bathrobe and hair curlers, flung the apartment door open, grabbed Addie around the shoulders. Al trailed behind. From the hall he said, "I'll go back for visiting hours. Unless the doctor calls."

Inside the apartment, Addie stepped out of her shoes, held up her hands. "Please don't ask me to talk." Doris folded her arms and stepped back.

Addie shut the bathroom door between them. She peeled off her blouse, ran the water until it was hot. She banded her hair back and scrubbed her face and neck, rubbing the sodden washcloth over and over her skin. The scratches on her palm from Ruth's nails stung. Her forehead and temples ached. Addie stumbled to her bedroom, peeled off the rest of her clothes, pulled on her nightgown, and crawled into bed.

Addie woke relieved that she had not dreamed. She hoped clean clothes and fresh makeup would prevent Mr. Reed from noticing her fatigue. Doris wasn't awake and Addie didn't take the time to make coffee. She found a note under the door in Al's hand—the telephone number of Ruth's ward. Addie shoved it into her bag as she hurried out of the building. Al's car was gone. She plopped into a seat on the tram without memory of walking the blocks to the stop.

Addie's heart raced with panic as she pushed into Hudson's employee lobby. Her eyes darted left and right. She had never seen Louis in the store, but now she worried he lurked in the corners. As her elevator ascended, Addie rolled her eyes, thinking how giddy she had been over him. Even if he hadn't turned out to be "Mr. C," she had let her good sense slide away over Louis's good looks, charm. She would be cautious in the class, stay under his radar. And if she did face him, she would tell him straight that she wanted nothing to do with him. After last night, Louis would figure out her connection to Dunn's. That she knew about his gambling. Would he leave her alone or make trouble for her?

The sight inside the Print Shop interrupted her worry.

Joe shouted at an army of men wielding mops in a flood of water. Water seeped from the overhead pipes onto them and the ringing telephone on the counter. Finished orders bundled in front of the counter were a soggy mess of soaked paper and running ink.

Joe pointed to a patchwork of rags and cardboard laid at the far edge of the flood. "Walk along that to go to Mr. Reed's office."

Addie followed the puddled path on tiptoes. Men were hauling the paper stocks to the back of the shop and covering the presses with tarps. From outside his office, she heard Mr. Reed yelling into his telephone. She stopped. She had never heard him raise his voice or use such a tone.

He hung up, saw her, waved her in. "The plumbers are on the way." He tapped the order book on his desk. "Lucky I forgot to put this on the counter last night. You work in here for the time being." He came around the desk and pointed to his chair.

The counter telephone had not stopped ringing. Addie and Mr. Reed looked at each other. She went to his desk phone, dialed the switchboard, asked them to connect Print Shop calls to Mr. Reed's office telephone. As she hung up, it rang. Four calls later, Addie realized she was still wearing her coat and hat.

The relentless rush and the compromised working conditions tested the fortitude of the crew. Mr. Reed prioritized the wet orders to rerun on the few working machines. The plumbers took over the front with their ladders and equipment, blocking the door. Addie heard Joe cursing under his breath as he ran back and forth.

Ruth and the baby hovered in the back of Addie's mind. If anything changed with the baby, Al or Doris would call. Unless the operator didn't put outside calls through. Addie called an operator she knew from the tower to ask that any call for her go to Mr. Reed's line. Each time she picked up the receiver, Addie held her breath until the caller identified as a Hudson's employee.

At midday, Addie huddled over a box lunch at the desk. Generous Mr. Reed had offered them to the entire shop. The men with pails said no, thank you, but Addie saw the appreciation of the gesture in their nods and smiles. At three o'clock she stole time to telephone Doris. No news. Addie would meet her at the hospital after work.

When the clock neared five, Mr. Reed came into the office, sat in the chair across the desk from Addie. She smiled to herself at the temporary reversal, turned the order book his way. He took off his spectacles, rubbed his eyes, wound the wires back over his ears, pushed the bridge back on his nose. "Today was one of our most trying. But we persevered."

"We did, Mr. Reed."

"Mrs. Reynolds has reminded me that your mid-semester examination is on Tuesday."

Addie clutched her pencil. Why would Mrs. Reynolds bring that up with Mr. Reed? She kept her voice calm. "Yes, Tuesday."

Mr. Reed glanced at the wall clock. "Then I imagine you plan to study this weekend. Go on home, Miss."

Except for two runs to the ladies' room, Addie had not had a break all day from the voices on the telephone demanding their posters and sell sheets and price lists. She looked into Mr. Reed's kind eyes and her own spilled. Tears dribbled down her cheeks. Mr. Reed looked at her, rose to close the door, sat again. Ruth, the baby, the raid, Louis, the fight, her worries, all tumbled out of her. Addie swabbed at her cheeks with the handkerchief Mr. Reed set in front of her. When she had poured out her woes, she heaved a great sigh and sat back.

She met Mr. Reed's gaze and what she had done hit her. She felt her cheeks burn with embarrassment. "I am so sorry, Mr. Reed. Forgive me. I didn't mean to—"

Mr. Reed cut her off. "Louis Carter was fired today."

Addie stared at him, wide-eyed. Mr. Reed nodded, went on. "Mrs. Reynolds informed me. Mr. Carter no longer represents Hudson's in the college program."

Addie clasped her cheeks with both hands, rubbed her fingers along her temples. Mr. Reed rose, filled a paper cup with water from the cooler in the corner, and handed it to her. She downed it, then dared to ask, "Why was he fired?"

"Mr. Carter's cash accounting was out of order."

Addie groaned, "Oh, no." What if Mr. Reed no longer had confidence in her, after what she had told him? "Mr. Reed, honestly, I didn't know anything about his work in the store."

"Louis Carter's misdeed has no connection to you." Mr. Reed checked his pocket watch. "Go see your sister, Miss. Study over the weekend. Monday will be an easier day in the shop. You'll have extra time at lunch."

Addie retrieved her handbag from under the desk, took her hat and coat from the rack. "Thank you, Mr. Reed."

He waved an arm. "We will see you on Monday."

Addie made her way to the down elevator, thankful for Mr. Reed's understanding. Her embarrassment lingered, but by telling him the story she had stepped away from the shadow Louis's actions might cast over her if Mrs. Reynolds discovered their friendship. But Louis, she reminded herself, was no friend. "Cash accounting out of order" and his gambling meant he had done the unthinkable—he had stolen from Hudson's. She knew Tom reacted to seeing her with Louis because he knew what Louis was capable of. And, knowing Tom, he enjoyed landing a few for what Louis had brought down on Dunn's. Preventing her from getting into Louis's convertible had been her rescue, after all.

She had been so angry with Tom and then laid on his chest as naturally as Ruth leaned on Al.

A beeping horn snapped Addie to attention. At the curb, Doris waved from the passenger seat of Al's sedan. Addie hurried to hop into the back seat and Al nudged the car into the traffic. Doris turned her head to say, "The little one is holding her own."

Addie breathed a sigh of relief. She asked, "Have you heard from Tom?"

Al glanced over his shoulder. "Tom can take care of himself."

Addie fumed. "That's not what I asked. Did you hear from him?"

Al and Doris exchanged a look. Al said, "Not yet."

"Hudson's fired Louis Carter today."

Al shook his head. "Over money?"

Addie caught his eye in the mirror. "His cash accounting was out of order."

Al blew out a whistle.

Addie asked, "Are you going to open Dunn's?"

"Ma will open for us tomorrow night. She and Patsy will work."

"What if the tough guys come looking for Tom?"

"Ma has that covered."

Addie said, "Even if there's no trouble, one night isn't enough." Dribs and drabs of beer sales would not make the bar's overhead, let alone bank the amount Al needed to buy Ruth a house.

Al chuckled. "Patsy is pretty darn good behind the bar. If she's pushing mugs, we might make enough to restock the kegs for more than one night a week." He shrugged. "If you've got any ideas, tell me."

Addie folded her arms, stared out the window. He didn't seem worried, so why was she stewing? Mr. Reed had advised her to see her sister and to study. She took heart from a vision of Mr. Reed pulling a compass from his vest, instead of the pocket watch, reorienting her to the priorities, once again.

They were allowed to visit Ruth in the ward one at a time. Al went to her first. Addie and Doris looked through the nursery window. The incubator sat nearest the nurses' station at the back of the nursery, *Katherine Jane Kealy* written on a card taped to the side. Craning their necks, they could see her face. No stuffed animals, knitted blankets, or cute bonnets allowed inside with her. Doris clutched Addie's arm. "She's holding her own. She'll be okay."

Addie said, "I want to hear what the doctors say."

Doris looked at her. "Have faith—and hope, for Ruth's sake."

"I want to be ready for the worst."

"Why not hope for the best?"

Addie shifted away from Doris's grasp. "Of course, you're right." She said that to end the debate, but she didn't agree. Watching the priest drip oil onto the baby's tiny chest, she had prayed for the first time since her stepmother stopped taking her to church. And she didn't know if praying when you were desperate counted. Praying and hoping for the best was only a waystation on a journey you were forced to take, like the newsreels of the enemy marching prisoners of war. She could not pray or hope the baby to health. No one could.

They went to the fathers' room. When Al came in, he paced, punched one fist into the other. "This is killing me. I can't help Ruth, I can't help the baby."

He went on to tell them that Dr. Tullen had called in specialists from the University of Michigan's maternity hospital to examine the baby. Katie, he called her, had passed the danger of the first critical hours. The nurses had begun feeding her Ruth's breast milk with a dropper. Little Katherine would stay in the incubator until she gained at least a pound. Her lungs would develop, but some degree of breathing difficulties would persist. Ruth's migraines, and the pills she took, may have brought on the early labor. The progress of Katie using her legs and arms, raising her head, her eyesight, would be known in the months ahead.

Doris said to Addie, "Go to Ruth." She put an arm around Al, led him to the coffeepot.

In the ward, Ruth whined, "The nurses attach a pump to my breasts to collect the milk. Do you know what that feels like? I cry through it. They say I'm not helping the baby, that my nerves will dry up the milk."

Addie, her hand inside her bag to bring out Dr. Spock's book, thought better of it. Ruth would not feel calmer reading Dr. Spock opine that a woman becomes a real mother when she holds the baby to feed at her breast.

"The nurses draw the curtains around my bed when they bring the babies to the other mothers," Ruth said. "They wheel me to the nursery window for a few minutes once a day to see her."

When Addie handed off the visiting time to Doris, she hurried to the ladies' room and thumbed through Dr. Spock's chapter on premature infants. Nothing, it said, was certain before the child was two years old. She took a deep breath. Katie had a long way to go. Addie stuffed the book into her bag, made her way back to the waiting room.

Al sat staring at the radio, seeming not to hear the static breaking up the broadcast. When he looked up at her, with dark circles under his eyes, the crease in his brow, no smile taking over his face, Addie's shoulders slumped. She sat in the chair next to his.

Al shook his head. "Ruth will stay here a few more days. The baby will be here for who knows how long. The bills are piling up. If I don't go back to work on Monday, I won't be welcome to come back."

"Ma and Patsy will sell the kegs. That's something."

Al folded his arms, smirked. "Little Dunn's and mighty Hudson's both taken in by Louis Carter." He kicked his legs out, stretched. "That's the icing on the cake."

"Hudson's can take the loss. You can't afford to be closed."

"That's the wrong way to look at it."

"How so?"

"I can't afford to open. So, I'm not going to."

Addie turned to him. "What do you mean?"

"I sold Dunn's." Al met Addie's stare. "Ma made me an offer today. I called her a while ago to take the deal."

"How does she plan to pay you for it?"

"Didn't get that far with the details. Just told her I'd take the offer."

Addie shook her head. "No, no, no. Ma doesn't have the money on her books to make you a good offer."

"It's a very good offer."

Addie exhaled a long sigh. "Then she's been hiding cash from me. I suspected, when she bought the tailor's building, then ovens and refrigerators appeared. I got so busy, I let this go. I will sort this out with her." She rubbed her brow. "What about Tom?"

"He knew we were at the edge. He'll get his share."

Al rose and fiddled with the radio dial, but the static persisted, and he flicked the knob to turn it off. He stood with hands in his pockets.

Addie asked, "Are you sorry?"

Al shrugged. "A family man goes to a steady job Monday through Friday, brings home a regular paycheck. A family man does not run a tavern." Then he said, softer, "We had a lot of good times." He picked up his hat. "Let's go see our baby, then I'll say goodnight to Ruth." He crooked his arm for Addie to take.

As they walked toward the nursery, Al said, "I've got my eye on a house." He winked. "With a big tree in the front."

CHAPTER 21

Addie pedaled her bike to a stop in front of the diner on Saturday morning. A crew of men were carting out the worktables and wooden cubbies from the tailor's building next door. A bin on the street caught debris thrown from the second-floor windows. The new owner stood on the sidewalk with hands on her hips, her thin cotton kitchen dress bulked up with an army-green man's cable-knit sweater.

Ma held up a hand when she saw Addie. "I see the purpose on your face, Missy, so before you start telling me what I can't do, come inside, and hear what's what."

With coffee and the paperwork, Addie listened and understood where Ma got the cash for the ovens and for Dunn's. She raised her brows, scanned the top sheet of paper set before her, when Ma said, "My old man died. His land came to me." Ma had never mentioned a mister.

"Ya, I washed my hands of him a long time ago. Both of us was raised in copper country, far as you can go in the Upper Peninsula, married there. We came down here for work. He didn't settle in, couldn't stay with a job, kept talking about

290

moving us back to the U.P." Ma slapped a hand on the table. "No way was I taking up the rugged life again." She sat back, arms folded. "I started out selling pies from my truck. Before my good-for-nothing man left, it was pies paying our bills. He took off up there with our savings, bought land. Never did nothing with it."

Ma pulled a letter from the pile. "This came with the deeds. Old bastard put my name down with his." "Mister" had a small-town lawyer hold the deeds for his parcels of waterfront property up north. Together, they were worth a tidy sum. "Didn't know it till he died. Then I cashed in."

The money was in the bank. The transactions satisfied Addie, and relieved her worry about the payment due to Al. Ma had made Al a very good offer, just as he said. Now, the block from the diner to Dunn's belonged to her. *Nothing stands in Ma's way*, Addie thought. She asked, "Why did you buy the tavern?"

Ma waved her arm at the street outside the window. "Dunn's been on this block for fifty years. Al was not going to keep his head above water." She sat back. "Small potatoes compared to the big boys like Hudson's, but I have the same bug. I like making money."

"What if Tom comes back?"

Ma shook her head. "He's welcome with me, but I don't count on him coming back."

Ma had a point about Al not making it, even if Tom wasn't in hiding. But Addie had a feeling Tom would have wanted to hold on. If he came back, he could be part of Ma's business. *If he came back.*

Ma said, "Me and Patsy will open tonight, with the kegs on hand, Patsy behind the bar." She pulled a larger sheet of drafting paper from the pile on the table. "These are the renovations we're making to the tailor's shop. Upstairs, in the old apartment, we'll make an office for you."

"Ma, I don't work here."

"Not like Patsy and the girls, but this enterprise needs an office."

Addie smiled at "enterprise." Ma's ventures were certainly expanding. Ma went back to the kitchen and left Addie to work. She did a quick updating of the books, ate one of Patsy's grilled cheese sandwiches, and promised she would spend more time the next week organizing Dunn's books. Ma and Patsy sent Addie home with a pumpkin pie to encourage her studying.

Addie pedaled in a wind so cold she expected to see snowflakes. Cardboard witches and carved pumpkins decorated houses and storefronts along the way. The exam would be over by Halloween. The midterm counted for half the class grade. With any luck, she'd do well enough to sail on that grade to the end of the semester. "We can't count on luck, Miss," Mr. Reed always said. But she leaned on luck and study working together.

Addie stowed her bike and clomped up the stairs. She entered a silent apartment. Ruth had forbidden Addie to come with Al and Doris to the hospital until after the exam. Addie got to her books. She paced while memorizing her notes. She re-read chapters, telephoned Mary to sort out her confusion on a formula. In the evening, her confidence in her preparation boosted, she warmed a bowl of soup and paged through the newspaper she had skipped reading that morning.

Someone knocked on the door, startling her. She opened it.

Al was in the hallway, unlocking his door. "Doris will be right up. We found out Ruth can come home on Tuesday. Katie

Jane will stay. Ruth will go in to give milk every day at the hospital."

"That's wonderful news. What about you going to work?"

Al shook his head. "Monday morning, I'll go to the office and square things so I can bring Ruth home midday on Tuesday. After that, I buckle down."

"How is she?"

"Not as weepy. Loretta visited today. Seemed to ease Ruth's mind."

"Loretta has a big heart." Al gave Addie a quizzical look. "I mean, Ruth says that about Loretta."

"Yeah. She's got her hands full, but she'll do anything for Ruth." Al looked away. "As will I." He pointed to Addie, "As will you, after your exam."

Addie laughed. "Goodnight, Al." She closed the door.

On Sunday, she woke at dawn sweating under the quilts with an ache in her neck. Her night had been restless. On the edges of her mind, she imagined a series of distressing scenes of her failure on the exam. An early walk to the Belle Isle Bridge, she decided, might clear her head. She pushed out of bed and dressed for the chilly morning.

The cold temperature prodded quick steps. Jack-o'-lanterns with jagged teeth perched on the porches of the houses made her think of the watchful eyes of the swordfish. She tried to fix her mind on *after*. After the exam, she would visit the baby; after the exam she would help Ruth. She would get Ma's businesses in order. Buy a new suit to wear for class. Returning home, she marched into the apartment and made breakfast. She went back to her books with coffee. Wise Doris kept her distance by heading out to visit friends.

Addie had read her notes so many times the pages shuffled in her head like a deck of cards. Her leg jiggled; her toe tapped under her desk. She paced through the apartment, sat again with the fidgets. She repeated the pattern through the hours until sunset, then slapped the textbook closed. Her hands shook as she gathered her notes into her bag, intending to read them again the next day, during the longer lunch time Mr. Reed had promised.

Mary telephoned on Monday evening for their last-minute review. Before bed, Doris offered Addie the use of her special bath salts to soothe her nerves. Addie lazed in the tub, shampooed her hair. Calmness surrounded her like a shield she could carry into the fray.

On Tuesday morning, Addie entered the lecture room fifteen minutes before the start. The glare of the overhead lamps, the stony faces of the teaching assistants lined up at the front, and the word "Silence" chalked in tall block letters on the board swept away her calm. She scanned the room. Louis Carter was not the only student missing on exam day. Addie guessed that about a third of the seats were empty.

Addie fixed on the beacon of Mary waving to her from their usual seats. "Where is everyone?" she whispered as she sat down.

Mary murmured, "If you drop the class before the midterm, it's not on your record. If you take this exam and fail, your average sinks. Guess they cut their losses."

Addie saw Bored One make his way to a seat at the side. She didn't see the fourth student from Hudson's anywhere in the room.

The teaching assistants took advantage of the empty chairs to instruct the students to sit one seat apart. Addie and Mary piled their bags and coats on the seat separating them. Both placed two pencils with erasers and a fountain pen on their desk. Mary smiled at Addie. "Cake and coffee after we ace this." Addie raised her brows in agreement. Her two morning cups gurgled in her gut.

The room fell silent when Professor Morse strode in. He stood at the podium with arms crossed as the senior teaching assistant announced the test instructions. The students had the full class time to work. Keep the test paper face down until the signal to begin. When finished, hand the test to the proctor and leave the room. Questions? Addie's eyes flicked left and right. No one moved.

With Professor Morse's nod, the assistants came down the aisle, distributing a bundle of papers to each row. Mary took one, handing off to Addie with a wink that was no comfort to Addie's thumping heart. She stared at the blank backside of the test paper waiting for the prompt: "Begin."

Pencil in hand, Addie scanned the first question. She called up details, shuffling through her mental notebook until she pictured the correct information. On to the next. Her neck and shoulders tensed, and she crossed her ankles to settle more comfortably in the seat. Out of the corner of her eye, she saw Mary tap her pencil on the page, write. The further Addie progressed in the questions, the surer she was of the answers. She almost giggled at seeing two problems the teaching assistant had drilled them on in the practicum. He had given them a preview, and she had paid attention.

Addie's eyes flicked to the clock. More than half the time gone. She had two questions remaining, requiring the working of accounting formulas and a written explanation of her conclusions. When she finished, she remembered Mary's tip to recheck all her answers, and she ran her pencil over each one. Her test paper was complete with minutes to spare. Her mental notebook closed. A sideways glance told her Mary was on the last problem. Addie closed her eyes, breathed out. She wanted coffee, and to never again feel as nervous as she had about this test. She opened her eyes at Mary's tap on her arm. Together, they went to the proctor and handed over their test papers. Bored One was scratching out something on his paper, smudges of blue ink on his hands. He glanced up, caught her eye with a sharp look. Addie straightened her shoulders and strode from the lecture room.

Heading to the cafeteria, Mary proposed that they not discuss the test until they got their results. Addie's mood lightened with every forkful of the cake and Mary's banter about making a Halloween costume. Mary was headed to the library, expecting Addie to go too, but Addie made an impromptu decision. "I want to be there when my sister comes home."

That afternoon, Ruth and Addie sat propped side-by-side on pillows in Ruth's bed.

"I cried so much that Dr. Tullen told the nurses to take me into the nursery to see Katie." Ruth clutched Addie's hand tighter. "When the nurse put her in my arms, her eyes opened! Addie, those few minutes were heaven."

Addie whispered, "You're her mother."

Ruth said, "But she doesn't know me. I wish they would have let me stay with my baby."

"You'll be there every day. Katie's getting stronger with your milk." Addie didn't mention Al's worry about the cost of days in the hospital. "What can I do to help?"

Ruth pointed at a box on the bureau. "Put that breast pump together. I feel the milk let down." She pulled her nightgown away from her chest. "See the wet spots?"

Addie opened the box. "I've never seen *this* sold at Hudson's." She laid out the pieces. Following the directions for assembling the apparatus, she clamped, screwed, and twisted. "This looks like a bicycle tire pump attached to a baby bottle!" she said when she finished.

Ruth eyed the measures marked on the bottle. "I'm supposed to try for two ounces." She got up from the bed, settled into the armchair with a pillow under her arm. "Set the bottle against this pillow. I need both hands to work the pump."

Addie wedged the bottle in Ruth's lap, squished it tight against the pillow. Ruth unbuttoned her nightgown. "Don't laugh; it's an ugly nursing bra." She unhooked the left cup to bare her swollen breast. Ruth winced as she fit the glass part of the pump atop her nipple. Her other hand grasped the body of the plunger, thumb on top. After three slow pushes, milky fluid trickled into the bottle. Ruth breathed in and out, found her rhythm. "Leave me for a few minutes."

Addie went to sit on the davenport, picked up Dr. Spock's book from the side table. She opened to the page with Ruth's bookmark, "Breastfeeding." She scanned a few pages and closed the book. The mother's diet was important for producing the baby's nourishment. Was Doris doing the grocery shopping, or Al? Addie went to the kitchen to check the supplies. Milk, orange juice, eggs and butter in the refrigerator, a bag of potatoes in the keeper, a loaf in the breadbox. Addie reopened the book and jotted Dr. Spock's foods for nursing mothers on a pad. She would ask Doris about cooking for Ruth.

Ruth waddled into the kitchen carrying the pump and bottle. "Not much. That was just a try-out." She poured the milk down the drain. Ruth nodded toward the book. "The nurses gave me a bag of feeding bottles for storing my milk. They must be sterilized every day. Page 113 in Dr. Spock. Doris borrowed a sterilizing pail from Muriel." Ruth leaned against the counter and sighed. "I don't know how I'm going to take care of the baby and do all the chores, like the book says."

Addie turned to the page, scanned the sterilizing instructions. "I can do this."

Ruth folded her arms under her heavy breasts. "But I am supposed to do it myself. When Katie comes home, feeding every three hours, day and night, changing the baby, washing the diapers, the clothes, and, oh, yes, *relaxing*, so I'll make enough milk. Dinner for my husband, and before he comes home, dressing and doing my hair and makeup. And a clean apartment!"

"Who said you can't have help?" Addie closed the book. "Dr. Spock is not here looking over your shoulder."

"What about Al? He'll think I'm not a good mother." Ruth started to cry. "Or wife."

"Al is the last person you have to worry about," Addie said. "Al is devoted to you, and to the baby." She faced Ruth, put her hands on her sister's shoulders. "I didn't trust Al. For a long time. The business with Mabel, and you getting married in secret ruffled me. But I have seen him come through for you, time after time. He loves you. And if he walks in after work to find you in this nightgown with a healthy baby in your arms—that is all he wants."

Ruth put her arms around Addie and leaned onto her shoulder. "A healthy baby in my arms is all we both want."

"Besides, I can do chores and Doris can make dinner." Addie felt Ruth relax. Ruth lifted her face away, rubbed her cheeks dry.

"Before we bring the baby home, help me get organized."

"Right now, I'll make you some eggs."

As Ruth nibbled her eggs, Addie sat with a cup of coffee. "How is Loretta getting along?"

"She's put on a brave face. One of her cousins broke with the family, comes over to help. Leonard hired a girl for laundry." Ruth sighed. "But Loretta's not only brave. Loretta adores her baby. She worries about the future, but she'll see her child through."

Ruth sat back, her face serious. "I wrote a long letter to Dan to tell him everything that's happened this year. I hope he'll understand."

"I know he will."

The sisters looked at each other. Addie sensed Ruth thinking about their mother. Addie said, "You and Loretta, not following in your mothers' footsteps."

"Loretta said something like that, too. Writing to Dan, for the first time I felt so clear of the past, not angry."

Addie thought back to the night of Katie's birth, when she saw her mother's face reflected in her own. Listening to Ruth, Addie realized features like eyes and dimples were not scars. "You have broken the mold."

Ruth shoveled the last of the eggs into her mouth, wiped her lips. "We'll make a new one, a day at a time."

That evening, Addie felt a contentment as she closed the door on Ruth serving Al the supper Doris had made. Al had beamed at Ruth when he came in the door. Motherhood and Ruth were finding their way together. They would bring their baby home and do their best for her. In her happiness for her sister, Addie had almost forgotten about the midterm. For the first time in weeks, her neck didn't ache.

During their supper, Doris picked up on Addie's mood. "I've got pumpkins to carve and half a bushel of apples to peel for canning on the back porch. Want to help?"

Addie grinned. "At home, my job was to scoop out the seeds and pulp. There's a picture of me with both arms inside a huge pumpkin."

Doris laughed. "I'd like to see that." She tilted her head in thought. "Wait here a minute. I want to show you something."

She went to the hall closet, brought to the table a black leather bag the size of a small hatbox. Doris lifted a box camera from inside, held it out for Addie's inspection. "My husband bought this. It's a Kodak Brownie."

Addie took the camera. "Have you made any pictures?"

Doris pulled a booklet from the bag. "No, but with a new baby in the family, this seems like the time to learn."

Addie took the booklet and scanned it. "I can buy the film and flashbulbs at Hudson's." She tapped the camera. "Ruth will be thrilled to have baby pictures."

Later, getting ready for bed, Addie thought about the difference between looking forward and looking back. She remembered a long-ago summer day at her grandparents' farm. She and her brother George were hiking to the pond for a swim. He led her away from the path, worn over the years, to what he said was a shortcut. She was used to following his lead and tramped behind him through the brambles of blueberry bushes. He pushed aside the scraggly top branches to clear his way, but she was a foot shorter and caught the thick scratchy edges.

Behind him she had whined, "Why did we come this way?" and "I'm getting scratched!" and "Let's turn back."

George scoffed at the scrapes on her face and arms. "You got yourself this far." He pushed aside branches to reveal the pond just ahead. When she jumped into the cool water, she forgot the sting of her skin. Sitting on the rocks drying off later, George told her, "Never look back. Figure out the way forward." She hadn't understood then that he was talking about life's brambles.

Now, she lay on her back in the dark, listening to the clank of rising steam in the radiator. Addie considered that Ruth, Al, Doris, Ma, Mr. Reed, even Mrs. Reynolds, had figured out their own ways forward. Addie had gotten herself to Detroit. She landed a good job, one that got her to college. She'd had help, sure, like George showing her the shortcut. But now the blank ledger page in her head was hers to fill.

CHAPTER 22

Addie went to Hudson's Bake Shop to order cupcakes on the day before Halloween. Mr. Reed liked her suggestion of giving treats with the orders delivered to departments. At the entrance, Addie faced a cardboard Patsy holding out one of Ma's pies. Al had been successful in getting Hudson's to sell them. Addie chuckled at the jaunty tilt of Patsy's head, her grin, the free hand on her hip. Ma cranked out pies with the new ovens as fast as Al made the sales. Featuring Patsy in the posters must have been his idea.

Addie counted a dozen pumpkin and apple pies on the display table. The woman at the counter told her Hudson's had already reordered pies twice that week. Addie saw the strategy behind Ma's buy-out of Dunn's: freed from duties at the tavern, Al had time to expand the number of stores selling the pies. Ma's growing bakery crew, trained by Ma and corralled by Patsy, kept pace with the growing flow of orders.

Al had missed a few paydays because of what happened at Dunn's and the baby coming early but had wheedled a hold on his job at the advertising agency. Addie figured Al's commissions on pie sales plus the sale of Dunn's had added enough to his bank account that he could afford the down payment on a house and at least some of the furniture. But he also had to pay the hospital and doctor's bills.

Space in Al and Ruth's apartment was squeezed tight. Getting ready to bring the baby home, Addie had helped her sister set up the crib in the bedroom on Ruth's side of the bed. Doris sewed a changing pad to fit atop Ruth's dressing table. Ruth emptied the drawers of cosmetics and filled them with diaper pins, tins of baby powder, tubes of diaper rash ointment. Loretta's gift, a baby buggy, was parked in the alcove where Addie had slept, full of crib sheets and blankets they had no place for. The effort exhausted Ruth. She collapsed into the rocking chair Doris had brought down from the attic. Addie went over the baby checklist—they hadn't crossed off as many things as there were still left to buy.

On Halloween morning, Addie slid onto the cold seat in the back of Al's sedan while he settled Ruth in front with a lap blanket. Next to Addie was a box of Halloween cookies Doris made for Ruth to give to the nurses. Al would drop Addie first at the college, then, before he went to work, he would see Ruth in at the hospital to spend the day with Katie. She was one week old.

Al looked at Addie in the rearview mirror. He tossed a paper over the seat into Addie's lap. "Can you order the stuff we need? On my account."

The baby checklist. "I'll do it tomorrow. Everything?"

Al and Ruth exchanged a smile. "Everything."

Addie folded the list into her bag. The pie money was a lifesaver. When the boxes arrived, it would take some doing to find space in the crowded apartment.

"Are you nervous about your exam grade?" Ruth asked Addie.

"Yes. No. I don't know." Addie shrugged. "I'm tired of being nervous."

Al pulled alongside the curb in front of the Main Building at Wayne University. Addie squeezed Ruth's shoulder and stepped out with their good luck wishes in her ears. She hurried along the walkway to where Mary was tamping out her cigarette. The friends linked arms. "Ready or not," Mary said.

The practicum classroom buzzed with the chatter of the students huddled around desks, waiting for the teaching assistant. They fell silent and sat down when he strode in with the bundle of test papers under his arm. His dour face scanned the room, and he slapped the bundle onto the desk. "Most of you should be scared today."

Addie felt a stab of heartburn.

The assistant walked along the rows, checking names on the papers against faces, thrusting them at the students. "Those who scored below ninety percent will stay for my full review of the test. Those who scored above ninety percent, you are free to leave, unless you have a question."

When he came next to Mary, he retrieved her paper and Addie's from the pile, handed both to Mary with a jerk of his head. A red 94 was inked above Mary's name. Addie held her breath as Mary slid Addie's paper from beneath, then gasped to see the red 96. Mary grabbed her hand and Addie squeezed hard. She pulled together her coat and bag, made for the classroom door with Mary right behind her.

In the hallway, they hugged and bounced on their toes. Normally stoic Mary pulled out a handkerchief to wipe her eyes. "Didn't I tell you?" she said. "I knew we could do it."

Addie leaned against the wall to catch her breath. Two others left the classroom and went down the stairs. Addie whispered, "Only four of us?"

Mary pointed to the bulletin board behind Addie.

Tacked on the cork was a typed list of student names, their sponsor organizations, and their test scores. The first ten students earned grades above ninety percent. Addie ran her finger across her name to the ninety-six. The next person also achieved ninety-six. Hudson's was his sponsor. Addie and Bored One had earned the same grade.

Mary looked for the names of the others sponsored by her company. All of them were below eighty percent. "I'm head and shoulders in front," she said. She stepped back with a satisfied sigh. "And so are *you*."

"Maybe." said Addie. "That guy got the same grade."

"Hudson's started four, two took the midterm." Mary tapped a note typed at the end of the list. "Says here they sent the grades to the sponsors. They'll be happy with two in the top ten. You've proved you deserved the spot." Mary slung her bag over her shoulder. "Come on, back to the grindstone."

Mary was probably right about Hudson's satisfaction with having two of their employees at the top, but pulling even with Bored One bothered Addie. Then again, she thought, it might bother him more, prick at his disdain for Mrs. Reynolds putting Addie in the program. Showing him up was a kick.

After a quick lunch, Addie and Mary took their usual library table. Addie pulled out her test paper, reworked the mistake that had cost her a perfect score. Calculating the percentages, even if her grade on the final exam slipped a few points, she figured her semester grade would be above ninety percent. Her leg jiggling under the table drew a look from the girl next to her, and Addie put her hand on her thigh to calm it.

Across the table, Mary scribbled in her notebook. Confident about where college was taking her for the next thirty years, Mary never flagged. Addie envied her focus. Mary wagged her pencil. "Hello? Study time."

Addie opened her textbook to the reading for the next class. "Thank you."

Mary squinched her face in a question.

Addie said, "For the push." Mary smiled and went back to her notes. Addie stretched out her jumpy legs, resolved not to look up before their break.

That evening, gaggles of trick-or-treaters were running house-to-house on the block when Addie turned onto the boulevard. She tingled at the sight of candle-flickering jack-o'-lanterns, spooky in the surrounding dark. Her brother George used to taunt them with ghost scares when they walked the dark roads at home on Halloween. Ruth would kick at George and march down the road chanting, "Ghosts aren't real, ghosts aren't real!" It turned out that a ghost had shadowed Ruth until she realized she could let it go.

At their gate, Ruth sat on a lawn chair with the basket of cookies to hand out. Addie plucked one and took a bite. "Aren't you cold out here? I can take over."

Ruth shook her head. "Tell me about your grade. Good news?"

Addie handed over her test paper. Ruth clapped her hands. "This makes Mrs. Reynolds and Mr. Reed look good for their decision to send you. That will go a long way."

"That's pretty much what Mary said."

"The men at the top know everything Mrs. Reynolds does. And vice versa. She wormed her way into the family's trust because she's not afraid to do the dirty work."

"Like firing Louis."

"No doubt she was the one who took care of that.

"Only me and the guy from Finance are still in the program."

"Reynolds'll turn your success to her advantage."

"How do you know?"

Ruth grinned. "Five years of reading the Hudson's tea leaves—and Susan giving me the lowdown."

Addie said, "We haven't talked about Hudson's since … they fired you. I was afraid of making you feel worse with my babble about work."

"I miss the store." Ruth pulled at her loose blouse. "And my better clothes. I'd enjoy seeing you have a career."

Addie sighed. "A career? It's more like Hudson's boxed me into this college program. Mr. Reed says it's a big opportunity." She shook her head. "I don't know."

"He's right. You have the brains to get ahead. *They* selected you. Get the grades, wait for your chance." Ruth got up, set the cookie basket on the chair. "I need the bathroom. Hold the fort."

Addie munched another cookie. How would she know her chance, if it came? "Reading the tea leaves," Ruth had said. Addie was not used to thinking from an advantage point of view, like Mrs. Reynolds, or Louis, who toted up leverage in their mental ledgers. Hudson's had placed Addie in this game, but Addie had to make her own moves. It was like balancing assets and liabilities or figuring out the best play in a card game. Unlike Louis, she was cautious. Best to watch and wait.

In the weeks before Thanksgiving, Hudson's departments began gearing up for the Christmas sales flurry. The Print Shop was already behind in running both the regular jobs and holiday-related orders. The crew oiled its works and got on track. The increasing deluge of orders and frenzied telephone calls made Addie understand that July Fourth had been a dress rehearsal for the main event. Mr. Reed insisted the men take their lunch each day because he often had to ask them to run through the afternoon break and into overtime. At the lunch bell, they straggled out but returned from the tower brisker. Joe, Addie, and Mr. Reed rotated counter duty during lunch. Addie made up for her short week by bringing her sack lunch and taking the most turns. Half of November had gone by before she made it to the tower for lunch.

The greetings from the different tables, the friendly asks— "How's your schoolin'?"—and the abundant cookies and cakes that were shared heartened Addie. She sat near the draft blowing through gaps around the lofty windows, letting the air sweep out the tension that had collected in her during the morning. Her textbook was in her bag and she ignored the tug to open it. With a slice of pumpkin bread in hand, she paged through the newspaper. A young colored man approached her table.

She recognized him as the son of a woman from the Laundry. He and Joe often talked baseball at lunch. Addie had passed him trundling carts of fresh smocks on the stock elevators.

He stopped, keeping the table between them, and waited. Addie said, "Hello."

He nodded. "Miss, sorry to interrupt."

Addie brushed the crumbs away. "Addie. Harold, right?"

"Yes, Miss. Can I ask you something?"

She nodded.

"Could I read the textbook for your course?"

"My accounting book?"

"Yes. After the course, would you loan it to me?"

Addie hesitated, puzzled. Looking past him, she saw his mother watching from the other side of the room. She had been the first to welcome Addie to the tower with the cookies.

"If you don't mind my asking, why?"

Harold shifted on his feet. "I keep books over in our part of town. Try to help the folks." He straightened up. "I was first in my class at Miller High School."

"The folks?"

"Negro businesses need bookkeeping, same as anywhere in Detroit."

Addie had never been to the colored part of town. But she was interested in what he was saying. "I keep books, too. For a diner, a tavern, and a pie business."

Harold smiled. "Didn't know you had side jobs."

Addie smiled back and shrugged. "I need the experience."

"I'm getting plenty of experience," he said. "But I won't be getting college."

I won't be getting college. Addie got the fourth spot in the college program because Mrs. Reynolds said she found no suitable man. Had Mrs. Reynolds even considered Harold in Laundry? Not likely. Hudson's had a pecking order and the hum-drum departments, like Print Shop and Laundry and others tucked away in the working areas of the building, were way down on the list. She wouldn't have been considered if Mr. Reed hadn't pushed her forward.

Addie said, "Okay." Harold raised his brows as though he was unsure what she meant. "After the final, you can borrow the book. And my notes from the lectures."

Harold smiled. "Thank you, miss."

"Addie," she said again, and glanced over to see Harold's mother smiling, too. "If you want, we could talk here at lunch. About bookkeeping."

He nodded with a smile. "Thanks again." He gestured a hat tip and strode away. He gave his mother a thumbs-up sign.

Addie flashed on a mental picture of her class assembled in the lecture room. Young white men, many of them veterans, a handful of girls like her and Mary, one Negro man who always took the same seat in the back corner. She had never thought about how that lone man got there or what his prospects were. But he had made it through the mid-term.

Addie flushed with chagrin about her wavering and whining about the class. A chance that few could hope for had fallen into her lap. Hudson's paid the tuition and her time to attend. Ruth was right—Addie had to see where it would lead.

Joe motioned time to get back as he tossed his wrappers in the trash. In the stairwell he said, "Harold finally worked up the nerve to ask you."

Addie said, "You knew what he wanted?"

"Yeah, I play pool with some of our guys over in Black Bottom. He wasn't sure how you'd take it." At the elevator, Joe pushed the call button. "He's got his pride. I told him you don't look down on people."

Addie flushed. "Thanks."

Joe said, "Harold's got big plans for his own business. Already lined up most of the shops in his neighborhood."

Addie gazed at him with new appreciation. "Joe, you're a good man."

Joe put on his Mr. Reed face and voice. "Thank you, Miss." She laughed, and Joe smiled. "You ain't bad yourself."

When they stepped off the elevator on their floor, Al was pacing in the corridor. Seeing him, Addie told Joe she'd be along in a minute. She pulled Al's sleeve. "Is something wrong?"

"Dr. Tullen says we can bring Katie home. Ruth's waiting for me at the hospital."

Addie clapped her hands. "Wonderful news!"

Al twisted his hat band. "It is, it is." His face and neck were flushed. "I wish I still smoked."

Addie put her hand on his arm. "Are you nervous?"

"I've been treading water, day to day. This is diving into the deep part of the lake."

Addie nodded. "You're a strong swimmer. So is Ruth." She looked at her watch. "I've got to get back. I'll hurry home after work."

"Thanks a million, Addie." Al waved his hat as he entered the elevator.

Addie went into the shop smiling, eager to hurry through the work and run out the clock. When she left the store—Mr. Reed shooed her out at five when he heard the news—sleet coated the sidewalks and clogged the tracks, causing the tram to slog along. On the ride, Addie made a mental inventory of Ruth's bedroom. The crib was made up with padded bumpers and flannel sheets. Piles of swaddling blankets and a basket of clean diapers stood ready. They had filled a drawer with the warmest baby gowns Hudson's offered.

When Addie burst into Ruth's apartment, Al sat in the rocking chair, beaming at the bundled Katie in his arms. Doris stepped out of the kitchen with a finger to her lips. Ruth came out of the bathroom and hurried Addie out of her coat. She whispered, "Come look at our beauty."

The sisters leaned over the swaddled baby. Al carefully tilted Katie's face toward Addie's gaze. Addie's hand flew over her mouth and tears stung her eyes. Katie's scrunched red face had filled out and softened to a healthy pink. Wisps of brown hair coated her head, and her eyelashes would have made movie stars envious. One tiny fist tucked was under her chin. Addie reached out a fingertip, stroked Katie's hand.

Ruth squeezed Addie around the shoulders. "We'll put her into the crib, then have dinner." Addie tiptoed into the kitchen with Doris while Al and Ruth carried Katie to the bedroom.

Addie would never forget how Ruth glowed that night. She and Al finished each other's sentences, telling the story of Dr. Tullen examining Katie and pronouncing her fit for home care at six pounds two ounces, the nurses sending them off with flowers and boxes of diapers. Al said, "The nurses will get pies for a month."

Addie listened to the chatter around the table with a mix of happiness and longing for Tom. The memory of her hand in his, his arm around her on the night Katie was born, hovered. Ruth was focused on Katie, but Addie had expected that by now Al would have told her where Tom went. He hadn't. She could ask, but how to explain why she wanted to know? Why *did* she want to know?

"Couldn't he come back now?" Talking stopped. Addie realized she had said that out loud.

Doris kept her eyes on her plate. Ruth looked at Al. Al said, "Yeah, the storm blew over, but he's set where he is."

"Al, what do you mean, 'blew over'?"

Al shrugged. "Ma and I hear that when Louis Carter's money dried up, so did the vendetta."

"Does Tom know?"

"He knows." It was a relief to hear that Tom was no longer in Louis's sights. For Tom to be "set where he is," Al had given Tom his share from the sale of Dunn's.

"Ma will have him back; she told me."

"He's got other ideas."

"Tell me where he is," Addie said.

Doris cleared her throat, rose from the table, began clearing the dishes. That meant Doris knew.

Addie locked eyes with Ruth. "Don't leave me out of this."

Ruth touched Al's arm. "Al protected you. But now, I agree—you should know."

Al said, "That night, Tom took a train to Bay City, got rides from there to Houghton Lake. He's helping Guy and Norma for the winter."

"Just for the winter?" Addie's cheeks flamed seeing the curl of Ruth's lips. Ruth knew Addie's interest in Tom was not brotherly. From the day she first met him at Dunn's.

Al didn't have Ruth's intuition. "He hasn't said what he'll do in the long run." With that, he changed the subject by asking Doris if she had called Loretta about Thanksgiving.

She had. "Two families giving thanks together makes me happy. Especially with two babies!"

Katie's cries pulled Ruth away from the table. Doris had the dishes soaking and Al picked up a dishtowel to dry. Addie went for her bag and jacket.

Ruth sat in the rocker nursing Katie. She held out a piece of notepaper to Addie. "Take this." On it was written the address of Guy's camp. Katie fussed. Ruth murmured to her, adjusted her position. Katie didn't settle, squirmed and wailed. Ruth put the crying baby on her shoulder and went to the bedroom.

Addie fingered the paper. Tom knew it was safe to return, but he hadn't. He had not written to her. Had he and Doris been writing? She didn't want to face Doris anymore that night. She went across the hall and closed herself in her room.

When she had leaned on Tom that night in the hospital, her fears for Ruth had overwhelmed her sense. She told herself she was being as silly about Tom as she had been about Louis. *I can't afford distractions.* She had to concentrate on keeping the pace of Hudson's holiday rush, studying, and doing Ma's bookkeeping. Just as well if Tom stayed up north. Addie stuck the paper with the address into her desk drawer.

Early on the cold Thanksgiving morning, Addie gave in to her fatigue and turned over for more sleep, satisfied with a dream vision of the parade from Hudson's second-floor perch over Woodward Avenue. When she went to the kitchen for coffee, Doris had pancakes ready and two casseroles already in the oven. Addie tuned in the radio broadcast of the parade while Doris hummed and peeled and chopped. She and Addie wrestled the eighteen-pound bird into the oven. Addie chugged coffee while setting the dining table with Doris's best dishes. When Al and Ruth arrived, Al propped Katie's bassinet next to him on the davenport, tented it with crocheted blankets while Ruth put on an apron to help in the kitchen.

Loretta and Leonard bustled in with their crying baby in a basket. At Mary Margaret's cries, Katie woke, wailing too, and Al picked her up, bounced her on his shoulder. Ruth threw the guests' coats and bundles in Addie's direction, took Katie from Al, and hustled Loretta and her baby into Addie's room. Al and Leonard looked at each other. "Coffee, or a cold one?" Al asked his friend. Leonard gave him a look, Al grinned, and went to the refrigerator.

Addie hung the coats on the rack. As she unpacked the bags Loretta brought, Leonard said, "Loretta made what she always makes for Thanksgiving. I hope you like Polish food."

Addie inhaled the aromas escaping from the covered dishes. "Smells delicious."

Al came back with two bottles and glasses. Leonard swigged his beer from the bottle. Al tuned the radio to the Lions football game, asked Leonard for his bet.

Before dinner, Addie brought out the Brownie camera. Ruth and Loretta sat the babies on their laps and commanded the men to pose for the different shots they wanted. Addie steadied the camera against her waist, moved the view box until she had the miniature faces in her sight. The mothers glowed, holding still against the fussing babies. The fathers straightened their ties, stiffened, forgot to smile. Addie saved the last two shots on the roll to pose the group around the table as Al cut the turkey.

Al and Leonard anchored the ends of the table. Doris put Addie next to Loretta. When Al made the toast, Addie was surprised to sip wine from her glass. Across the table, Doris winked.

If Loretta was missing her traditional family gathering, she didn't let on. Loretta babbled non-stop with stories about their neighbors, calling on Leonard to affirm the scandalous details— "Len, tell 'em, it's true!" The two mothers ate and drank like bears awakened from hibernation. When the laughter rose too loud, they shushed each other with giggles, peeked into

Mary Margaret's basket on the davenport and, next to it, Katie's bassinet. The babies slept through.

Addie sat back, fingering her wineglass. Tom should be here. At least he wasn't alone for Thanksgiving. She pictured him in front of the fireplace with Guy and Norma. She missed Tom's way of teasing her. Or she was sappy from the wine. Or both.

She poured another inch into her glass when Ruth wasn't looking.

CHAPTER 23

Addie's days blurred by in a flurry counting down to the final exam. Mary the taskmaster paced their strict schedule of reading and practice reviews. She cajoled Addie into adding an extra thirty minutes to their library sessions. "We have to be on point with the old material and have the new stuff down cold," Mary insisted. Ruth's instinctual clock allowed Addie snippets of time with baby Katie before she'd shoo Addie back to her books.

Hudson's relentless Christmas advertising lured crowds into the store. Tinsel, ribbon, and trimmings in gold and red glittered from the pillars, railings, and ceiling on the first floor. Holiday tunes broadcast from the Music Store spread cheer through the speaker system. Half of the twelfth floor had been closed after Halloween to build the Christmas Trim Shop and Toytown. Various Webbers appeared for the official opening of Toytown, posing with the store Santa for the newspaper photographers. Addie and Joe watched the formalities from the side as they unloaded a batch of sales posters under the glare of the senior clerk, who snarled "We expected this delivery last night!" In the elevator, Joe whistled. "The season will be worse for them than for us." Addie raised her brows. Joe added, "Not by much."

The Print Shop added a skeleton crew on Saturdays to churn out handbills for the daily special sales and events. The store's strolling employee choir was so popular that Mr. Reed came back from an executive meeting carrying an order for thousands of Christmas carol song sheets bordered with Hudson's advertising. When he announced the extra run, Joe yelled, "Battle stations, men!" There was no time to question or groan. The men fell in.

On Addie's class days, her fellow students bandied around clues they believed Professor Morse gave to the final examination test questions—"If he spends over five minutes on a topic, it's on the test." Mary snorted at the silliness. "Accountants have to know all of it." Which helped not a bit to still Addie's nerves.

What did help Addie was swapping ideas with Harold. When she took lunch in the tower, he would come to her table and launch into a problem he'd run into with books for a tailor or a barber. Getting the right answers in the class had its satisfactions, but figuring out bookkeeping questions with practical, down-to-earth Harold boosted Addie's confidence.

Snow fell hard and fast on the morning of the exam. Addie threw aside the wool skirt she had chosen to wear and put on trousers she tucked into her boots, not caring if Professor Morris disapproved. Doris cooked breakfast, insisting that Addie couldn't think properly with only coffee in her stomach. She was bundling her scarf around her hat and neck in the downstairs vestibule when Al came in carrying a snow shovel. "Car's dug out, let's go." From the passenger seat, Addie saw Ruth waving from her window. Addie waved back, smiling at the efforts of the three of them to send her off.

Mary and Addie trudged into the Main Building amidst the crowd of snow-covered, anxious students. Radiators clanked with the effort to overcome the chill in the corridors, melting the wetness from hundreds of woolen coats and boots into puddles. Christmas decorations taped over doorways and on bulletin boards tantalized with the holiday cheer they hoped to enjoy, after.

Three hours later, drained, Addie and Mary leaned on the wall in the hallway outside the classroom. Mary said, "I had no breakfast. I feel sick." Addie started toward the lounge, but Mary shook her head. "Let's get out of here."

Addie took Mary's arm, grabbed the banister with her other hand. She focused on each step down, trying to calm her breathing. She had sweated through her blouse, and it stuck to her back. Before venturing into the storm, they wrapped themselves in their still-damp coats and scarves.

Snow blanketed the paths. Mary headed them to a diner around the corner. When they ducked inside, the cook pointed at hooks on the wall for their wet coats. Two men at the counter sat hunched over coffee mugs. Mary and Addie took a booth next to the window. After they ordered grilled cheese sandwiches and hot chocolate, Mary sat back, arms folded. "Every question he threw at us was in our drills."

Addie nodded. "It was like he copied our notes."

"Somehow that made me more nervous. I kept thinking there would be a trick question we never studied."

"There was no trick. We just got ourselves all worked up."

Mary grabbed Addie's hand. "We have to wait for the grades to be sure, but my dear, I believe we aced it."

Addie grinned. "As Mr. Reed would say, 'Well done, Miss, well done.'"

The two friends parted at the streetcar stop with wishes for a Merry Christmas. Addie was not due to work, and she had already bought everything on her gift list, but at the store she got off the tram. She maneuvered through the throng of shoppers crossing Woodward and ducked into the customer entrance, taking a shortcut into a corridor behind the sales counters for the stairs to the Mezzanine. She waited her turn at the counter in the Photo Shop. The salesman handed Addie an envelope with the photos developed from the roll she took on Thanksgiving. "Film for Christmas is going fast," he said. Knowing Ruth would want plenty of photos that day, she bought two rolls.

Addie wound her way to the Engraving stockroom and peeked around the curtain separating the space from the sales area. Mike, the clerk, was helping a customer, samples spread across the sales table. She sat in the rolling chair at his desk, knowing she was welcome in his cubby to use the discontinued stationery whenever she wanted to write something.

From her bag Addie pulled an envelope that had come in the mail the day before, addressed to her in Miss Ames's precise cursive. She sliced the envelope from her high school teacher with the Hudson's engraved letter opener Mike kept on the desk. Inside was a Christmas card with a note of congratulations. Addie had forgotten that she had sent a Hudson's postcard to Miss Ames about being selected for the college program. "Of all the girls I taught, I had the highest hopes for you. I would dearly love to hear about your continued progress."

Maybe it was the kind interest of the teacher she so admired, and that her worries had tightened inside like holding her breath; or the grinding schedule of work and the rigors of the class, the expectations of the sponsorship; or how hard she worked for the grades, pretending to ignore the snubs from men in the class; or her doubts about the future—Addie grabbed a sheet of stationery and spilled it all into a letter. *Sometimes*, she wrote, *I dream there is a mountain falling behind me and I run and run, but I can't get clear of it.*

Five pages fast-scribbled, Addie sat back. She found a tissue to blow her nose, breathed away the sting of tears. Miss Ames would understand. Addie addressed an envelope, found a stamp in the desk drawer. The street level floor was a chaos of shoppers jamming the aisles. Addie shook her head at the memory of her first-day wish for a job in sales. She slipped the letter into the mail chute on her way out of the store.

Katie's wail carried into the hall as she climbed the stairs to Ruth's apartment. She let herself in. Ruth sat on the davenport holding the nursing baby with one hand and a pen in the other. Milk stains and ink smudged her dressing gown. Christmas cards were strewn on the cushions and onto the carpet. Addie took the pen from her sister's hand and capped it. Ruth adjusted the baby and sighed. "The cards should have been mailed last week."

"Do you want me to help?"

"Could you? Because I am a complete failure."

Addie began gathering up the cards. "Don't say that."

"How do people have more than one?" Ruth's voice was weary. "I am at the end of my rope."

They looked at each other. Ruth nestled Katie on her lap. The baby quieted, drifted off.

Addie opened her bag and pulled out the packet of photographs taken on Thanksgiving. She bundled the pile into her hand like a deck of cards and drew the top photo into Ruth's view. One by one, she set them out on the cushion. Ruth oohed over the shots. "You're good with the camera."

"Which one do you want to send with Dan's card?" Ruth pointed, and Addie sorted the photos for him, for Jane and George, and which to give to Loretta. "And these two for Tom." Ruth looked at Addie. "Did you write to him?"

Addie didn't reply.

"It seemed to me you had something you wanted to tell him."

Addie scoffed. "What would that be?"

Ruth shrugged. "I don't know, but *something* happened before he left."

Addie rolled her eyes. "Give me your address book. Let's finish the cards."

Ruth put Katie in the crib. She made a make-shift desk with a cushion on her lap to sign the cards while Addie addressed the envelopes. Ruth slipped the two photos inside the card for Tom. "I signed your name with mine and Al's," she said, holding out the card. Ruth had saved her the fuss of deciding whether to send him a greeting card. Relieved, Addie wrote out Tom's name, in care of Guy's address, licked the envelope, and sealed it.

Ruth went to change her clothes before Al came home. Addie moved around the living room picking up newspapers, tidying the pillows on the davenport, removing coffee cups from where Ruth had left them on the lamp tables. Doris bustled in with the dinner she had cooked. "How did the exam go?"

Addie said, "Oh, we did fine! I've almost forgotten about it."

Doris chuckled. "That's a relief." She spotted the pile of Christmas cards. "I'll give those to the postman in the morning." She picked up the bundle, Tom's card on top. "Did you write to him?"

Addie folded her arms. "Who?"

Doris raised her brows. "Never mind."

The shop worked overtime for the remaining days before Christmas. Mr. Reed declared, "The switchboard will hold all calls during lunchtime until Christmas Eve." Joe whistled when he heard. "Never done before. But we've never had this volume."

Addie took refuge in the blessed silence of the stairwell for quick bites at lunch. She had another spot in the employee corridor on nine where she could listen to the Piano Salon staff fingering holiday tunes. In the shop, she hummed under the clacking of the machinery, trying to hold on to the Christmas spirit.

The Laundry ladies took charge of organizing a Christmas Eve party in the tower. Most of the departments were on staggered hours; to include everyone, the festivities began at mid-morning and ran through the afternoon. Decorations scrounged from old displays plus an abundance of tinsel and Christmas tree light strings surrounded a space cleared for dancing. When Addie got to the party, people were on their feet to the radio music. Joe was digging into a plate of sweet potatoes and ham. She scanned the room looking for Harold.

He was standing with a few of the folks near the desserts. Harold laughed at something one of them said. She skirted around the people filling plates. When he caught sight of her, Harold's face lit with an easy sociability. "Merry Christmas, Miss!"

Addie knew he was teasing. She motioned him to a table at the side where he joined her. Addie held out her accounting textbook, tied with a bright red ribbon. "Merry Christmas, Harold."

"Just what I wished for." He laughed, pulled off the ribbon, flipped through the pages, and made a low whistle. "You way ahead of me with all of this."

"Not really," Addie said. "I wish …" She met his eyes. She wished that handsome, capable, funny Harold was getting college, too. That giving him the book didn't feel like second-best. That she knew how to tell him he deserved his dreams as much as anybody.

Harold smiled, shrugged his shoulder. "That's how it is." He tapped the book. "Thank you." He tucked it under his arm. "I'm gonna stow this away so nobody spills on it." He took two steps and turned back to her again. "Merry Christmas, Addie."

"Merry Christmas, Harold."

Addie danced with Joe, but he won the impromptu swing contest with the counter girl from Carpentry. Joe was smitten. He kissed her under the mistletoe. Addie tugged him from the party with less than five minutes left in the lunch period.

In the stairwell, Joe snapped his fingers. "Got me a date for New Year's Eve. Wanna go with us? That guy in Maintenance will take you in a minute."

Addie knew who he referred to, and she had no interest. "Nope, no, do not."

"How many dates have you had since you moved here?"

"None of your business."

"C'mon, you gotta have some fun."

"And *you* gotta help me get a lot of orders out *today*."

The last order left the shop thirty minutes before closing time on Christmas Eve. Not only had they finished every Christmas order, but the crew had also delivered the orders for the sales starting after Christmas. Mr. Reed called for the machines to shut down. The men gathered their coats and lunch pails, murmured Christmas greetings to each other. Mr. Reed came to the counter with a bundle of green envelopes. As the men filed past, he shook their hands, gave each one an envelope. Addie and Joe lined up next to him, added their holiday good wishes. The burly men taking her hand in their callused ones, wishing her Merry Christmas, brought tears to Addie's eyes. Mr. Reed and Joe, the men, Harold, and the folks in the tower—she had come to respect the people she spent her days with, different in their ways, all hard workers, kind.

When the men had gone, Mr. Reed turned to Addie and Joe. "Another Christmas season in the books. Well done." He held out envelopes to them. "Merry Christmas to you."

Addie took his hand with the envelope. "Oh, Mr. Reed, I am so grateful to you. Thank you. Have a wonderful Christmas. And a good vacation."

Mr. Reed gave her hand a firm shake, then Joe's. "The shop is in your hands until the New Year." He checked his pocket watch. "Go on home. I'll turn off the lights."

Before they parted on the street, Addie kissed Joe on the cheek. "Merry Christmas, Joe."

He grinned and said, "Hope Santa is good to you."

Addie rode the streetcar thinking about the presents she still had to wrap. At the gate, she was cheered by the glow of colored lights cast over the snowy yard. Doris and the neighbors on the higher floors had placed their Christmas trees in front of their living room windows. Addie thought about asking some of the neighbors to go caroling before they went off to Midnight Mass.

But a worried Doris met her at the top of the stairs. "Ruth and Al rushed to the hospital with Katie—she couldn't get her breath."

Addie and Doris spent Christmas Eve waiting by the telephone. Al called just before midnight. "Katie's breathing, thank God, but she's staying for at least the night. They've got her in an oxygen tent."

The doctors relieved the baby's wheezing enough for her parents to bring her home on Christmas afternoon. Ruth was a wreck. She held swaddled Katie tight to her chest, only her face visible, but the baby worked an arm free and shook her fist. Ruth barked orders, and Al and Addie sprang into action. He moved the crib to the curtained alcove in the living room; Addie pinned blankets all around the sides to block drafts.

Ruth wouldn't leave the baby except to use the bathroom. Doris shuttled the pans and dishes for Christmas dinner across the hall and served it in Ruth's kitchen. Ruth took her plate to the rocking chair next to the crib, where she kept vigil. Addie exchanged a look with Al. "She hasn't slept," he said.

Addie shook her head. "Ruth's in a panic."

Addie crept around the alcove curtain and crouched next to Ruth, who looked at Addie with wild eyes. "I thought she would die in my arms. I didn't know what to do." Ruth sobbed.

"But now you know. Al said the nurses taught you what to do." A nebulizer sat ready to mist medicine for Katie's lungs beside Ruth's untouched plate.

"I'm so tired." Ruth rubbed her eyes.

"Ruth, come with me to the kitchen. Doris brought the wine you like."

"I have to stay with her."

Addie peeked into the crib. "Katie's sleeping. She's breathing fine." Addie coaxed Ruth from the rocking chair. "You're exhausted, and you need to eat. We can take turns checking on her from the kitchen."

Al was standing outside the curtain. He took Ruth in his arms and walked her to the table.

The Christmas snow began a deep-freeze that iced the windows in the apartments no matter the full bore of the old coal furnace. Ruth hibernated with her baby. When Katie awoke crying, Ruth picked her up and walked the floor, holding Katie upright, counting her breaths, alert for a wheeze.

Doris cooked their meals. If Katie was asleep, Al might have Ruth's company at the kitchen table, bobbing out of the chair to check the baby between bites. Doris shook her head at this and at their sleeping arrangement. "Ruth sends Al to their bed and stays in the chair next to the crib," she said to Addie. "This isn't good for them."

Addie lay on the davenport in the evenings, staring at the lights on the Christmas tree. Addie continued confiding in Miss Ames; writing letters was a sort of diary. Addie described the turns in her relationship with Ruth, through the migraines, the pregnancy, and the birth. The fears they both harbored about their mother. "Ruth is so scared," she wrote, "she's exhausting herself. Doris says we need to have faith and hope for the best. But I see Ruth trying to push away the worst that could happen. I don't think she knows any other way. I don't think I do, either." She and Ruth had sore spots on the inside that had been patched, like the tight stitching the Laundry wove on the coveralls torn by the wear of rough work. Mothering sick Katie pulled at Ruth's stitches.

The mailman trudged along the boulevard on the Saturday after Christmas. Addie was clearing snow from the walk and met him at the gate. He handed her a bundle. "Post from up north finally made it through." Addie thanked him and took the mail to the boxes in the vestibule. Sorting through, she pushed envelopes into the slots. In the pile were three postcards, winter scenes on Houghton Lake. Her heart raced. She turned the cards over: one addressed to Al and Ruth, one to Doris, the other to Addie. The same message on all, "Merry Christmas and Happy New Year," and Tom's signature.

Addie had started a letter to him, then crumpled the paper and threw it away. She had hoped he would write to her. Sending her a Christmas greeting on a postcard was being polite, not personal. She slipped the card for Ruth and Al under their door, took the one for Doris into the apartment with her other mail. Addie headed off questions from Doris by handing her the stack of envelopes and announcing, "Holiday postcards from Tom came today." As Addie took off her boots, she said, "We all got the same card."

Doris read her card, looked at Addie. "He didn't say anything about the baby pictures."

Addie slung her coat onto the hook. "He didn't say anything." In her room, she propped the postcard against the lamp on her desk as a reminder of her foolishness.

Doris hosted a New Year's Eve card party. Only Patsy ventured out in the nasty weather. Ma had closed Dunn's for the night; she figured what little business they would get was not worth opening. Addie ate and played card games with Doris and Patsy, but her attention was across the hall. It was the first time in years Al was not at Dunn's. A year ago, he and Ruth had celebrated there. Doris had taken dinner to them before the card game, but Addie doubted they would be awake for midnight, unless Katie fussed.

After the holidays, Al began coming home late. "Don't wait dinner for me," he told Doris. Ruth didn't seem to notice. Doris threw up her hands. "Make sure your sister is eating," she told Addie. "I'm staying out of their business."

Addie trudged to the curb one morning, determined to confront Al as he dug the night's snow from around the sedan. He didn't see her behind him and threw back a shovelful of wetness that covered her. She grabbed handfuls of snow and pelted him.

"You want a snowball fight?" he yelled.

"I'll keep 'em coming unless you tell me what's going on."

He slammed the shovel into the snowbank. "What are you talking about?"

"You, out late every night. If you're two-timing Ruth …"

"Jesus, Addie, is that what you think? Of all the stupid—"

"What are you doing?" She threw an ice ball at his feet.

"Looking for a house!" Al yanked open the driver's door and started the engine.

Addie let the snowball crumple in her hand, opened the passenger door.

Al fumbled in the glove box and pulled out a paper. He held it out to Addie. "This is the place."

A drawing of a brick house with the sale information below. Addie bit her lip. "Sorry."

Al let her wait for a few seconds before he smiled. "Still got that checklist?"

CHAPTER 24

Detroit, July 1, 1947

The Stars and Stripes unfurled over the windows of the seventh floor with a lurch of the ropes. Clusters of men stationed on the scaffolding above the sidewalk reset their grips and hollered at one another for the next pull. Addie and Joe stood amid the cheering crowd across Woodward Avenue, watching the crew guide the unbundling of the American flag on Hudson's façade.

As the last stripes rolled open, Addie anticipated her summer. July Fourth falling on Friday gave her three days off. She had received the pay increase Hudson's bestowed at her one-year anniversary in the store. New summer outfits waited in layaway. There were two months of normal working hours until the start of her fall classes.

Five days a week in the Print Shop would be heaven compared to the grueling schedule she had ground through since January. Addie and Bored One, with Mary and the other top students, had been "accelerated" in the second semester—two classes, three days on campus. Mary organized them for group study in a research room in the library. Addie spent her nineteenth birthday with her study group during the week before the final exams. Bored One had decided to join a men-only accounting club instead. She finished the two terms one point ahead of him in the grade postings.

Hudson's renewal of its sponsorship for their second year had set off a showdown between Mrs. Reynolds and Mr. Reed. "Hudson's interest in the success of the two employees going forward in the program requires a change," Mr. Reed read to Addie from Mrs. Reynolds's memorandum. Addie and Bored One were to transfer to Personnel under her supervision. Mr. Reed put the paper down and gazed at Addie. "Miss, do you wish to transfer to Mrs. Reynolds's office?"

"No, Mr. Reed, I do not." Addie lowered her voice. "Is she doing this because of ..."

Mr. Reed sat back, hooked his thumbs in his vest pockets. "That will not be an issue."

Joe had busied himself near the closed office door during Mr. Reed's call to Mrs. Reynolds. "He didn't yell like he did at the plumbers last summer, but he threatened to take it upstairs."

Addie stayed in the Print Shop.

The harsh winter had at last sputtered out on Mother's Day, with flurries sprinkling the budding daffodils and tulips in their yard. Doris, Al, and Addie had tried to make the day special for Ruth, but the cold derailed their walk to Belle Isle with Katie in the buggy. Ruth had refused to go out all winter. Even Loretta had no luck inviting Ruth to her house or for a night out with their husbands. She telephoned Addie. "You've got to talk to your sister."

Addie tried and Ruth pursed her lips. "You, too? Loretta and Doris don't leave me alone. I know what I'm doing."

Dr. Tullen had made house calls whenever a panicked Ruth telephoned his office, worried about Katie's breathing. He arranged for one of the specialists to re-examine Katie. Al took a day off work to drive Ruth and the baby to Ann Arbor. Ruth came home flustered. "There *might* be new medicines soon. What good is that?"

Al gave up on the house he had chosen. "Ruth wants to be closer to the hospital." He drove Addie to work most mornings, but it had become a silent routine of shared worry about Ruth.

A week ago, Ruth had come to Addie with the shears. "Would you cut my hair? I don't have time to fuss with it."

"Doesn't Al like it long?"

Ruth sniffed. "With all I have to cope with, he'll live with it."

Addie had cut Ruth's long dark locks into a cap of short curls. Pleased with the style, Addie was in the bathroom trying to replicate the cut on her own hair when Doris took over. "You won't need curl clips, or my giving you a perm."

Joe had whistled when Addie entered the shop. "My sister would say you look like a real career gal."

Now, the bottom edge of the huge flag flattened against the brick and the men scrambled to tie the guy lines. People sang along with the music of "It's a Grand Old Flag" blaring from Hudson's windows. Addie checked her watch. "I'll see you in the shop." Joe gave her a thumbs-up.

She walked the long way around to the Farmer Street entrance, hands in her pockets. She fingered a postcard from Miss Ames, sent from Chicago. She and a teacher friend were on a train journey to California; her letters to Addie would pause for the summer. This was bad timing. Addie realized her last letter hadn't reached Miss Ames before the trip.

In it, Addie had put her muddled feelings for Tom into words. The pen seemed to move on its own as she wrote, like playing with a Ouija board. Addie asked Miss Ames to help her understand why she thought so often about Tom. She didn't know him well. They had been alone together only one afternoon on Belle Isle. On the night of Katie's birth, Addie had turned to him. She shivered at the memory of his arms around her. In her daydreams, she and Tom rode their bikes, laughing. She longed for him to hold her hand.

He would come to her mind while she was on a date with one of the college boys. Addie and Mary had become popular with men in the program. Mary laughed at the attention. "They act like two girls with high grades landed here from outer space." But they played along for fun. Addie and Mary agreed only to double dates, picked up and dropped off together, Mary spending the night with Addie and Doris. Addie enjoyed the movies, the dinners out, the chatter. But she stiffened away from a hand creeping along the back of her seat, pulled back from a kiss.

Addie sighed, half-wished she was on that train with Miss Ames. Last night, Doris had announced that Tom would come to their July Fourth celebration.

Addie waved her employee pass at the guard and took the stairs. On the Mezzanine, she made her way to the Engraving storeroom; Mike had an order for her to pick up. The store's fan system didn't reach Mike's stuffy cubby. She peeked around the curtain separating the cubby from the sales area; Mike was with a customer. Addie sat in the desk chair to wait. She tugged at the hair along the back of her neck. What was she thinking cutting her hair this short? She would look to Tom like a baby Shirley Temple.

She pushed back hard from the desk and the chair slammed into the shelves behind her. A box of envelopes crashed to the floor. The curtain opened and Mike stuck his head in. "You okay in here?"

Addie grabbed at the spilled box and collected the pieces from the floor. "Fine, fine."

Mike picked up the last stray envelope. "Very attractive hairdo."

Addie blushed. "Do you think so?" She knew from his chuckle that he heard the doubt in her tone.

"If you're trying to impress someone, he'll like it." Mike winked as he handed her the order sheet.

"I gotta run." Addie ducked into the back corridor and trotted to the elevator.

The door to the Print Shop was propped open and men, pushing handcarts, ferried boxes to a waiting elevator. Mr. Reed stood in the hallway, extended his hand to take the Engraving order. The counter telephone rang. Addie hurried inside to pick up the call—another last-minute order. Mr. Reed came in, scanned her notation in the order book, and called for Joe.

It was only Tuesday; the shutdown for the Friday holiday seemed far off. Addie answered the telephones—a second line had been added—and wrote the orders with only half her attention. The fan on the counter moved stuffy shop air across the back of her neck. She hooked the heels of her sandals onto the rung of the stool, but the jiggle in her leg went on.

Joe brought an order back with a question about the calculation. "Not like you to mess up the numbers."

Addie corrected the sheet and slid it across the counter. "We're busy."

Joe looked like he wanted to say more, thought better of it, went to the back.

Addie gripped her pencil. She kept her head down to concentrate. In front of the counter, one of the men was sweeping the floor. Addie wished for a broom in her mind to sweep away thoughts of Tom.

Before she heard Tom was coming, she had been looking forward to the yard celebration. Addie and Doris had been making the grocery list when Doris said, "Oh, Tom called. He's driving Norma and Guy down for the Fourth. Said Norma won't wait any longer to hold the baby."

Addie covered her surprise by asking, "Why would they leave their camp in July?"

Doris shrugged. "Tom didn't say. But Guy's been having some heart trouble."

"How do you know that?"

Doris looked at Addie. "I wrote to Tom. He wrote to me a few times."

"You never said you were writing to him."

"Ruth has no time for letter writing. I thought somebody ought to stay in touch with him." Doris held out her hands. "I like Tom. Not his fault he had to run."

Addie didn't know what to say. Doris continued calling out items for the grocery list, and Addie wrote, thoughts swirling in her mind. She remembered Doris tending his bruises, Tom hugging Doris, calling her "my angel." That had to be it: Tom was coming back to see Doris. Doris, who had had a younger husband, had her sights on Tom.

Five o'clock in the Print Shop. The men shut down the
machines. The sudden quiet roused Addie from her brooding.
She tidied the counter, handed the final order tally to Mr. Reed
as she walked to her locker. The men waited while she got her
handbag and hat before they crowded into the locker alcove to
collect their lunch pails. She called out "Goodnight" to Joe and
Mr. Reed as she passed them and made her way to the elevator.
Addie sighed, hoping they would not think her rude. She would
clear her head and come in tomorrow with better attention.

The trolley ride was the usual crowded crush. She tumbled
out at her stop, shook out her skirt, and ambled home. She came
past the hedge to open the yard gate and stopped.

Doris and Tom sat side-by side on the stoop, baby Katie
on Doris's lap.

Tom waved a toy bunny in front of Katie, and she made
her little-baby grin. Doris laughed and bumped Tom's shoulder
with her own. In the second before they saw her, Addie turned
up her lips in a tight smile.

A swarm of neighbor kids were playing with a ball in the
side yard. The ball flew in front of Addie and bounced on the
walk. She dodged around the kids running for it and walked
the few steps to the stoop.

Tom stood, hands at his sides, and she felt the urge to move
in close, let his arms slip around her. But her pride frowned at
him. "What are you doing here?"

"Well, hello, fine, thanks for asking."

Doris shook her head at Addie behind Tom's back. Addie
ignored her. She met Tom's eyes and waited.

"Where's your bike?" he said.

"On the back porch. Why?"

He glanced back at the stoop. "I've got our picnic." A rucksack sat there, and a bike lay in the grass. "Thought we could ride to Belle Isle."

"Just like you to assume things." Addie pinged with delight at the invitation, but she couldn't resist the taunt.

Tom smiled. "It's a fine evening."

Addie looked at Doris. "Where is Ruth?"

"Al bought a house! Ruth saw it this morning. They made it final at the bank this afternoon. I told them no dinner here tonight, have supper out. I've got Katie until they come home."

Addie said, "That's wonderful for them."

Tom grinned at her. "Belle Isle?"

She knew that he knew she would go. "You'll have to wait. I'll change my clothes."

Tom moved aside on the walk. Passing close to him, she forced her eyes forward. Inside, Addie took the stairs two at a time, flew into the apartment, kicked off her sandals, flung her hat and bag onto the chair. Her shaking hands grabbed at the buttons on her dress. Through the open window, she heard his voice murmuring to Katie. Addie pulled on denim pedal pushers and a flowered blouse. She threw shoes out of her closet until she found the canvas loafers. She ran to the bathroom, freshened her face powder and dabbed rouge on her cheeks, ran her fingers through her short curls, and pulled the front strands over her brow. She gripped the sink and stared into the mirror. *It's only a picnic.* She breathed deep until the giddy flutter in her chest calmed.

Addie walked downstairs and took another deep breath before she opened the vestibule door. Tom had Katie on his hip, bouncing her gently. He grinned at Addie. "Katie seems well."

"Better now. The winter was hard. I'll get my bike."

Doris met her coming through the side yard, wheeling Addie's bike. Doris handed off the bike with a knowing smile.

Addie took the handlebars. "Did you invite him here tonight?"

"He just showed up."

Addie raised her brows, pushed her bike to where Tom stood ready with the rucksack on his back. Katie sat in the baby buggy. Doris waved to them and pushed the carriage into the side yard. Tom wheeled his bike to the street, and Addie followed. She pushed off, with Tom just behind her. He caught up and matched her pace.

The sun still blazed as they crossed the bridge onto the island. They wove their bikes between clumps of walkers and other riders taking advantage of the balmy evening. Addie figured Tom had a picnic spot in mind, and soon he motioned her to turn off the main avenue, onto a side path along the lagoon. Tom slowed. "How about here?"

Addie nodded.

They dropped their bikes on the grass. Tom pulled an old army blanket from the straps on his rucksack and spread it open. Addie kicked off her shoes and sat down. Tom, on his haunches, untied the strings on the pack. "I won't pretend I made this picnic. Patsy packed this for us." There were the diner's thick sandwiches wrapped in waxed paper, and wedges of pie in foil, with a thermos of iced tea. Addie watched him lay out a dish towel, open the sandwiches for her to choose. When he handed her a tin cup, their fingertips touched. Tom said, "I thought about this picnic all winter." Addie took the cup with a smile.

As they began eating, she studied his profile. He had already tanned some, though his nose was sunburned. Tom's hair curled along his neck and waved over his brow. Working at Guy's camp had kept his arms muscled. He was the same, and yet different. She wanted him to think the same about her.

Tom said, "So, Ruth and Al got a house. Katie is beautiful. I'm happy for them."

Addie nodded. "They've got what they wanted. Are you sorry about selling Dunn's?"

Tom shook his head. "At first, I was. Not now." He leaned closer. He looked at her with the kind eyes she remembered and something else that pulled on her, like the way Joe looked at the girl from Maintenance. Her heart thumped. "I hated running that night," he said.

"Everything happened so fast."

He sat back, stretched out his legs. "Yeah, it did. You know that fireplace up at Guy's? I've spent the winter staring into the flames, thinking."

They ate the sandwiches and pie while Tom talked. Guy, he told her, was a master woodworker. "Did you know he carved the oak leaves into the bar at Dunn's? When we took it over. I helped with that, but he's taught me the craft in his shop." Guy had a buddy who had started a woodworking company after the war. "The factory's over in Adrian—about eighty miles west. I got a job there." Tom laughed. "They've got contracts to build furniture for Hudson's." He sighed. "I didn't see a future for myself before. Now I do."

Addie's shoulders slumped. He'd make a new life, meet someone. He was telling her to forget him. It made sense to forget him. She had her future to think of.

She busied her hands wrapping the leftover half of her sandwich. "How nice for you. I'll finish college and work for Hudson's until I set up my bookkeeping business full time." She tucked the sandwich into the rucksack and met his eyes.

"I heard you've done well." Tom held her gaze. "You didn't write. I thought you were mad about—"

"*You* didn't write to *me*. You wrote to Doris." She twisted the cap on the thermos.

"I answered her letters. She's the one told me I had a shot with you."

Doris. Her friend, not her competition.

Tom sat up, leaned on an arm, his hand behind her, his shoulder close to hers. "Is she right? Do I have a shot with you?" Heat inched up her back.

Addie turned her face to him. *Ready or not.* "I've missed you."

She was happy to say it aloud, to give that to him, no matter how he took it.

Tom's smile lit up his face. He reached for her hand, and she entwined her fingers with his.

Many years later, when they had had the life they wanted, she would remember the fireflies sparking here and there under the canopy of leaves, the sound of doves cooing, and the jaunty way she flung her arm around his neck on the night she first kissed Tom.

Acknowledgements

I am indebted to The Department Store Museum (http://www.thedepartmentstoremuseum.org/), developed by architect and historian Bruce Allen Kopytek, and to The Detroit Historical Society, for online access to the archives documenting the J.L. Hudson Department Store, as well as the streets, buildings, and life in 1940s Detroit. Mr. Kopytek has also published *Hudson's - Detroit's World Famous Department Store* (https://editionsbk.com/).

The hundreds of photographs available from these sources, and from the Burton Historical Collection at the Detroit Public Library, and on the site of Historic Detroit (https://historicdetroit.org/), were invaluable for realistically setting the story.

The photographic history inspired my writing and made me feel profoundly sad that the amazing Hudson's store is gone.

The wonderful team behind *River Avenue*, editor Paula Stahel and cover designer Roy Marshall, graciously agreed to work on *The Bookkeeper*. I am so happy they did and thank them for their patience, humor, and expertise.

The idea that became *The Bookkeeper* took shape toward the end of the time I was writing *River Avenue*. I am grateful to the readers of *River Avenue*, especially those in Pennsylvania who reached out to me with their responses to the story. Readers surprised me by wanting to know more about what happened to the kids, beyond the bits revealed about their adult lives. *The Bookkeeper* is another part of their story.

I wrote chapters of *The Bookkeeper* at the Main Library in Clearwater. Clearwater is a welcoming community for authors, and the Clearwater Library is our greatest asset. I am most appreciative of the support from librarians Thomas Shepherd and Leslie Walbolt. That appreciation extends to the members of the Beach Library Book Club for their insights as readers of fiction, and to the book clubs that hosted my author talks.

Endless thanks to my greatest cheerleader, my son, Jasper Walton Klein, who pushes me forward and leads my marketing efforts. Jasper is the blessing on my life, and the reason.

Made in the USA
Columbia, SC
18 August 2023

21813118R00209